# ANNA JACOBS

*One Special Village*

Ellindale Saga Book Three

HODDER

First published in Great Britain in 2018 by Hodder & Stoughton
An Hachette UK company

This paperback edition published in 2019

6

A CIP catalogue record for this title is available from the British Library

B format ISBN 978 1 473 63091 8

Typeset in Plantin Light by Palimpsest Book Production Limited, Falkirk,
Stirlingshire

Printed and bound in Great Britain by Clays Ltd, Elcograf S.p.A.

Hodder & Stoughton policy is to use papers that are natural, renewable and
recyclable products and made from wood grown in sustainable forests. The logging
and manufacturing processes are expected to conform to the environmental
regulations of the country of origin.

Hodder & Stoughton Ltd
Carmelite House
50 Victoria Embankment
London EC4Y 0DZ

www.hodder.co.uk

Dear readers

I hope you enjoy the third book in this series which is set further up an imaginary Pennine valley from the town of Rivenshaw (also invented) in a tiny village I've called Ellindale. All the stories in this series are set during the first half of the 1930s. It was fascinating researching that era.

My great-grandmother on my mother's side and other Gibson ancestors are buried in a village called Cross Stones, which is near Todmorden and which gave me the idea for Ellindale. The little cemetery at Cross Stones (not used now) still lies above the village on the very edge of a windswept moor. It's a fascinating place to visit.

In this story I was looking at the village as a whole, and basing my feelings about neighbourliness on the streets my family and I lived in, where all the neighbours kept an eye on each other – and on each other's children! It was hard to misbehave because some adult would step in and tell you off if you tried it. I didn't do much misbehaving because I had my head in a book most of the time. I was more likely to trip over something as I started reading my books on the way home from the library.

I was useless at riding a bicycle with gears, and I can't count the number of times one of the men in the district would stop me and tell me I was using the wrong gear. It never sank in how the gears functioned and I never enjoyed riding a bicycle, so gave up trying and walked everywhere – especially to the library.

I've added two more family photos at the end of the book, since readers seem to have enjoyed the others. I couldn't resist my mother's primary school photo from about 1930. She's the middle child in a dark dress in the middle row. Doesn't look happy, does she? And then I saw one of the earliest photos of me and my parents, with my dad in his army uniform, so I thought I'd share that. It was taken just before he was posted overseas to the Middle East and I didn't meet him again until I was nearly five.

Since I wrote my last 'Dear Reader' letter I've had my DNA tested. I am amazed to find that ALL my inheritance comes from Lancashire. I thought with several Irish surnames in the family tree, I'd have Irish ancestry, but no – I have none at all. I am as 'pure Lancashire' as it's possible to get. Who'd have thought?

The characters in this story are also as 'pure Lancashire' as I could make them. I based them on my memories of the people in my family and on our neighbours. I think modern big towns and cities have lost some of that neighbourliness, which is why TV programmes about people looking to move to the country are so popular.

Enjoy your third visit to Ellindale. It was supposed to be a series of three books, but the story overflowed. There were things still to tell and a new character hovering around, wanting to join in the fun, so we've extended it to four books. Book four is called *One Perfect Family*.

NB. If you're interested in what England was really like in the 1930s, try reading JB Priestley's 'English Journey'. He went round England and wrote about what he saw in a most entertaining manner, thus providing me with a great research resource and an enjoyable read. Thank you, Mr Priestley!

This book is for my son-in-law, David Glossop,
who was the inspiration for the character of Wilf.
David is the best I've ever seen at putting machinery
together, understanding how it works and repairing
or modifying it. He's also great at moving spaces
around in his head and building things. But best of all,
he married our daughter Sas and gave us our grandson,
another David.

# I

Lancashire: 1932

As Harry Makepeace waited outside the Ward Sister's office to speak to the doctor, he looked down the long children's ward at the slight figure of his daughter, lying in a bed halfway along, and his heart twisted with pain.

She'd been taken bad at school and they'd had to call the ambulance to take her to the hospital. One of the older lads had been sent running to the factory to tell him, but by the time Harry got to the school, the ambulance had taken her away, and he had to catch two buses to follow it into Manchester. His employer would be furious about time lost.

If Cathie had been at home, he'd have tried the Potter's powder, burning it and letting her inhale the smoke. It usually helped a little. But this remedy was working less and less well and he was at his wits' end as to how best to help her.

The local doctor was an old man and he just shrugged when Harry took Cathie to see him. 'We can't perform miracles, Mr Makepeace. Don't let her run around too much. Keep her calm. Some children get hysterical easily.'

Hysterical! This wasn't hysteria; it was an illness.

When Harry asked him for the name of a doctor who specialised in treating asthma, the local doctor took umbrage. 'Do you think I don't know my job! Not one really understands asthma and many think it psychosomatic, which is what I just said, a hysterical reaction. It's better if parents of such children treat them more strictly.'

Which was ridiculous. As if Cathie did it on purpose.

She'd never needed to go to hospital before or he would have tried to do something about it. He was going to find another doctor for her from now on, he decided.

'Mr Makepeace.'

He looked up as someone called his name and Sister beckoned him into her office. He stood in front of her desk, looking down at the two people seated behind it. There was another chair at the side of the room, but they didn't ask him to sit down. He held back his anger at that rudeness, reminding himself that Cathie was what mattered.

'Your daughter has had a severe asthma attack, Mr Makepeace,' the doctor said slowly and loudly, as if he were speaking to an idiot.

'If you don't mind telling me something about asthma, doctor, I'd appreciate it. I need to know as much as possible so that I can help her.'

The doctor studied him and he looked steadily back. Unlike some people he wasn't cowed by doctors. They were only human beings like him.

'Well, some people are starting to wonder if asthma is a disease of the lungs but no one's sure. Personally I've noticed it's worse where the air is impure.' The doctor looked down at the admission form and tapped it with his forefinger. 'Where you live is in the middle of an industrial area, is it not, and no doubt very smoky?'

'Yes. But I need to live near the place where I work. I'm an electrical engineer. I keep the machines in a factory running.' He always called himself an engineer, as they had done in the army where he'd been trained during the final two years of the war.

'Indeed. But that isn't a good place to bring up a sickly

child, with the mills and factories belching out black smoke every day. The air there is dirty and when it's breathed into the lungs, it dirties them in turn. This may be making matters worse in your daughter's case. When I visit patients near mills, even I feel stifled sometimes and there is nothing wrong with my lungs.'

'I see.'

'Fortunately we were able to treat her with ephedrine and give her oxygen to breathe. Your own doctor will be able to prescribe it for you.'

'He hasn't done so far. He says the attacks are due to hysteria.'

'Ah. Old gentleman, is he?'

'Yes.'

'Perhaps a younger doctor might be of more assistance?'

Although the sister was clearly impatient for him to leave, the doctor took the opportunity to stretch his arms and ease his shoulders, which gave Harry time to take this in.

'Maybe cleaner air would help, doctor. Cathie wasn't as bad when we used to send her to visit her grandmother in the summer, only the old lady died and I don't know anyone else who lives in the country.' He shook his head sadly. 'Eh, what must I do?'

'Get her out of the city to live in the fresh air of the countryside, even if you have to send her away to do it. It's her only hope. If we hadn't given her oxygen today she might not have pulled through.'

Harry could only stare at him in dismay.

'She isn't a strong child, as you must realise. Motherless too, I gather. How are you coping?'

'We have a neighbour who helps. She's kind, like an auntie to my Cathie.'

'The child was clean enough when brought in,' the sister said, as if reluctant to admit Cathie was well cared for. 'Given what doctor says, and your lack of suitably placed relatives, it might be better for you to put her in the care of an orphanage in the country, Mr Makepeace. She's old enough at nine to understand why and you could probably visit her occasionally.'

'What? Nay, I'm not sending her away. She's all I've got since her mother died and I love her dearly.'

'There are other considerations as well as her health. Men aren't the best people to bring up girls of her age anyway. She's going to need a woman to show her how to deal with a woman's body soon, not to mention teaching her how to look after a house when she marries.'

The doctor was scribbling on the admission form so Harry turned back to the sister. 'Can I take Cathie home now?'

'You'll have to ask doctor.'

Harry had to wait for him to finish writing, scrawl his signature and look up. 'It'd be better to leave her here till tomorrow. We have oxygen to hand if she has another asthma crisis.'

The sister stood up and gestured towards the door, her large starched headdress flapping up and down like a bird's wings, and not a friendly bird, either, but one waiting to pounce on its prey. 'That will be all for now, Mr Makepeace.'

The doctor was already reading the next paper from the pile and there were others queuing outside to see him.

Heartsick, Harry went down the ward to speak to his daughter, trying to hide from her how worried he was. Cathie seemed lethargic, her face pale, her thin body not making much of a lump under the bedclothes. This wasn't like his lively little darling.

He wasn't giving her away to an orphanage. Never! She coughed and he added mentally, well, only as a very last resort.

He sighed as the bell rang for the end of visiting hours,

most of which he'd had to spend waiting outside the sister's office. He bent to kiss Cathie. 'I'm sorry to waste visiting time, love, but they insisted I had to see the doctor while he was here. I'm to come back for you tomorrow morning and take you home.'

Tears trembled on her eyelashes. 'Oh, Dad, please take me home now. It's horrid here.'

'They say it's best you stay in case you need oxygen again. Your breathing hasn't settled down yet. Even I can hear the roughness.'

'I hate it here. They care more about straightening the bedcovers than asking how you are. And you'll lose another day's work. Mr Trowton will be furious. I'm sorry, Dad.'

'What are you sorry for? You didn't do it on purpose. Just concentrate on getting better and leave me to deal with my boss. Getting better's your main job now.' He couldn't resist giving her another kiss. 'Be a good girl.'

Harry walked slowly out of the hospital, trying to get his mind round the new problem as he waited for the first of two buses home. If the doctor was right, something could be done to help Cathie. So he was going to do it, whatever it took.

There had to be a way to get her out into the country without putting her in an orphanage; there had to be.

He'd lost his wife to pneumonia two years ago. Dora had faded so quickly, he'd been left stunned by his loss, with a seven-year-old child crying for her mummy and depending on him for everything. That was when Mrs Pyne next door had stepped in for the first time, because Trowton had just sacked her on a whim, something he'd been doing more often lately. The woman was a saint.

Harry would give everything he owned, every drop of the blood in his veins, to make Cathie well again. But exactly how to do that was difficult to figure out. He had a job here and was lucky to have it when so many couldn't find work, even though his employer was a mean old sod, and getting meaner with every year that passed. If he left Trowton's, how would he live? He didn't think he'd get sacked, though, because he was good at his job and there were a lot of old machines to keep going.

He arrived home to a silent house. It felt wrong to have no smiling daughter running to fling her arms round him. It was a two-up, two-down terraced dwelling near the factory, which was a smallish place, specialising in soft furnishings – curtains, cushions and all sorts of bits and pieces.

Mrs Pyne knocked on the door to enquire about Cathie, so he asked if she'd look after the child when he brought her back the next day, which of course she was happy to do.

'You're a wonderful neighbour, you are,' he told her.

'Get on with you! Let alone I'm fond of Cathie, it's a poor sort who doesn't help a neighbour.'

But he could see she was pleased with his compliment.

When he went back inside, he stood in the kitchen feeling numb, not knowing what to do with himself.

He'd intended to make do with a couple of slices of bread and jam for tea, but his stomach rumbled and he told himself he needed to keep up his strength. He nipped along to the corner shop for one slice of ham and a couple of carrots. He didn't bother to cook the carrots, just washed them and crunched away between bites of ham sandwich.

He looked at the second carrot before he put it in his mouth and grimaced. Even the food was poor stuff if you lived in a place like this. When his father was alive, they'd had fresh vegetables all through summer and autumn from the old man's big country garden, whatever was in season. He still missed that Sunday visit, coming back with shopping bags full of food.

Now they had to make do with what the local shops offered. Maybe good fresh food would help Cathie as well as fresh air. It wouldn't hurt, that was sure. He'd have to make the effort to go to the market on Saturday afternoons to buy fresh stuff, though it meant a long walk.

He cleared up methodically after eating. His wife had been insistent on keeping a clean house and he'd seen how Dora did things, so he'd continued to tackle the various jobs the way she'd have wanted. He took care of most of the housework himself, with Cathie's help now she was bigger, and to hell with the other men laughing at him and saying that was women's work.

The only thing he couldn't do himself was the washing – he just didn't have the time – so Mrs Pyne did that every Monday with hers for a small payment, which she was glad to earn, and he also paid her a little something for keeping an eye on the child before and after school or during holidays.

They didn't tell anyone about those payments, because Mr Pyne was on the dole and subject to the means test. If the authorities had found out, they'd have docked the money Harry gave her from her husband's dole payment. Mean devils, they were, always suspicious! As if the poor chap was out of work on purpose and wouldn't have preferred to go to a job.

He looked round the room and sighed. It was clean and tidy but that was all you could say about it. Dora had managed to make things look homely, but he didn't seem to have the knack.

People kept urging him to marry again, but he didn't intend to look for a wife simply because he needed someone to see to the house. Imagine living with a scold like Tom Blake's wife, however cleanly her ways, or a poor housekeeper like Don Roason's wife, who might have a lush body but was stupid and forgetful. Or, worst of all, someone who didn't love Cathie. No, thanks.

He sat down and tried to read a newspaper he'd picked up on the bus. Fortunately someone had left it behind. But his thoughts wandered, because he was all churned up about what to do.

He ought to be able to find a job somewhere else because during the war, the army had trained him as an electrical engineer. He'd not had to do a lot of actual fighting, thank goodness, but had been kept busy in England maintaining equipment used on the home front. He'd been lucky, very lucky indeed. He hadn't thought so at the time, though, as his friends had been posted all over the place and saw a bit of the world, while he was left in Aldershot, working his way through his training.

Harry smiled at the memories of Sergeant Deakins who'd been in charge of his group. He was strict but gave those in his unit the most thorough training in electrics you could possibly get. At the time Harry had fretted against the restrictions, because he'd only been a lad, hadn't he, too stupid to know when he was well off? He'd lied about his age and enlisted at fifteen, so well grown that no one had questioned his age. He reckoned the sergeant had worked out that he was under age, though, and had kept him under his wing.

Even if Harry's parents could have afforded to pay for an apprenticeship, they'd not have let him do one. They'd wanted him to work with his dad on the smallholding they'd rented for decades and had been sure the war would be over before he was old enough to be called up. They'd been furious when he ran off and enlisted.

He'd never gone back to live at home again. After he was demobbed he found a job in Manchester running in electricity to houses and lived in lodgings near his work. It wasn't long before he met and married Dora. He'd actually been nineteen then, though folk thought him twenty-one, and she'd just turned eighteen. They'd been happy together and he still missed her.

It was a sorrow to them both that she'd only given him the one living child and had lost two others after Cathie. Neither of them had expected that because Dora seemed a fine, healthy lass in other ways. He'd have liked more kids but there you were.

When the doctor said another baby would probably kill Dora, Harry took care not to start any, even though preventive measures weren't cheap at a shilling a protector.

But she'd died anyway, poor lass, and her only twenty-eight. Pneumonia was a scourge.

With Mrs Pyne to help look after Cathie, he'd stayed in the same house. Except that now he knew it was bad for his child's health here, he would have to leave.

There had to be a way. He'd *make* a way.

And what was he doing sitting thinking about the past when it was time for bed? He'd have a busy day tomorrow.

# 2

Harry had to take part of the following morning off to pick up his daughter and Mr Trowton didn't like it, threw a fit and said he'd fine Harry five shillings for the inconvenience, but there you were. She was too little and weak to travel home alone.

Then something distracted Trowton and he broke off in the middle of ranting about ungrateful employees who *deserved* fining. He was very strange at times as well as a bit forgetful. But with a bit of luck he might forget the fine. He'd sacked a woman last week, telling her to leave at the end of the day, then asked her to do a special job for him when she came to work the next day and hadn't mentioned sacking her since. It was all very strange.

When Harry got to the hospital, Cathie was sitting on a hard chair near the entry to the ward waiting for him.

The sister came out of her office to see him.

'Doctor says she's doing all right but I'm to remind you she needs to get out of the smoky air.' She thrust a piece of paper at him. 'This is the address of a very good orphanage in the country.'

Cathie burst into tears.

He didn't throw the paper back at the sister, which was his first instinct, because Cathie might wind up here again. He just muttered, 'Thank you,' then took his child's hand and hurried away from the dratted woman.

Outside the hospital Cathie stopped to hold on to his arm.

'She said you'd have to send me away to an orphanage in the country. Promise you won't do that, Dad, *promise*.'

'Of course I won't send you away. I didn't say anything in there because I didn't want to upset Madam Starchy Knickers in case you had to come back here.'

The tears stopped at this rude nickname, and it won him a watery smile.

'I couldn't manage without you to boss me around, loviekins.'

As they found a double seat and sat down together on the bus, Cathie leaned her head against his shoulder and sighed, still clinging tightly to his hand.

Oh, how he loved the feel of that little hand in his! Yet how frail and weightless it seemed today. He didn't think he could carry on if anything happened to her.

That settled it, time to use Dora's money. When she died, he'd vowed never to touch the insurance payment, had considered it blood money, and put it straight into the savings bank.

Dora had taken the two policies out without consulting him, one on his life and one on hers, for the sake of their child. He'd considered it a waste of money and it had been one of the few things they'd argued about. He'd never expected to collect on a policy but she insisted on keeping up the payments, however much they had to scrimp.

But now, that damned blood money might be his only chance to help Cathie. He wasn't sure how to do it yet, but he'd find a way.

Two days later, Harry was called in from the workshop by the owner. A stranger was standing by the office window, looking thoroughly fed up.

'Ah, Makepeace. This is Mr Selby. He's been looking at the old car that belonged to my brother, thinking of buying it. Only the engine won't start. I had it working only last week, didn't I, so there can't be much wrong. Could you just have a look at it? You're good with machinery.'

Harry didn't contradict him, though this was a barefaced lie. The car in question, a Fairbie, hadn't been used since the brother died.

'Happy to, Mr Trowton. I'll just go and get my toolkit.'

'I'll come with you,' the stranger said. 'I know quite a bit about cars, actually, but I don't have any tools with me and I don't want to get my good clothes dirty. I've never seen a car quite like that before.'

'It was built a few years ago by a small company near here that's gone out of business now, like a lot of them have,' Harry said. 'The car used to be a good runner. Not fast but steady and was known for its good brakes.'

Behind them, Trowton nodded approvingly at that remark.

Mr Selby followed Harry through the workshop and out to the long narrow yard at the side, where all sorts of bits and pieces were stored.

Someone had given the car a polish and tidy up, Harry noted. As if that'd make the engine run properly. 'I'm not a car mechanic,' he told Mr Selby, wanting to be fair to both parties, 'I'm an electrical engineer. But I'm good with machinery and I do understand how car engines work, so I'll be happy to have a go.'

They got the bonnet open and Harry shook his head as he looked inside. Trowton could at least have had the motor cleaned.

'We can both see that the car hasn't been used for a while,' Selby said in a low voice, 'but I guess you didn't dare contradict your employer.'

'In times like this a man has to hang on to a job.'

Selby walked round the vehicle. 'I'd have left when it

wouldn't start, but the bodywork looked to be in good condition and strongly made. If I can buy it cheaply and get it to my workshop in Rivenshaw, I can pull the engine to pieces and get it working properly again. The parts don't look too badly worn.'

'I know Mr Trowton's brother didn't drive very far in it,' Harry offered. 'Now, let's see what we can do.'

They chatted as Harry examined and fiddled with and cleaned the various parts of the engine.

'What's your job here, exactly?' Mr Selby asked. 'For a man who isn't a motor mechanic, you seem to be making a good fist of checking it over.'

'I like machinery, have a feel for it. My job is keeping the factory machinery running, mostly smaller stuff like sewing machines and electric irons, because the factory runs on electricity. This place used to be reasonably profitable, even during the war. But nobody's thriving these days.'

'You're the head mechanic?'

Harry chuckled. 'In practice yes, but not in name. That'd mean Mr Trowton having to pay me more. *He* calls himself the head mechanic.'

'Places like this aren't doing so badly in the south of England,' the visitor said thoughtfully. 'And the big factories producing motor cars, like Fords, employ hundreds. Only I wanted to live near the moors. The air's bracing there, suits me better. I'm a northerner, heart and soul, I reckon.'

'Where exactly do you live, if you don't mind my asking?'

'Rivenshaw. It's in one of the Pennine valleys in Lancashire, near the border with Yorkshire. Good honest folk round there.'

Harry put that on his mental list of places to check out.

It took two hours of work to get the engine going, even with Mr Selby's helpful suggestions. The owner came out twice to see how things were going, scowling at Harry as if it was his fault it was taking so long.

Then at last the engine coughed, as if protesting at being woken, and started chugging somewhat unevenly.

Mr Selby sat in the driving seat, touching the accelerator a couple of times when it faltered and listening as if he knew how engines should sound.

In the end he switched it off, poked his head out of the window and beckoned Harry over. 'You did well. Want to earn a bit extra this weekend delivering it to Rivenshaw for me?'

'I think you'd be better fetching a lorry and loading it on that, or towing it behind a bigger car. I doubt it'd get out to Rivenshaw under its own steam.'

'If I came and towed it, would you sit in it and steer it for me? Driving under tow isn't as easy as it looks. I have a partner in my used car business, but Charlie's a terrible driver. I'd not trust him to do it.'

Harry thought quickly. 'I work Saturday mornings so it'd have to be Sunday. And we'd need to start off early so that I'd be back before nightfall. I have an ailing child to look after, you see – and before you ask, my wife's dead, so it's all up to me. My neighbour would look after her in the daytime though. And I could maybe borrow a friend's motor-cycle to get back home and put it on the boot rack at the back of the Fairbie. I'm afraid I'd have to ask you to pay him five shillings to hire it. I haven't got the money to spare. You know how bad the trains are on Sundays.'

'You're on. I'll be over here by eight o'clock on Sunday morning. Do you want me to pick you up at home or meet you at the factory?'

'Would it be too much trouble to pick me and the motor-bike up from home?'

'Not at all.'

'Thanks.' He gave Mr Selby his address and was thinking aloud when he added, 'I'll be able to look at the countryside as I go. The doctor says fresh, clean air is my daughter's only chance. She gets dreadful asthma attacks, so I'll have to find somewhere in the country to live.'

'I'm sorry to hear that. Do you know where you want to go?'

'Eh, no. Anywhere that will help my Cathie and provide me with a job will suit me. Last week she nearly died and was rushed to hospital. The doctor told me her only chance was to move to the country out of this smoky air. I've started looking in the paper for jobs and there doesn't seem to be anything at all going out near the moors let alone in my line of trade—'

He realised he was talking too much. 'Sorry. I shouldn't bore you with my troubles. Please don't tell Mr Trowton what I said. It's just that my little lass is on my mind and it slipped out.'

'Of course I won't mention it. Good luck with your job hunting.' Mr Selby slipped a ten-shilling note into Harry's hand. 'Thank you for your help today.' He added two half crowns. 'For the hire of the motorbike.'

Ten shillings was over-generous as a tip and Harry hesitated, hating to act like a beggar. Then he thanked Mr Selby and accepted it. He was going to need every penny to move and set up another house, and Mr Selby had a well-fed, healthy air that said he wasn't scrimping a bare living, so could afford to tip well.

Harry still couldn't think how to find a job, but this Sunday would give him a start on looking for a place to live. He was planning to visit the smaller nearby towns on Saturday afternoons or Sundays to see what he could find.

He put the old car away and watched Mr Selby make his way to the office to haggle with Trowton, then he went back to his own work.

At the end of the day, Mr Trowton saw the other workers off the premises and came to find Harry, who was making his final rounds to check that everything was switched off properly.

'Well done, Makepeace. I sold the car to him.'

'That's good.'

He hesitated, then slipped two shillings into Harry's hand. 'You did well.'

'Thank you, sir.'

His employer was a mean bugger, Harry thought as he walked home. Two shillings when he must have got at least twenty pounds for the car. Even a stranger had given a bigger tip than that. And Harry put a lot of extra time in here without complaining.

But at least Trowton's factory was still doing business and though the number of workers had been cut drastically, there were still twenty women employed there, and three men for heavier work and deliveries, including Harry. The women cut, sewed and ironed, making up loose covers for furniture, curtains, cushion covers, antimacassars, whatever Trowton could find a market for.

They had other jobs to do for his cousin who had a similar place in the south, which was a big help. The other Mr Trowton had plenty of work, and could get some things made up in the north more cheaply than he could produce them himself without extending his factory.

Harry was still managing to keep the machinery going but some of it was getting very old and outdated. He worried about those machines. They all did. Who could afford replacements in times like these?

If the factory closed down before he'd found another job, what would he do?

When he got home, Harry knocked on Mrs Pyne's door. He didn't usually bother to pick up Cathie, just knocked and shouted that he was home. But today he needed to ask her about Sunday. She was happy to earn an extra shilling looking after the child, but his daughter cried when he said he'd have to leave her on the one day they usually spent together.

In fact, Cathie had been tearful and lethargic ever since she came home from the hospital. This made him even more certain he needed to get cracking and find a way to move. She might have recovered, but she wasn't thriving.

In fact, she looked so wan he began to think he might have to move without finding a job first.

That thought was frightening, but not as frightening as the thought of losing Cathie.

# 3

As she carried their plates to the table, Leah Willcox paused, as she often did, to stare out of the kitchen window at the moors. She loved to gaze down the slope and see their tiny village of Ellindale bordering the road down the hill. Such a pretty view! And such a nice set of neighbours. She loved living here.

Spring Cottage was the highest dwelling in the narrow Pennine valley. She'd grown up in the small town of Rivenshaw at the lower end, but after her marriage she'd fallen in love with the rolling open spaces of the Pennines, which stretched beyond their land across what locals called 'the tops'. She'd hate to live anywhere else now.

After sitting down, she ate her first sandwich in a few hungry bites then sneaked a sideways glance at her husband. He'd taken a couple of small bites and pushed the rest of his to one side. Lately he'd only been picking at his food and it showed in the gaunt lines of his body.

'If you don't feel like cheese sandwiches, I could make you something else, Jonah.'

'What? Oh, no thanks. I'm not all that hungry today.'

'You need to eat to keep up your strength.'

'Don't fuss, dear.'

She suppressed a sigh and finished off her sandwiches before clearing the table. She was seriously worried about him. He'd made it clear to her when they entered into a marriage of convenience that he wasn't likely to make old bones. Men who'd been gassed during the war rarely regained their health. But she hadn't expected such a sudden decline.

The trouble was that she'd grown very fond of him and it hurt to see him suffer.

As she was thinking of going back across the yard to her little fizzy drink factory, he said suddenly, 'I'd better tell you, Leah: I'm not going to do Charlie's accounts for his pawnshops from now on. I find it too tiring to drive into Rivenshaw. I'll come into town with you when you go to the library if I need to change my books, or get someone else to drive me.'

'You're giving up driving completely? Why?'

'I, um, don't feel safe driving. I'm getting coughing fits more regularly now and I nearly ran off the road the other day when I had a bad one. Just imagine if I bumped into another car or knocked someone down.'

'Oh.'

'The coughing usually happens when I exert myself.'

She'd heard him coughing, of course she had. He tried to get up quietly when it happened in the night, but she was a light sleeper. He'd been bringing up blood for a while, but it had got worse lately. She'd seen the stained rags the morning after and provided a bucket to throw them in and plenty of clean rags. She hadn't said anything, had just done it, because she knew he preferred not to discuss his weakness.

She realised he was waiting for her to speak, one eyebrow cocked as if expecting other questions. She contented herself with a little nod. As her dear father would have said, what can't be cured must be endured. If Jonah could endure his declining health without complaint, so could she.

He'd been going on quite well, considering, till he came down with a bad cold just after Christmas. It'd taken him a long time to recover and since then he'd looked frailer.

What did surprise her was that Jonah still made love to

her occasionally. It didn't happen very often, but he turned to her sometimes. She'd given up hoping for a child and so had he, but he seemed to find comfort in gentle lovemaking, and she didn't mind.

She knew that he'd deliberately distanced himself from her from the very beginning of their marriage, as if trying to make sure she would be able to manage without him one day. It was the sort of thing he would do, always thinking of others.

When he wasn't working he would sit in his big armchair looking out over the moors, whose views seemed to change with the weather. He occupied himself with the newspaper and his books, not uttering a word of complaint as his health went relentlessly downhill.

She felt helpless to do anything but go along with this. She didn't want to waste whatever time was left nagging him and she never, ever let him see her cry. He had enough to bear.

'I'll still help you with your accounts for the factory, though, Leah. I'm not completely useless.'

'Good. I don't like fiddling with figures. I enjoy making our drinks much more.' She was lucky that her days were busy running the small fizzy drinks factory she'd opened with Jonah's encouragement in one end of the huge old barn. It kept her mind off sad things. Most of the time, anyway.

In summer she also had to keep an eye on the small youth hostel they'd opened last year in the other end of the barn, but that was still closed for the winter. They were a new thing, youth hostels, which gave poorer people a chance to spend their holidays tramping round the countryside and staying in the hostels, which were not only cheap but also safe and decent.

They'd open their hostel again at Easter and this year she'd have to find a woman to manage the place and keep it clean. She wouldn't have the time to deal with that now that the drinks were selling so well. She'd ask her friends if anyone knew a suitable woman to do it.

Another reason she wasn't going to take on the responsibility for the youth hostel was that Jonah might need her.

She realised he'd said something. 'Sorry, I was wool gathering.'

'I said: the sales of our drinks have been excellent lately.'

'Thanks to your brother.'

'Thanks first of all to the excellent drinks you make.'

'Yes, but your Charlie has an amazing gift for making money. No wonder his pawnshops are thriving.'

'He was right about making our bottles look fancy and selling mainly to the better class of person, wasn't he? They still have money to spare for little treats. You're making a nice steady profit now and when times get better, you'll make an even bigger profit.'

'It matters more to me that my drinks give employment to a few people in our village. I wish I could find a way to provide more jobs.'

'Give it time and—' He broke off to ask, 'Is that a car coming up the hill?'

She went to peer out of the window. 'Yes. It's your brother. Oh, my goodness! He only just missed the gatepost.'

They both chuckled, which broke the tension nicely. Charlie had knocked one of their gates off its hinges a couple of months ago. He was a terrible driver. Thank goodness he somehow managed not to hit pedestrians, just walls and gates, which couldn't jump out of his way.

She smiled at the way he took his spectacles off before he got out of the car because he hated wearing them, then came hurrying towards the house. He never walked slowly. He'd be visiting Spring Cottage more often now Jonah had stopped working in the shop, she guessed. He cared deeply about his ailing older brother.

★

Charlie just about bounced into the house, clearly in one of his ebullient moods. 'I'm glad you're not at work across the yard, Leah. I don't want to say everything twice over.'

'What have you done now? Don't tell me! Let me make us all a cup of tea first, and maybe a scone to go with it?' She tried not to look at Jonah as she said that.

'Not for me, love,' he said.

Charlie looked at his brother, his anxiety slipping past his smile for a moment. 'I'd not say no to a snack. Marion buys scones from the bakery. They're all right, but yours taste better.'

Charlie munched his way through half the scone, then suddenly set the rest down on his plate, excitement radiating from him. 'You two are the first to know, apart from my wife, of course: I'm going to buy Flewett's shop on Rivenshaw High Street.'

They both gaped at him.

'I didn't know he was selling up,' Jonah said.

'I heard he was thinking about it and nipped in quick with an offer.'

'Isn't it rather big for a pawnshop? And anyway, you've already got one in Rivenshaw.'

'I'm not opening another pawnshop,' said Charlie. 'I'm going to keep on selling the same sort of things as Flewett did. People are buying more electrical goods every year, you know. Who wants to sweep a carpet by hand when they can push a modern vacuum cleaner across it and get it cleaner? I shall change the name of the shop, of course, to Willcox's. And my motto will be "Willcox's for Everything Electrical".'

'Very catchy,' Leah said, seeing he expected some comment.

Jonah was frowning. 'Why is Flewett selling up? Isn't the shop doing well?'

'The shop's doing all right, though it'll do better when I'm in charge. It's his wife. She's not well and they're going to see if she does any better in the sea air. They've already bought a house in St Anne's.'

Jonah continued to frown. 'Unless your Marion has inherited some money, I can't see how you'll finance it. I've been doing your accounts for long enough to know exactly how you stand financially. You don't have much spare money after setting up the second-hand car yard last year and buying some stock. So how can you even think of buying another shop?'

'I've taken out a mortgage on my house, that's how, and Todd's going to sell my car and find me a smaller, cheaper one. Not one as small as my Marion's Chummy, mind. I draw the line at that. An Austin maybe, he says. He's looking round for something nice and steady.'

'Don't do it,' Jonah begged. 'Times are still bad. You've stayed out of debt so far, and you don't *need* another business. If you must buy another shop, wait until things improve to do it. You've more than enough money coming in every week with your pawnshops and car sales.'

Charlie waved one hand dismissively. 'Flewett's shop is much cheaper now than it would be in better times, that's why I'm buying it. Last year the government came off the gold standard and they've brought the interest rates right down, so I reckon business will only improve from now on. Didn't I tell you that was what the government should do? I couldn't have afforded to borrow money at eight per cent, but I'll only be paying two.'

'But Charlie lad—!'

He covered Jonah's frail fingers with his strong ones and gave his brother's hand a quick squeeze. 'I'm taking a risk, I know, and that's not your way. But I feel it in my bones that things are going to improve. They've never had it as bad in the south as we have in the north and you should see how well electrical goods are selling there. I had a good look round the shops last month when we visited Marion's auntie.'

'But—'

'But nothing, Jonah lad. Change is in the air, even here, though it'll take a while yet. When most people have jobs again, they'll buy all sorts of domestic equipment and I intend the people in our valley to buy from me. Prices of all sorts of goods are going down because modern factories can make them more cheaply. I tell you, it's the time to invest not sit in a corner dithering. You tease me about becoming a millionaire, but I'm going to do it, Jonah.'

'I could never bear to get into debt or take such a big risk.'

'I know. It's not in your nature, lad, never was.'

'How much will you be borrowing?'

The answer shocked him into exclaiming, 'No!'

Charlie flapped one hand in the air as if to brush away his brother's objections. 'Look, Flewett's is an established shop and there isn't anyone else selling electrical goods in the whole valley. And think how many things there are to sell now: kettles, irons, washing machines, radios, gramophones. Even ordinary people are buying fridges these days, and of course electric cookers are much cleaner than gas. I'm going to sell them all and anything else people care to invent. Housewives are crying out for labour-saving equipment because it's getting harder and harder to find a maid.'

He grinned at Leah. 'Didn't I tell you to have more electric sockets and light points put in than the engineers suggested when they brought electricity up here to Ellindale last year?'

She nodded. 'And you were right about how convenient it is, too. I'd not like to go back to heating my iron on the fire and Jonah uses that electric toaster nearly every day, because he doesn't feel hungry when he gets up but has a snack later.'

'There you are. What did I tell you?'

'But to borrow such a lot of money,' Jonah protested. 'I'm surprised the bank manager let you.'

Charlie grinned. 'It's thanks to your clever wife I got the loan.'

They both looked at him in puzzlement.

'It doesn't hurt that your fizzy drink company has been making me a steady profit since I became your partner, Leah my pet, it doesn't hurt at all. The bank manager was very impressed by the figures I gave him from that and my various other businesses.'

Jonah's voice was sharp. 'You've used the fizzy drinks company as security!'

Charlie shrugged. 'I shan't go bust. It's perfectly safe.'

Leah swallowed hard. She didn't like the thought of him doing that either.

There was silence, then Jonah shook his head and stopped trying to reason with his brother. But he continued to look worried.

She wondered what would happen to her little factory if Charlie's business failed and he had to pull his money out. Would the bank seize it in payment? Would she lose everything she'd worked for? She didn't understand how that sort of thing worked and would have to ask Jonah to explain it to her later.

Then she looked at her brother-in-law, with his fine clothes and expensive shoes. What people noticed most of all was the air of confidence that always surrounded him.

No, he wouldn't go bust. Charlie hadn't failed at anything so far, though people had often shaken their heads at what he was doing.

And he wouldn't fail this time, either. Not their Charlie.

# 4

The next person Charlie went to tell was Todd Selby, his partner in the second-hand car business they'd started up. He heard noises coming from the workshop, so didn't bother knocking on the door of the tumbledown house behind the big paved area.

Todd was wearing his overalls and was bent over an Austin Seven.

Charlie looked at it scornfully. 'That looks a right old mess.'

'The owner had an accident. I'll soon get the motor fixed, not much damage there, then I'll take it round to Stan's. For a blacksmith, he's good at doing car bodywork repairs. He's going to specialise in that when times improve.'

'That's not one of our cars, though.'

'No. Word's getting round that I repair cars as well as sell them, so I'm earning a pound or two here and there. I'm going to fetch another car on Sunday, a Fairbie. A friend told me about it so I rang the owner and went to see it when I was in Manchester at the beginning of the week.'

'Never heard of that make of car.'

'It was made by one of those little companies that sprang up after the war. It's a few years old but it's hardly been used. It's a solidly built little vehicle but it doesn't go very fast, and when the bigger companies like Morris and Austin brought out better and cheaper cars, they couldn't compete so had to close down.'

He wiped his oily hands on a rag. 'Now, what can I do for you today, Charlie? You haven't pranged that car of yours again, have you?'

'No, of course I haven't. But I wondered if you could sell it and get me a cheaper one for the time being. I need some extra money.'

'I heard you were going to buy Flewett's?'

'Yes. But there isn't much stock so I'm going to need to spend a bit more than I'd expected filling the shelves.'

'The Fairbie might suit you, then. But we'll have to do your present car's bodywork up before we sell it.'

'I'll have a look at the Fairbie, see if I like it.'

'I'll be picking it up on Sunday.'

Charlie smiled. 'There's good money in repairs. Flewett offers a repair service too. He did that sort of work himself, with the help of an assistant. He says the assistant can handle it and I promised to give the chap a try.'

Todd paused, spanner in mid air. He'd met the assistant, Gordon Bexley, and didn't like the fellow, who had a shifty look to him. He suddenly remembered the chap who'd helped get the Fairbie going. 'Well, if Bexley doesn't work out, I know an electrical engineer who's looking for a job in the country.'

'What? Who?'

'The chap who helped me with the Fairbie. He was trained by the army so he knows his stuff. At the moment he's working at Trowton's where I bought the car, only he's looking for a job in the country so that his sickly daughter can get some better air to breathe.'

'I think that's what doctors tell people when they don't really know how to help them,' Charlie said gloomily.

Todd gave him a quick sympathetic glance. Everyone knew Jonah Willcox was failing. 'Well, good fresh air can't hurt, can it? This chap lives right in the middle of Manchester

near to where he works at the moment and talk about smoky
air! It's as bad as I've ever seen.'

'What about his wife? Will she be happy moving to the
country?'

'He's a widower. Manages on his own with a bit of help
from a neighbour.'

'Well, it'd be asking for trouble to employ him, then. A
man needs a wife to look after his house, especially if he has
a sick child to look after as well. I'd not want to take him on,
even if I did need a repairman. But I won't. I've got one.'

Todd shrugged. 'Suit yourself. But you'd better let me keep
an eye on what you buy. You don't know a thing about electrical equipment and you don't want to stock anything
shoddy.'

Charlie grinned. 'I was counting on you for that. I'm taking
over the shop next week. Flewett is very keen to hand over
quickly and get his wife into the sea air.'

On Sunday morning Todd set off while it was still dark and
drove into Manchester. He didn't mind early mornings and
it took little more than an hour to get there at this quiet time
of day. He could foresee a nice profit in the car he was picking
up today.

Inevitably as he drove along the nearly empty roads, his
mind wandered and he started to ponder on his life and
where it was going. There was something about the peace of
the beautiful English countryside which did that to you, and
a good think about life never did anyone any harm.

After the war, he'd spent a decade travelling the world until
his mind calmed down and he got over the horrors and
carnage he'd witnessed. That had taken longer than he'd
expected but gradually he had stopped feeling a desperate
need to move on from one place to the next every few weeks
or months.

His need now was to settle down and perhaps if he was lucky find a wife and start a family – if it wasn't too late. He was thirty-three now, after all. He hoped it wasn't, but that would depend on meeting someone special. He didn't intend to marry purely for the sake of it. You could always hire a cleaner.

During his travels he'd met many women and some had openly thrown themselves at him, and not only because of the shortage of men after the war, either. But not one of them had made him want to stop travelling and settle down with her. Strange that, because he did enjoy women's company, in every sense of the word.

Since he'd come back to England, acquaintances kept introducing him to their unmarried female relatives and he wished to hell they'd stop doing it. The poor women were usually embarrassed and he'd been upset about the way they were being treated by their families as problems to be disposed of.

Why were people so bothered about what they called these 'surplus women'? He'd seen articles about 'the problem' in newspapers and magazines. It wasn't a crime to be single, for heaven's sake. No one considered unmarried men a problem in that way. Not that there were all that many unmarried men in his generation.

He blamed the government. If they would lead the country into wars and use their young men as cannon fodder, what could they expect but thousands of women left without a chance of finding a husband?

As if fate was mocking him, for the first time in ages he'd found one particular woman whom he admired greatly since coming to Rivenshaw, only she was already married – Jonah Willcox's wife. The two brothers had chosen well, finding women with a bit of sense in their heads, nice looking too, though that was less important to Todd.

He gave a wry smile as he turned into the street where Harry Makepeace lived. How arrogant his thoughts sounded, as if he only had to click his fingers for a 'spare woman' to come running into his life.

He pushed those thoughts aside and concentrated on what had to be done today, waving to Makepeace, who had come to the door as soon as he drew up outside the house. He could see not only the light motorbike but a few straps to hold it in place.

A little girl came out of the house, kissed her father and went next door, using the knocker once and going straight inside. She turned to wave goodbye before she closed the door again.

You could see the love between those two and Todd suddenly felt a pang of envy. To love and be loved must be wonderful. He might have more money than Makepeace but he had no one to love him, because he had no close relatives left now.

That poor child looked frail, though, and he could see why her father was worried.

If he ever had any children, would they be strong or weak, clever or stupid?

Oh, he was in a silly mood today. He had to pull himself together and forget these foolish fancies.

He got out of the car. 'Good morning. Let's get this motorbike strapped on. I think it'll fit into the back of my van more easily than on the Fairbie's luggage rack.'

'Right you are, Mr Selby.'

'We're both ex-soldiers. Harry and Todd are good enough names to use, don't you think?' He stuck out one hand.

Harry grinned and shook it. 'Nice to meet you, Todd lad.'

At the factory, Mr Trowton was waiting to let them in to get the car, dressed in his Sunday best.

Once again the Fairbie wouldn't start without a bit of persuasion and Trowton kept pulling his pocket watch out to check the time as the two men worked on it. Then he started walking up and down, muttering to himself.

As soon as the engine was running, Harry backed the vehicle out carefully so that Mr Trowton could lock up and go home, surprised when he didn't even say goodbye. The man's behaviour was getting more unpredictable by the week.

Todd stood listening to the engine. 'Let's see how far it gets under its own steam.'

'I don't think there's enough petrol in it to go far,' Harry said. 'I checked on Friday.'

'I've got a couple of cans of petrol in my boot. Switch the engine off and we'll put some in, then give the car a try?'

That was another good thing about the Fairbie. You didn't have to contort yourself to get petrol into it. 'Whoever designed this had a few good ideas,' Todd said.

'Yes, but he didn't give it a big enough engine for its weight, I reckon, so it'll only ever chug along gently and slow right down on steep hills.'

It was, Todd realised, a perfect car for Charlie. It was much harder to kill yourself, or anyone else, in a vehicle that was going more slowly than others and anyway, Charlie didn't even try to go fast. It made Todd smile to see his friend drive, because he always leaned forward, clutching the steering wheel like a drowning man holding on to a lifebelt.

If Todd could get the Fairbie to run reliably, this would definitely be the perfect car for him.

It was a pleasant surprise when the car started first time after they'd put in some petrol.

'Let's get going while we can,' Todd said and got into his Model T Ford van to lead the way.

*

The Fairbie lasted about ten miles, roughly half the way there. This was nine miles more than Harry's most optimistic hope for it, so he was pleased. He'd enjoyed driving, which he hadn't been able to do for years, but the skill soon came back to you.

When they tried to start the car again, it coughed pitifully and refused to start.

'Tow time,' Todd said cheerfully. 'You're a nice steady driver.'

'I learned in the army and when you worked on the home front they weren't having you doing anything risky, in case you damaged their vehicles. Men had to save the risks for fighting on the front.' He looked sideways at Todd. 'I think you were in the trenches.'

'Yes. Not a good place to be. And you?'

'No. I signed up under age and my sergeant kept me away from the front.'

'You should count yourself lucky. It's no shame not to have gone out there, because we needed people to look after our equipment as well as do the fighting.'

Harry gave him a wry smile. 'I mostly worked on the cooking equipment. How's that for a war effort?'

'They say an army marches on its stomach, and that's not an exaggeration. How old were you when you joined?'

'Barely fifteen.'

Todd whistled softly. 'And no one realised how young you were?'

'I was well grown by then and considered myself a man. But I didn't fool my sergeant.' Harry shrugged, got back into the Fairbie and they set off. The more he chatted to Todd, the more he liked the man.

It was clear that Todd had towed vehicles before. He drove carefully with due regard for the vehicle behind him, so Harry had plenty of time to take in the scenery. It wasn't lush countryside so close to the moors, but he'd always liked the lovely rolling curves of the uplands. They seemed to soothe your eyes and soul both.

When he saw a sign for Rivenshaw, he felt pleased to have arrived well before noon. That would give him time to look around at other places on the way back.

The used car yard had a big square of black tarmac in front, with a car standing sentinel on either side of the entrance, and a couple of others neatly parked further back. There was a tumbledown house at the rear of the yard and a big, newer-looking shed to one side.

Todd got out of the van and stretched, so Harry put on the handbrake and went to join him.

'We did it.'

Todd nodded. 'I never doubted we would. Let's push the Fairbie into the shed and get your motorbike out of the van.' He pointed to the shed. 'That's my workshop. It's a bit cold in winter but it serves for the time being. We only opened for business last year, you see.'

When the Fairbie was under cover, he beckoned to Harry. 'Come into the house and I'll brew us a pot of tea, then pay you.'

'Thanks. A cup of tea would be welcome, but I won't stay long if you don't mind. I'd like to look around on my way back, see if there's anywhere I'd like to move to.'

As they sat down at the kitchen table to drink their tea, Todd said, 'This is a nice place to live.' He hesitated then added, 'I could give you an odd day's work now and then, probably one day a week. Picking up a car for instance, or helping with repairs.'

'I didn't train as a car mechanic.'

'But you have a knack for machinery and that shows.'

Harry nodded. He did enjoy his work and found it easy to understand machines of all sorts.

'But that'd not be nearly enough for you to live on, I know,' Todd said.

'It'd be a start, which is more than I've got now. How definite is that offer?'

'Very definite. I'm building up a repair business as well as selling cars, and it's either feast or famine, so it'd be good to have someone to turn to for help with a rush job. But it'll be a year or two before there's full-time work for another man with me.'

'I'll definitely bear that offer in mind. Thank you.' Harry held out his hand and the two of them shook on the bargain.

'Why don't you drive up to the top end of our valley and have a look round before you go back. It'd only take you half an hour, maybe less. There's a large village called Birch End halfway up and right at the top, a small village called Ellindale. They're nice folk up there. It's where I'd live if I had money to spare, only I get the house here free for the time being.'

Harry looked at the clock on the mantelpiece. 'I might just do that.'

But in spite of the part-time job offer, he wasn't going to jump into living near here because a day's work here and there wouldn't be enough to bring up a child on and Dora's insurance money wouldn't last for ever. He intended to make detours all the way home, and ask questions.

It was equally important to ensure there'd be somewhere for them to live without it costing an arm and a leg. Rent was always a prime consideration in the weekly budget.

# 5

A quarter of an hour later Harry was driving slowly up the gentle slope from Rivenshaw into Birch End. It looked a pleasant enough place, with what looked like a cluster of better class houses at one end, a few terraces of small dwellings, and a few older dwellings of all shapes and sizes.

But there weren't a lot of shops or businesses, other than a jumble of small workshops at the Rivenshaw end, and somehow it didn't appeal to him as a place to live.

He immediately took to Ellindale, however. The approach to it had an outlook over the moors, looking up some gentle slopes on his left and down across undulating countryside on his right.

It seemed as if the village was the last place the narrow road led to, so he stopped the motorbike, got off and propped it up carefully, then had a good stretch. Taking several deep breaths, he smiled, feeling as if he could taste the freshness of the air. This would be a good place for Cathie to live, no doubt about that, but what would he do for a job, even if Todd did keep his promise of a day's work a week?

Sadly, this place was even less promising for jobs than Birch End had been. There was only the one shop and no other businesses at all that he could see, unless you counted what looked like a few small farms set on the nearer part of the moors. He knew nothing about farming but everyone knew the wages paid to labourers were poor, so they wouldn't have money to spend on electrical appliances for their homes.

The shop was closed on a Sunday of course. Pity. He could have found out a lot there, he was sure. Local shopkeepers always knew what was going on.

He saw an old man sitting on a bench in a sheltered corner of the open space near the centre of the village and went across to him.

'Good afternoon, sir.'

The old man nodded. 'Afternoon.'

'Mind if I ask you a few questions?'

The man studied him, 'About what?'

'This village.'

'Well, I've lived here all my life so I know it as well as anyone you could find. It's a special place, Ellindale is, I reckon: honest people most of 'em, good neighbours to one another, an' the moors to rest your eyes on even when you're too old to walk across them.'

He paused for a moment to stare into the distance, sighing softly. 'I'd not like to live anywhere else, 'deed I wouldn't.' Then he frowned at Harry. 'Why would you be wanting to know about our village?'

'I've got a nine-year-old daughter who's not well. She needs to live in the fresh air, the doctor says. There seems to be plenty of that here.'

'Does she have TB?'

'No, asthma.'

'Ah. Knew a chap as had TB. Died young he did, poor soul. But I don't know anything about this asthma.'

'Are there any cottages to rent here?'

'No. Most of them have been lived in by the same family for years. A few lucky ones own their own cottages.'

'Pity there's nowhere free.'

'Even if there were, how would you earn a living? There's no jobs going here, more's the pity, young fellow.'

'I'm an electrical engineer. I could maybe find work down in Rivenshaw.'

'I've not heard of many jobs going there either, an' if there were they'd soon be snapped up. But then I don't know much about what your sort of engineers do, I must admit.'

'Repair things mostly. There are a lot of new electrical gadgets being sold these days.'

'Some of us still manage all right with the old ways, though I do like an electric light of an evening, that I will admit. What does your wife think of a move to the country?'

'My wife died a couple of years ago. There's just me and my daughter.'

The old man chuckled. 'Better not think of moving here, then. People allus seem to be finding husbands and wives for theirsen when they settle here.'

'No chance of me doing that.'

An even longer chuckle greeted this. 'They all say that. But Nancy at the shop just got wed to Mr Harris as owns the laundry in Rivenshaw. She's left her young cousin in charge of the shop she set up here after her first husband died. And Mr Carlisle, him as inherited Heythorpe House up the hill, has married his housekeeper. I had a good Ellindale lass by my side for forty year an' I still miss her, I do that.'

He paused, looking sad, so Harry waited. He enjoyed talking to old men, but you couldn't hurry them. You could learn a lot from them if you were patient and they often had a wry sense of humour about life that he admired.

'If you've any money saved, you could ask Farmer Kerkham about his bit of land an' build a hut there to be going on with.'

'What do you mean?'

'He's been trying to sell a corner of his farm for a year or more to bring in some money. It's not part of the family farm, came to him from an old auntie. It's cut off from his land by a stream that comes from a spring at the far corner from his house, and it's not good farming land so it's not much use to him. He has a well next to his house so he doesn't need the spring, though it's good water. And his wife doesn't want to keep her chickens on the bit of land and have a long traipse across a field every day to feed them and collect her eggs.'

Another pause to collect his thoughts, then, 'It's not even big enough to graze a sheep or two. It's like a square with one of the top ends squashed and the other going higher up to a point. There's an old wall round it, built I don't know when. A long time ago, it must have been because no one remembers a time it wasn't there.

'But some of the wall's ripe to fall down if you give it a push. Well, a bit did fall down in one corner a few years ago when some lads were larking around on it.' He added with another of his faint smiles, 'Kerkham, the farmer as owns it, belted them lads good and hard, so no one's gone near his wall since.'

'I'm surprised no one's taken the stones from the wall and used them.'

'Eh, no one would dare touch it. Bad-tempered sod that Kerkham is an' allus ready to use his fist to settle an argument. Any road, to cut a long story short, he'd rather have the money than the land. He's scratching a living at the best of times, and these aren't the best, are they?'

He paused again, then snapped his twisted fingers. 'I near forgot. There's a shepherd's shelter on it, three walls and a roof, facing away from the main winds.'

'How big is this bit of land, give or take?'

'Big enough for a house an' a fair-sized garden with a bit to spare. I could show you if you don't mind walking slowly. It's not far but I can't move fast these days, not even if you paid me.'

'I'd be grateful.'

Harry waited while the old man pulled out a big white handkerchief and blew his nose loudly, then stuffed it in his pocket.

'I'll have to wheel my motorbike so I can't walk fast either. I'm Harry Makepeace, by the way.'

'Simeon Waide.'

He helped the old man up and they set off. It was a cold day but fine and his companion was well wrapped.

'I'm the oldest person in the village, you know.' Simeon paused to get his breath after a hundred yards.

He was panting slightly so Harry waited patiently.

'Turn ninety next year, I will.'

'Congratulations. That's a great age.'

'My grandma were ninety-four when she died, an' still had all her wits about her.'

A hundred yards to the south of the village, the houses ended and Simeon passed the end of a narrow earth track then stopped again, waving one hand to the right. 'This is it.'

Harry hadn't even noticed the weathered sign as he drove up. 'Land for sale, £5. Apply Kerkham Farm'. The writing was untidily painted on bare wood, as if done by a child, and there was a crude arrow nailed to the top of the sign, pointing away from the road and down the track.

Simeon hobbled across to sit on a pile of stones. 'It's all the land inside the wall that he's selling.'

Harry kicked out the stand and stood the motorbike carefully on the verge, then walked up and down along the road, staring at the rough square of land, which grew narrower away from the road. There was no gate but the wall had fallen inwards at one corner so he clambered over the stones there.

As the old man had said, the ground was rocky at one

side. He knew nothing about gardening but you might be able to dig some of the stones out and use them to help build the walls of a small house. Or get a stonemason to do the building.

At the end away from the road he saw a three-sided construction, not much higher than his head. He turned back to Simeon. 'Is that the shepherd's shelter?'

The old man looked where he was pointing. 'People reckon that's what it is. Must ha' been well built, because it's stood there since before my great-grandfather's time an' it's in better condition than the wall.'

The three-sided shelter stood a couple of yards in from the perimeter wall and the old man was right. It must have been well built because none of it had sagged or fallen. It was built of the local stones and was about four yards by three, with a sloping roof made of uneven pieces of slate.

He went to inspect it more closely. Immediately he walked inside, he found himself out of the wind and when he looked up there were no signs of leaks or loose slates. There was a chimney with a flat stone below it that had probably been used as a hearth, judging by the darkened wall behind it. To one side was a big flat stone set on two upright supports, presumably to be used as a seat for any sheltering shepherds.

He moved out again, following the sound of water gurgling. A spring surrounded by a circle of rocks welled up, forming a tiny stream only a few inches wide that ran down the slope. It began about two yards in from the wall and trickled out of the enclosed land through a narrow gap in the bottom wall.

He cupped a handful of water and took a mouthful. It seemed sweet, and looked clear and sparkling.

'We've got a few springs up here,' Simeon called. 'Good drinking water, they are. That's why they set up the fizzy drinks factory at Spring Cottage up at the top end of the village. You haven't been up that way yet but they've got a much bigger spring than this.'

'I'll go up and look at the other end of the village before I leave.'

Harry paced out the land, which was about thirty paces wide at the front and forty going back. Plenty of room for a house and garden, and a workshop too maybe.

He went back to sit next to Simeon. 'This has given me something to think about. Thank you.'

They sat in a companionable silence as he considered how it might work. He had an old tent. He could put it up to sleep in to start off with if they moved in the summer. If he put a rough wooden wall across the front of the shelter, it'd make a tiny house. Cathie could sleep there as soon as that was finished.

But he'd have to provide somewhere warm and weatherproof before the winter set in. He'd need another two rooms at the very least. They didn't need to be big, though. His present house had very small rooms.

The main thing was whether Cathie would do better up here. If he knew that, he might consider this piece of land seriously. But then she couldn't do much worse than in their present house. Perhaps if she ran wild for the coming summer out of doors, she'd regain her health.

'Do you think he'd take less than five pounds for it?' he asked.

Simeon shook his head. 'Not Kerkham. When he decides something, that's it and he won't change his mind. Five pounds is what folk usually pay for pieces of land up on the edge of the moors.'

Five pounds wasn't a bad price, Harry thought. He'd heard of one or two families buying a lump of land out in the country and living on it in tents then building huts to live in.

Well, he'd have half a hut already if he came to live here.

But he wouldn't have a job, only odd bits of work here and there. That was what worried him more than anything.

Hmm. He'd have to think about it.

'I'll walk you back to the village, shall I?' he asked Simeon.

'Nay, you've still got to ride home. Go up the hill and look at Spring Cottage before you leave, then go and put your thinking hat on. Nice meeting you, lad.'

'Nice meeting you, too, Mr Waide. Um, I'd be grateful if you'd keep it to yourself that I've been looking at this piece of land.'

Simeon laughed. 'Eh, I shan't need to tell anyone. Some will have seen you through their windows an' they'll spread the word.'

'Ah. Then would you mind telling them I said it wouldn't do for my purpose.'

'Aye. I can do that. Good luck whatever you do, lad.'

'Thank you, Mr Waide.'


Harry started the motorbike, which was a good little runner, and chugged up the hill. He stopped briefly on the other side of the village to gaze at a big house on the left, down a slope from the road. It looked well cared for. Would this be the Heythorpe House that Simeon had mentioned?

He went on till the lane petered out and saw a sign saying 'Spring Cottage Mineral Waters'.

There was the sound of a small machine clanking in the big barn to one side of the yard but no sign of anyone to talk to, and if he wanted to see any other places on his way home, it'd be wise to start back now.

On the way down he waved to Simeon, who was sitting on his bench again, then couldn't resist stopping for a few moments as he got to the piece of land. It had a grand view over the moors. It'd be lovely to wake up to that instead of smoke-stained terraces of houses and their shadows.

Even if he used Dora's money to build a small dwelling, he would still be taking a big risk, though he'd have no rent to pay and that would make a big difference.

No, what was he thinking of? It wasn't at all practical to think of bringing a sickly child to live there when he didn't have a job.

But he had to do something about where they lived. Had to. Her life could depend on it.

# 6

That same day, in a village on the other side of Rivenshaw they buried an old man. He had been a quiet sort of person, not disliked, but not particularly well liked either. He'd kept himself to himself and made certain the daughter who kept house for him did the same.

Feeling relieved more than grieving, Nina Halshall watched them bury her father, then as soon as she could she turned to her brother. 'Do you and Patricia want to come back to the house for a cup of tea?'

'I've got to go home and collect the children from our neighbours.' Patricia dug her elbow into her husband's side. 'Des has something to tell you.'

Nina turned to him. He avoided looking her in the eyes so she knew it wasn't going to be good news. What now? she wondered.

When they got back she put the kettle on and put a meagre measure of tea into the pot because she hadn't been able to get to the shop for a few days.

He paced up and down the kitchen, then vanished into the front room and came back when she called out that his tea was ready.

She took her place opposite him at the scrubbed wooden table. 'Well, Des? What do you have to say to me?'

'Um, Dad gave me his will a few weeks ago.'

She stiffened. 'I thought I was dealing with that.'

'He changed his mind about what he wanted after my

children were born, felt they needed the best we could give them since a spinster of your age would never have any. He knew I'd see you were looked after, so he left everything to me.'

She set her cup down with a clatter, unable to frame a word. Was it for this that she'd cared for a domestic tyrant all these years, ever since her dear mother died? Her voice came out as a croak. 'So he's left me nothing?'

'As I said, he knew I'd look after you.'

'And how are you going to do that? Father's pension from the railways dies with him and you've no room for another person in your house.'

'We'll be moving in here now, because Dad's left the house to me. He was right to buy it.'

'He was able to buy it because Mum and I scrimped and saved for years. I have a *right* to a share of it.'

'Well, he didn't leave it to you and I'm sticking to his wishes. It'll be a relief for us not to have to pay rent any more.'

'Where do I go? There won't be a bedroom left for me if you all move in. Will you be turning me out on the street?'

'As it happens Owen Rogerson is looking for a wife. He's offered for you. So you'll be well cared for.'

She stared at her brother in disbelief. 'I wouldn't marry *him* if he was the last man on earth! He's seventy if he's a day and a meaner man I never heard of. He's even more tight-fisted than Father.'

'You don't have much choice, Nina. In times like these we all have to do what we must to put bread on the table. Owen has a sound little house and is still running his shop. He expects you to help him with it.'

'In other words, he gets a shop assistant without having to pay her any wages. No, thank you. I won't marry him. Never, ever.'

'You're not thinking straight. A man like him is all a woman of your age can expect since the war. You refused two offers of marriage from perfectly decent chaps when you were younger and now see what's come of it.'

'Mam was ill. I had to look after her. And I'm not at death's door yet, thank you very much. I can still earn a living, if I have to.'

He shifted uneasily but didn't comment.

'I definitely won't marry Rogerson, Des. And you can't make me.'

'There's no choice. They're cutting my hours again. We'll have a hard time managing, even with this house. Patricia wants to move in tomorrow. She's arranging it now.'

'I'll leave first thing in the morning, then.'

'Leave? What do you mean *leave*? You've nowhere to go.'

'I'll tramp the roads and sleep rough if I have to rather than marry him. You'll be shut of me then.'

'I forbid you to go.'

'I'm nearly thirty, Des. You can't forbid me to do anything.'

He sat there and stared at her, plucking at his lower lip as he did when he was upset. 'Patricia will be furious. She'll find some way of stopping you.'

'How can she? She can hardly tie me up?'

'You know what she's like. She *always* finds a way to get what she wants.'

There was another silence as she tried to work out why Patricia was so keen for her to marry. Then it came to her. 'How much is Rogerson paying her to arrange this marriage?'

'Not much. But she won't get the money till you're wed to him.'

'I see.'

'And she wants whatever money you have left from the housekeeping right now. After all, it comes to me, she says.'

'Well, she's unlucky because I've nothing left.'

'I don't believe you.'

After a struggle that he won because he was bigger than her, he got her purse out of her shopping bag and tipped its contents over the table. A shilling, two penny pieces and a halfpenny.

'If you take it, I won't even have the money to buy something for my tea.'

His face tinged with red, Des scooped up the coins and put them in his pocket, muttering, 'Dad did leave me everything, after all. And there'll be something to eat in the house.'

She folded her arms and stared at him, saying nothing, just looking.

Des wriggled uncomfortably, broke eye contact and moved towards the door. 'We'll be round in the morning. Don't touch the furniture till then. Rogerson is coming to help us and may perhaps buy a piece or two, since we'll have more than we need. You'd better be looking your best and you'll need to speak nicely to him, if you know what's good for you.'

'I will *not* marry that man.'

'You will. We'll make you if we have to beat you black and blue.'

She stood at the door, dry-eyed, arms folded tightly to hold herself together as he left. He was the most hen-pecked man she'd ever met, even though he was twice the size of his wife. As her brother, Nina would have expected him to treat her better than this, though. Beat her black and blue, indeed.

He stopped and turned to look at the house and she spat on the ground to show her utter contempt of him. A big tide of red washed over his face this time. She'd never in her life spat at anyone before, but then she'd never felt so sickened by anyone before, either.

He hadn't even given her a penny back to buy something for her tea.

She'd known there was some secret between him and their father but not that they'd arranged for Des to take away her home and every last penny in her purse, leaving her with nothing to do but marry a horrible old man.

Only they were wrong if they thought they'd backed her into a corner where she'd give in meekly. They couldn't make her say the words that married her to a vicious old man, whatever they did to her.

But she wasn't waiting to find out. She would have to run away before they moved in.

Within two minutes of Des leaving, her friend and neighbour was knocking on the kitchen door. She called 'Come in!' but didn't get up from where she had slumped in a chair.

Brenda stood looking at her. 'What has that brother of yours done now? Or should I ask what his wife has made him do?'

Nina explained.

Letting out a cry of disgust, her friend thumped the table a couple of times. 'I'd break every plate in the house if it were me.'

'Don't tempt me.'

'What *are* you going to do?'

'Leave. See if I can find a job, I suppose. I'd tramp the roads rather than marry *him*.'

'You can sleep on our front-room floor if you need to.'

'Can I sleep there tonight? I'm worried about what Patricia will do when Des tells her I refused to marry Rogerson. I'll feel safer with you.'

Brenda sat frowning, then said slowly, 'I've an idea. You know Jim's Auntie Carrie is personal maid to Lady Terryng, who's one of the kindest people I've ever met. So is his aunt, kind I mean. I used to work for her as well. That's how I met Jim. I'm sure they'll both be happy to help you. I'll take you to see his aunt and her ladyship tomorrow.'

'They've never even met me. Why should they take me in and help me?'

'They've a reputation for being kind to those in trouble. I saw when I worked there how Lady Terryng used to help people. I'm sure they'll be able to help you find a job as a maid. I quite enjoyed being a maid, whatever people say about it. We ate well and there was always someone to chat to. Such work would be far better than marrying Rogerson, surely? What's more, if you live in, it's all found and you could save your wages.'

'Anything would be better than marrying that man. I'm so grateful, Brenda love.'

'What use is someone who won't help a friend? I think we should go to see her straight away. I'll put my Sunday clothes on and ask my neighbour to look after the kids till I get back.' She glanced at the clock. 'There's a bus leaves every hour from the Park Road depot. Hurry up and pack. We can just make the next one.'

Brenda went back to her house and Nina locked the front door as she passed it on her way upstairs, just in case Patricia came round to scold her. She even slid the bolt across because she knew Des had a key and she wouldn't put it past her sister-in-law to simply walk in.

Upstairs, she grabbed her father's old suitcase from the top of his wardrobe and put it on her bed, cramming her clothes into it anyhow. It didn't take long because she didn't have many. The sooner she got away from here, the easier she would breathe.

When she'd put in every garment she owned, she knelt and lifted the loose floorboard, taking out the little cloth bag which contained the money she'd saved from the housekeeping. Only a few pounds. Not much to show for a decade of acting as unpaid servant, but better than nothing.

She was going to shove it into the suitcase but on second thoughts she pinned it inside the top of her knickers.

She glanced out of the window and gasped in shock as she saw Des and Rogerson turn the corner into the far end of the street and start down it, looking grim and determined.

Abandoning her books and trinkets, she grabbed the suitcase and clattered down the stairs as fast as she could. She went out the back way, making sure to close and lock the door with the spare key, and taking that with her. Then she opened the gate of the yard quietly so that the latch didn't even clink. After closing it equally carefully behind her, she listened.

Even from the back laneway, she could hear someone shouting angrily and hammering on the front door. She supposed one of them would come round to the back in a minute or two, so she lugged the case into Brenda's yard, relieved that none of the other neighbours were around.

She didn't knock on the back door, but opened it and went in, saying baldly, 'My brother and Rogerson have turned up. I think they intend to force me to marry that horrible old man. I put the bolt on the front door and locked the back one, but now I don't know what to do.'

'You can stay here, as I told you.'

'We'd better lock the doors, then.'

'They won't break into my house. You'll be safe here.'

'But how are we going to get out and catch a bus without them seeing us?'

Brenda sank down on one of the kitchen chairs. 'I don't know.'

# 7

Des didn't bother to knock but used the key his father had given him to open the front door. Only it wouldn't open. He rattled it and tried again.

'Must be bolted,' Rogerson said. He banged on the knocker but there was no sound from inside, no sign of anyone peeping through the front-room curtains, either.

Des said nothing. He couldn't seem to think straight today. He didn't like doing this to his sister, but what else was he to do about Nina? She couldn't live with them, because Patricia wasn't having another woman in *her* house. And Nina would have found it hard to get employment even in better times. It'd be impossible now, so she'd be a burden on them.

Rogerson jabbed him in the ribs with a bony elbow. 'Do you have a back-door key?'

'Yes.' Des took the key out of the front door and indicated a second one hanging on the key ring.

'We'd better go through to the back, then. If that one's bolted, you'll just have to break it down.' Rogerson gestured towards the narrow passage that led through the middle of the terrace of small houses and they walked through it. 'Come on!'

The back gate was closed but not locked. The back door was locked.

Des stared at it, reluctant to use his key.

'Go on,' the old man prompted. 'See if you can let us in.'

'Yes.' But still Des hesitated.

'What the hell are you waiting for? Unless she's still inside, she can't have bolted the door she left by. You haven't even tried it.'

Des was getting worried about whether Nina would be safe. 'Look – you'll treat her kindly, won't you?'

Rogerson let out a sniff of laughter as if his companion had made a joke. 'Women and dogs need to know who's master.'

Des's heart sank, but he knew Patricia would kill him if he didn't do what Rogerson wanted.

Once they got into the house, he stood still for a moment. The place felt empty. You could sometimes tell. He looked at the man next to him, such a nasty old man. Suddenly he hoped his sister had got away. 'I'll go upstairs. You look round down here.'

'I'm coming everywhere with you. We'll do this together.'

Which made Des realise that Rogerson didn't trust him. Well, the old sod didn't trust anyone, did he?

The older man moved round the downstairs rooms, walking a little stiffly, and Des followed him. Then they went upstairs and Des held his breath. But Nina wasn't there either, thank goodness.

When they came downstairs again, Rogerson said, 'You've got younger legs, Halshall. Go and check the cellar.'

Des switched on the single light bulb and edged carefully down the narrow stone stairs, with his companion peering down from the top.

But there was nowhere for his sister to hide in the small cellar; it was only used to store a few odds and ends. Even Rogerson could see that from where he stood.

Des went back up the stairs, feeling relief that Nina had definitely got away and hoping that didn't show in his face. He was sure to get the blame for her escape from Patricia, though how he could have prevented it, he couldn't see. 'She must have left.'

'Well, she can't have gone far because she obviously took the time to pack all her clothes and you can't have been away for long after you told her what was planned, if you really did come straight round to see me. Which neighbours is she friends with?'

'There's a young woman next door. Can't remember her name, but they're on good terms.'

'That'll be where she'll have run to, then. But she'll not cheat me of my due. Your wife promised I could marry her and I'll hold you both to it. Let alone she'll be useful in the shop, I miss having a woman in my bed.'

Des dared to say, 'Even if we brought her back, we couldn't force Nina to say the words.'

'You find her and bring her to me. I'll do the forcing.'

'Now look here, I'm not having you hurting her.'

'She'll not do as she's told without a few thumps. Don't worry. I won't injure her seriously, just knock her about a bit, teach her to mind me.'

Des looked at him pleadingly, but Rogerson glared at him. 'Your wife isn't as soft as you are, thank goodness. Any road, you go into next door's backyard and walk straight into the kitchen. I'll go to the front.'

There was a knock on the front door and the two women looked at each other in dismay. But it was the errand boy from the shop a few streets away bringing Brenda's shopping.

It was Nina who thought of it. She grabbed the boy's arm. 'Do you want to earn a shilling?'

''Course I do. How?'

'Have you got any money?' Brenda whispered to her. 'If not, I can lend you some.'

'It's all right,' Nina whispered back. 'I've got a few shillings I saved from the housekeeping. Des doesn't know about that.'

'Oh, good.'

The lad looked from one to the other, waiting for instructions.

'I'll give you a shilling if you'll lend me your clothes and the bicycle. I need to get out of the street without anyone recognising me. I can put my suitcase in the big iron carrier on the front of your bike and cover it up with your other packages. If I'm wearing your overall and cap, no one will look at me twice. I'll meet you in the park and give you back your clothes and the bicycle there.'

He looked down at himself dubiously, then shrugged. 'You can have my overall and cap but I'm not taking my trousers off, not for anyone.'

'Nina, you can wear my Jim's best trousers,' Brenda said. 'They'll be a bit big but we can hold them up with a belt. You'll have to be quick changing, though, love. It won't take them two long to search your house. I'll nip up and get the trousers.'

A couple of minutes later an errand boy left the house whistling tunefully, put a cloth-wrapped package in the carrier and pedalled rapidly along the street.

Relieved that her friend had got away, Brenda quickly locked the front door and went back to help the lad fabricate a story in case he was stopped when he left the house. Then she went to keep watch through the front room window.

When she saw Rogerson come out of next door, she ran to open the front door just as he reached out to use the door knocker.

As he jerked back in surprise, a lad came out holding a cardboard box with a picture of a kettle on it. 'I'll bring it back when it's been repaired, missus,' he called out as he'd been instructed.

The man standing outside the front door grabbed his arm, studying his face.

'Hey! You let go of me.'

The man realeased his grip. 'Sorry. I thought you were someone else.'

The lad hurried off down the street and Brenda tried to shut the front door, but Rogerson held it open.

Des came panting round from the ginnel between the houses. 'The back door's locked.'

Brenda glared at him. 'Have you been trying to get into my house? How dare you?'

She squeaked in shock as Rogerson pushed her inside and followed her. The expression on his face frightened her and she backed away.

'Where is she?' he asked.

'Who?'

'My sister,' Des said.

'How should I know?'

'Search the house, Des,' Rogerson ordered. 'Don't forget to look under the beds.'

'You can't do that.'

'Oh, can't we? Who's going to stop us?' Rogerson took another step towards her and she moved hastily to the other side of the kitchen table.

After an apologetic glance at Brenda, Des hurried round the house and came back shaking his head.

Rogerson glared at Brenda. 'She can't have got far. Who was that first lad, the one on the bike?'

'The grocer's lad.'

'I checked the second one and it was definitely a lad, so you go after that other one to find out if it really was the grocer's lad,' Rogerson told Des. 'Go on! Run as fast as you can! He won't have got far if he keeps stopping to deliver things.'

But though Des looked high and low, it took him a while to find the delivery boy. When he did, it turned out to be the one from the grocer's shop, as he'd been told.

'Sorry. I'm looking for someone.' He let go of the lad's arm and hurried back, worrying now that Patricia would make his life hell for losing Nina.

The next thought came unbidden. And Nina's life would be hell if Rogerson forced her to marry him. He was glad his sister had got away, glad he was, though he'd never say that to his wife, of course.

When he got back he found Rogerson still standing in the kitchen with Brenda at bay behind the table.

The lie came easily to him. 'I caught up with him. It was just a lad. I looked all over the place, but I didn't find my sister. I can't think where Nina could have gone.'

'I'm back!' a voice called and a man came into the house, wearing his working clothes and needing a wash. When he saw his wife looking afraid and two men he disliked standing as if they were bullying her, he scowled at them and moved across to her side of the table.

'What's wrong, love? What are these two doing here? Are the kids all right?'

She burst into tears and flung herself into his arms. 'The kids are next door. These two pushed their way in and they won't go away. They're looking for Nina and they think I'm hiding her. And I'm not. They even went up and searched the bedrooms.'

'*They did what?*' he roared.

She pointed to Rogerson. 'That one pushed me into the kitchen and I nearly fell. I thought he was going to thump me.'

Her husband moved quickly across to Rogerson and gave the old man a shove that sent him crashing into the wall. 'Get out of my house, you, and don't ever come back into it again. If you ever so much as approach my wife again, anywhere, not just in here, I'll knock you to kingdom come.'

Another hard shove sent Des stumbling after him. 'Get out, damn you!'

'Sorry. It was a mistake.' Des ran out of the house.

Rogerson stopped outside on the pavement to yell, 'I'll find her and fetch her back. You tell her that, missus.'

Jim went along the street a little way and watched them to the corner then came striding back to demand, 'What the hell is going on?'

Brenda explained. 'So you see, Nina couldn't marry a man she hated.'

Jim could only gape at her. 'They can't do that to Nina or to any other woman. This is 1932 not the Dark Ages. And fancy a brother trying to force his sister to marry a man she hates.'

'He's weak, that Des is. It's that wife of his who's doing this to get rid of her. Eh, all those years Nina's looked after her father and he hasn't left her a penny.'

'I never thought much of Des Halshall but I now know he's more than a coward, he's rotten through and through.'

'Unfortunately he's moving in next door with his shrew of a wife. And guess what, Des even took the last few coins out of her purse, though she had less than two shillings in it.'

'The mean devil. What is she going to do now, though? Has she anywhere to go?'

'No. Her father didn't let her have friends apart from speaking to the neighbours. Eh, I'm going to miss her.'

'She could go and stay with my parents till she works out what to do. They haven't got much – well, who has these days? – but they have a sofa she could sleep on an' my mam wouldn't let anyone hurt her. She's fearsome when her temper's roused, my mam is.'

Brenda plonked a kiss on his cheek. 'You're a lovely man,

you are. And your parents are lovely too, but I have a better idea. I was going to take Nina to your Auntie Carrie, and see if she and Lady Terryng could help. Now you'll have to take her to Wemsworth instead in case those two catch up with her.'

'Nay, it'd be better if you went. You're used to her ladyship. I always feel out of place in that great big house when we visit my aunt.'

'I don't know why. The other servants at Netherholme have always treated us well. You'll *have* to do it, Jim. I'd be terrified of Rogerson and Des catching me an' Nina travelling there. They're stronger than we are. Look how they pushed into this house.'

'Oh, all right. Where is Nina hiding?'

'I told her to wait for me in the park at the children's playground, but it'll be getting dark soon. Oh, no! How are you going to get out of the house? I bet they'll be watching it to see if we lead them to her. What are we going to do, Jim?'

'*You* are going to stay here and lock all the doors. I'll go to the pub and give them the slip by sneaking out the back way.'

He gave her a quick hug and added ruefully, 'Eh, lass, you've led me into more scrapes since I married you than I got into during the whole of my life before.'

He grinned suddenly. 'I've another reason for doing it, think on. That Rogerson fellow once gave me a good thumping for nothing when I was a little lad. Said I'd cheeked him. I wouldn't have dared. I'll be glad to stop him hurting your friend.'

She put her arms round his neck and planted a big, sloppy kiss on his cheek. 'You're a good man, Jim. I'm so glad I married you.'

'Aye, well, don't get into any more scrapes for a while after this, eh? And put a sandwich together while I change out of my work clothes, will you? I'm not helping your friend on an empty stomach.'

'Um, I lent Nina your other trousers when she dressed up as the delivery boy. She'll give them back to you in the park. But you'll have to go in your work trousers.'

'She's wearing my trousers? Women! Nothing's sacred.' He clattered upstairs to change his shirt and get his best jacket, so that at least his top half looked all right, and came down to grab the sandwich.

'I only hope I can do this in time to catch the last bus back or I'll be sleeping under a hedge.'

'Don't go till I've fetched the children back from the neighbour's.'

He followed her out, locked the door and handed her the key. 'You'll be nattering forever and I don't have much time. Get Walter next door to come and see you inside, then lock the front door again and don't open it unless it's me or someone you trust.'

Nina stood at the back edge of the children's playground watching for the delivery lad. When he came she returned his overall and cap, paid him his shilling and watched him leave. She pulled down her skirt and wriggled out of Jim's trousers, folding them over her arm.

After a while she found a bench out of sight of anyone passing along the main path of the small park and sat huddled on it, waiting for Brenda or her husband. She was sure her friend wouldn't let her down, but it seemed a long time before anyone came into view.

For one dreadful moment she thought the tall man walking along the path towards her was her brother and jerked to her feet. Then she realised it was Jim from next door and waved to attract his attention.

He cut across the grass, which was patchy and faded after the winter. 'Are you all right, Nina lass?'

'I am now you've come.'

'And you're still wanting to go and ask my aunt for help?'

'Yes, please. I can't think of anything else to do, because I don't have any references or way of getting a job.'

'We'll catch the bus then.'

He picked up her suitcase as if it weighed nothing, and indeed, considering it now contained all her worldly goods, it wasn't all that heavy.

'Come on, then. There's a bus leaving in ten minutes.'

Without a word she trudged along beside him, hoping desperately that they'd not meet anyone she knew.

He paid for the bus fares and when she offered to pay her share, he shook his head. 'You'll have a hard enough time managing.'

'Thanks.' That small kindness and the care with which Jim helped her up the steps into the bus brought tears to her eyes after the way her brother had treated her.

They sat side by side, mostly silent, as the small one-decker bus chugged its way out into the countryside.

# 8

Leah drove down into Rivenshaw, telling Jonah she was going to do a bit of shopping and would then visit the woman who had once been her neighbour and whom she'd always called 'Auntie Hilda'.

She'd made an appointment to see the doctor first, wanting to ask him how best she could look after Jonah without letting her husband know what she was doing.

Dr Mitchell looked at her sympathetically. 'There isn't much more you can do, Mrs Willcox. Just let your husband do what he wants, keep him warm and well fed, and don't let him go near any people who have colds.'

'How long could we hope for?'

He hesitated.

'There's something else, isn't there?'

'I'm afraid so. His heart isn't working very well. It's beating rather unevenly. I mentioned it but he said it was the least of his worries and he'd get back to me if it caused him trouble. That was last year and he hasn't spoken to me about it again, but he must feel the rapid beating at times.'

'There are times when he stands still suddenly and presses one hand to his chest.'

'Yes. A common reaction to atrial fibrillation. Does it last long?'

'I don't think so.'

'Then we must hope it isn't getting any worse. How are *you* keeping? It must be worrying you or you'd not have come to see me.'

She shrugged. 'I'm all right. I'm rarely ill. But as you say, I'm worried about Jonah and you know how it is when there's an invalid in the house. The one looking after them gets a bit tired now and then.'

She'd eaten something that disagreed with her a couple of days ago, probably the last of the potted meat and it had made her queasy. Thank goodness Jonah hadn't eaten it too.

She stood up. 'Thank you for seeing me.'

'If you think there's anything else wrong, don't hesitate to come to me because Jonah won't unless he's desperate.'

'No. He's very thoughtful; doesn't like to trouble people.'

She had a cup of tea at her adopted aunt's then left her to cook for her lodgers and went out to the car.

It didn't want to start and when she did get it going, it hiccupped a bit, before settling down. She'd get Todd to have a look at it. She'd been meaning to have it checked for a while.

Just after she'd left Rivenshaw and was driving past the farms between it and Birch End, the car made a grating sound and stopped dead.

'Oh, no!' She managed to get to the edge of the road before the car stopped completely. Sighing, she gave it a minute or two, then tried again to start it. Nothing happened.

She looked up and down the road but there were no cars coming either way. Should she wait for someone or walk back into Rivenshaw to Charlie's shop and get him to call his partner? If anyone could fix the car, it'd be Todd.

Fate must have been on her side, because a man she knew came driving down the hill. She got out and waved to him to stop, explaining her problem.

'I'll go and tell Mr Selby. He fixed my cousin's car up last week and it's running perfectly again. You get in your car and wait. It may be spring but it's turned cold again.'

Leah knew it'd take at least a quarter of an hour for him to send Todd out to her, so she settled into the driving seat and tried to wait patiently. She kept glancing at her wristwatch and finding only a couple more minutes had passed.

She was feeling the cold, hadn't dressed warmly enough because she had a car. She'd not make that mistake again. Yes, and she'd put an old blanket in the car, too, in case she broke down again. Easy to be wise after the event. She glanced down at her watch. Three more minutes had passed.

Eventually she saw what looked like Todd's neat little van coming up the hill towards her. Yes, it was him. Thank goodness!

Todd stopped in front of Leah's car so that he could reach his tools easily if needed.

She got out of her car, arms crossed as if to keep herself warm.

'What's wrong with the car? Do you have any idea?'

'I've no idea. It didn't want to start when I was leaving Auntie Hilda's but then it did start and it seemed to be going all right, so I set off home.' She spread her hands helplessly. 'It's never let me down before.'

She didn't look as well as usual and was shivering, so he got out the old blanket he kept in his van. 'You look cold. Here. Put this round your shoulders.'

'Thank you.'

He shook out the blanket and wrapped it round her. For a moment they were close together and it happened as it had before – he felt the attraction zip between them.

She felt it too, he could tell, because she coloured slightly as she said, 'Thank you!' and stepped quickly back.

He busied himself looking at her car, but it wasn't anything he could fix by the side of the road, so he went back to her. 'I need to take it into my garage. You haven't been getting it serviced lately, have you?'

She frowned as if trying to remember, then shook her head. 'I keep meaning to but we've been so busy and it was running pretty well till today.'

'Would you be all right guiding the car if I towed you slowly down to my workshop? I can drive you home after that.'

'Yes, of course I'll be all right.' It couldn't be all that hard, could it?

'I'll attach the tow rope then we'll wait till the road is clear and turn to face the other direction as we pull out slowly. Good thing the edge of the road is firm here. Don't worry. I won't go fast.'

She nodded and gave him back the blanket. 'Thank you for that. I'll be all right now. It'd get in the way of me driving.'

She managed better than he'd expected. She was a very capable woman in many ways, and he admired that about her too. In fact he hadn't seen anything about her to dislike, except the fact that she was already married.

When he pulled her car into the garage yard, she got out and he saw her shiver again. 'I could make a quick cup of tea to warm you up.'

'No. Better not. Jonah will be worrying and he hasn't been well.'

'You could phone him from here.'

'Yes, of course. I should have thought of that. All right, then. A cup of tea would be very welcome. I do feel chilled through.'

He put the kettle on then they phoned Jonah, setting his mind at rest.

While the tea was brewing Todd took her bag of shopping out of her car and put it into his van to make sure he didn't forget it, then went back and finished making the tea.

It was lovely to sit and chat to someone. He was usually alone here.

He gestured round them. 'Sorry it's such a dismal place, but neither Charlie nor I want to waste money doing it up at the moment.'

'It wouldn't cost much to distemper the walls in here. That'd brighten the place up.'

He glanced round. 'You're right. It would.'

'And those old curtains could do with a good wash.' She went across to examine them. 'They're sturdy cotton. If they were washed carefully, they'd come up quite well. Take them to Harris's laundry. They'll see to them for you.'

He chuckled.

She looked at him as if to ask what was amusing him.

'They talk about "a woman's touch". It didn't take you more than a few minutes to work out two simple things to improve this dreary place.'

'Sorry. I shouldn't interfere.'

'No need to be sorry. You're right and I'd love to make it brighter in here. I'll do what you suggest. Would you like a refill?'

'No, thank you. I'd rather get on our way, if you don't mind.'

He did mind. He didn't want her to leave. They hadn't said much, let alone talked about anything personal and yet he'd felt comfortable with her, as if he'd known her for years. If things were different, he'd be courting her.

He'd better watch himself carefully from now on. He didn't want anyone else guessing how he reacted to her. Nor did he want to embarrass her in any way. She had enough on her plate with a sickly husband to care for.

Why was life so difficult? Why couldn't he find a woman with no ties to be attracted to?

# 9

The bus chugged along steadily on through the twilight. It had few passengers so didn't need to stop very often. When he recognised the small village of Wemsworth ahead, Jim got the suitcase down from the overhead rack ready to get off.

The bus stopped next to the church and he helped Nina down and indicated a side road. 'This way.'

She couldn't help asking, 'Are you sure your aunt will want to help me?'

'Yes. She's my great-aunt actually, but she hates me calling her that, says it reminds her how old she is, so I just call her aunt.'

He turned off into a private drive that had huge, wrought-iron gates open to the world. She hoped that was an omen, that the owner would be open to helping her. Oh, she was being stupid, clutching at straws to give herself hope.

When they got to the house, Jim led the way round to the back.

Before they reached the kitchen door a man looked out of the stables and called, 'Did you want something?'

'I'm Carrie's nephew. I need to see my aunt.'

The man came across. 'Oh yes, I can see you more clearly now. It's Jim, isn't it?' He opened the kitchen door, leading the way in. Once inside, he called, 'Anyone know where Carrie is? She has a visitor.'

An older woman peered out of a doorway, face flushed as

if she was hot and called, 'Mabel, go and fetch Carrie. Sit down in the passage here, Jim and . . .?' She looked rather suspiciously at Nina.

'Miss Halshall, who is a friend of my wife's.'

Three minutes passed slowly by the big clock on the wall. Nina felt desperately anxious. What would she do if they didn't help her? The only thing she knew was that she wasn't going back, not for anything.

An older woman came bustling down the stairs, looking at them in surprise. 'Jim? I didn't expect to see you here at this time of the evening.'

He went across to kiss her cheek and introduced Nina. 'Can we speak to you in private, Auntie?'

She cast him a quick, suspicious glance and led the way into a small room to one side.

'Nina's a friend of Brenda's and she's in trouble through no fault of her own.' He explained quickly what had happened, ending, 'Brenda thought you and Lady Terryng might be able to help her friend find a job in service.'

Carrie leaned back in her chair studying Nina and what she saw seemed to satisfy her because her expression softened and became more friendly. 'We'll definitely help her. We can't let people behave like that to decent young women.'

'Not so young,' Nina said. 'I'm nearly thirty.'

'That seems young to me. Don't look so worried, dear. I'm sure we can help.'

Jim cleared his throat to get their attention. 'Um, what time does the last bus go, Auntie?'

'Oh dear! It's gone already. It was the one you arrived on.'

Jim's shoulders sagged. 'Can I sleep in the stables, then, do you think? What time's the first bus in the morning? I can't afford to be late for work.'

'No need to worry. I'm sure her ladyship will ask Falding

to drive you back once she hears why you've come out here at this hour. She's in charge of the orphanage now, you know. You'd not recognise the place since she took over. That man was starving those poor children as well as beating them.'

She got up. 'I'll ask cook to give you both a bite to eat while I'm explaining to her ladyship.'

She whisked out of the room and Nina let out a shuddering sigh of relief. 'Your aunt seems very sure her employer won't mind me turning up.'

'She should know. She and her ladyship are as much friends as employer and maid.'

The kitchen maid took them into the servants' dining room and brought some hearty soup and thick slices of bread. By the time they'd finished eating, Carrie was back.

'Falding will drive you home, Jim, and we'll look after Miss Halshall.'

He smiled and stood up. 'Thank you. Brenda will be delighted. And I'll really enjoy going back in style.'

Nina thanked him again for his help and hoped she'd kept her expression calm as she said goodbye. But as he walked out she felt very vulnerable, alone in a house full of strangers.

Carrie patted her shoulder. 'You'll be all right here, my dear. Come and meet her ladyship.'

Lady Terryng was much younger than her maid, around forty Nina guessed. She had a rather plain face till she smiled, then you didn't care how she looked, just wanted to smile back at her.

'You must feel terrible after what's happened,' her ladyship said once Nina was seated. 'Don't worry. You can stay here and help out generally till we find you a job.'

'But what job could I do? I'm not trained for anything, not even the sort of housework needed for a lovely place like this.'

'You've been running a smaller house for years. Are you any good at that?'

'Well, yes. And I'm very thrifty, too. I've had to be.'

'Would you *mind* going into service? Many women do these days.'

'Of course not. I'd do anything to keep away from my brother and that horrible old man.'

'Well, there you are. We'll definitely be able to find you something.'

'I don't know how to thank you.'

'You can come across to the orphanage with me and help out with the boys while we wait for something to turn up. That'll be thanks enough. Because of the shocking way they've been treated, they still find it hard to trust people. Some of them can barely read and write, so we're working on that, as well as feeding them up and making sure they run about and get used to behaving like boys again.'

'I'd be happy to help, though I don't have much experience of children.'

'I'm sure you'll cope. You won't be working alone. Now, you look tired. Carrie will find you a bedroom – do you have enough clothes?'

'I managed to pack all my clothes because I don't have many. I had to leave my books behind, though, and I'll miss them. Books can be a great comfort. Is there a library in the village?'

'No, but you can borrow my books while you're here. I have plenty in the room we call the library.'

Half an hour later, Nina was in a bed in one of the attic rooms used for servants, enjoying snuggling down in the crisp, clean sheets that had been well warmed by a stone hot water bottle.

She'd escaped. She really had. And somehow she trusted her ladyship to keep her safe. It was wonderful to have someone else to help you, instead of having to struggle alone.

She fell asleep between one thought and the next, a smile on her face.

# 10

When Harry got home from Ellindale, it was almost dark. He took the motorbike back to its owner first and found the man in a cheerful, chatty mood.

'You're just in time, lad. I'm going to be moving down south soon to stay with a relative and I'll be selling the motorbike and the one with the sidecar as well. I've happened on an old motor van and managed to fix it up. I'm going to be delivering stuff for my relative.'

'You've let lucky.' Harry looked at the motorbike with a sidecar. Life would be a lot easier if he had one of those, by hell it would. But he couldn't risk buying one until he saw how things panned out in Ellindale.

He walked home. It was only a few streets but the day had been tiring and it seemed further. How dull and dirty everything looked in the fading light! There was a smokiness in the air even though this was a Sunday when the mill chimneys weren't belching out thick clouds of smoke. But there were still thin trickles of smoke here and there as the various mills kept the boilers going on low ready for the morning.

The people he passed seemed pale and worn. Those he'd seen in Ellindale had looked rosier, even though their clothes were just as shabby and their faces gaunt. They must be spending more time out of doors in clean air and they looked the better for it.

Would his daughter look rosier if they lived in Ellindale?

Would she really be better simply by breathing in fresh air there? He had to believe it.

When he went next door, he found Cathie lying on the sofa looking utterly limp.

'That poor lamb had another asthma attack,' Mrs Pyne said in a low voice. 'Luckily it wasn't one of her bad ones. I've kept her quiet since then.'

He knelt by the sofa to hug his daughter and she clung to him tightly, her breath rasping in her throat still.

'I was frightened, Daddy. You weren't there.'

'When she got better I let her read an old newspaper my husband picked up in the street last week,' Mrs Pyne said. 'It kept her mind off things.'

'I read lots of it, Daddy,' Cathie said. 'Nearly every page, though I didn't understand some parts of them. I liked the adverts best.'

'Did you? Adverts for what?'

'All sorts of things. But the one I liked best was someone selling railway carriages for people to live in.' She giggled. 'Just imagine buying a railway carriage. Where would you put it?'

He felt as if he'd been struck by lightning and had trouble keeping his voice steady. 'Show me that advert, my little loviekins. I've never seen one offering railway carriages for sale before, either.'

She turned over the big sheets of newsprint carefully, and showed him a page full of narrow columns separated by black smudgy lines containing lists of adverts for many different items. 'There it is, Daddy.'

He picked up the paper and read it carefully: *Railway carriages for sale, suitable for holiday homes.* £10 plus small delivery charge.

His hands were shaking as he turned to Mrs Pyne because it seemed as if fate had thrown one answer at him. 'Could I have this page of adverts, please? There's something I want to look into.'

'Of course you can. Keep it. I was only going to use it for lighting the fire anyway. I shan't miss one page.'

He ripped off that page carefully. 'Thank you. And I'm grateful to you for looking after my Cathie so well.' He slipped a shilling into her hand and she put it in her apron pocket, patting it as if it were something alive.

A shilling made a big difference when you were struggling to survive on the dole. He wished he could afford to give her more, because she gave him far more than a shilling's worth of caring for his daughter.

After Cathie had gone to bed, he sat down to read the advert again. He must have read it at least a dozen times and even though he knew it by heart, he still followed the words on the page as he muttered it aloud, because the dark print made the advert seem more real than simply going over it in his head.

This could solve one of his main problems: where they would live if they moved to Ellindale. If he dared take the risk, he'd be spending some of his precious money but they wouldn't have to pay rent.

Well, he had no choice. Cathie's asthma attack today seemed like a final warning.

He'd have to go to Ellindale again next weekend to see if he could buy that piece of land. No use doing anything about buying a railway carriage until he had somewhere to put one.

Him spending another Sunday away would upset Cathie, and he wasn't even sure whether to tell her what he was thinking of doing in case she blurted it out to someone. He had to be very careful because he didn't want to lose his job before he was ready to leave Manchester, before he had somewhere for them to go.

★

Two days later he had another idea. If it was fine at the weekend, he'd spend three shillings more than last time and hire his friend's motorbike with a sidecar instead of the small motorbike. In all fairness Cathie ought to see the village before he took steps to move there.

If he wrapped her up well, she could ride in the sidecar and he was sure the outing would cheer her up. He'd seen the vehicle and it looked to be in good condition, and it was well-sprung, therefore safer and more comfortable to ride in than the unsprung cheaper ones.

He sat Cathie down that very evening and explained what he was thinking of doing.

'You mustn't tell anyone about Ellindale, not even Mrs Pyne. Nothing is certain yet, anyway; we're just looking into it. But I could lose my job on the spot if Mr Trowton found out I was thinking of leaving the factory. Eh, he'd throw a fit, that one would.'

'I won't tell anyone, Dad.'

'Some of your friends are bound to see us leaving, so tell them we're off for a run in the country to give you a breath of fresh air. Don't tell them where we're going, just say we'll be driving round the countryside.'

She looked at him wide-eyed and thoughtful. It was a few moments before she nodded acceptance of this precaution.

A little later she asked suddenly, 'Is Ellindale a nice place, Dad?'

'Very nice indeed. The old man I talked to said it was special because people are good neighbours and are kind to one another.'

'We have a good neighbour here.'

'Yes, I know, but we don't have clean air to breathe and you need that more than anything. We'd have the moors nearby and they're lovely, the moors are, Cathie. The old man said it made him feel good just to look at them. They made me feel good, too.'

She nodded, looking brighter. 'It'll be an adventure, Dad, won't it? Like in the books I get from the library. I never thought I'd have a real adventure.'

'You're right. But remember not to tell anyone where we're going or why. Promise me.'

She crossed her heart solemnly.

'There's my lass.'

One day during his half hour midday break, Harry nipped along to the nearby Yorkshire Penny Bank where he'd deposited Dora's insurance money three years ago. One hundred pounds they'd paid him for his wife's death. He'd nearly thrown the cheque back at them because it seemed like blood money, but even in the throes of grief, he couldn't act that stupidly.

He'd never touched the money though, and it'd taken a desperate emergency to make him consider using it now. If Cathie's deteriorating health wasn't more important than his feelings about the insurance money, he didn't know what was.

He asked to see his balance first and when the teller had filled in the various interest payments in his savings book, Harry took it to the counter at one side of the room to study it.

He hated even touching the damned thing, but forced himself to open the little book and study the figures the clerk had written in today. What he saw made him gasp and stare at it in shock. He'd known interest would be paid on the deposit, of course he had, but he hadn't been able to bear thinking about specifics and anyway, the interest rates had kept changing in the past three years from what he'd read in the newspapers, so it was hard to keep track.

He now had a balance of just over £110. It might be blood money, but Dora would have been the first to tell him to stop being so stupid and use it to help their daughter. And she'd have added, 'Told you we might need it if one of us died.' She'd been wiser than him in some ways.

She seemed like a distant ghost now, he'd been so busy since she died, working and looking after their daughter and caring for their home – a task he'd never had to do before. You thought you'd never get over the loss of losing a wife, but the sharpness of his grief had softened. Nature was kind to you in that way. He couldn't have lived the rest of his life in such agonising pain as he'd experienced in the weeks following Dora's death.

After some thought, he filled in a withdrawal form and took £10 out, asking for a five-pound note, three pound notes and four ten-shilling ones. He'd never had that much money in his pocket at once in his whole life. He put the banknotes in the wallet, and slid it carefully into his inside jacket pocket. It felt like a heavy lump against his breast as he walked back and he had to resist the urge to clutch it to keep it safe as he moved.

When he went to bed that night, he prayed for the first time since Dora's death. He wasn't a religious man, but it seemed right to ask for help in doing the best he could for his daughter.

Then he spoke to his wife. He'd had conversations with her in his head a few times since she died. 'You did the right thing taking out that insurance policy, my lass. I think your money will give me the only chance of saving our daughter's life. Thank you.'

He'd have sworn he heard Dora's voice faintly in the distance saying he was doing the right thing buying that land. It was only his imagination, of course, but even an imagined conversation could be comforting when you were making such important decisions all on your own.

*

On the Saturday afternoon he got out his old atlas of the counties of England and opened it at the map of Lancashire, showing Cathie exactly where they were going. She wanted to draw her own map from it, with the towns and villages labelled, so he let her. She loved to draw, so he kept the white wrapping paper some shops used when they weighed and wrapped the things you were buying, and they smoothed the paper out together with a cool iron.

As she went to bed that night, she put her map on the table and weighed it down with the sugar bowl. 'I don't want to forget this in the morning. I'm going to hold it on my lap so that I can see where each town and village is, how far we've gone and how far we still have to go.'

'Better get a good night's sleep then, love. It'll be a big day for us tomorrow.'

She nestled against him for a few moments. 'I love you lots, Dad.'

'I love you too, loviekins. Now, scoot! Up those wooden hills to blanketshire with you.'

On the Sunday morning Cathie was very excited but had learned the painful lesson of not giving in to excitement or her breathing would suffer.

Harry watched her anxiously. 'Remember, love. You have to keep calm and breathe slowly.'

'I'm trying, Daddy, but I think I can let myself get a tiny bit excited without it upsetting me, because it's a good thing that's happening, not a bad one.'

He left her with Mrs Pyne while he went to pick up the motorbike. He never left her on her own in the house because this wasn't the nicest part of town to live in.

He'd driven a motorbike with a sidecar before, so he had no trouble with it. Well, he'd driven just about any vehicle you cared to name in the army. Old-fashioned some of them were now, compared to modern cars, but he'd always enjoyed driving.

He tucked Cathie into the sidecar with a blanket over her knees. 'Away we go.' He put the lid down over her and pulled a face at her through the glass side panel.

She stuck her tongue out at him in reply then stared ahead eagerly as he set off. He caught occasional glimpses of her as he drove. She kept looking from side to side, a happy expression on her face, no signs of distress in her breathing. He'd be able to tell if there were, just from watching her.

He realised that she hadn't been anywhere in her short life except into the centre of Manchester and felt guilty about that, though he couldn't have managed things much differently since Dora died.

You had a very narrow choice of activities when you didn't have much money and had to save whatever few pennies you could in case you lost your job.

There was an even narrower choice when you lost your wife, who was also your housekeeper, because then you had to pay for help. He always told people he didn't want to marry again to stop them introducing him to their female relatives, but it wasn't true. Being married was a practical way to cope with daily life for a man.

Only to himself did he admit that he'd love to marry again for the company, he felt so desperately lonely at times.

But he wasn't going to do that unless he found someone he felt comfortable with. A woman's looks didn't matter nearly as much as a pleasant nature. You spent a lot of time with a wife and once you'd got used to a face, you never really looked at it closely again.

Only the trouble was, he couldn't imagine finding another woman he got on with as well as Dora.

# 11

Cathie jigged about in her seat in excitement when her father slowed down to indicate the sign by the side of the road saying 'RIVENSHAW' in big letters.

He didn't expect there to be anywhere open to buy a warm drink, not on a Sunday, but he'd brought along a big bottle of water, some sandwiches and some biscuits. They'd have a picnic if they could find somewhere sheltered, otherwise Cathie could eat in the sidecar.

The first thing he intended to do was go right up the valley to Ellindale and look at the plot of land again. Could it really have as lovely an outlook as he'd remembered?

He drove slowly, taking in the scenery, feeling excited when he reached the Ellindale sign. He stopped immediately after it and pointed to the old wooden 'For Sale' sign on the piece of land. It was still there, thank goodness.

After letting Cathie out of the sidecar, he helped her over the wall so that they could walk round the piece of land. When he turned round she had stopped to stare behind them at the moors that surrounded the village.

Her eyes were full of wonder. 'It's beautiful here, just like you said, Dad.'

'Yes. And how does the air taste?'

'Fresh, as if it's blown over lots of growing things.' She drew in deep breaths as she continued to gaze at the moors and looked so happy he didn't urge her to move on.

Then suddenly the peace was broken by a man's voice, shouting at them harshly.

'Hoy, you! What do you think you're doing on my land?'

Harry turned to see a middle-aged man with a red, weather-beaten face scowling at them, so pointed to the sign. 'It says the land is for sale. I'm looking to buy a piece of land so I thought I'd walk round this one. You can't buy something this important without having a good look at it first, can you?'

The man was clearly surprised and it was a moment or two before he spoke again, this time in a quieter tone of voice. 'Well, um, that's all right then. I've had to watch out for people picnicking on my land and leaving all sorts of messes, you see.'

'How much do you want for it?' Harry asked.

'What it says on that sign: five pounds. And I'll not take a penny less, because it's a fair price.'

'Yes, it is fair. I wouldn't quibble about that. With your permission, my daughter and I will walk round and have a good look. Then, if I'm interested, I'll come and see you. Do you live up that lane?'

'Aye. Only house there is, so you can't miss us.' He nodded and walked away, turning once to stare at them, then moving on.

Cathie had edged closer to her father. 'He looks very bad-tempered.'

'If we want to buy the land, it doesn't matter what he looks like. Now, come on. We must make a really thorough inspection.'

He explained to her what the three-sided building was for and she tried out the rock that looked as if it was meant to be a seat or table.

The little spring he'd noticed before beyond the shepherd's

shelter was welling up clear and sparkling. He bent to scoop up a handful of water. 'It tastes good to me. See what you think.'

She imitated him, taking care not to spill water down herself. 'It tastes lovely when it's cold like this. Can I drink this instead of the water we brought with us?'

'Why not?'

She didn't wheeze once as they walked to and fro, and he was listening carefully for any sign of it.

After they'd gone the whole way round they clambered back over the front wall to look at the land from the other side of the main road.

'I'm hungry.' She sounded surprised.

'Are you? So am I, now I come to think of it.' That was a good sign. She hadn't seemed really hungry for a while.

'Can we sit on the wall to eat our sandwiches, Dad, and look out across the moors?'

'The wind's quite chilly.'

'I don't mind.'

'Let's eat in the shepherd's shelter. We can sit on that stone bench and still see out.'

She perched on it, sandwich in one hand, smiling. 'This is bigger than my bedroom and I like sitting here, but what will we do for a house if we move here?'

'I'll go and fetch our picnic, then we'll talk about that as we eat.'

He sat beside her watching her eat with a good appetite. Her cheeks had some colour in them, too. So far so good.

'This is another secret for the moment,' he began, 'but I thought about that advert you found, the one for railway carriages. If we bought one and had it transported here, we could live in it. How would you like that?'

'Ooh, I'd love it!'

'We could use this shepherd's shelter as a kitchen if I built a wall across the open side and attached it to the end of the railway carriage.'

She looked round again, as if assessing it. 'That'd be nice. We'd need a window as well, though, or it'd be too dark.' Then a frown wrinkled her forehead. 'Can Mrs Pyne come and live here too?'

'I'm afraid not, but perhaps she could come and visit us once we're settled.'

Her face fell. 'I'd miss her a lot.'

'I know, loviekins, but nothing is ever perfect and you've not been well living where we are now. You'll feel better here with all the fresh air. That's what the doctor said anyway.'

'Where would I go to school?'

'I asked about that last time. There's a junior school in the next village down the valley.'

She nodded. 'Birch End.'

'Yes, and a secondary school in Rivenshaw. But I think I'd let you run free for a few weeks first and you could start school again in September when your health is better.'

He realised he was getting ahead of himself, because he still had to buy the land and sort out somewhere to live. Folding up the paper bags he'd put the sandwiches in, he placed everything in the shopping bag. 'I'll just put this back in the sidecar then we'll go and speak to the farmer.'

When he looked back there was a big break in the clouds and though it was still cool, Cathie was standing in the entrance to the shelter, her face turned up to the sun like a flower needing the brightness and light.

That sight made him even more certain that he was going to buy this land.

He went back, helped her over the wall and they walked hand in hand along the lane to the farmhouse. It was a poor sort of place, looking very run down. Well, it'd never be the sort of land that gave you a good living.

Cathie slowed down, smiling at the hens walking about in a run made of wire netting and oddments of wood. Then they came to a cat sitting in a sunny, sheltered corner suckling two kittens.

She'd let go of his hand before he knew it and knelt down to caress one of the fluffy little heads. The mother cat didn't seem to mind and swiped a lazy tongue indiscriminately over Cathie's hand and her kitten's head.

Harry let her enjoy petting the pretty little creatures for a few moments then said, 'Come on, love. We have business to attend to.'

Mr Kerkham opened the door before they got there. He wasn't looking angry now but wary, definitely wary, as if he didn't dare hope for a sale. He didn't say anything, seemed to be waiting for his visitor to speak first.

'My name's Harry Makepeace and I'm interested in buying your piece of land, on certain conditions.'

'I'm not taking less than five pounds.'

'I'm happy to pay you that, but it'll take me time to arrange to move, so I'd make it a condition that you keep an eye on the land till I come here myself. Mainly I'd want you to see that no one pinches the stones that have fallen off the wall or dumps muck in that spring or leaves any rubbish there. I'll need the stones for building a shelter and repairing the wall and I'm like you, can't abide a mess.'

'Aye. I can do that for you.'

'I'm assuming the spring water is clean enough to drink?'

'None cleaner. We have another little spring on our land. Lots of them up here. The spring water in Ellindale is so good that Mrs Willcox uses the one up at Spring Cottage, on the other side of the village, to make fizzy drinks and sell them to rich folk.'

'That's going to save me a lot of trouble about a water supply.'

A woman joined them, much too thin with a hungry look to her. She had a worn face and rough hands reddened with hard work. 'If you don't tell anyone you've sold it, Peter, folk will still keep away because you've already got them too frightened to come near it.'

He considered this. 'Aye. We could do that for a while, but we'd have to register the sale with the council an' someone there would be bound to let the news out.'

He snapped his fingers and grinned, suddenly looking years younger. 'But if I were to tell folk I'd sold it to my *cousin* an' say I'm watching it for him as carefully as I watched it for myself, I reckon they'd still keep away.'

Kerkham's face changed when he smiled, Harry thought, and he looked younger. Perhaps he was going through a bad patch. 'That'd be a big help. Thanks. I'll want a bill of sale properly witnessed. Is there anyone round here who'd do that?'

The other man frowned, then said, 'I think Mr Willcox up at Spring Cottage would know how to do that, an' him and his missus could witness it. You could trust them to keep quiet about it better than anyone else.'

His wife nodded. 'I'll send our Frankie up the hill with a note asking if they'll do that. And if so, we'll walk up to their house straight away and get it done. Well, we could do it if you have the money with you, Mr Makepeace.'

He nodded. 'I saw the land last week and came prepared.'

'Good. You can give it to us in front of them an' then the land will be yours.'

Frankie, a scrawny lad of about ten with an alert expression, listened to the message and repeated it to his mother's satisfaction. He was wearing cut-down trousers too big for him and his mother wrapped a long scarf round his neck, crossing it over his chest and fastening it at the back, before he set off at a run.

She turned to the visitors and asked, 'Would you like a cup of tea?'

'We'd love one, thank you.'

Her husband went out to see to his pigs while the kettle boiled and she whispered, 'My Peter's bark is worse than his bite. Only he don't like them village lads messing him about and things haven't been easy lately.'

Harry guessed from how weak the tea was that they were very short of everything and refused a biscuit. 'Actually, I could share the rest of our biscuits with you, because they'll only get battered into crumbs on the way back.'

'Are you sure?'

'Oh, yes.'

'Well, that's very kind of you. Thank you.'

He saw her lick her lips. He recognised deep hunger when he saw it. There were women who went short to feed their families. He'd read in the newspaper about one with seven children who just dropped dead one day because she'd been giving her share to them. In his books, that was just as heroic as anything that had happened in the war.

He saw it all around him, the quiet heroism of people enduring without complaint the troubles that lack of work and poverty brought. Shame on the damned government for making the dole so low that it wasn't enough to feed folk properly. As for that rule that they had to sell all but their essential possessions before they could receive money, it was one of the cruellest things he'd ever heard of.

He realised he was wool-gathering and pulled himself back to the moment. 'I'll just nip out to the motorbike and fetch the biscuits. I'll be glad not to see them go to waste.'

*

Ten minutes after he'd run up the hill, Frankie came back with word that Mr and Mrs Willcox would be happy to witness the document. There were two biscuits left on the plate and his mother passed them to him, which made his eyes gleam.

Mr and Mrs Kerkham walked up the hill and Harry followed them slowly on the motorbike. Two women gossiping at their doorsteps stopped their conversation to stare at him and when he called 'Good afternoon!' they nodded in return.

The whole village was neat and tidy, which meant the inhabitants looked after it, even now.

When they got to Spring Cottage, Harry got off the motorbike and was helping Cathie out of the sidecar when Mrs Kerkham came closer and whispered to him, 'Mr Willcox was gassed in the war, and he's not well. Tell the little lass not to stare.'

Most people of Harry's age had seen the unfortunates gassed in the war and recognised their laboured breathing. As he bent to explain to Cathie, he realised yet again how lucky he'd been to come out of the war uninjured. The give and take of life, he supposed you'd call it.

Mrs Willcox came to the door to greet them, smiling to see Cathie. 'I didn't realise we'd be having a youngster come to visit us as well. Rosa, have you a minute?'

A tall lass came to join her. The two women bore a distinct resemblance and Harry guessed they were sisters.

Mrs Willcox gave her companion an assessing look. 'You're due a break from your studies, love. Why don't you take the little girl to look round the fizzy drinks factory while we help Mr and Mrs Kerkham with their business? You can give her a drink of lemonade or whatever she fancies. What's your name, dear?'

'Cathie. Can I really see how you make fizzy drinks?'

'Yes, of course.'

Rosa eased her shoulders and smiled at the girl. 'I forget where I am when I'm studying. I'll be happy to stretch my legs. Come on, Cathie.'

Harry wasn't surprised at his daughter going off with her without hesitation. Rosa had a lovely warm smile, just like her elder sister. Besides, a treat like that was something his daughter didn't often experience. He wished suddenly that he could buy her all the treats in the world: sweets and bottles of lemonade and new clothes for a start.

Inside the house, Mrs Willcox offered them a cup of tea and though they'd just had one, the Kerkhams both accepted eagerly. When their hostess brought a plate of buns to the table, their eyes gleamed just as much as their son's had done at the sight of the biscuits.

Harry and Mr Kerkham explained to the Willcoxes what they needed and why he was moving up to Ellindale, after which Mr Willcox studied Harry more intently.

His voice was faint and raspy, and he looked pale. 'I hope you'll be happy here, Mr Makepeace, and that the fresh air will help your daughter. I'm sure it's helped me prolong my own life since the war.'

Harry saw his wife throw him a quick, sad look as he said that, and didn't need telling that her husband was on the downhill path healthwise. It showed in his face. There was often a transparent look to someone's eyes when they were at the end of their life. He'd seen too many men with that look to mistake it.

'I'll write you out a proper bill of sale, if you like,' Mr Willcox added. 'I've done them before.'

Mr Kerkham's face brightened. 'I'd be grateful. I'm not much of a one for writing, let alone legal stuff, and I'd rather not waste my money on a lawyer.'

As the tea was brewing Mr Willcox got out some paper and his writing equipment and wrote two copies of a simple bill of sale, one for each person involved, putting himself and his wife at the bottom as witnesses.

He looked up as he finished. 'We can do this quite quickly. Do you have the money, Mr Makepeace?'

'Yes.' Harry got out the first five-pound note he'd ever owned and handed it over, not giving in to a silly urge to kiss it farewell.

Mr Kerkham took a deep, wobbly breath as he accepted it. 'You don't have any smaller notes?'

Harry shook his head. He needed them himself.

'I can give you some change out of the fizzy drinks money,' Mrs Willcox said.

'Eh, thank you. That'd be a big help. No one I deal with can change a five-pound note.' He and his wife signed their names on both papers and Harry did the same, then let the Willcoxes witness them.

'There you are,' their host said. 'Signed, sealed and delivered. The land is now yours, Mr Makepeace. Welcome to Ellindale. I'll get you some envelopes to keep the bill of sale clean.'

As he started to get up, his wife said quickly, 'I'll get them.' She vanished into the other room.

They sat at the table for a few minutes, drinking cups of tea that were far stronger than the weak ones offered by Mrs Kerkham, and eating delicious buns.

From the way Mrs Willcox urged her guests to tuck in, he suspected she knew how tight money was for them. For all her smiles, there was a shrewdness to her that he respected.

When Cathie returned with Rosa, she came straight across to her father, nestling against him, still with no sign of laboured breathing.

'I had some ginger beer, Dad. It was lovely.' She looked across at their hostess. 'Thank you very much, Mrs Willcox. It was the best drink I've ever tasted.'

'I'm glad you enjoyed it.'

As they left, Mrs Willcox came to the door with them but her husband said goodbye from his chair by the fire. He looked white with exhaustion now.

'We'll look forward to having you as neighbours once your house is built, Mr Makepeace.'

'I can't afford to have a house built, Mrs Willcox, so I'm hoping to bring in a railway carriage to live in for the time being because I don't want to wait to move here.'

She looked surprised.

'They sell them for ten pounds plus moving costs.'

'What a clever idea!'

He nodded. 'After that I'll have to see if I can find work. I'm an electrical engineer and I repair household equipment as well as doing bigger jobs. Mr Selby in Rivenshaw has promised me a day's work here and there. Do you know him?'

'Oh, yes. He's my brother-in-law's partner in selling cars. He's, um, a very capable man.'

Harry was glad to hear that. 'Once I move here I'll have to get my name known to find other jobs.' He hoped he didn't look as worried as he felt whenever he thought of that impending lack of income. 'It's not a good time to leave a steady job, but Cathie was really ill recently, so I can't wait. And the owner is getting very strange as he grows older. It can make my job . . . difficult.'

'I'll mention you to my friends once you've moved here. People never know when they might need something repairing. Your motorbike will be good for getting around to jobs.'

'Thank you.'

Her assumption that the motorbike was his gave him a second idea. Motorbikes were much cheaper than cars, both to buy and to run. And you could fit a lot of tools and equipment into a sidecar. He'd have to travel here and there to do jobs for people – which meant he'd also have to find someone to look after Cathie after school. Perhaps Mrs Kerkham would do it if he slipped her the odd shilling?

Well, he'd worry about details like that later. His next job was to buy a railway carriage. He didn't know what he'd do if they'd sold out. He could live in a tent in summer as he'd heard of one man doing, but that wouldn't be a good enough shelter for Cathie.

'Aren't they nice people, Dad?' she whispered as he was about to close the top of the sidecar. 'Rosa was lovely. She told me she's studying hard because she wants to be a doctor.'

'Good luck to her then. We need more doctors in the world. And yes, the Willcoxes are lovely. Now, we'll have to get off home. I'll phone up and ask about the railway carriages tomorrow.'

She nodded and pulled up the blanket.

When he stopped at a crossroads half an hour later, he glanced at the sidecar and saw that Cathie was asleep. He hoped it wasn't his imagination, but her face seemed rosier than usual. Well, she'd been out in the fresh air for much longer than usual today, hadn't she?

And he hadn't heard her wheeze once.

# 12

Two days later Leah went back into the house from the factory and paused just inside the door, surprised not to see her husband in his chair by the fire.

She went into the front room where Ginny Dutton was dusting the ornaments and humming to herself.

'Have you seen Jonah this morning?'

'He's still in bed. I peeped in earlier but he didn't stir. Well, he does get up late sometimes, doesn't he? I decided to start in here so as not to disturb him.'

Leah frowned. 'How long ago was that?'

Ginny looked at the clock. 'Gracious me! It must have been a good hour and a half ago.'

'He doesn't usually stay in bed this late. I'll nip up and check that he's all right. He didn't sleep at all well last night, was very restless.' In fact they'd had a quiet chat at one stage and he'd held her hand, telling her how much he loved her, something he didn't often do.

She went quietly up the stairs.

Jonah was lying half across the bed as if he'd started to get up then fallen back. As she moved closer, she couldn't hold back a loud cry of anguish. '*Noooo!*'

He was dead. No mistaking that look. It was as if someone had made a bad copy of her husband's face, which was now slack and lifeless, lacking the gently humorous expression he normally faced the world with.

She felt for a pulse, of course she did, but she knew she wouldn't find one.

Ginny came up the stairs. 'I heard you cry out and— *Oh, no!*'

Leah couldn't think what to do. She could only kneel beside the bed with tears rolling down her cheeks.

Ginny put an arm round her. 'Get up, love. Come and sit down in the kitchen.'

'I have to stay with Jonah.'

'You can't help him now. Better not move him. Leave him for the doctor to check. Eh, see how peaceful he looks. Not many folk get to die so easily.'

Leah took a long look at Jonah then let Ginny guide her towards the stairs and follow her down. She felt disoriented, couldn't see beyond the pain. Well, who wouldn't be upset to lose a husband like Jonah?

She saw Ginny watching her with tears in her eyes.

'He was a lovely man, Mr Willcox was.'

How quickly people spoke of someone in the past tense, Leah thought. She told the simple truth. 'I can't think what to do, Ginny.' She searched in vain for her handkerchief and used the corner of her overall to mop her eyes.

'I think you'd better phone the doctor and Mr Charlie. You need help and they'll sort everything out for you. Let's take this overall off you first. You don't want to be caught wearing it at such a time.'

Ginny talked gently as she helped Leah out of the wrap-around overall, moving her mistress from side to side as if she were undressing a child. 'I'll put the kettle on while you make the phone calls, shall I? You'll be better for a good strong cup of tea with a dash of that brandy you never normally touch in it. It's good for shock, brandy is.'

Leah gazed at her blankly for a moment or two then the

words sank in and she nodded. 'Yes. Thank you, Ginny. I'll phone the doctor first, I think.'

She spoke to the doctor's wife, who was also his nurse. It was hard to get the words out, but as soon as Mrs Mitchell realised what had happened, she took over.

'Don't touch the body, Mrs Willcox. It'll be best to leave him just as you found him. I'll send my husband up to Ellindale as soon as he finishes surgery. He only has one more patient to see after this one, so he'll be there within the half hour.'

'Thank you.'

It took Leah a minute or two to work out what she needed to do next, then she called Charlie. But she burst into tears when she tried to speak.

'Leah? Is that you?'

'Yes. Oh, Charlie. It's Jonah. He's d-dead.'

Silence at the other end of the line then she heard him gulp and blow his nose very hard.

'Are you sure?' he asked at last.

'Yes. I've called the doctor, but he can't help Jonah now.'

'How, um, did my brother die?'

'He was tired so he stayed in bed a bit longer and . . . well, I think his heart just stopped as he started to get up this morning. He looks very peaceful.'

'Oh. Right. I'll, um, come up straight away.'

She heard Charlie sob as he put down the receiver. Well, he would. The two brothers, for all the differences in their personalities, were very close.

Leah wanted to wail and weep, oh she did. But Jonah would expect her to be strong now, so she went into the kitchen, where she accepted a cup of strong tea with brandy in it. She didn't like the taste and drank it as if it was medicine, hoping it would help.

It didn't, though. She doubted anything would get rid of the hard lump of anguish that seemed to be weighing her down. Jonah had told her from the start not to get too close to him, and she hadn't fallen headlong in love with him in that way. But they'd become such good friends, he'd been so pleasant to live with that she'd become very fond of him.

She waited, staring bleakly into the fire while Ginny tiptoed around tidying up.

Leah could smell the casserole she'd slipped into the slow oven on the cooker that morning. It was Jonah's favourite lamb and potatoes.

She didn't think she could eat it now.

The fire needed more coal on it and she attended to that automatically before sitting down again.

The clock ticked on steadily but time seemed to pass slowly and it felt to be ages till she heard the sound of a motor car in the yard.

Charlie had been driven up the hill by Todd and was wiping away tears as he got out of the car. He flung his arms round her and started sobbing, his whole body shaking. She had to guide him inside.

'He wasn't safe to drive,' Todd said in a low voice. 'If it's all right with you, I'll stay to take him back and please don't hesitate to ask if you need anything doing in the meantime. Anything at all.'

'Thank you. Has Charlie phoned Marion?'

'No. I asked Vi to get in touch with his wife.'

Ginny came across to whisper, 'Shall I nip across the yard and tell them in the factory what's happened, Leah love?'

'Oh. Yes. I should have thought of that, shouldn't I?'

'It's hard to think of everything at a time like this. What about Rosa?'

'Let's leave her at school. No need for her to know anything till she gets back.'

With another quick pat on her mistress's shoulders, Ginny went across the yard.

Charlie sat down in Jonah's chair and Leah wanted to tell him to get out of it, but from the way he was stroking the chair arm, she realised it was comforting him to sit there.

'Should I go up and see him?' he asked. 'I feel I ought to, only I don't think I can bear it yet.'

'Let's leave that till the doctor's seen him.'

'Who are your undertakers?' Todd asked. 'I can phone them if you like.'

'Oh. Good idea.' She looked at Charlie and repeated the question. He supplied the name of the undertakers his family used. Not that there were many to choose from in a small town like Rivenshaw.

Todd went through into the back hallway and she could hear his voice murmuring on the phone.

When he came back, he nodded. 'They'll get everything ready and come as soon as the doctor has finished and given them the go-ahead. I'm to ring them back. Unless you want to do that?'

She didn't. 'No. I'd be grateful if you did it. Thank you.'

'It seems he's already spoken to them about what sort of funeral he wants.'

She closed her eyes for a moment to take that in. Jonah had done everything he could to make this easier. Only it wasn't easy to lose someone, especially someone as kind as him. How could it be?

It was a relief when another car drove up and Ginny, who was standing near the window, said, 'It's Dr Mitchell. I'll let him in.'

Leah stood up, but she felt wobbly and the room started

to spin. If Todd hadn't steadied her, she'd have stumbled sideways. He helped her sit down again in her armchair.

Ginny opened the door and Dr Mitchell stood for a moment or two studying the people in the room before he walked in.

'My husband's in our bedroom,' Leah said. 'Shall I show you up?'

'She's feeling dizzy, doctor,' Todd put in, keeping one hand on her shoulder to prevent her standing up. 'I just had to steady her.'

'Shall I go with you, doctor?' Charlie asked.

'I've been here enough times to remember the way. Why don't you all wait here and I'll check – um, everything I need to. You look rather pale, Mrs Willcox. You should definitely stay where you are. I'll have a look at you when I come down again.'

So she waited again. Charlie paced to and fro, his arms clasped round his body as if he was holding himself together. Todd stood at one side of the fireplace as if keeping guard over her and her brother-in-law.

The doctor wasn't long.

She gestured to the chair opposite her and waited but he came across to take her wrist and check her pulse before he sat down.

'You're still too pale. It's the shock. No exertion for you today.'

She nodded and he sat down.

'It's as I expected. Heart. Jonah had been having trouble with it for a while, but asked me not to tell you. Um, if it's any comfort, Mrs Willcox, it would have happened very quickly and I doubt he'd have felt much pain. I'm not making that up to comfort you. You must have noticed how peaceful he looked.'

'Yes, I did. I'm glad.'

Charlie blew his nose loudly. He was feeling Jonah's death more than anyone, Leah thought, then realised the doctor had stopped talking and was waiting for her to pay attention.

She could feel herself flushing. 'Sorry. Do go on.'

'I've examined your husband recently so I can sign a death certificate without any more, er, formalities. Perhaps someone would let the undertaker know? Had your husband made any arrangements?'

'The undertaker said that he'd arranged his funeral with them,' Todd said.

Ginny surprised them by saying, 'And Mr Willcox told me if anything happened to him unexpectedly there was an envelope in the bottom drawer of the bureau. I can't think why I didn't remember that before.'

'You'll be feeling the shock, too, no doubt. Don't blame yourself.' The doctor pulled out his watch. 'I'm sorry to rush off but I have some house calls to make. I'll leave you in capable hands, Mrs Willcox. No, don't bother to see me out.'

When he'd gone, Ginny asked, 'Shall I get the envelope for you, love?'

Leah stood up and this time didn't feel dizzy, thank goodness. 'I think I'd like to get it myself, thank you. No, you wait here, Charlie dear.'

Her eyes met Todd's for a moment and the sympathy there, though unvoiced, seemed to hearten her for facing the difficulties she was sure lay ahead. Todd must have seen the worst things possible during the war, and it had taken him years to get over them, but he'd survived. Her situation was normal, if painful. She would survive, too.

But oh, it hurt. It hurt so much to lose him.

She went into the front room and opened the bottom

drawer of the bureau. There the envelope was, on top of everything, with her name written on it in Jonah's bold, spiky black handwriting. She bent to pick it up, cradling it to her chest. She wasn't usually fanciful but she felt for a moment as if he'd put his arms round her and was hugging her gently. He did – *had done* most things gently.

Should she open it on her own? she wondered.

No, Charlie needed to be part of this. Poor dear, he wasn't the sort to keep a stiff upper lip. It'd be better if he had something to do.

She went back into the big main room. 'Here it is. Charlie, will you open it for me?'

He nodded and tore the end off anyhow, taking out some papers. Then he put one arm round her shoulders so that they could read them together. There were two pages. The first was a letter; the second was a list.

*My dear Leah and Charlie,*

*If you're reading this, I'll be dead.*

*I want to thank both of you for being part of my life: the best brother and wife a man could ever have hoped for.*

*I want to ask you to do something for me as life continues. Grieve a little, yes. We all miss those we love. But then get on with your lives and live them to the full, savouring every precious second. Don't mope around. Life is too short without that.*

*More specifically, Charlie, I hope you will have lots of children and maybe you could name a son for the uncle he won't know? I'd really like that.*

*Leah, you must definitely marry again, and do it soon, before it's too late for you to have children. You will make a wonderful mother.*

*Now to practical matters. I've included a list of people you'll need to deal with as you settle my estate. My lawyer has my will and maybe it'll surprise you in a pleasant way, Leah.*

*Say farewell to my other friends and relatives for me!*

*All my love,*

*Adieu,*

*Jonah*

Leah and Charlie stood for a moment, then he folded the letter. 'May I keep this?'

She could see the desperate need in his face. 'Yes. But I'd like a copy, if you don't mind.'

'I'll get Marion to make you one.'

'Let me do it. You can have Jonah's letter tomorrow.' She'd have liked to keep the letter itself but Charlie's need was greater, she could tell. And it was the words that counted, after all, not the piece of paper.

He nodded. 'Thank you.'

'Shall I ring the undertaker now and confirm that it's all right for them to come and collect Jonah?' Todd asked. 'Then I think I should fetch your sister from school, Leah. If Rosa comes home by bus, someone is bound to tell her about Jonah and they'll probably just blurt it out. Word spreads quickly when someone so well liked dies.'

'Are you sure you don't mind doing that? Thank you. I'd better give you a note for her headmistress.'

'I meant what I said: I'm happy to do everything I can to help you and Charlie. I had a lot of respect for Jonah. He was a brave man.'

Leah went back into the front room, wrote a quick note and took it back to Todd.

Then she sat down again. 'I can't believe how weary I feel.' And yet it was only early afternoon. Strange, that. She usually had abundant energy. But she supposed grief took people in different ways.

'I'd like to go up and say a last goodbye to him,' Charlie said. 'I don't want to remember him in his coffin. Do you want to come, Leah?'

She shook her head. She didn't want to look at him again. Better to remember him alive, smiling, being kind to everyone.

They should all be remembered so warmly.

Ginny went back to finish cleaning the front room and Leah found great relief in being able to spend some quiet time on her own.

# 13

Jonah's funeral was to be held three days later and would be attended by nearly everyone from Ellindale, even though it would be hard for some to get down the valley into Rivenshaw when even bus fares were beyond their means.

When Leah heard from Ginny that many people were intending to walk all the way there and back to pay their respects because of this, she phoned Todd.

'How are you?' he asked at once.

'Sad. It's a good thing I'm so busy.' She paused, not used to asking for help.

'What can I do for you?'

'I need your advice. I was wondering if it's possible to hire a bus.' She explained about the Ellindale folk.

'If they don't mind being jolted about in lorries, I can get hold of one and drive them in that, and I have a friend who'll drive another if there are too many people for one vehicle.'

'There will be too many.'

'Then two lorries it is.'

'How much will that cost?'

'Nothing.'

'I don't want you to pay for it.'

'My time costs nothing and my friend owes me a favour.'

'Then I'll pay for the petrol.'

Silence, then he sighed. 'Very well. The funeral's at eleven, isn't it? We'll be up there at quarter to ten in the morning to pick people up.'

'Thank you.'

'And Leah?'

'Yes.'

'Don't be too proud and independent. We all need help at times, and we all like to be of help.'

'You're a kind man.'

It was all he could do for her, be kind and try to guess what help she needed.


Leah took a few minutes to pull herself together then walked down to the village and went into the back room of The Shepherd's Rest pub. Everything was more of an effort than she'd expected. She'd felt so tired lately.

Gillian Jarratt was in charge of handing out the daily milk here and though she was only sixteen, she was very capable. She was the daughter of Dilys and the granddaughter of Mrs Jarratt, who were the two maids at nearby Heythorpe House. Gillian also worked part-time at the pub.

She was preparing the milk which Finn, the owner of Heythorpe House bought every day for the children of the village. That act of generosity not only helped the children and their families, especially in keeping rickets and malnutrition at bay, but also helped a couple of local farmers with smallholdings. They now had a guaranteed market for their milk and didn't need to traipse down to Rivenshaw station with the churns each day to catch the early morning milk train, but could take it in turns to deliver the other's milk.

It had been decided to give the smaller children their milk in the mornings after the older children had left for school, so that none of the bigger lads could pinch a smaller kid's milk. When the older children got back from school, Gillian gave them their daily glass of milk.

Two days a week each child got an apple as well, and though the apples were a bit wrinkled by this time of year, the children ate them with relish, most of them consuming the cores as well and just spitting out the pips.

'Everything all right here?' Leah asked.

Gillian smiled at the children. 'Everything is fine. Did you want to see Izzy?'

'If she's free.'

'She's in the kitchen. Go straight through and call out. The bus has just dropped off the older children from school and I daren't leave them on their own or those lads will be into the milk.'

Leah turned to see children rushing across the village square to queue up, pushing and shoving one another till Gillian called out to stop that because she wasn't serving anyone who couldn't behave. That dire threat made most of them calm down.

How kind Finn was to do this, Leah thought as she went into the pub. He and his new wife, his former housekeeper, had gone to visit a friend of his in London, but Dilys had telephoned them and they were coming back early for the funeral.

She stopped in the doorway to call, 'Can I come in?'

Izzy yelled back, 'Of course you can.'

Leah went through to the kitchen.

'Are you all right, love?' the landlady asked.

She shrugged. No, she wasn't all right and she wished people would stop asking her. Jonah's death seemed to have upset her whole body. She felt tired all the time and couldn't keep her food down. All she wanted was to get the funeral over and done with, then spend a day or two resting and working out how to organise her new life.

'I wondered if you could provide some food for the people from the village after the funeral.' She explained how they'd be getting there and back, and invited Izzy and Don to join them on the lorry.

'How kind of you! And yes, we can provide the food. I'll order some bread and pies from the baker in Rivenshaw and get them to bring it up here early. How much do you want to spend?'

'Give them a good hearty feed, whatever that costs. Perhaps ham and whatever else is available. Get what you can from the village shop to give Lily the custom. I'll leave the details to you. And if any of the women slip some food from their share into their pockets, let them, as long as they eat part of it themselves.'

'I'll make sure of it. Some of the women would save the lot for their children. Gillian will have to stay here to keep an eye on everything, but she doesn't know Jonah like we do. You won't mind if she doesn't attend?'

'No, of course not.'

So that was another job done. Leah trudged slowly back up the slope, which seemed to feel steeper each day.

When she got home two hikers were waiting outside the hostel.

'Are you in charge here, missus?' one of them asked. 'It says in the rule book that hostels will be opening this month but you haven't got your sign up.'

'Is it April already?' Leah was amazed that she had lost track of the month. 'I'm sorry but I've been, um, we've had a . . . a bereavement and I haven't been able to get things ready in the hostel.'

They both took an instinctive step backwards. 'Oh. Sorry to have troubled you, missus. We'll go back down to Rivenshaw, then.' They turned and left.

But that reminded her of another thing she simply had to sort out. She needed a matron cum housekeeper to run the hostel. She'd have enough on her plate sorting out her new life. She'd have to manage the accounts as well as make the fizzy drinks from now on. She wasn't fond of paperwork.

After a few moments' thought, she rang up her friend Lady Terryng, ready to endure the usual questions about how she was. But Margot was mercifully short with her enquiries.

'You'll be tired of saying all that. Is there some way I can help, Leah?'

'I wondered if you knew of a capable woman looking for a sort of housekeeper's job.'

'What do you mean by "sort of"?'

Leah explained.

'Ah! As it happens I have a woman staying with me at the moment who's had to leave home suddenly because of bullying by her brother and his wife. She's called Nina Halshall and she's about thirty. She's been helping out at the orphanage while she looks for a job. I've found her pleasant, a hard worker and capable with it. She doesn't feel drawn to teaching, however, so your job would be ideal for her. Shall I drive her over to see you for an interview after the funeral?'

Leah rested her aching head on one hand and tried to concentrate. 'No need for an interview. I'll take your word about her efficiency, Margot, because I'm desperate for help. Youth hostels are such a good idea for giving poorer people the chance of a holiday and this is only our second year of being open, so I don't want people to think we're closing down already. If you bring her to the funeral she can come back in the car with us – I mean, with me.'

She still thought 'us' automatically. She had to get out of that habit, because it made her want to weep.

As she put down the phone, she nodded. Another thing sorted out, at least. She'd better go into Rivenshaw next and buy some black garments. Unthinkable not to be properly dressed for the funeral, and afterwards she'd have to wear black for a while, though that colour didn't suit her.

How terrible to think of how she looked at a time like this!

She decided to phone her sister-in-law to ask for help, because Marion was always very smartly dressed and would know exactly what to get and where to find it.

Leah picked up the phone again, and of course Marion was delighted to help.

It took such a huge effort to drive down the hill half an hour later to pick up Marion and go shopping that Leah began to worry that she might be sickening for something.

When she put the phone down after speaking to Leah, Margot Terryng went to find Nina, who was scolding a rather naughty little boy. It was a long time since he'd been free from being beaten for the slightest mistake, and the joy of this seemed to have gone to his head and made him act silly at times.

Nina turned and stood up when she saw who had joined them.

Margot made a shooing gesture to the boy, who ran off at once. 'I'm the bearer of good news, my dear! I've found you a job.'

Nina beamed at her. 'Oh, that's excellent! Unless it's teaching. I really don't think I'm cut out to be a teacher.'

'No, I don't think so either. I'm going to look for a strict but kind man to take those boys in hand. Anyway, the job is as matron of a youth hostel in a small village on the edge of the moors. I accepted for you because I know the woman who owns the hostel and I know the village. I'm quite sure you'll like living in Ellindale and be safe there.'

Nina was struggling to take all this in, let alone think clearly. 'What does a matron in a youth hostel do exactly? I've read about youth hostels being opened recently in various parts of the country but it's such a new thing, I'm not sure how they're run.'

'You'd have to do a bit of everything, I should think. Book

in the hikers and take their shilling for the night's stay, sixpence more if they want a meal. Make sure they keep the place tidy and clean, deal with the bedding, provide simple meals if asked – there will be all sorts of things to do really. There is a woman who does the rough cleaning, though, and the bed linens will surely go to the laundry. The hostel gets quite busy in the summer but it closes in winter, so the job may stop then, or they may let you stay on at reduced wages. If you want to, that is.'

'How much does it pay?'

'A pound a week and all found.'

'That sounds fair.' It seemed a fortune to Nina after her father's mean ways to have a whole pound each week to do what she wanted with.

'I need to tell you about the lady you'll be working for.' Her ladyship explained about Leah starting up the fizzy drink factory to provide a few jobs. 'Jonah Willcox has only just died and they haven't held the funeral yet. It'd be good if you could keep an eye on Leah and let me know if you think she's overdoing things. I've heard she's not looking at all well.'

'Of course.'

'I'll take you and your things over with me to the funeral, Nina, and afterwards you can go back to Ellindale in the car with Leah.'

And just like that, it was settled.

Her ladyship bustled on to the next job, telling her she might as well take the day off and get her things together.

Nina didn't move for a few moments, trying to take it all in. Then she realised she was dawdling and went to her bedroom to pack, not that it would take her long.

She'd have done anything respectable to support herself but this sounded to be a particularly good opportunity for someone in her position. 'All found,' she murmured, smiling.

Could anything be better than a job that provided accommodation and food as well as work? She'd easily be able to save some money.

At the end of the hiking season she'd have to think carefully about what to do next. She wasn't sure she wanted to stay so close to her old home as she would hate to run into her weakling of a brother who sometimes took his wife shopping in Rivenshaw. She would never forgive those two for trying to push her into marrying a nasty old man like Rogerson.

Selling her, that's what they'd been doing. She wondered yet again what she'd been worth.

Spending the warmer months on the edge of the moors would be very pleasant indeed. She might be able to go for walks across the tops during her free time – well, she assumed she'd be allowed time off now and then.

From what Lady Terryng had said, it sounded as if the man they'd be burying tomorrow had been greatly loved, not only by his wife but by everyone around him.

Nina didn't mind attending the funeral with her ladyship. How different it would be from her father's funeral, which had been the cheapest one available, barely better than a pauper's burial.

She was never going to marry and put herself in the power of a man. Her father had cured her of that idea.

# 14

Harry went out in his lunch hour and used a public phone box to ring the number in the railway carriage advert. His call was answered by a man who said they only had two carriages left from this batch.

'When can I come and see them?'

'Better come soon. They're selling quickly.'

'I could come after work today.'

'We close at six o'clock on the dot, mind, because they want to lock our gates.'

'I'll be there at half-past five.' He'd have to find an excuse to leave work early.

When he asked, Mr Trowton said at once, 'No, you bloody can't leave early! You've done enough of that recently.'

Harry tried to plead his case, promising to come in earlier the next day to make up the time, but Trowton was in one of his moods and ordered him curtly to do as he was damned well told or take the consequences.

Suddenly anger boiled up in Harry at the years of casual abuse like this. Trowton didn't care how rude he was to his employees or how he inconvenienced them, only about himself and making money. And in the past year or two he'd grown even more chancy, not to mention forgetful at times.

The temper Harry usually controlled boiled over and he surprised both of them by thumping one hand down on the table in the office and yelling, 'I've worked a lot of extra hours over the years and haven't asked for extra pay when a machine needed mending and it kept me back late.'

'We all work hard in times like these and you're not getting out of my factory till the hooter goes for leaving time.'

'All right, then. If you won't give me the time off, I'm quitting.'

There was dead silence in the office, then Trowton said harshly, 'Oh, no you're not. I'm firing you.'

'I'm glad you said that. It means you'll need to pay me until today.'

'Who's going to make me?'

'The law.'

'You wouldn't dare bring in the law.'

'Oh, but I would. And it'll cost you more than the week's pay I'm owed to hire a lawyer to defend the case, which you won't win anyway. The law's the law, even for employers like you.'

'You impudent devil!'

There was dead silence in the office and Harry waited, folding his arms and refusing to cave in. Indeed, he was feeling rather exhilarated. For years he'd been putting up with this man's rudeness. Trowton knew about Cathie and if he didn't care about a child's health, he wasn't worth working for, so Harry was going to stop right now.

'I'll make sure you don't get another job in the area, you can be sure of that, Makepeace.'

'I'm leaving the area – but only *after* I've got my pay.'

'You'd better leave quickly then because I know your landlord and he'll chuck you out if I ask him to.'

'Listen to you, threatening something which might kill a sickly child and then you'll go to church on Sunday all dressed up fine and look down your nose on decent folk like your workers. You're a damned hypocrite and you make me sick.'

Trowton breathed in deeply and turned dark red. Harry

thought for a moment he was going to erupt into rage, but instead he closed his eyes briefly, then muttered, 'Worth it to get rid of you.' He unlocked his money drawer, slammed the bag of money on the desk. He enjoyed flaunting this to his employees who had trouble putting bread on the table, the rat. He pulled a smaller bag out of it, counting off what was owed to Harry, minus five shillings.

'It's short five shillings.'

'You can take that or nothing. I'm fining you for insolence.' He reached out as if to take the money back.

Harry picked his wages up quickly and turned on his heel, going to his locker to clear out his things. He became aware of someone standing close behind him and found that Trowton had followed him.

'I'm making sure you only take what's yours.'

'I've never stolen anything in my life.' Harry crammed nearly everything into his canvas bag, bundled up what was left in the spare ragged overalls he kept there for emergencies, and strode out of the factory, still tailed by Trowton.

Work had stopped and everyone on the shop floor watched him go in dead silence.

'Get on with your work!' Trowton yelled and all the heads bent over their work again.

They weren't allowed to speak while working and didn't dare break that rule because they'd all seen others frog-marched to the door for no reason other than Trowton needing to take his anger out on someone.

It gave Harry satisfaction that Trowton hadn't tried to manhandle him. He'd damned well better not.

The metal gate to the factory yard slammed shut behind him.

'Good riddance!' Trowton yelled.

Harry turned and smiled.

'What have you got to smile at?'

'You'll see.' He knew Trowton would say something very different when that end sewing machine stopped working. It was sounding rough and Harry had been going to attend to it today because he knew how to baby it along.

Trowton could do straightforward repairs to his own machinery, but nothing fancy. Just let him try to keep that particular machine running. He wasn't a good enough engineer for that.

Harry carried on down the street, moving more slowly now, his brief elation fading. He wasn't sure whether he'd just done the most stupid thing in his life or the best. Leaving work now would get Cathie away from the smoky air more quickly and speaking his mind to Trowton had made him feel good, but there would be no more money coming in for a while.

He took his things home, told Mrs Pyne what he'd done, cut short her exclamations of shock and set off for the railway yard.

First things first.

He had no idea how long it would take to get a railway carriage in place and set it up for living in. Or if there'd still be a carriage left for sale by the time he got there.

He really would be in trouble if there wasn't.

He arrived at the address he'd been given just after two o'clock in the afternoon and found himself facing a huge open space, criss-crossed by railway lines. The patterns made little sense to him and worst of all, there were no signs to indicate what each area was for. It took him a few minutes to find someone to ask even, then he was directed to one side and told to shout for Albert.

Albert turned out to be an older man, as friendly and polite as Trowton had been unfeeling and rude. He showed Harry the two remaining railway carriages, both in need of refurbishment, inside and out.

Harry went all over them, even lying down to peer under-neath. As far as he could tell, both were sound structurally, though one had some damage. He turned to the older man. 'Which would you recommend I buy? That one has dents at one end and looks as if it's nearly caught fire.'

'Nay, it's not for me to say which. I'm just supposed to sell them.'

'I have a sick child and I need to get her out into the country to breathe the fresh air. She'll be living permanently in one of these. Please. Tell me if one is better than the other. For her sake. I'll not have a lot of money left for repairs.'

Albert hesitated. 'How old is she?'

'Nine.'

'I have a granddaughter that age.' Albert glanced over his shoulder and muttered in a low voice, 'The far one looks worse because it's dented at one end and has a bit of damage inside, but actually it's a better buy. There's less rust in the bodywork and the bogies underneath. And best of all for your purpose, it's got open seating.'

He paused to let this sink in and added, 'And as you can see, it's got a clerestory window all along the centre of the top, so you'll get a lot more light inside. The other carriage looks in better condition, but that's just the outside. It has separate compartments and it doesn't even have a corridor inside to connect them. You can't get from one compartment to the other except by getting out of the carriage and in again.'

Harry went to peer into it and could see what he meant, so moved on to the other one to inspect the damage.

Albert patted the carriage he favoured as if it were a pet dog. 'This one was for carrying first-class passengers, so they made a better job of the inside. Most of the upholstery is still perfect except on two of the eight seats where it got damaged by some miners. Seems they were angry at the owner who was riding in luxury while they starved. They got on board, but only for a few minutes and someone bashed the outside panels at the same end with a hammer, denting them. Don't take my word for it. Get in and have a good look around. You'll see the difference in quality between the two.'

Harry climbed into the carriage he'd recommended and walked up and down it. There was even a lavatory compartment at the damaged end, with the toilet pan intact. Now, that'd be useful. He'd be taking out some of the seats anyway, so it didn't matter that the upholstery on two of them was badly slashed and scorched.

When he climbed down again, Albert was waiting for him. 'Well?'

'I can't thank you enough for your help and advice. I'll take this one. I have to get the site prepared. Can I leave the carriage here till next week?'

'Yes – well, you can as long as you've paid for it in full. Do you want it delivered?'

'Yes, please.'

'Where to?'

'A village called Ellindale, up the top end of the valley beyond Rivenshaw.'

'Ah. We can deliver it to the station in Rivenshaw, but not up one of them narrow Pennine valleys. We've come to grief with them before. You'll have to sort something out yourself for getting it to Ellindale from there, I'm afraid, lad. See if you can find a farmer with a big tractor or someone with a big lorry and make a couple of strong trolleys to fit under the bogies, then you can drag the carriage up the road.'

Harry's heart sank. Nothing was going well today.

His feelings must have shown because Albert said suddenly, 'Look, we've had trouble selling this one because of the damage, so we'll make a special agreement to deliver it to

Rivenshaw for free, but you'll have to collect it quickly. These are the last two and the railway company wants the siding cleared for other uses.'

Harry counted out the money into Albert's hand, accepted the receipt, took another quick walk round the carriage and started for home.

He kept shivering with the worry of it all. Was he doing the right thing? How could you tell when it was something you'd never done before, never even heard of anyone else doing?

On the way back he thought about the to-ing and fro-ing there would be to get things moved, so made another decision. He detoured to ask the chap who hired out the motorbikes if he still had one with a sidecar for sale and to his huge relief it was still unsold.

They dickered for a while over the price and in the end Harry got it for ten pounds, so he'd need to go back to the bank to withdraw more money. He put down a deposit of one pound.

But at least the fellow he was buying from trusted him enough to let him go to the bank on the motorbike, which made things a lot easier. He smiled as he chugged along on it. The engine sounded smooth and the brakes were good.

He took a quick look inside his bank book as he walked out of the bank and his happy mood faded. A hundred and ten pounds had seemed such a lot of money but it was pouring out at a rapid rate and he hadn't the faintest idea how he was going to get the carriage up the valley to Ellindale.

When he reached the motorbike he stopped dead on the pavement. At that moment he was suddenly quite sure he'd done the wrong thing in defying Mr Trowton as well as in buying the railway carriage and motorbike. Talk about burning your bridges!

How much would he have left by the time the railway carriage was in place and habitable? How long could he make that money last?

Oh, hell! What would he do if he still hadn't found work and ran out of money completely when he was living in Ellindale? There were men who'd been out of work for five years and more. You read about them in the papers.

No. He mustn't look on the black side. The motorbike was a necessity. He needed it for many reasons: bringing materials and equipment back to the plot of land to put his new home together, getting to repair jobs to earn money, all sorts of things.

Someone called, 'You're blocking the path,' so he got on the motorbike and set off back to pay the owner.

First thing in the morning he'd drive over to Rivenshaw and see what he could arrange about delivering the railway carriage. Surely there would be someone there who could help him?

In the meantime he was going to pretend to Cathie that everything was just fine and it was good for them to be moving sooner than planned.

That was going to be hard. He didn't usually lie to her.

There were no guarantees in this life, however hard you tried to do the best for your family, but he had to remember that her health was bad where they were living now. That was the most important thing of all: keeping Cathie well.

And this was the only way he could see to do it.

When he got to Rivenshaw the following morning, Harry went straight to Mr Selby's garage to ask if the job offer still held. But it was closed with no notice to show why. Surely a man like that hadn't gone bust?

He found out from a neighbour that Todd wasn't available because it was the day of Mr Willcox's funeral. Eh, that poor man. He must have been close to death when he helped Harry.

As he drove away from there, he saw the funeral procession coming slowly along the main road. He wasn't surprised by how many people were following the hearse if Mr Willcox had been as kind to others as to him. He stopped the motorbike and dismounted, taking off his cap and standing with head bent in respect until they'd passed.

Mr Selby was driving a lorry filled with people, but he noticed Harry and raised one hand in salute as it chugged past.

After the way was clear Harry drove up to Ellindale to have a look at his plot of land and maybe do a little preparatory digging with his newly purchased spade. He'd bought a few tools he'd never needed before since he hadn't had a garden or needed a home workshop. They were from the local pawnshop, so the spade wasn't brand new, but it was sturdy and had no visible damage.

He'd brought some other bits and pieces with him from home, filling the sidecar to save on the removal costs. He intended to ask Mr Kerkham if there was somewhere on the farm he could store them safely. He'd offer sixpence a week for that and felt fairly certain his new neighbour would agree.

Harry parked the motorbike and clambered over the wall on to his land. The first thing he intended to do was work out exactly where to put the railway carriage. Close to the shelter, he decided, pacing it out – only how would he get it there?

He'd have to knock down part of the wall to get it on its new site and make sure the area was as level as possible. But some of the front wall was crumbling anyway, so he'd put an entrance for the motorbike and sidecar at that part. He could build proper gateposts and put in a gate later.

Before much time had passed, he'd decided yet again he

must have been mad to get himself into this. But he was excited as well as worried. Very excited.

Suddenly someone called out, 'Hoy, you!' and he jerked round in shock.

A man was looking over the wall. 'Can I ask what you're doing here?'

'Who are you to ask?'

'Daniel Pollard. I live in Ellindale and you don't. So who are you and what are you doing digging here?'

His voice had been civil but determined and Harry answered calmly, 'I've bought this land.'

'What's your name?'

'Makepeace.'

He was rewarded with a nod. 'Ah. Coming to live here soon, are you, Mr Makepeace?'

'I hope so.' Harry waited and when no explanation was furnished, asked, 'You haven't said why you want to know what I'm doing here.'

'Me an' my friend have been left here to keep an eye on the village while so many people are away at the funeral.'

'I'm surprised you think you need a patrol in a small place like this. But you can ask Mr Kerkham to confirm that I'm Makepeace when he gets back from the funeral.'

'There are some folk as think they'll find easy pickings here while people are away. I've had to chase one chap off already, a fellow who lives here, too. Disgusting to go thieving on the day of Mr Willcox's funeral. Well, that chap didn't get away with it and no one else will neither. We look after our own here in Ellindale.'

Harry liked the sound of this, so explained a bit more about who he was and why he was coming here.

His companion's face brightened. 'You'll be having a house built, then. There are local chaps who could do some of the heavy work for you.'

'I can't afford a proper house. I've bought an old railway carriage, only how to get it up here from Rivenshaw station is beyond me at the moment. I'll have to ask around and see if there's anyone who can take on the job.'

Daniel stood frowning in thought, then said slowly, 'Well, if you can pay to get that done, I've a brother as needs work. Wilf's a strong devil and he's good with wood and building things. If he were rich, he'd be an artist, I reckon, because he also carves figures out of wood.'

'You'll have to introduce me to him.'

'I will. He'll do anything to stay off the dole, our Wilf will, as long as it's legal. His wife takes in washing for a couple of ladies in Birch End, or does anything else she can get. Sometimes there's no work to be had an' Wilf has to go without. He says he'll starve to death before he claims the dole, because they'd make him sell his wood-carving tools an' the bits and pieces he's carved for whatever he could get, then he'd have no way of doing his carving.

'Do you think your Wilf would know how to move a railway carriage? They're ruddy great things.'

'He's the most likely person round here to be able to figure it out. He allus seems to know if something will fit and how best to get it into place. Has done since he was a lad.' He tapped his own head. 'Got the gift for it, he has. If he'd come from a rich family, I reckon he'd have been trained as an engineer.'

'Well, perhaps he'll come and see me about it. It's how to get the carriage up here that flummoxes me. The man who sold it to me said to make two big trolleys, and I've got the carriage's measurements, but I don't know how big the trolleys would need to be or what exactly they'd be like. I'm an electrical engineer not a carpenter. Are there any farmers round here with tractors or big strong horses?' Every time he thought about it, something else occurred to him that'd need doing.

Daniel stood frowning. 'I'd not know how to do it, either. What time are you planning to leave today? Will you still be in Ellindale after the funeral?'

'Probably. I'm going to start digging out the foundations today.'

'How much was it going to cost to get the carriage delivered till they found out it was up here?'

'Three or four guineas.'

Daniel let out a soft whistle. 'So if Wilf can work out how to do the job, you'd pay him the same amount?'

'Yes, willingly. As long as he doesn't damage it or get it stuck somewhere.' Harry shivered, suddenly aware of how cold he felt. 'Is there anywhere I can get a cup of tea? That wind fair cuts you to the bone.'

'Village shop's open at this time of year. They're allowed to open on Sundays from April to October to make sandwiches and cups of tea for hikers. You don't get many folk hiking over the moors this early in the year, but you get the odd one, an' you get a fair few in the warmer weather. I'm sure Lily will find you something to eat and drink. She didn't go to the funeral either, felt she had to keep the refreshment side of the shop open for her aunt. Them folk from the council don't like shops closing when they're supposed to be open.'

'I'll go and buy a pot of tea and then come back here to do a bit of work while I'm waiting for your brother.'

Daniel nodded. 'Don't leave till we've seen you. He wouldn't let you down.'

There was a pleading tone in his voice.

'I'll give your Wilf a chance,' Harry said quietly. He went to the shop and treated himself to a pot of tea and was unable to resist a big currant bun. And very nice it was too.

Then he went to see Kerkham and as he'd expected the man jumped at the idea of earning sixpence a week for providing storage space in one of his ramshackle outhouses.

When Harry had finished unloading his things and putting most of them in the outhouse, he went back to stand out of the wind in the shepherd's shelter on his land, wondering if this Wilf really would know how to move the carriage from Rivenshaw up the hill without damaging it. It wasn't a steep hill, but the road had several curves and it wasn't all that wide, either, in some places.

Then he realised he was wasting time and went to pace out again where the carriage would go and began digging out the foundations. After all, there was only one place he could see the carriage fitting, because of the rocky uneven ground, and that was in front of the shelter. He'd have to dig out a cesspit at the back of the shelter, too, and move the lavatory out of the railway carriage into it, perhaps.

Good thing he wasn't afraid of hard work.

# 15

Inevitably a funeral for such a well-loved man was a particularly sad occasion, and yet it was wonderful to see so many people there. Leah had vowed not to weep, but simply couldn't hold back her tears. Charlie sobbed openly and his wife put her arm round his shoulders and kept it there.

The sight of the two of them standing so close together made Leah feel sad because she had no one to do that with now. But then Rosa put an arm round her and she told herself she was being stupid because she still had her sister.

She fumbled desperately for her handkerchief, unable to remember where she'd put it when she last used it to dab away a tear. Someone passed her a clean one from the pew behind her before Rosa could get hers out. When Leah turned to say thank you, she realised it was Todd. He'd been a tower of strength in an unobtrusive way ever since Jonah's death.

She mouthed a 'thank you' and mopped her eyes, then paid attention to the service and the lovely things people were saying about her husband. Every one of them was true, too, which wasn't always the case at funerals. Jonah had been helping people unobtrusively for years.

She had to make a huge effort to move out of the comparative shelter of the pew and follow the coffin out into the churchyard. She was glad when Charlie offered her his other arm and they formed a threesome as they walked to the graveside at the head of the long procession of people. Rosa fell in behind them.

The sun came out as they took their places around the grave. Leah lifted her face to it for a moment, finding its warmth comforting.

Lady Terryng took one look at Leah's sad, drooping figure and told Nina they'd be better coming back to see her the next day. 'She's very pale, doesn't look at all like her usual self.'

When everyone went out to see the coffin put into the ground, her ladyship managed to have a word with Marion Willcox and explain the situation.

'Miss Halshall could come and stay at our house tonight. It's a long way for you to go to and fro.'

'You don't mind?'

'Of course not. Miss Halshall is desperately needed to help in the hostel, so I'll drive her up there tomorrow. I was going anyway to check that Leah is all right, so it's no trouble at all. I think you're right not to introduce her today, though. I've never seen Leah so dazed and uncertain. She's normally one of the most capable women I know.'

'I'll take Nina to your house, then.'

'Yes. I have to go and stand beside Charlie now. He's dreadfully upset.'

'Men don't usually cry openly.'

'Charlie's unusual in many ways. He doesn't mind showing his emotions, whether happy or sad. It took me a while to get used to it, because my parents aren't at all like that.'

Leah had to lean on her brother-in-law as they stood beside the grave, she felt so weak. He shot her a quick, concerned glance and she couldn't even find the energy to speak to him, let alone reassure him that she'd manage somehow to get through this.

Marion had lingered to speak to Lady Terryng and now

rejoined them, standing the other side of Charlie and whispering to him.

It was a familiar part of the burial service so Leah didn't have to concentrate to do the necessary tossing in of earth and bow her head for the final prayer.

Even then, she felt shocked that it was over. Jonah had gone now in every sense. She couldn't seem to think clearly what she was supposed to do after the ceremony ended.

As she turned to leave, everything seemed to waver around her and she cried out as she felt herself falling.

It was Todd who realised that she was about to faint and caught Leah before she could fall into the open grave. Without taking his eyes off her, he said, 'Go and fetch your car, Charlie. I think we should take Leah to see the doctor. She hasn't been looking at all well since Jonah died.'

'Yes. Yes, of course. I should have noticed.'

'Go!'

By the time Todd got her into the car, with Marion driving, thank goodness, not Charlie, Leah was starting to regain consciousness but he and Rosa still needed to hold her between them in the back.

She stared up at him in a drowsy, uncertain way, then her eyes gradually started to focus properly again. As she took in where she was, she asked, 'What happened?'

'You fainted. We're taking you to see Dr Mitchell,' Todd said.

'No need for that. I'll be all right in a minute or two.'

'You haven't been well for a while,' Todd said.

Charlie turned round from the front seat. 'You get no choice about it, Leah. You're seeing the doctor and that's that.'

'But—'

'It'll only take a few minutes,' Todd coaxed, 'and it'll reassure everyone. You look very pale today.'

'Chalk white,' Rosa put in.

'I couldn't face breakfast. I can have something to eat then rest once I get home. That'll set me right.'

Marion gave her a strange look. 'We're there now so you might as well go in to see the doctor. Charlie, run inside and tell Mrs Mitchell what happened.'

'Where's my handbag?' Leah muttered.

'I've got it,' Rosa said. 'I'll hold it while you see the doctor.'

'Thanks, love. I'm sorry.'

'What for? Feeling upset at Jonah's funeral? That's normal for a wife, isn't it?' Tears were welling in Rosa's eyes. 'We're all upset.'

Within minutes Leah was sitting in the doctor's surgery answering his questions, with his wife standing near the door in her nurse's role.

Yes, she'd felt a bit nauseous lately.

Yes, she'd been more tired than usual and was it any wonder?

'And how are your monthlies, Mrs Willcox? When did you last have one?'

'They're—' She broke off and frowned at him. 'They've always been irregular. I can't remember exactly when the last one was. It's been a difficult time because I could see that Jonah's health was failing fast.'

'Had you still been having, um, relations with him in bed?'

'Yes. That surprised me but he still wanted to . . . to love me.'

Dr Mitchell patted her hand. 'Try to remember roughly how long it is since your last monthly.'

She tried to calculate and to her surprise, had to admit, 'It must be about three months, I suppose.' She gave him a shocked look as it began to sink in what he was getting at.

'Let me examine you. At that stage I should be able to tell whether you're expecting.'

*Expecting?* The word seemed to echo in her head. It couldn't be true, though, just couldn't.

She felt mentally numb as she let him touch her stomach gently, and everything still felt unreal as she got dressed and sat in the chair again.

He was giving her such a knowing look, she muttered, 'I can't be.'

'You're definitely expecting a child, my dear, and you're probably closer to four months along than three.'

Tears welled in her eyes.

'Does having a posthumous child upset you?'

'What upsets me is that Jonah didn't know. It'd have made him so happy.' She burst into great gulping tears, dampening still further the big handkerchief Todd had given her.

Mrs Mitchell put an arm round her shoulders. 'Shh now. Shh, dear.'

But it was a while before Leah could stop weeping. 'It seems so unfair that Jonah didn't know.'

'Perhaps he does?' the doctor suggested. 'If we're to believe in a heaven, then surely he'd know by now that he'd left something precious behind.'

Leah didn't know what to think about that; she didn't have any strong religious beliefs. 'I'm too tired to . . . to consider the situation now. What I'd like most of all is to lie down and sleep.'

'Good idea. Why not spend the rest of the day in bed, looking after yourself and your baby?'

The word echoed in her mind. *Baby! She was having a baby.*

The doctor nodded to his wife who went and called in her sister and sister-in-law.

When they came into his room, he said bluntly, 'I think Mrs Willcox needs looking after. She's expecting, which is partly why she fainted. And I doubt she's been eating properly. That must stop.'

Rosa gaped at him, then let out a happy little cry. 'Why, that's wonderful!' She put her arms round her sister and plonked a kiss first on one cheek then the other.

Marion's voice was gentler than usual. 'We'll look after you, dear. You can both come and live with us, if you like. We'll definitely take you home with us today and cosset you.'

Leah clutched her sister's hand, glad of the warmth of it. 'Thank you, but what I want most is to go home and rest in my own bed. I'm so very tired. Don't worry. Rosa and Ginny will look after me.'

She hesitated, then asked her sister-in-law, 'Will you go and tell the men why I fainted, please? I feel such a fool for not realising sooner. I'll just wash my face, then if someone can drive me and Rosa home, I'll go straight to bed.'

'Do you want to keep it a secret in the village for the moment?'

At that Leah smiled, truly smiled for the first time in days. 'Even if I tried, they'd find out. Once one person knows, so does the rest of Ellindale. Don't ask me how they do it, they just do. Anyway, I don't want to keep it a secret. I want to tell the whole world.' Perhaps Jonah would hear the echoes from wherever he was. Oh dear, she was being silly again.

Todd had found someone else to drive his lorry up to Ellindale, so that he could drive back home in it. When Marion protested, he shook his head. 'You're all upset today and I'm a very safe driver. Let me do this.'

She gave him a strange, considering look, then shrugged. 'Very well.'

'Congratulations,' Charlie told Leah. 'It's the best news there could be today, the very best.' He paused then added in a choking voice, 'It means something of Jonah will live on.'

Todd's congratulations were more subdued. Well, he wasn't a family member, Leah thought, so why should he be as happy as the others about it?

'I'll carry you out to the car,' he told her abruptly.

'There's no need. I can—'

But he'd already picked her up and Charlie was leading the way, opening the car door. People in the street were watching, so she stopped protesting. This time Todd put her in the back with Marion and Rosa, then went to sit in the driver's seat.

'You'll not be going to the funeral feast in the village now,' Marion said firmly, taking Leah's hand and patting it absent-mindedly. 'We'll call in and tell them what's happened.'

'I'm not going to argue. I feel as if I need to sleep for a million years.'

As the car stopped at Spring Cottage, Rosa got out and ran into the house to tell Ginny what had happened.

Leah wriggled out of the back seat before anyone could stop her and looked down at Todd, who had just opened the driver's door.

'Thank you for driving us back. And for everything else today. Ginny will look after me now. Rosa!' She waved her sister over. 'Would you go to the funeral meal to represent me?'

Rosa studied her face, then gave a little nod as if reassured. 'All right. Here's your handbag.'

'She can come with us,' Charlie said.

Ginny had come to the front door by then and called, 'I'll look after her, Mrs Willcox, don't you worry. The Shepherd's Rest is putting on a real feast.'

'The family will be represented, that's the main thing,' Charlie said.

Todd drove down the gentle slope into the village and

stopped outside the pub. But as they got out of the car he turned to stare back up the slope at Spring Cottage, and wished he could have stayed with Leah.

Then his face became expressionless and he followed the others inside.

Leah looked at Ginny. 'It doesn't seem fair, does it?'

She didn't have to explain. 'No, not fair at all. He'd have loved a child.'

The two women had a little cry together, then Ginny pulled back. 'Is it a secret?'

'No. I'm happy for everyone to know. But I'd like to go up and lie down now.'

'Rosa told me that doctor wanted you to eat something before you do that, Leah love. You're eating for two now, don't forget.' She frowned. 'Or do you want me to call you Mrs Willcox now you're in charge of everything?'

'Of course not. We're still friends, aren't we?'

'Yes, we are.' Ginny gave her another of the quick pats on the shoulders by which she often expressed affection, then went to prepare some food.

Though she still didn't feel hungry, Leah forced down a scone with butter and strawberry jam on it to placate Ginny, then insisted on going up to bed on her own.

She took off her new black clothes carefully and laid them over a chair, finding comfort in donning her old faded pink flannel nightdress.

Footsteps sounded on the stairs and she looked up as Ginny came in with a stone hot water bottle.

'I thought this might be a comfort.' She didn't linger.

It was a comfort, but the greatest comfort of all was to lie peacefully in bed, feet on the warmth of the bottle, looking out at the moors. Nobody needed anything from her for the moment. She could really, truly rest.

'Oh, Jonah, I hope you do know that I'm carrying your child,' she whispered as she let her eyes close.

When Ginny came up ten minutes later to see if Leah wanted anything else, she found her fast asleep, her face peaceful.

The older woman went back down to report this to the woman who'd walked up from the pub to see if there was anything she could do to help.

The kind offer of help brought tears to her eyes because Biddy was one of the hungry ones, who gave most of the food her family could afford to her husband and children and often went without herself. She was so thin that people were getting worried about her.

'You go and get some food into you. You need it. And you'll oblige me by eating up the second scone I buttered for Leah. She left it and I'm not hungry.'

'You could eat it later.'

Ginny set her arms on her hips and said firmly, 'You can eat it now, Biddy. If you don't eat more regularly and take your share of the food, you'll not be much use to your family.'

'They're only children.'

'So they need you alive, not dead.'

Biddy ate the scone, closing her eyes in bliss.

Ginny shook her head as she watched her neighbour walk away. That woman had given up her chance of a good meal at the funeral feast to see if she could help Leah. Eh, people could be so nice it made your throat ache with keeping back the tears, it did that, Ginny thought. She didn't manage to keep them all back this time.

# 16

While most people from the village were at the funeral, Daniel came to find Harry. 'Wilf's helping Don at The Shepherd's Rest to set things up. He can't waste the chance to earn a bit. He says you should come and join us there. The whole village has been invited to a funeral gathering, with food and drink provided, but you could buy a half pint for yourself and then no one would mind you being there, especially if you're with me. I'll be able to introduce you to your future neighbours and you can talk to my brother Wilf once he's not needed.'

'Are you sure it'll be all right? I don't want to intrude on such a sad occasion.'

'It'll be fine if I take you and you pay your own way,' Daniel repeated. 'Trust me.'

'Well. All right.' Harry could afford one half pint in such a good cause, though he would have to sip it slowly because that was all he was buying.

To his relief, it was as Daniel had said: people accepted his presence and seemed pleased to meet their new neighbour. Nice, decent folk they were, shabbily dressed, many of them thinner than they used to be from the way their clothes hung on them, but carrying on bravely.

Surely this would be a good place to live? He sipped his beer, listened to people and waited for Wilf to be free.

★

Marion and Charlie went to the gathering at The Shepherd's Rest to represent the family, taking Todd and Rosa with them. As they entered the big main room, everyone fell silent and the men stood up in respect.

'How's Mrs Willcox?' someone called. 'I heard she fainted after the funeral.'

'She did, but she's at home now, having a lie down and rest,' Charlie announced.

Izzy pushed to the front of the crowd. 'She's not ill, is she?'

Some people were still chatting to one another and others shushed them, anxious to hear the answer.

Marion came to stand beside her husband, knowing the news would sound better coming from a woman. 'My sister-in-law isn't ill exactly, but she's expecting. She's been so busy looking after Jonah, she hasn't been thinking about herself, so didn't realise.'

'Eh, that's grand, that is,' old Simeon said at once. Then he frowned as he worked out what that might imply. 'Does that mean Jonah didn't know about the babby?'

'I'm afraid not.'

Simeon stood up, not without difficulty, holding on to his neighbour's chair to steady himself. 'Then we must have a toast to her health and the babby's safe arrival. Has everyone got something to drink?'

There were nods and calls of 'Yes' but some shouted, 'Hold on a minute!' so they waited for one or two latecomers who hadn't been served yet.

Simeon let them all settle then banged his walking stick on the table to get their full attention. 'As the oldest person in the village I shall take it upon myself to propose two toasts. Neighbours, I ask you to drink first to Mr Willcox. God rest his soul.'

Glasses were raised and the toast echoed.

More banging with the walking stick was followed by, 'And

now we'll drink to Mrs Willcox's health, *and* to that of her precious child.' He held up his glass and took a good long pull of beer.

His words were echoed by everyone there.

Harry, watching from a corner, where he was standing with Daniel and clutching the glass of beer he'd bought, was very touched by this and raised his own glass instinctively. As he watched the others he realised they were drinking very little each time, presumably to make their free drinks last, so he wasn't the only one taking small sips. Eh, what times these were!

Two women started bringing out plates of food and he was impressed by the orderly way they were received. It took him a moment or two to realise that Daniel was trying to introduce him to another tall, well-built man.

'This is my brother Wilf. After he and I have eaten, we could go and have a good look at your land and discuss what needs to be done to get the carriage up there. If anyone can help you out, it's him.'

'And if I can find a way to earn a bob or two, and help a new neighbour at the same time,' added Wilf, 'I shall be doubly pleased about it.'

'I can definitely pay you a little for help,' Harry promised, well aware that he couldn't do all the jobs on his own. 'My big problem is how to get the railway carriage up to Ellindale.'

'We'll find a way,' Wilf said confidently. 'I'll enjoy doing that.'

When they'd finished their beers and the two brothers had had some food, the three men strolled down to look at Harry's piece of land. Daniel and Wilf knew it quite well already, because like everyone else they passed it regularly on their way up and down the valley. But they hadn't walked over it since they were lads, given Mr Kerkham's ferocious attitude towards trespassers, so that was the first thing they did.

Harry found himself next to Wilf with Daniel following them a couple of paces behind. Eh, it'd been a long time since he'd enjoyed a conversation as much. Wilf was a practical man with the same need to describe something by shaping it in the air as Harry's wife used to tease him about.

More than that, he had never met anyone who could move shapes around in his head and come up with ideas for how to fit them together so quickly. He certainly couldn't.

In the end Harry put his thoughts into words. 'If I could only move out here, I could employ you for a week and get three times as much done as I would on my own, Wilf lad.'

'The weather's warmer now that summer's nearly here, so you could camp out in the shelter while we're getting the carriage footings set up. It'd be easy enough to make it weatherproof for the warmer months if you put a rough wooden wall across the open end. I don't think your daughter would suffer from sleeping there if she had plenty of warm covers, not unless we have a late snowfall in the next week or two, and Mr Carlisle would let you take shelter in his house if we did.'

'Who's he again?'

'Lives in Heythorpe House, on the other side of the village. He's been visiting relatives, but has come back for the funeral. Him and his wife were the ones sitting at the table with Charlie Willcox and his wife. And you know Todd already, don't you?'

'Oh yes, I noticed that group.'

'Mr Carlisle's a kind man. He's the one as provides a glass of milk every day for every child in the village.'

'That *is* kind. But how could we make the open end of the shelter weatherproof without it costing a fortune?' Harry wondered aloud.

'I know where there's a load of wood going cheap. It looks as if most of it'd only be useful for firewood, but if you don't mind a jigsaw puzzle of a wall, I could fit the good bits together to block off the end of the shelter. You could use the bits that are left for firewood. We'd have to dig you a cesspit outside, though, if you're going to be living here. That won't wait.'

The three men laughed. Anyone who'd been in the army knew how to dig those.

Harry tried to picture living in the shelter. 'We'd need a window in the wall.'

'I'd have to think about that,' Wilf said. 'You don't find windows lying around.'

'Yes, you do!' Daniel exclaimed. 'There's one lying doing nothing up at Spring Cottage. It's got a cracked pane, but you'd not mind that, would you, Harry? They took the window out of the end of the old barn and put a much bigger one in when they mended the wall there. Mrs Willcox might sell it to you cheaply. Ben, who lives up there, is a stonemason and he was telling me even before Mr Willcox died that they're not planning to do any more building.'

'Could you ask them about it?'

'Aye, o' course I could.'

'If I only had a little money coming in, I'd feel better about all this,' Harry said with a frown. 'I started off with just over a hundred pounds, but twenty-five of it's gone already on the land, the motorbike, the railway carriage and other bits and pieces, and I need enough to live off till I get established round here.'

He didn't say it but he thought it, as people often did. *He needed a way to manage till times got better.* Surely they would?

Just as Wilf was about to say something, a voice hailed them from the road. 'Is that you, Harry Makepeace?'

Harry spun round to see that a lorry had stopped on the road next to his land. When the driver switched off the engine and jumped down from the cab, Harry moved forward smiling. 'Eh, Mr Selby! I came to see you today but you were otherwise engaged. I was sorry to hear about Mr Willcox. I only met him last week but he did me a kindness.'

'Jonah helped a lot of people in his own quiet way. We should all be as well thought of as he is after we die.' There was a moment's silence and the other men bobbed their heads in silent agreement, then he went on, 'How are things going? Do you know yet when you'll be moving up here?'

'We're just trying to organise that.' Harry gestured to Wilf. 'I've bought a railway carriage for me and my daughter to live in, because I can't afford a house. But they can only deliver it as far as Rivenshaw station, so I have to find a way of getting it up the hill.'

'Good idea about the railway carriage. Anything I can do to help?' He gestured to the lorry. 'I doubt this one would be strong enough to tow a railway carriage but we could move your furniture across from Manchester in it, if you don't mind risking it being rained on, that is.'

Harry gaped at him, unable to believe what he was hearing. 'Are you sure?'

'Yes. Any chance you could come and work on a motor with me before we do that? I've got a difficult refit and could do with an extra pair of hands to get the engine in and out, then put in new parts. It may take more than one day to finish the job. I don't suppose you could come till the weekend but if you could stay overnight, I could move your things over here the following week.'

'I could come back tomorrow, actually.' Harry explained about getting the sack.

'If you'll do that and work with me till it's fixed, I'll pay you the daily rate we agreed before. Then I'll bring the lorry over to move your things at the weekend, and I'll not charge you for that.'

'Are you sure? Well, thank you. That'd be grand.'

'What about your furniture? You won't be able to fit much of it into the shelter, but I could store it for you in my spare bedroom. There's nothing in there except bare boards and I certainly don't need the space.'

Harry closed his eyes for a moment out of sheer relief, unable to believe his luck, then explained about Wilf helping him find a way to transport the railway carriage up the valley to Ellindale.

Todd nodded to Wilf. 'I've heard you're good at sorting problems out, as well as wood carving.' He held out his hand and they shook. 'You live in Ellindale as well, don't you? Right, then, if you tell me your address, I'll know where to come if I want to build something cheaply without being over-charged. Some folk think because I'm Charlie's partner I've money to waste, but I'm not rich like him.'

'I'm easy to find. I live opposite the village shop. The house with the red front door.' Wilf grinned. 'I didn't choose the colour; I was given a half empty tin of paint and the door needed protecting from the weather so the landlord paid me a few bob to paint it.'

Daniel chuckled. That door was a joke in the village.

'You can leave a message for me if you phone the village shop, too. I'll give you their telephone number.'

'I have the number already.' Todd turned to Harry. 'I'll see you tomorrow morning, then, Makepeace. Come as early as you can. I'm always up by six.' With a cheery wave he got into his lorry and drove away.

'Now, that's another nice chap,' Wilf said. 'Selby's not been living in the valley for long but folk speak well of him.' He turned and waited for Harry to decide about the shelter.

Harry took a sudden decision. 'Can you get that wood and put up a wall for me across the shelter?'

'Yes.'

'How much will it cost?'

'I'll find out. Not much. Ten bob at most for the wood. It's just lying there doing nothing so he'll be glad to sell.'

Harry fumbled in his pocket and took out a pound note and a ten-shilling note. 'Here. If you can get it for less than ten bob, keep the change. I'll pay you ten bob to build the wall and the rest is for nails and fixings, maybe even that window you told me about.'

He watched the other man's eyes brighten at that, which meant they were both satisfied with the bargain. Harry had never thought to get a wall built so cheaply. And it meant they'd have extra space once they moved into the railway carriage. They could maybe use the shelter for their kitchen if the carriage was close by.

'I'll be working at Mr Selby's tomorrow, Wilf, if you need anything else or if that's not enough money. I'll spend tomorrow night here in the shelter to save one lot of to-ing and fro-ing from Manchester, not to mention the cost of petrol. My neighbour there will look after my daughter, I'm sure.'

'Sounds a good plan to me. Do you have the exact measurements of the railway carriage?'

Harry gave them to him and he repeated them a couple of times to fix them in his mind.

'I won't forget them. Now, let's get a bit of the foundation dug out.' Wilf eyed the ground, measuring it mentally. 'If I nip home for my spade and crowbar, then we can spell one another and get a start at the digging. We'll keep the rocks we lever out of the ground to repair the walls with. They've been let go and some of them are in a sad state.'

'How much would it be fair to pay you for the digging?'

'Nowt. This is to welcome you to the village.' He stared down at his hands. 'Any road, it's good to have something useful to do. I'm not one to sit around idle waiting for work to drop down from heaven. An' the money I earn from helping you with that wall will mean another week when I don't have to apply for the government's damned charity. I've managed without it so far, thank goodness, because my wife picks up bits of work here and there as well. She's a good lass, my Enid is.'

Harry had to swallow a couple of times to get rid of the lump in his throat and thank the two brothers for their help. He still couldn't believe how helpful people were here.

He joined Daniel and Wilf in a bout of digging that got more done than he'd expected, but kept an eye on the time. When he had to leave to get home before dark, he tried to give them each a couple of bob, because they'd worked hard, but they still refused to accept any money. All he could persuade them to do was accept enough for a pint apiece on him. If they chose to give it to their wives for food instead, that was their business.

He drove gently back to Manchester, not hurrying because he was tired, but feeling a lot better than he had done this morning.

Perhaps he hadn't made a mistake in leaving Trowton's, after all.

# 17

Nina didn't know where she was when she woke up, but then it all clicked into place. The funeral. Poor Mrs Willcox fainting like that. And now, here she was sleeping in another stranger's house. What an uncertain life she'd led since she ran away from home.

But she didn't regret doing that, no, not a bit. All she regretted was not doing it sooner. She'd wasted her best years on being her father's drudge, and in the end he'd cheated her.

She noticed a pretty little clock on the bedroom mantelpiece. Six o'clock. When she got out of bed, she realised a towel had been hung over the footboard of the bed, a lovely big soft towel such as she'd never used in her whole life before. Whoever had done it hadn't woken her. She slipped into her coat, because she didn't own a dressing gown, and went along to the bathroom she'd been shown last night, pressing her cheek against the towel's softness before setting it down and starting her ablutions.

As she used the facilities, she couldn't help stroking the luxurious fitments. How wonderful to obtain hot water without any need to beg her father for a penny to put into the gas meter so that she could switch on the geyser.

The people who owned this house weren't short of money, she thought as she went back to her bedroom and got dressed. What had Lady Terryng said about Mr Willcox? Oh, yes. He owned two pawnshops, half of a used car business and had just bought a shop selling household electrical goods. No wonder his home was so nice.

And even Mrs Willcox worked now and then, apparently. She was becoming known for designing business signs and notepaper, as well as Christmas and birthday cards, for people with money to spare. All this even though she'd recently had a child. My goodness, this was a busy family. Fancy a married woman being able to have a career of her own like that! Most were just their husband's servant or did part-time work like scrubbing on top of their household duties. Some of them even had to hand over the extra money they earned to their husbands instead of spending it on food for the children.

Nina had been cheated by the two men closest to her and didn't intend to get married and become someone's drudge again – even if she was to be offered the chance. Which she probably wouldn't be, given the shortage of males around her age.

She stood and listened from her bedroom doorway and thought she could hear someone stirring downstairs. It'd be that nice young maid perhaps. Nina had had a drink from the cold tap in the bathroom, but was still thirsty. She might go down and see if she could get a cup of tea from Clara.

What would today bring? A new job, she hoped. That was the main thing she needed.

The maid was happy to make her a cup of tea, allowing her to drink it in the warmth of the kitchen and chattering away as she continued to work.

When Nina volunteered to help with the breakfast, Clara gave her a few small tasks but didn't seem to need much help. The work here couldn't be onerous and obviously the maid was happy in her job.

What would it be like working at a youth hostel? Nina

wasn't exactly sure what she'd have to do and asked Clara if she knew anything about such places.

'I've read in the newspapers about them being set up, but I don't know much more than you about how they're run. We sometimes see hikers walking up the valley towards the moors and I suppose some of them sleep in the hostel. Goodness, they do wear big, heavy boots, even the women!'

She mimed clumping along heavily and they both laughed.

'What time are you going to see Mrs Willcox, the one at Spring Cottage, I mean?' Clara spoke about the widow in hushed tones.

'I don't know. When your Mrs Willcox arranges it, I suppose.'

'That poor lady. She hasn't been married long – last year, was it, or the year before? – and now she's a widow. I wonder if she'll still go on making fizzy drinks. I shouldn't think she'll be short of money, though. He was a Willcox, after all.' She cast a quick glance over her shoulder before adding, 'They're not short of a bob or two.'

'So I hear.'

'The master lets us have a bottle of their ginger beer or lemonade sometimes for a treat. Me, the nursery maid and Cook share it, a glass and a half each we get from one bottle. Lovely, it is.' She licked her lips.

'Does Cook get up later than you?'

'No, she lives out and comes in daily because the master has known her since they were kids and he likes her cooking. I can easily cope with breakfast because he only ever wants a ham sandwich and the mistress favours toast and honey. It's good practice for me, because I'm learning to cook. I intend to better myself and become a cook-house-keeper eventually.'

She glanced at the clock. 'I'll just take up their cups of tea now. You pour yourself another then you can tell me what you'd like for breakfast. They have theirs at seven-thirty because the master likes to make an early start.'

After the owners of the house had finished their breakfast, Nina was summoned to the morning room.

'Did you sleep well?' Mrs Willcox asked, but it seemed a dutiful question, not one in whose answer she was really interested.

'Very well, thank you. Such a comfortable bed.'

'It should be, the price we paid for it,' Mr Willcox said. 'It's good to see it getting some use. I rather fancy buying one of those new rubber mattresses the big rubber companies have started making. I had a lie on one in a shop in Swindon. No springs jabbing into you on those.'

'And it'll be squashed flat rubber if you get any fatter,' Mrs Willcox said sharply as he got up and went towards the electric bell push on the wall to summon the maid. 'You're not having another sandwich, Charlie.'

'Have a bad night, did you?' He sighed regretfully and sat down without pushing the bell.

'Your son is the one who had a bad night,' she said even more sharply.

'Oh? I didn't hear a thing.'

'You never do.'

'Why were you the one to get up? What do we pay a nursery maid for if not to do that?'

'She got up the night before and for part of last night. She can't go without sleep for two nights running. Besides, poor little Arthur was upset. We think he's teething. They're not supposed to start so young, but you can't mistake the signs.'

'Ah. Well, you can have a nap later today, can't you?'

She rolled her eyes and shook her head. 'You're not the only one who has things to do today, Charlie.'

Mr Willcox hastily swallowed his last mouthful of tea and glanced at the clock. 'Shall I phone Leah yet, do you think?'

'Well, it's ten past eight. She'd usually be up by this time, but if she's still asleep, Ginny will answer your call and take a message.'

Nina was amazed at how abrupt Mrs Willcox was with her husband and how tamely he was taking it. She doubted her mother had ever answered her father back like that in their whole married life. If she had done, he'd have given her a stinging backhander.

She couldn't imagine Mr Willcox thumping anyone. He looked sad today, as you would after losing your only brother, but he had the sort of face that seemed born to smile.

Leah was sitting in the kitchen with a glass of ginger beer, which seemed to help settle her stomach, when the phone rang. 'I'll get it, Ginny.' She went into the back hall and picked up the receiver. 'Oh, Charlie. Yes, I slept like a log, thank you.'

'We have your new matron staying with us. What time do you want us to deliver her?'

'Oh, my goodness! I forgot about her completely yesterday. I was supposed to bring her back with me after the funeral. Ginny had got everything ready for her, too.'

'You had enough on your plate with that fainting fit, so we brought her home with us. Are you all right now?'

'I'm fine. There's nothing like a good, long sleep for setting you up.'

'Shall I bring Miss Halshall up after breakfast, then? Oh, hang on a minute. What is it, dear?'

Silence, then he came back on the phone. 'Marion says she'll bring Miss Halshall up because she's coming to check for herself that you're all right and she doesn't want the poor woman scared out of her wits by my driving. When would suit you?'

'Any time is fine.'

Leah heard him repeat this to his wife.

'Marion says she'll be up in about an hour.'

'Good. I'll look forward to seeing her. Don't forget to apologise to Miss Halshall for me.'

As she was putting the phone down, Leah heard him mutter, 'I'm not that bad a driver!' and found herself smiling, something she'd not expected to do today. He would never admit that he was a terrible driver, but she'd noticed that he never tried to drive far out of the valley, as if he preferred to stick to the roads he knew.

Charlie came back into the morning room. 'Leah slept well and is looking forward to seeing you, Marion. The matron's room is ready, Miss Halshall. Ginny finished it off yesterday. Oh, and Leah says sorry for forgetting about you yesterday.'

'She wasn't well. I quite understand.'

He went to kiss his wife's cheek. 'Got to go now. I'll be at the electrical shop for most of the day if you need me. The place is in chaos. I'm taking Vi with me. If anyone can organise a better system for running it, it's her.'

'All right. Have a nice day.'

'Can I ask who Ginny is?' Nina said.

'She's the general maid at Spring Cottage. You can't do better than ask her help or advice if Leah isn't around. The woman is an absolute treasure. I'm blessed with my servants, too. Clara is so efficient and cheerful with it, and the nursery maid's a dear, really good with little Arthur.'

It amazed Nina how many nice things these people said about one another or their servants. Her father had never had a good word for anyone, her included. 'Shall I get ready to leave straight away?'

A baby's wail rang out faintly from upstairs.

'We'll go in about half an hour, Miss Halshall,' Marion said. 'I want to see my precious darling first. He'll be all fresh and cuddly after his bath.'

The nursery maid brought in the son and heir, and Mrs Willcox soon had him cooing and laughing.

'His tooth's come through, ma'am,' the maid announced. 'See. There's the corner of it.'

Charlie must have heard this because he came back from the hall to peer inside his son's mouth, shaking his head in bafflement. 'He made all that fuss for one tiny tooth and now he's *laughing*? I don't understand babies.'

The front door banged behind him and the sound of clashing gears could be heard almost immediately from the side of the house. Marion sighed. 'Just listen to him. He can't even start off smoothly, let alone handle the car when it's moving.'

The sound of a horn being tooted several times floated back from the street.

'There. You see. I didn't want to frighten you to death by letting him take you up to Ellindale, Miss Halshall. Even with his new spectacles, he's hit their gatepost several times over the past few months going into the yard and it's a really wide entrance. You'd think he was aiming straight at it.'

'Wouldn't he be better with a driver?'

'Ha! Try telling him that. He always says he's improving, but he isn't.'

When they did go outside, Nina joined her mistress in a neat little car, quite the smallest she'd ever seen, called a 'Chummy'. She was looking forward to her first sight of the upper valley where she hoped to make her home for several months at least, if not longer.

Mrs Willcox didn't clash the gears at all, Nina noticed. Indeed, it was a very smooth drive up the hill from Birch

End, and the scenery was as pretty as she'd hoped. Such lovely views. She was glad Mrs Willcox didn't try to chat.

When they reached Spring Cottage, they saw a man loading crates of fizzy drink bottles into a van, helped by a plump youth with a rather vacant face. 'Spring Cottage Mineral Waters' was written on the side of the van with a pretty design around it.

'What a lovely sign.'

Mrs Willcox beamed at her. 'I designed that. My first sale, it was.'

'I wish I could draw.'

'I'm glad some people can't or they'd not pay me to do it.' Marion came to a halt, switched off the engine and got out of the car. 'They're late starting off on their rounds today. It'll be because of the funeral, I suppose. This way. Bring your luggage.'

Nina hastily slid out of the car and followed her, hoping she wouldn't have to bring her one battered suitcase back to the car again. Mr Willcox had said the room was ready for the matron, so they must need someone quickly.

Marion tapped on the cottage door and went straight in, introducing Nina to the slender, sad-looking woman who'd fainted so dramatically after the funeral. This other Mrs Willcox looked a lot better today, but was still rather pale.

'You must think I'm terrible, ignoring you like that yesterday,' Leah said.

'You fainted. I don't call that ignoring me,' Nina said.

'No. I suppose not. But I still feel guilty. Thanks for letting her sleep at your house and bringing her up today, Marion love.'

'What else would family do? We'll have you round to tea in a few days.' She studied a small wristwatch. 'I can't stay. I just wanted to see with my own eyes that you were all right.'

'I'm fine, love.'

'Don't try to do too much today.'

'I'm better keeping busy. It takes my mind off Jonah.'

There was a moment's silence, then Marion squeezed her sister-in-law's hand in a wordless gesture of comfort and left.

Nina turned to her new employer and waited. Well, she hoped Mrs Willcox would be her new employer.

'Do call me Leah. I don't like to stand on ceremony.'

Nina was surprised at that. 'Are you sure?'

'Yes, of course I am. And your first name is Nina, I believe?'

'Yes, it is.'

'Pretty name. Now, leave your suitcase here and I'll show you the youth hostel before we have a chat. It's at the right-hand end of my little factory.' She pointed across the big yard. 'The building used to be the main barn for a farm. It's well over a hundred years old, perhaps as much as two hundred, but very solidly built. Ben Lonsdale had only to repair one corner when he was renovating the barn for me. He lives next to the youth hostel in that low building at the side. He's a stonemason.'

'Mr Lonsdale lives here too?'

'Yes. He's just starting up his own business after finishing his apprenticeship and we had space for him, so he paid us by renovating an outhouse to live in. Jonah—' Her voice faltered for a moment, then she took a deep breath and went on, 'Jonah said that was worth a year's rent. It'll be good to have someone else living up here. It can get very quiet in the evenings.'

Nina looked round and mentally agreed with her. She wouldn't like to live on her own in such an isolated place.

'We have electricity up here now, thank goodness, so you'll be able to listen to the radio.'

'I'll have to save up for one.'

'Ah. I can lend you Jonah's.'

'I can't ask you to do that!'

'You didn't ask; I offered.'

That would be wonderful. Her father had refused point-blank to have a radio, despising such modern inventions and preferring to read his newspaper in the evenings.

Leah led Nina across the yard and showed her round the hostel. There were two dormitories, one for men at the far end and one for women upstairs, with a day area containing a big table and a place to brew tea or make sandwiches downstairs, shared by everyone. An inner door that could be locked at night cut off the stairs to the women's dormitory.

'The women should be told to keep the door locked at night from their side.'

'Yes. I see.' She was beginning to feel hopeful about the job.

'I'll leave it to you to tell them that. There won't always be both men and women staying anyway. We only have room for eight in each dormitory and as we're new and not on one of the more popular hiking routes, so far we've never been full.'

There was a small hallway next to the stairs with another door at the end that led into what had once been a storage area for various pieces of farm equipment. It had now been turned into two comfortably furnished rooms for the matron. One was a living room with a small kitchen to one side and the other was a bedroom. It had its own entrance into the women's ablution area as well.

'I thought the matron might like to make meals for herself sometimes, especially when there's no one staying in the hostel. But if you'd rather eat with us – that is me, my sister Rosa and Ben – you'll be welcome as long as you take pot luck. Ginny usually gets us something ready, but she goes home at teatime.'

She looked round then turned back to Nina. 'If I've forgotten anything, just ask.'

Nina had to ask, 'You mean I've definitely got the job?'

Her companion looked surprised. 'Well, yes. I took Lady Terryng's word that you're a good worker. She's a shrewd judge of people. Didn't she tell you that?'

Nina surprised herself by bursting into tears of relief, so her companion took her back to the main house and she found herself confiding in Leah about what had brought her here.

'I won't let you down, Mrs Willcox,' she promised earnestly once she'd finished.

'I'm sure you won't. And please remember to call me Leah. Just one other thing: do you know how to drive?'

'Me? No. I've hardly ever ridden in a car, even.'

'Well, I think we'll get Todd to teach you, if you don't mind.' She cradled her stomach briefly, even though she wasn't showing much yet. 'As I grow bigger, I may find it useful to have someone else able to drive me into Rivenshaw to do the shopping or to go for the doctor if there's an emergency. Unless you don't want to drive?'

'I'm nervous at the thought of it, but I'd love to try.' This job was sounding better and better.

'That's all right, then. Now, I'll ask Ginny to give you some food supplies and she'll help you set up the hikers' kitchen at the hostel while I have a quiet rest. I'm still a bit tired after . . . everything.'

So Nina took her suitcase across to the hostel and Ginny came with her to explain what food staples she'd already put in the matron's room.

'I hope you know how to cook,' she said.

'Oh, yes. My father was very fussy about what he ate. I don't know any fancy recipes but I'm not wasteful.'

'We're only supplying simple evening meals, sandwiches

and soup or stew probably, and we'll use tinned soup if there are only one or two people, or they turn up late. So you see, we don't need a fancy cook. But till you settle in, if there are more than two or three staying, don't hesitate to come to me or Mrs Willcox and we'll advise you or help you provide the food. We can always phone the village shop to see if they have any bread left, if necessary, and they sell tins of stewing steak.'

That was an expensive way to provide meat, Nina thought, but if there was no butcher you had to do what you could.

Ginny looked at her shrewdly. 'If you don't mind me saying so, love, you look as if you've had a hard time recently. It's a fine day, so why don't you stroll down through the village and call in at the shop? Introduce yourself to Lily who runs it for her cousin, and have a look at what they stock. When you come back here, you can make yourself familiar with every corner of every room in the hostel.'

'A gentle stroll sounds wonderful. Are you sure Mrs Willcox won't mind? She said to call her Leah, but I hardly like to do that.'

'She really does prefer it.'

'Right.'

Ginny carried on talking, 'She married above herself as they say. But *I* think Mr Jonah got a good bargain in her. She won't be checking on you every minute. She trusts people to do their work. She'd normally go through all these details with you herself, but at the moment, what with Mr Jonah dying and her finding out she's expecting, she's not herself, but you can always ask me. Have you met her sister Rosa yet?'

'I don't think so.'

'Very clever young woman, that one is. Only twelve but already saying she wants to be a doctor. No one from Ellindale has ever become a doctor before. Wouldn't it be grand if she succeeded?'

'I think it's wonderful that women can have the chance.' Her father had said some very rude things at the mere idea of females 'pretending to be doctors'. But why not? Women were no more stupid than men and were more used to caring for people, now she came to think of it.

Ginny snorted scornfully. 'I reckon women can do nearly everything men can and just let anyone tell me different.'

She looked like a small, fierce hen as she said that and Nina smiled involuntarily.

'I think doctoring will suit Rosa. If we women had got the vote sooner, we'd have changed a lot of things. And for the better, too. Look at the mess this country is in now. But at least we've got the vote now and I'm not going to waste mine.'

She patted Nina on the shoulder. 'Sorry. I didn't mean to go on at you on your first day. Don't look so nervous, love. No one will expect miracles of you, just hard work and learning how to do things. We're all still learning about youth hostels, after all.'

'Thank you, um—?'

'Just call me Ginny and I'll call you Nina, if that's all right.'

'I'd like that. I'm grateful for your kindness and I won't hesitate to ask your help if I need it.'

'Well, if we can't be kind to one another, what are we worth? Now, do you think you can manage to settle in? I can't stand here chatting all day, not that I haven't enjoyed talking to you because I have. Just come across whenever you need anything. Or even if you just feel like a bit of company. I'll tell you if I'm too busy.'

Nina watched her amble across the yard, smiling again. She liked Ginny, and her new employer too.

Then she walked round the hostel again, feeling truly proprietorial this time and ending up in the matron's quarters, where she spun round out of sheer joy. It took her only a few minutes to unpack her clothes, she had so few of them. She never had owned many, let alone pretty ones.

She might find out where the nearest market was and buy a few new clothes. Her underwear was pitifully ragged, for a start.

After she'd closed the last drawer and put her suitcase on top of the wardrobe, Nina set off down the lane into Ellindale. She passed a big house on the right about a hundred yards along and it wasn't far from there to the first village house.

In the centre was an open space. She was hailed by a very old man sitting there, on a bench.

'Are you the new matron?' he called, in the overloud tones of one slightly deaf.

'Yes. I am.'

'Got a name?'

She told him and found out his. She didn't mind his nosiness because what else would a man that old have to do with his time but watch the world go by? Simeon wished her well as if he meant it when she said she had to get on and that made her feel welcome here.

She went into the shop, waited till the young woman behind the counter had served a customer, then introduced herself.

'Ah yes. Ginny said you'd be arriving today. How about a cup of tea to welcome you to the village?'

Lily also gave her a squashed bun without charging her, as a welcome. Nina wasn't really hungry, she rarely was, but she ate it to be polite. There were a couple of tables to one side for people to sit at and have refreshments.

'We get quite a few hikers in the summer and they're always hungry. Sometimes people from the hostel come in as well, or go to the pub. It was such a good idea, that hostel, brings hikers to spend money in this shop and another job into the village, plus some cleaning work for the married women. We've a lot to be grateful to Mrs Willcox for. She's the one who always got the clever ideas, you know, not her husband. Though he supported her. Lovely man, he was.'

Someone else came into the shop just then so Nina sat at one of the tables and sipped her tea, listening to three customers chatting to the young shopkeeper. She was introduced as 'the new matron of the youth hostel' and was feeling more comfortable with the title now, more than just comfortable – proud of it.

It was a nice village, or it would be when people weren't so hungry. It wasn't just food hunger, it was hunger for work, for something to fill their empty days. She could tell from the way two small groups of men were standing around at corners, looking downhearted. She'd seen that all too often.

When the last person had left the shop, Nina bought a quarter pound of mint imperials, her favourite sweets. It was extravagant when she hadn't even earned her first week's pay yet. Her father had never allowed anyone but himself to have treats, but she felt it set the seal on her first day here to spend money openly on her own pleasures. She strolled slowly back up the hill sucking one of the round white mints, thoughtful now.

She had been given a warm welcome by every single person she'd met. That made her feel comforted about coming here in such a hasty way. If she ever could, she'd like to help other people, too, as she had been helped, especially the men who were out of work. In January the Prince of Wales, who was the patron of the National Council of Social Service, had spoken at a meeting in the Albert Hall. He'd called on the British people to regard unemployment as a 'national opportunity for voluntary social service'.

She'd read in the newspaper at the library a few days later that there had been a heartening response all over the country, with people starting to set up centres to provide educational opportunities for the unemployed and their womenfolk. There had been 114 centres set up for men and 35 for women in Lancashire alone.

She'd wished she could contribute locally, as Mrs Willcox had, but it had been all she could do until now to squeeze out the time from caring for her selfish and demanding father just to go to the library. At least her father hadn't been able to find anything wrong with her taking advantage of the free loans of books.

It made her feel good to have found herself a job and a home so quickly!

# 18

The day after Jonah's funeral Finn Carlisle left his wife to continue going through the contents of the large house he'd inherited. She was his former housekeeper and had been itching to get on with this, but he'd wanted her to meet some cousins he'd recently got in touch with first.

He'd told her to get rid of anything she didn't want, and they'd agreed to give such items to those in most need in the village. She understood all too well what it was like struggling to feed your children, because she'd been in that position when he first employed her, abandoned by her husband.

This house still contained too many of its former owners' possessions because he had never been sure what to throw away and what to keep. He'd cleared out a few rooms when he moved in, the ones he wanted to use, but hadn't finished the job because he hated going through other people's possessions and anyway, there were other things that needed doing.

He left Beth to it and decided to go out for a breath of fresh air. He called for the dog he'd bought for Reggie, but which had become his by default now that Reggie spent the school terms with his aunt, Lady Terryng.

Tippy came rushing at the sound of her name and followed Finn outside. At the top of the drive he turned to stare back at Heythorpe House and she went to sniff her way through the grass at the side of the road. It still surprised Finn that an uncle he'd never known had left everything to him, not just the house but quite a lot of money as well. He'd never thought to be so comfortably circumstanced for he'd worked as a policeman till his first wife died. He didn't care much about spending money on himself, because he had everything a man could desire in his new wife and a decent roof over his head. But he was starting to get pleasure from having enough money to help people who had little or nothing in these hard times.

Which reminded him . . . He wanted to call in at the back room of the pub first to check that the system he'd set up was working and the younger children from the village were receiving their daily glass of milk.

He heard laughter before he got there and didn't make himself known but watched Gillian cope with the group of boys and girls, teasing one ragged little lad, making him giggle, while keeping an eye on the whole group. Some women were like that, even when they were only sixteen like her, able to command children's attention without being cruel.

She caught sight of him. 'Mr Carlisle! I didn't expect to see you so soon after your return.'

'I wanted to find out how these scallywags were getting on.'

The children had fallen silent and some were even standing up straighter, watching him warily. A couple of little girls already had milky moustaches, while others were clutching full glasses tightly in both hands.

He waved one hand at the group. 'Carry on drinking your milk, children.' Then he turned to Gillian. 'Is there anything else you need?'

'We've got the milk organised, sir. But can I have a word, do you think, once they've finished and gone home?'

'Is something wrong?'

'Not exactly, no. Just an idea I had.'

'Well, I'll look forward to hearing about it. I'll go and say hello to Don and Izzy, then come back to you when the children have left.'

'They don't stay long once they've had their milk.'

When he returned ten minutes later from speaking to the publican and his wife, he found Gillian clearing up, washing the glasses in a bowl of hot water, rinsing them in another bowl and drying them carefully.

'I'll do that.' He took the tea towel out of her hand and picked up a wet glass.

She looked surprised but let him dry the glasses while she finished washing the last few dirty ones.

'Tell me,' he said as she hesitated.

'Well, I was wondering if you could spare a little more money to help the children?'

'Oh? In what way?'

'Their clothes. Children grow out of things all the time and after years of being short of money, some of the mothers are running out of hand-me-downs and finding it hard to replace the worn-out clothes. There's a second-hand clothes stall at Rivenshaw market, and it'd not take much money to outfit the worst cases.' She gave him a wry smile. 'Some of their backsides are nearly on show, it's so bad.'

'What an excellent idea!'

Her sigh of relief was so heartfelt he grinned at her. 'I'm not an ogre, as you should know by now, Gillian, nor did I grow up rich, so I do understand what life can be like. How much do you think it'll take to buy the necessary clothes?'

'I don't know. I need to make a list. I'd try to keep it under twenty pounds. Just the worst cases.'

'No need to skimp. Be careful with the money, yes. But if they need clothes, don't hesitate to help them, whatever it costs. In fact, why don't Beth and I drive you down to town next market day and we'll all shop together.'

'That'd be good. Beth is very practical.'

'I am too, I hope.'

She didn't comment on that, clearly still a little in awe of him.

Money could do that, he'd found, set you apart, however hard you tried not to flourish it at people. Beth had never stood in awe of him, though, even when she was his house-keeper. He didn't think his delightful new wife would be afraid of anyone.

When he strolled on down the hill, Finn felt delighted at the thought of finding another way to help the village. He'd always been fond of children, but had lost his unborn child and his first wife at the same time. Now he was daring to hope to have children with Beth. She'd borne two already to her first husband and said she carried them easily. He prayed that was true.

While he was walking, he saw two men digging on Mr Kerkham's land and crossed the road to find out what was going on. People didn't usually go on to this piece of land at all, because Kerkham made such a fuss.

One of the men straightened up and he saw it was Daniel, who worked for him sometimes, so he clambered across the wall to chat to them. 'You two are brave, invading Kerkham's territory!'

'It's not his now, Mr Carlisle. He's sold it. I thought everyone knew that by now.'

'Good heavens! I go away for a couple of weeks to meet my long-lost cousins and our little world changes. I didn't think he'd ever find a buyer. Who was it? Someone from round here?'

After they'd explained about Harry Makepeace, Finn looked at what they'd done. 'Did he hire you to do this?'

They both looked a bit sheepish.

'He's hired me to get him some wood and make a wall to

fill in the end of the shelter so he and his daughter can sleep in it for a few nights,' Wilf said. 'Only I can't fetch the wood till I get my handcart back from my neighbour. He paid me to let him borrow it today.'

He looked down at the shovel he was holding and shrugged. 'I've nowt else to do with my time, so I thought I'd lend Harry a hand and clear some more ground for his foundations.'

'That's kind of you. Perhaps he'll pay you a few bob.'

'I can manage to do a favour for a new friend without asking for payment,' he said rather stiffly.

'Yes, of course you can. Still keeping off the dole, Wilf?'

'I am, yes. It's hard, though. If my friend at the market hadn't sold a couple of my carved animals, and Enid hadn't got an extra load of washing to do, we'd have had to ask for help last week. It's hand to mouth, that's what it is, and the uncertainty is wearing.'

'It must be.'

'And there's a new means test man coming to the valley soon. We don't know what this one will be like. The old one turned a blind eye when someone slipped you a bit of food, but I've heard about some sods who'll take the cost of the food out of your dole payments – even of things like the milk you give to the children.'

Finn made a sympathetic noise and decided to watch out for something like that with the new means test man. Surely no one could grudge children a glass of milk!

He was wondering how else he could help people. Clearly he couldn't provide jobs for all of them, but he hated to see the men hanging around on the village green in little groups or standing together outside their houses with shoulders slumped. He knew how it fretted them to have nothing constructive to fill their days, apart from the necessary trip into Rivenshaw to sign on for the dole every week.

He'd been thinking about starting one of the clubs for the unemployed he'd heard about, with activities that gave men something worth doing or taught them a skill, but he wasn't sure how to set about that. It was on his list of things to look into now that he'd settled into his new marriage.

People in the whole valley were dreading the arrival of the new means test man, he knew, but Finn was hoping he could make an ally of the fellow. The one who'd just died had been a colourless creature, weary and worn, looking old though he'd only been fifty. The poor fellow had looked sickly for a long time and had just dropped dead one day. He'd more or less obeyed the law about the means test, when it wasn't too much trouble, and had been neither nasty nor helpful towards those who had to pass the various tests that treated long-time unemployed men so cruelly.

As if the lack of a job was the men's fault! You couldn't get yourself a job when there were none going. He realised Wilf had spoken to him and was waiting patiently for an answer. 'Sorry. What did you say?'

'I'm going up to see Ben after tea. He's working on a little job in Rivenshaw today so he won't be too late back. I want to ask his advice about the footings.'

'Well, I shall enjoy watching progress here.'

Finn turned round and strolled slowly back up to his home, the dog gambolling around behind him. It was a nice dog, should have had a child to play with, and he'd promised Reggie a dog. But Margot Terryng was too busy sorting out the orphanage's problems to keep an eye on it while her nephew was at the grammar school.

He was missing Reggie's company, had intended to adopt him, only the lad had turned out to be Margot's missing nephew and heir, so now Finn had to forgo the pleasure of bringing him up and be content with him visiting them here occasionally. This was only right, because Reggie had to learn the ways of better-off people, not to mention how to run the family estate when he inherited it. But he did miss the lad.

He and Beth had dropped Reggie off at his aunt's on the way back from visiting some distant relatives who'd been trying to find him for months to make sure Finn was all right. That was kind of them but he was glad he hadn't needed any help after his first wife died.

He'd been surprised at how comfortably the various relatives were living, with all the men in work. Things were so much better in the south and Midlands than up here in the north because of there being more jobs available, especially jobs in the manufacture of motor vehicles.

Finn told himself to stop day dreaming and find his wife. He wanted to discuss buying new clothes for the children with her.

A short time after Mr Carlisle had left, Wilf paused in his digging. That sounded like Ben's van. He ran down to the wall and signalled to his friend to stop.

The van pulled up a short distance past the piece of land. Ben switched off the engine and jumped down from the cab.

'Finished your day's work already?' Wilf teased. 'My goodness, you live a lazy life.'

Ben gave him a wry look. 'I'm getting enough work to manage on and more coming in now that people know I've set up as a builder here in the valley. How are things going for you?'

Wilf shrugged. 'Not too bad. I've got a week or so of work coming up with the new owner of this land and I'm fair set up about that. I get fed up of tramping round Lancashire day after day, and as for sleeping under hedges on the nights I go further afield, it's damned uncomfortable, that is.'

'What's the new fellow like?'

'Seems a nice chap, hard-working.' He explained the

situation to yet another person – eh, he'd be saying this in his sleep if he kept having to go over it! – then went on to his main purpose. 'I wanted a bit of advice about the footings, if you can spare a moment.'

'Show me.' Ben climbed over the wall and they walked across to the shelter.

'There'll be a wooden wall to put across the shelter first, quite a small job but I want it secure, then there'll be footings and a retaining wall to support the old railway carriage he's bringing up to live in. There's only going to be about a two-foot difference in height, because it's one of the more gently sloping parts of the land. But the footings will need to be good and strong and I want to be certain my ideas of how to do it are right. I'd not like to let Harry down.'

'How big is the carriage?'

'He gave me the exact measurements.' Wilf pulled the scrap of paper out of his pocket and held it out.

'Why not dig the ground out?'

'He wants to use the shelter as a kitchen after he's got the carriage here, so he wants it all on one level.'

'Yes. That'd be better for daily living, I'm sure.'

Within minutes Ben was walking up and down, working out with Wilf how best to do the footings. Wilf wouldn't have been far out in his rough calculations, but Ben had a couple of suggestions for improving matters, and explained how to make the retaining wall at the lower end strong enough, and suggested a rim wall to set the carriage on, perhaps topped with old railway sleepers.

'Harry hasn't got a lot of money,' Wilf warned him. 'He won't be able to pay you for your help.'

'Like you, I can spare a bit of time to help a neighbour.'

'Good lad. How's Mrs Willcox going?'

Ben shrugged. 'Missing Jonah, as you'd expect. She looks sad. If we can get her interested in helping the newcomers, perhaps it'll give her something else to think about. Todd says he'll pop in to see her whenever he's up in Ellindale. He says Jonah asked him to keep an eye on her, but I reckon he'd have done that anyway. I've always thought he was a bit smitten.'

Wilf smiled. 'I've wondered too. My missus used to say Leah and Jonah were allus more like friends than lovers but when Todd looks at Leah you can sometimes see how he feels about her.'

'Time will tell if she can return his feelings. She's only in her twenties, isn't she? Plenty of time to remarry and have a few more kids.'

When they'd done all the planning they could, Ben glanced at his wristwatch.

Wilf watched enviously. Wristwatches were so much more practical than pocket watches. Men who could afford them had started using them after the war. He had a secret longing to possess one, but didn't even own a pocket watch now, had had to pawn his dad's old watch to keep from going on the dole. At least Charlie Willcox paid fair prices – for a pawn-shop owner.

'How about I go and leave my stuff at home, then run you down to get that wood?' Ben suggested. 'There's plenty of room in the back of my van if I take my tools out.'

'Eh, that'd speed things up nicely. I'd have had to make two journeys with my handcart. If we can drop off my spade and crowbar at home on the way I'll go on working till you're ready. I don't like to leave them lying around, even in Ellindale. They're good tools those are. If I have to go on the dole, the new means test man will probably force me to sell them before I get any money paid out.'

'He won't be popular if he does things like that.'

'Well, no means test man is ever liked, but some are worse than others. I hope this one won't take pleasure in ordering folk around or making them sell their favourite bits and pieces of furniture. I heard one chap made a friend of my wife's over Rochdale way sell her grandmother's vase. It only brought in sixpence and she cried for days about losing it, poor lass.'

'It's a wicked law, that one is.'

Wilf nodded. 'They made her get rid of one of her beds as well, which left her without enough beds for her kids. Her oldest lad sleeps on a pile of rags on the floor now, because he won't sleep in a bed with three little 'uns, says they kick and twitch in their sleep, not to mention wetting the bed sometimes.'

They both stood scowling for a moment or two at the injustice of that, then Ben clapped him on the back and added encouragingly, 'Ah well. We'll come through it and one day we'll get our normal lives back. Charlie Willcox reckons things are starting to improve already, now Britain is off the gold standard and interest rates have gone down. I pray he's right.'

'Aye. So do we all. Is that why he bought the shop?'

'I think so. But it's a run-down old place with some old-fashioned stuff in it. I'd rather have started fresh, if it were me. I did hear a whisper that he was disappointed in the stock and it wasn't what he'd been told.'

'He should go after the chap as sold it to him.'

'It'd cost more to pay a lawyer than it'd be worth. And Flewett's gone to live near Blackpool now.'

Later, as Ben drove away after helping to unload the wood, Wilf stared at the pile of timber, then kicked a stray offcut on to the main pile and said to his brother Daniel, 'I think I'll sleep in the shelter tonight. There are folk who might be tempted to pinch some of this wood and waste it on firewood.'

'That damned Judson for a start. Want some company?

It's a fine night, and even if it rained we'd be dry inside that shelter.'

'Aye. It'll be like when we were lads together, lying out on the moors looking up at the stars. I'll stay here while you go for your evening meal, then I'll nip back for a bite to eat while you keep watch. We're late finishing so you must be famished.'

With a nod, Daniel tramped off, whistling cheerfully.

It wasn't dark but it was well into twilight and people were mostly back in their homes by now, so when Wilf heard footsteps coming down from the village, he remained in the shelter, watching and listening. The person was trying to move quietly and why would he do that unless he was bent on mischief?

Well, you're not moving quietly enough to fool me, he thought.

Whoever it was stopped on the road near the piece of land and stood there in silence for a good two or three minutes.

Then Wilf saw someone clamber quickly over the broken wall in the corner and bob down behind some fallen stones. Silence again. The intruder must be listening to make sure he was alone.

Well, he could guess who it was.

Knowing the terrain on the piece of land rather better than the other person did, after all his work today, he waited until the man started moving again, inevitably making some noise.

Wilf used those sounds to mask his own move out of the shelter as he crept towards the pile of wood. He heard the soft clunking sound of pieces of wood as they were picked up. When he judged the thief had his arms full, Wilf pounced, grabbed the collar of his jacket and shook him hard. The intruder let out a terrified yell.

'I thought it'd be you, Judson.'

'Let go of me.'

'Why should I? I've caught a thief. I should shout for help and tell whoever comes to ask Lily at the shop to phone the police.'

'It's only a few pieces of wood. The wife wants to make some soup for the children but we've no fuel to cook with. Have pity on the children.'

Wilf laughed out loud. Judson's wife was famous for her inability to cook and the poor way she fed her kids. 'You'll have to think of a better excuse than that. Your wife can't even boil water.'

'Look, I'll put the wood back and I promise I won't come here again.'

A voice called suddenly, 'What's going on there?'

'I've just caught a thief, Mr Carlisle,' Wilf called back. 'Come and see. I bet you can guess who it is.'

Finn climbed over the wall and came across to join them, followed by the dog. 'I'd have guessed correctly. Good thing I was out for a last stroll, eh?'

'Do you think we should call the police?' Wilf nudged him because it was too dark for a wink to show. 'I'll keep hold of him and you look inside his jacket. He hasn't managed to shake out all the pieces of Mr Makepeace's wood yet. There are some in his poacher's pockets, too, I daresay.'

'Think of my children if they were without a father,' Judson pleaded desperately.

'They managed without a father when you were in prison for a couple of months recently and probably ate better without you there to take most of the food. They'll manage again.'

'Hmm.' Finn pretended to think about it. 'Maybe we can let him off with a final warning, Wilf. What do you think? You've got me as a witness so the police will take it more seriously if he's ever caught thieving again in this village.'

'Give me a minute to think about it. And while I'm doing that, you can damned well take the rest of the wood out of your jacket, Barry Judson!' Wilf ordered.

Cringing away from him, Judson did this. When he'd finished tossing out the smaller pieces of wood, he repeated in a whining tone, 'It was for the kids.'

'More likely you'd have sold it to buy a beer.' Wilf let go of the collar and shoved him away so hard he tripped over a rock and fell.

As Judson scrambled to his feet and ran away, Wilf shouted at the top of his voice, '*Do not come back here again. I'll be keeping watch.*'

Judson scrambled over the wall as if expecting to be grabbed at any minute, with the dog chasing after him, yelping happily at this new game. He panicked and fell over again on the other side with another screech, but got up and was running again within seconds, this time limping noticeably.

'We could do without that one in our village,' Finn said. 'He'll never change.'

'No, he won't.'

'I thought he'd been locked away for a few months – for poaching, wasn't it?'

'Must have been let out again. Heaven help his wife. He's not only a poor provider but he thumps her regularly.'

They both shook their heads in disgust.

'What were you doing here anyway, Wilf?'

'Guarding the wood for the new owner. Me and Daniel thought someone might try to steal it. People have scoured the countryside for miles around and there's hardly any dead wood to be found these days.'

'Shall I bring you something to eat? We had some food left over from our tea.'

Wilf hesitated. He hated taking charity, but a meal was a meal and it'd save his wife a couple of slices of bread. He had to watch Enid like a hawk to make sure she fed herself properly and didn't give her share to someone who needed it more. 'Thank you. That's very kind of you, Mr Carlisle.'

'It's kind of you to watch Mr Makepeace's wood.'

'Makes me feel useful, for once,' Wilf said before he could think how it sounded. He tried not to complain about anything or to sound self-pitying, but it was hard to keep a cheerful face on things all the time, it was indeed.

Then he thought about how he'd saved the wood from being stolen tonight and he cheered up a little. He was still of use here and there.

# 19

The following morning, Harry set off from Manchester at dawn and was back in Rivenshaw by half-past seven, ready to start his day's work with Todd and determined to make a good impression. Cathie had slept next door at Mrs Pyne's, so he'd set his alarm for half-past five and contented himself with a piece of bread and a scrape of dripping before setting off.

The sidecar was once again loaded with household bits and pieces. He trusted Kerkham to look after his possessions.

When he got to the used car yard in Rivenshaw, he found Todd only just getting up and was persuaded to have a boiled egg with toast before starting work.

'Everyone works better on a full stomach,' Todd said firmly.

'How did you know my stomach was empty?'

'I guessed when I saw you lick your lips. I was right, wasn't I? You're eating as little as you can to make the money spin out.'

Harry shrugged. No use denying it. He wasn't the only one who'd had to cut back on food. There were a lot of thin people around.

He enjoyed the morning's work on the car engine. He might not be a motor mechanic by trade, but thanks to his experience in the army, he usually found any type of smaller machinery easy to understand.

Though Harry was acting mainly as labourer and odd job

man today, he knew enough to make himself more useful than Todd had expected. And when he didn't understand something, Todd was happy to explain so he learned a lot, which was always a pleasure to him.

As the light started to fade, Todd called an end to the work, looking at the car engine with satisfaction. 'We did well today, achieved more than I'd expected. When times get better there'll be good money to be made from repairing cars and I'll be ready for it. Now, let's go and get something to eat from the baker's before you drive up to Ellindale. They do a really tasty meat pie and I asked them to save me two.'

'I'm still full from the last lot of food you bought me at lunchtime.'

'Liar.' But Todd said it with humour in his voice. 'Come on. I shall work you hard tomorrow as well, Harry, so I won't be wasting the money I spend on feeding you. Where are you sleeping tonight?'

'In the shepherd's shelter.' There was something very satisfying about the idea of sleeping on his own land. It might not be good farming land, but his house would have wonderful views across the moors.

Todd paid for the meat pies and led the way outside. 'See you in the morning.'

Harry stepped back into the shop to buy some of the broken pieces of bread and pastry that were lying in a basket, labelled a penny a bag, for his breakfast. He bought some for Wilf and Daniel as well. They wouldn't care if the bread was stale tomorrow.

Then he drove up to Ellindale.

He'd enjoyed today's work, and the company of a man who had travelled all over the world after the war and had some interesting tales to tell.

Now he'd enjoy the first night in his new home.

★

When he got to Ellindale, to his surprise he found Wilf sitting on the outer wall of his land.

'Is something wrong?'

'No. But we caught a thief here last night, so me and Daniel are keeping watch.'

'What was there to steal, for goodness' sake?'

'Wood. Folk have been going out scrounging in the countryside for firewood, but this fellow thought it'd be easier to take some of yours. It's that Barry Judson I told you about. He's a lazy sod. Even if there were jobs going, he'd be last in the queue. Never trust a word he says.'

'Thanks for looking after my wood. I'll just drive along to Kerkham's house and unload my things from home, then I'll come back and have a chat, if you've the time. He's letting me put my stuff in an old shed till we can get the railway carriage here.'

He pulled the paper bags of bread off the top first. 'These were going cheap in the baker's so I got bags for you and Daniel as a thank you for your help.'

Wilf gave a stiff nod, but accepted the gift. 'Thanks.'

When Harry came back there was still enough light for him to study the ground in front of the shelter, which had clearly been dug up. Someone had started levelling it where the railway carriage was due to go. He turned to the other man in surprise. 'Did you do this?'

Wilf shrugged. 'I'd nowt better to do with my time. And no, before you ask, I don't expect payment, though the bread pieces will be welcome.' His voice grew sharper. 'It felt good to do something useful, if you must know. Some days I feel I'll go mad with boredom, and if I go tramping across the moors, it wears out my shoes, and new leather to repair them costs money. You never realise how the pennies mount up till you've not got enough of them to keep body and soul together.'

Something occurred to Harry. 'Well, I can give you some shoe leather, if you're short of it. I have plenty put by from the scraps of leather used at the factory.' He'd had to pay sixpence a bag for the pieces to Trowton, but they'd still been a bargain.

'Are you sure you can spare them?'

'Oh, yes. I bought a few bags of offcuts while they were going cheap. Trowton had done a bad job of planning the layout for some upholstery pieces, you see, and there were some decent sized pieces going, for once.'

'I won't say no to that. Would there be enough for my wife's shoes as well?'

'Sure to be. It's quite a big bag and full. I'll get it out of Kerkham's shed tomorrow morning before I go. I've got several bags of leather pieces left, so I won't miss it.'

He could see by the way his companion was fighting to stay calm that shoe leather had become a serious problem, so turned his back and walked slowly along the footings as if studying them. He waited a moment or two at the other end before asking, 'How did you know what to dig out?'

'I asked Ben Lonsdale. He's the stonemason I told you about. He had some hard times when his master died and the son who inherited chucked him out, so he understands what it's like to go short. At least with a trade behind him Ben hasn't had to go on the dole.'

'I'm praying I never have to, either.'

'Better pray hard then. Jobs aren't easy to find in the valley. I have to tramp a bloody long way sometimes to find work. Or sit at home and clem for lack of food till my Enid gets paid for doing someone's washing and we can buy a loaf.'

There were a lot of people going hungry, Harry thought, even capable chaps like Wilf. He said good night and settled himself in the shelter, lying so that he could see the road.

Eh, the stars were bright tonight! He'd intended to lie

watching them, but felt himself getting sleepy. His last thought was what a satisfying day it had been.

In the morning Harry nipped along to the farm to search among his stored belongings, knowing the Kerkhams would be up early. He was pleased to find that his memory hadn't betrayed him and took out one of the drawstring bags of leather pieces he'd collected. They were all sorts of colours, but Wilf and his family wouldn't mind what colour they walked on or patched the toes with.

He hid the bag carefully under some pieces of wood at the rear of the shelter, not wanting that Judson fellow to sneak in and find it.

Harry went back to his motorbike and made sure all the things he'd need today were packed in the sidecar, then chugged up into the village, stopping at the house with the red door opposite the shop, hoping he'd remembered correctly about this as well.

To his relief, Wilf opened the door and looked at him in surprise. 'Something wrong?'

'No. I found that bag of leather pieces and hid it in the shelter behind a pile of wood. I've got other bags, so I won't miss that one. There may be enough for your brother as well. I thought you'd like to sort it out before you took it home.'

Wilf's face brightened. 'Eh, that'll come in so useful. We're all desperate for shoe leather. Our Daniel had some other good news last night as well. Mr Carlisle is going to buy clothes for all the children who're growing out of them, especially the ones with no bigger brothers and sisters in the family to pass clothes down to them.'

'I'm glad to hear that. He seems a kind chap.'

'Known for it. That milk makes such a difference to the children's health.'

Harry wondered as he drove away why Wilf didn't have

any children, but it wasn't something you could ask a man. It was nice to see the pleasure his new friend took in his brother's good fortune.

He chugged back down the hill past his land, thinking Mr Carlisle wasn't the only kind person here. Without expecting any payment, Wilf had watched over the pile of wood and dug out some footings. If he ever wished anyone well, it was that man.

Then he pushed away all thoughts except what Todd would need him to do today.

The two of them finished work on the car engine in the early afternoon and Todd said they'd go and buy a sticky bun from the baker's to celebrate. On the way they stopped to have a word with Charlie Willcox who was standing at the doorway of his shop looking a bit down.

'Everything all right, Charlie lad?' Todd asked.

'Not as good as I'd expected. Bexley, the chap who's supposed to do the repairs, is a slow worker. Today someone brought back an electric toaster he told me he'd fixed – only it still wasn't working properly. Now he's saying it can't be mended so I'll have to give them their money back.'

'I could have a quick look at it for you,' Harry offered. 'I'm used to electrical equipment.'

Todd introduced the two men and added, 'If you need another pair of hands to do repairs, Harry is moving up to live in Ellindale from Sunday onwards and he's good with electrical equipment of all sizes.'

'Oh?'

'I was trained in the army,' Harry explained.

'Ah. I'll bear that in mind, then, but I promised the chap who sold me the shop that I'd keep Bexley on and I'm a man of my word. I'll have to give him a bit of a longer try-out.' But he didn't look happy.

'Harry will be living in a railway carriage on that land near Farmer Kerkham,' Todd put in. 'If you need him, you can ring the village shop and they'll send him word.'

Willcox nodded, but it was clear his mind was elsewhere. 'Come in. See what you can do.' He didn't sound hopeful.

The man in the workroom at the rear of the shop scowled at Harry. 'It's worn out and can't be repaired. Stupid things, toasters, always going wrong. What's wrong with a toasting fork and a good hot fire?'

Harry forced himself to speak mildly. 'I might as well have a look.'

The man didn't move.

'Well, let him get to the tools, Bexley,' Charlie snapped.

Muttering something under his breath, the man moved away from the small workbench.

It took Harry only a short time to find the fault and mend it. He glanced sideways and wondered if the man's eyesight was poor or he was just incompetent. 'Here. Try it.'

They watched as the toaster glowed inside for a couple of minutes, then the apparatus bounced up again.

'Tell your customer to clear out the crumbs regularly,' Harry told Charlie. 'There's no machine made that doesn't need regular checking and cleaning.'

Bexley reached out for the toaster, but Charlie grabbed it first. 'I'll take it round to the customer myself. We can't have him saying we don't know how to mend things.'

As Harry left the workshop, Bexley threw a dirty look at him.

He'd made an enemy there, Harry thought, which was a pity when they were both in the same trade.

Charlie slipped a florin into his hand. 'Thanks. I'm grateful. If we have any more problem pieces, I'll call you in. He's supposed to be an electrician but he doesn't seem to understand modern machinery.'

Todd waited till they were out of earshot to say, 'I'm getting a bit worried about Charlie. I think he's bitten off more than he can chew with that shop, and as for employing that lazy fool, I'd not have done it.'

'The shop looks shabby, could do with brightening up a bit on the outside.'

'Aye. And on the inside too. But most of all, he needs a proper electrical repairman. Pity.'

Harry shrugged. He was pleased to have earned two shillings, and pleased to have met Mr Willcox, too. If there was ever a job going at the shop, he reckoned he'd be in with a chance. It'd be an interesting job, too, repairing different sorts of household equipment.

Oh, well. He could hope. And he had enough on his plate at the moment arranging the move.

They took their buns back to the car yard and while Harry's hands were sticky with sugar, Todd slipped another precious ten bob note into his jacket pocket.

Harry froze, a little worried at what this might mean. 'I thought you were paying me by fetching my furniture across.'

'I am. That's extra, a bonus because you did well, much better than I'd expected. And it was a trickier job than I'd anticipated, too. Your quick thinking and help saved me at least another half a day's work if I'd been doing it on my own.'

'Yes, but—'

Todd smiled at Harry. 'Don't look a gift horse in the mouth, eh? Finish that bun now and get back to your daughter.'

'Thank you.' He took another big bite.

'I'll be at your house around nine o'clock on Sunday morning, think on, to bring your furniture across to Ellindale. You'd better sort out the stuff you want to store in my spare bedroom and make sure we load that last.'

'I will. Thank you.'

As he drove back home, Harry decided he was in much the same position as Wilf, except that he had some money behind him, thanks to Dora. Well, folk out of work had all learned not only to accept but to welcome charity in the form of gifts, call them what you liked. They had to, in order to survive.

And he was out of work now. That didn't feel good. His money wouldn't last forever.

If he ever got a comfortable, permanent job again, he'd make sure he helped those who hadn't managed to find one, by hell he would.

When he arrived home, Harry looked anxiously at Mrs Pyne.

She understood what he wanted to know first of all and said in a low voice, 'It's all right, Harry. Your Cathie's had a good day today. She's happy and excited about the move.'

'So am I.'

'I'm going to miss you both dreadfully, love.'

'I'll miss you too. We're moving on Sunday.' He hated to see the tears well in her eyes at that.

Her voice wobbled as she asked, 'This weekend?'

'I'm afraid so. I got the chance for a friend to bring his truck over on Sunday so it won't cost me anything. I can't miss such an opportunity. I'll go and give my notice to the rent man first thing tomorrow. It'll be a waste of a week's rent, but there you are. It'd cost more than that to hire a removal van.'

She nodded so sadly, he said, 'Once I'm settled, maybe you can get that son of yours to drive you over for a visit.'

'He'll not give up a whole Sunday to do that. He's grown very selfish, our Frank has.'

Her son had been selfish all his life but Harry didn't say that. 'I'm sorry to hear it. But we'll find a way to see one another again, I promise you.' He'd slipped a half crown into her apron pocket without saying anything while they were talking and her only acknowledgement was a slight nod and a little sigh.

Then Cathie heard her father's voice and came pushing out past Mrs Pyne to get to him. He picked her up and couldn't resist swinging her round and round till she squealed with pleasure. Then they went home to pack.

When he'd brought his tools in and padlocked the motorbike to a convenient lamp post, he sat beside her on the lumpy old sofa and explained about their move. She had a dozen questions about where they were going to live and was thrilled at the thought of them camping in the shepherd's shelter. He hoped she'd stay thrilled when faced with the reality of how roughly they'd be living.

After she'd gone to bed, he began to gather things together in the kitchen, ready to pack. He was exhausted by the time he got to bed. It had been a busy two days, but worth it. He'd earned a little money, made a start on his home and made some new friends.

He hoped for all sorts of things in the future, but most of all, better health for his Cathie.

# 20

Harry slept so soundly he was startled to realise it was daylight and he'd been woken by someone knocking on his front door. He squinted at his alarm clock. What on earth did they want at this early hour?

He rolled out of bed, yawning, but since he wasn't dressed yet, he stuck his head out of the window to see who it was rather than going downstairs.

One of the women from the factory looked up. 'Mr Trowton wants to see you.'

'Do you know why?'

She put one finger to her lips, beckoned to him and pointed to the front door. He assumed that meant she didn't want to shout out her message for all to hear. He put his overcoat on over his ragged pyjamas, which he only wore to be decent with a growing daughter, and ran down to speak to her.

'What does he want?' he asked in a low voice.

'He's got a problem with that machine you kept having to mend. It's broken down again and he can't fix it. He's tried several times. You should have heard him curse.' She couldn't hold back a smile at that. 'He says to tell you that if you'll apologise, he'll give you your old job back.'

'Tell him I've got a new job and I'm moving away on Sunday.'

She looked astonished at that news, then dismayed. 'Oh, Harry, I daren't do it. Couldn't you come and tell him yourself? He'll be so furious he'll probably fire me if I tell him that.'

'I'll pop round to see him after I've given Cathie her breakfast. But not because I want the damned job. I'm doing it to save you from losing yours.' He had been disgusted for years at how Trowton fired women for imagined faults, but he had got a lot worse at such chancy behaviour lately.

'Thanks, Harry. We're all missing you. Good luck with your new job.' She hurried off.

He went back indoors and lit the gas burner, putting the kettle on it and taking a mouthful of water straight from the tap because he was suddenly thirsty. That made him realise how much sweeter the water from the spring on his land tasted.

He looked round the kitchen, permanently dim because of the shadow of the tall wall round the factory next to Trowton's. There was bright, clear daylight shining down on his new home in Ellindale. People needed sunshine and you didn't get much when you worked long hours in a factory.

After breakfast he insisted Cathie go round to Mrs Pyne's while he went to see Mr Trowton. He never liked to leave her on her own. She was too precious.

He was shown straight into the owner's office but as usual wasn't invited to sit.

'I'm glad you've come to your senses, Makepeace.'

'About what?'

'Didn't she tell you what I wanted to see you about?'

'Something about a machine breaking down.'

'Stupid bitch! I was offering you your job back, as long as you apologise.'

'Thanks, but I've got another job now.'

Trowton gaped at him. 'Where? No one round here is taking on workers.'

'Aren't they?' He didn't intend to tell Trowton any details so he said, 'I went a bit further afield to find a job.'

'Doing what?'

'Working on machinery and electrics.'

'How much are they paying you?'

'That's my business.'

'Well, I shan't give you any references when you could perfectly well come back and do the same work for me. And shame on you for abandoning your duties here.'

'I shan't need references.' Duties, indeed! This factory was nothing to him now. Suddenly he'd had enough of even talking to Trowton and stood up. 'If that's all, I'll get back to my daughter.'

At the door he had an idea and stopped. 'For ten bob I'll fix that machine of yours one last time.' So that the women who used it had work, not to help this arrogant man.

When Trowton glared at him and said nothing, he shrugged and turned to leave.

'Wait! All right.'

'I'll want paying in advance.' He knew Trowton's tricks of old. Any penny he could steal from a worker's wages, he did, usually by making up 'fines' for imagined mistakes.

'I don't pay in advance.'

'Suit yourself.'

He was right outside the door before Trowton yelled, 'Oh, very well. Just this once. Come back.'

Harry returned to the office, pocketed the ten shilling note, then went out into the factory to work on the machine. Trowton stood behind him, breathing laboriously, as he always did when concentrating. He was watching every move Harry made. That might help him a bit in future but this machine had several minor problems that cropped up, not just this one.

When he'd finished, Harry straightened, easing his aching back, and started up the machine. It worked perfectly so he nodded to his former employer and left without another word.

He walked out past rows of silent women. Their heads remained bent and they continued working hard. No one so much as looked up or even whispered a farewell as he passed, and he understood why. They were terrified of losing their jobs, poor things.

It felt good to have another ten shilling note in his pocket. He'd come out the winner today.

Every shilling counted, but shillings winkled out of Trowton were especially sweet.

The next day Harry was again woken by someone hammering on his front door. He stared blearily at the light shining through the curtainless window and realised he'd overslept and it was even later than yesterday. Groaning in annoyance at himself, he got out of bed and poked his head out of the window to see who it was.

He was shocked to see two policemen standing there. 'Just a minute.'

He didn't ask what they wanted, because he didn't fancy them calling out his business for all the neighbours to hear.

When he opened the front door, he was surprised at how darkly one of them was scowling at him.

'You'd best let us in,' the taller one said.

'Um, yes. Yes, of course.'

Cathie peered over the bannisters. 'What is it, Dad?'

'I don't know yet. You get dressed, love, and I'll see what these officers want.' He led them into the front room, which was stripped bare except for the old sofa and a couple of boxes.

'Going somewhere, are you, sir?'

'Yes. Moving to a new job in another town. Look, it's going to be a busy day. Can you just tell me what you want and then I'll—'

'You've been accused of theft.'

'*What?*' He could only gape at them for a minute. 'Who accused me? What am I supposed to have stolen?'

'Some valuable tools from the factory where you used to work.'

'When was that?'

'Three days ago, or rather, three nights ago. The factory was broken into after hours.'

It must be Trowton who'd accused him. He straightened up. 'It's not true. I've never stolen anything in my life, from him or from anyone else.'

'Mind if we search the house?'

'Yes, I do mind.' He was about to tell them he'd not even been here three nights ago, but something made him hold back the information. Who knew what else Trowton had accused him of and how carefully the cunning devil had built a case against his former employee.

He watched as one man went straight out into the backyard, into the lavvy, and came back brandishing a package wrapped in newspaper.

'I've found them, just where he said they'd probably be.'

Trowton must have put them there, damn him. He'd set Harry up for an accusation of theft.

Fury ran through him and following it, icy cold fear. He couldn't work out how best to proceed. If he just said straight out that he'd not been here three nights ago, Trowton might change his story. No, better to wait and see what they did next. He wanted witnesses from now on to anything he said or did.

Cathie crept into the room and ran across to cuddle him. He held her close and tried to think things through. His whole future depended on what happened today, and the police would take Trowton's word against his any time, he was sure. And if they locked him away, they'd put Cathie in an orphanage. That didn't bear thinking of.

Only, if he told them the truth, how could he persuade them to accept his word for it? Would they even investigate if he said he'd been away from home?

Then he heard the sound of a truck in the street outside and sagged in relief when it stopped outside his house.

Someone knocked on the door and he moved to open it.

One of the policemen barred his way. 'Stay there, please, sir. I'll answer it.'

Harry heard Todd's voice and the policeman saying Mr Makepeace couldn't speak to him at the moment and to come back later.

In desperation he yelled, 'Todd, come in. I need your help.'

'Look, sir! Do not—'

'I need to see Mr Makepeace.' Todd appeared in the doorway, with the policeman behind him scowling and straightening his helmet.

'What the hell's going on here?' Todd demanded.

'Mr Makepeace has been caught thieving,' the policeman said.

'I didn't do it,' Harry put in quickly.

Todd nodded to him as if accepting that without question. 'Oh? When did this theft happen, officer?'

'Three nights ago, sir.'

Todd looked across at Harry and asked him directly, 'Who accused you?'

The taller policeman said, 'You keep quiet! It's none of his business.'

Harry said rapidly, 'My former employer accused me, the one who sacked me and now wants me back.'

'Ah.' Todd smiled at the policeman, not a nice smile. 'Well, three nights ago, Mr Makepeace slept in Ellindale, after working all day with me in nearby Rivenshaw on repairing a car. Then he worked with me on the same vehicle all the

*Anna Jacobs*

next day. So he couldn't have stolen anything from round here at that time.'

The policeman looked cynical. 'A friend will say anything, tell any lies.'

'What about other people from the town who saw him as they walked past? I can bring a former policeman who'll swear on oath that he *saw* Mr Makepeace in Rivenshaw that day.'

'A former policeman?'

'Yes. And another witness to where Mr Makepeace was is Mr Carlisle, who used to be a policeman and is now a land-owner in Ellindale. You can get someone to phone Mr Carlisle from the police station.'

'And by the time we do that, you'll have phoned him yourself and arranged for him to provide an alibi for Mr Makepeace.'

'Are you deliberately trying to arrest an innocent man? If so, it won't look well in court when our lawyer *proves* where he was.'

'Lawyer!' one echoed in surprise. 'How would a man like him have a lawyer?'

'Because I'll be very happy to engage one if Mr Makepeace needs help proving his innocence.'

'Why should you do that?'

'Because *I* shall be employing him from now on and I need his skills.'

'But Mr Trowton said—' The policeman broke off realising he'd betrayed the accuser.

'I already knew who'd have accused me,' Harry said. 'He's the only person who has a grudge against me.'

The policemen shuffled their feet, not seeming to know what to do.

Todd took over again. 'Look. I'll wait here with one of you, so that there's no chance of me contacting anyone in

Rivenshaw, and the other one can go back to the police station and ask the sergeant to phone Mr Carlisle from there.'

'I suppose we could do that,' the older man allowed.

Todd folded his arms. 'Then do it. I haven't got all day. Which of you is going and which of you staying?'

His confidence about what needed doing to prove Harry's innocence seemed to be having an effect on them. The older one took a step towards the door, 'I'll go, John.' He stabbed his forefinger towards Todd and Harry. 'Do not leave the premises, either of you.'

'Won't you want the phone number and name of the former policeman?'

'Ah. Yes, of course.' He came back looking embarrassed.

Todd pulled out a small pocket notebook and scribbled in it, ripping off the page. 'This is the number and if you don't phone him, the lawyer will make mincemeat of you in court.'

That won him another scowl. 'Make sure they both stay here, John,' the older policeman warned his companion before he left.

'You heard him,' the younger policeman said.

'Why would I want to leave?' Harry asked. 'I'm moving house today, so I've plenty to keep me busy. I presume I can go upstairs and get dressed, though?'

'Um. Get your daughter to bring your things down then you can get dressed in here. I don't want you passing any messages to a neighbour.'

Was there no end to the man's suspicion? Anger was still simmering in Harry, burning even higher when the policeman searched his clothes before letting him put them on.

While her father was getting dressed, Todd took Cathie to the window to show her the truck her furniture would travel in. Then Harry sent her upstairs to bring her last few things down.

The nightdress and pyjamas made a sad pile of well-worn

clothing on the bottom step as they waited for the other policeman to return.

It seemed to take a very long time.

At last the policeman returned and with him was the local sergeant, a man Harry knew by sight.

'Just a couple of things to sort out, sir.'

Harry looked at Todd in puzzlement. Surely they weren't still unsure about his innocence?

The sergeant said to the young officer. 'Are those the tools and is that the newspaper they were wrapped in?' He waited a moment then snapped, 'Well, go over and check that it's the same wrapping and tools.'

'Yes, sarge. It is. I didn't let him touch them.'

The sergeant sighed wearily at the man's slowness and picked them up. 'Right. Show me exactly where they were found.'

'This way, sarge.' He led the way out into the backyard.

When they came inside again the sergeant was scowling. 'Is the window of your lavvy always propped open, Mr Makepeace?'

'Yes. For obvious reasons.'

'Then anyone could have put the tools on the windowsill from outside.'

The younger policeman was looking worried now.

'My constable should have reported this to me before accusing Mr Makepeace. I'd have got to the bottom of it more quickly otherwise. I'm sorry you've been inconvenienced, sir.'

The constable echoed the apology in a faint voice.

'When I spoke to Mr Carlisle on the phone, a man I worked with some years ago and respect greatly, he corroborated the story, Mr Makepeace, and said you were definitely in Ellindale and Rivenshaw for two days and one night. So it seems that someone is trying to get you blamed for a crime you didn't commit. And I consider it my duty to try to find out who.'

He picked up the newspaper the tools had been wrapped in and tapped it with one forefinger. '*The Times*. Not the sort of newspaper people in these streets would buy, even if they could afford it.' Then he picked up one of the newspapers Harry had been using to wrap plates and cups in. 'The *Daily Mirror*. More your sort of thing, I should think, Mr Makepeace, eh?'

'Yes. You can ask at the corner shop. I buy a copy there now and then.'

The sergeant stared down at the tools and their wrapping. 'Surely the man I'm thinking of wouldn't be so stupid as to use one of his own newspapers?'

'I never respected his intelligence,' Harry murmured, 'only the fact that he paid my wages.'

'Precisely. Well, I think we can safely say that you were not involved in this supposed theft, Mr Makepeace. However, I shall need your new address, just in case there are any other queries.'

Harry sighed. 'I wonder if I could give it to you in confidence, sergeant. I'd rather not reveal to Mr Trowton where I'm going. Especially after what's happened this morning.'

'That will be fine. Please write your address down in my notebook and I'll keep it to myself unless it's needed by a magistrate or someone with similar authority.'

He turned to Todd. 'And if I could have your address as well, sir? Just to be sure I can find you if we need you to back up Mr Makepeace's explanation again?'

'Certainly.'

# 21

When the policemen had left, Harry sat down on legs that suddenly felt shaky. 'I don't know what I'd have done if you hadn't turned up just then, Todd.'

'You'd still have been cleared, but it'd have taken a bit longer, that's all. Quite a few people saw you in Ellindale, people of importance socially, whose testimony would be valued just as much as this Trowton fellow's.'

'But in the meantime they'd have locked me away and what'd have become of my Cathie?'

'Don't dwell on it. We managed to sort things out.' He waited a moment or two, then asked, 'Have you had any breakfast, Harry?'

'What? No. I was working late finishing the packing and I overslept. The police woke me, so I haven't even had a cup of tea.'

'Well, let's put the kettle on, then you and Cathie can get something to eat before we load your things on to my truck. Unfortunately, it looks as if it's going to rain. I've got some tarpaulins and I'll do my best to protect your belongings, but I—'

Harry suddenly had to run out into the backyard and be sick in the lavvy.

When he came back inside, he felt ashamed about this reaction. 'Sorry.'

Todd said gently, 'It takes some people that way after danger has passed. I brewed a pot of tea. It'll be ready now.

That'll set you right. A man can't work as hard as you need to on an empty stomach.'

Harry nodded, grateful for this tact, and turned his attention to his daughter, who was hugging her arms round herself looking worried.

He pulled her close for a hug. 'We'll be all right now, Cathie love. It was all a mistake, as the sergeant said.'

After that he got on with things, working as quickly as possible. He couldn't wait to leave this house and hoped he'd never have to come back here again.

Inevitably they were later setting off than they'd planned but Harry didn't care. He hugged Mrs Pyne, shook her husband's hand and climbed on to the motorbike. His daughter was now sitting in the sidecar, surrounded by all sorts of household oddments. The back of the truck was full, too. Who'd have thought his small house contained so much stuff? He probably should have thrown some of it away, but it was too late for that now.

It was a while before he became aware of anything but the road ahead, then he realised they were nearly out of Manchester. He felt guilty because he hadn't noticed a thing about the road. He'd have to be more careful than that, or he'd risk having an accident.

When he looked sideways, his spirits lifted for the first time that morning because he could see his daughter's eager face through the sidecar window. He sneaked further glances when they slowed down at a crossroads and when they had to wait a few minutes for a herd of cows to amble across the road. Each time she was staring out, looking first at one side of the road, then at the other. When they stopped and she saw him looking at her, she waved one hand and gave him a big, wide smile.

He nodded back at her satisfied, well, more than satisfied,

absolutely delighted, to see her looking so excited. Then he turned his attention firmly back to the road, more mindful of what he was doing from then on.

Something deep within him settled into a happier mode now they were away from Manchester. Open fields and distant glimpses of the moors seemed to soothe his very soul.

It was early afternoon before they arrived in Rivenshaw, because the heavy loads meant they'd had to drive more slowly than usual. By that time Harry was stiff, dying to get off the bike and have a good long stretch.

They stopped at Todd's house first to unload the things that were going to be stored there. Harry was keeping only the barest necessities, because they wouldn't be able to fit much into the small shelter.

Cathie used the facilities, which were outside at the rear, and skipped her way back across the yard to join them, as happy children often did.

'Why don't you sit in the kitchen to wait for your dad?' Todd suggested. 'We'll unload this lot then have a quick cup of tea and something to eat.'

'We've got some food,' Harry said quickly.

'I'm sure you have. But so have I. I thought Cathie could keep an eye on the kettle for us and shout when it boils. You might like to try one of these iced fancies, love. There's a pink one in the paper bag that's just right for a little lass like you.'

She licked her lips. 'I haven't had one of those for ages.'

'Well, there are three, one each. I can't remember what colour the others were. Go and see if you fancy the pink one. They're on the table, on that plate covered with a bowl. If you're hungry you can eat yours now, while you wait for us.'

The two men kept unloading things until the spare room

was stacked high with very shabby looking furniture. Harry hadn't noticed how worn and scuffed it had become and in contrast to the newish lounge suite in Todd's front room, it looked even worse. One day, he vowed, he'd provide better stuff than this for his little lass.

Once they'd put everything in the room, he let Todd persuade him to have that cup of tea and the cake, followed by a scone with butter and jam. He felt this was taking advantage of Todd's generosity and said so but the other man just laughed. Eh, Todd's cheerfulness was a tonic, it was that.

'Me and Cathie are having them, so you can either watch us eat, Harry lad, or join in.'

One day, Harry vowed, he'd repay his companion for such kindness, which went beyond anything he'd expected from a near stranger – though Todd felt like a friend already. It happened that way sometimes.

'When we unload up at the shelter, Harry, just tell me if there's anything you need bringing back. It's hard to judge what'll fit into such a small space.' He looked up at the sky. 'We're due for some more rain later, I think, but we should manage to get your stuff unloaded and under cover before it starts.'

'I feel guilty at taking up all your day!' Harry said.

'Actually, you'll not be taking me out of my way. I want to call on Leah afterwards and see how she's going on. She'll probably come down to introduce herself to you in a day or so.'

He grinned as he added, 'And so will half the village. They're looking forward to seeing who's moving in. There isn't a cinema up at this end of the valley, so they watch each other's doings instead. They're nosey but nice. Well, most of them are, anyway. There's a nasty little chap called Judson that most of us have had run-ins with at one time or other.'

*

When they got to Harry's land they found that the stones from the crumbling wall had been piled neatly to one side, away from the road. A group of men, including Wilf, were either digging or taking a breather. The entrance they were making would give Harry a place to park the motorbike off the road, and maybe he could find some more cheap wood to make a simple gate with a padlock to keep things safer at night. Or get Wilf to do it.

'I can't afford to keep paying them for help!' he whispered to Todd.

'You won't need to. It's their way of welcoming you. In better times the women would have brought plates of food to help a new neighbour settle in, but they don't have any food to spare, so the men are lending you their muscles instead. Come on. I'll introduce you.'

'You knew about this, didn't you?'

'I guessed it might happen. I'm getting to know folk round here. They made me welcome too.'

After introductions, Wilf took Harry to take a closer look at the wooden wall now covering the open side of the shelter. He seemed worried about the work he'd done. 'I could have done a much better job with proper wood, but that'd have cost you a lot more.'

Harry stopped to study it, amazed at how neatly it had been done. The man was a genius at building things. 'I think you did wonders and so cheaply, Wilf. I'm grateful for that because I'm counting every penny and never imagined a wall could be built for that price. It's plenty good enough for me and Cathie and I can't thank you enough.' He shook his companion's hand.

Wilf relaxed visibly. 'That's all right, then. I enjoy working with wood.' He traced the grain on one piece with loving fingers. 'This was part of a big tree once.'

'How much did the window cost?'

'Nothing. It was just lying around behind the sheds at Spring Cottage, and when Ben told Mrs Willcox what you were doing, she said you could have it, because she has no use for it and it'll save her having to get it carted away. The glass is cracked but only across one corner, and it hardly shows.'

He fumbled in his pocket. 'I've writ down what I spent on screws and such, and you have a couple of bob change due to you.'

Harry pushed it back to him. 'Keep it.'

Wilf sucked in his breath sharply and it was a minute before he asked hesitantly, 'Are you sure?'

'Of course I am. You've more than earned it. You've saved me pounds. Any road I managed to earn another few bob myself yesterday, so it's only fair you get something too.'

Wilf swallowed hard and then noticed another man standing in the road a short distance away from the entrance. 'Argh. Trust him to come noseying around. He's called Judson and he's not liked round here. He's probably come to see if you've anything worth stealing.'

That was the fellow Todd had warned him against. Harry stared at the thin, shabby figure, hands thrust deep in pockets as Judson scowled across at the group of men. 'I'll remember his face. He'd better not try anything.'

He turned towards his daughter, who was looking longingly at the new door. 'You open that door, love, and go straight in.'

'Can I really?'

'Of course you can. It's your home now.' He followed her inside and the two of them stopped near the door, turning from side to side as they studied the small room. It was only about four yards by three with a hard earth floor. The window in the new wooden wall let in plenty of light but he hoped they'd not have to live in such cramped quarters for long.

'Can we give it a name?' she asked.

'Of course. What would you like to call it?'

'Well, I was thinking about it on the way here and since we're going to live in a railway carriage, we should call it "Railway Cottage", don't you think?'

He savoured the sound of it, repeating it slowly, '"Railway Cottage". Yes, love. That's a nice name for our new home. Not that we've got our railway carriage here yet.'

Todd had stayed just outside, close enough to hear them. 'I like the name, Cathie. Houses that stand on their own usually do have a name.'

She gave a little skip on the spot. 'Goody. I've always wanted to live in a house with a name. You read about them in storybooks and they sound so much friendlier.'

Wilf had also come across to join them. 'I cleared out the fireplace and stacked the leftover small pieces of wood to the side. I hope you don't mind, Harry, but I lit a little fire to try the chimney out, it's such a rough old thing. But it burns all right, so it isn't blocked. It just looks a bit rough. I could put a cap on the top of it to keep the rain out, if you like.'

'Yes, please do that.'

'You'll need to find an old-fashioned trivet and fire-irons to use for cooking. I can look out for some if you like.'

'I've got those already, thanks. They were my grandfather's and I never liked to throw them away, though we had gas in our row of houses for cooking. I'll have to learn to cook on an open fire.' Harry looked at the fireplace ruefully. 'I'm not a good cook, but there you are. I manage and I haven't poisoned my little lass yet. She doesn't complain, bless her.'

'How about I get my wife to give you and the little lass a few cooking lessons? Our Enid does miracles with whatever food we get.'

'I'd be really grateful if she'd do that once we've got the carriage here. That has to come first.'

Wilf hesitated. 'There's just one other thing I wanted to ask. There are a few pieces of wood left over that I could use for my carving, lumps of wood, they are, not planks. I like to carve, you see. It helps to pass the time, especially when the weather's bad. And sometimes I get a few shillings for a piece, which a friend sells at market. That helps a lot.'

'What do you carve?'

'Animals, birds, figures of people, whatever takes my fancy. It's getting suitable chunks of wood that's the difficulty. I could maybe pay you a few pence for these few.'

'No need for that. Take the pieces that are suitable.'

The answer came sharply. 'I wasn't begging.'

'I shall be if a piece you've carved takes my fancy.'

Wilf's face brightened. 'Eh, I'd be happy to give you one.'

'I bought a carving of a sheepdog at the market,' Todd said.

'That's one of mine.'

'I didn't realise you'd done it. They were all very good.'

Wilf flushed. 'Thank you.'

'Now, let's help you sort this place out, Harry lad,' Todd said. 'Your Cathie's too little to lift the furniture and boxes.'

'I'd be grateful.' Harry suddenly noticed the sound of digging outside. The other two men must have started work again. 'I feel guilty letting them work for nothing. If I sent Cathie to the shop for a loaf for each of them, would they take it?'

'Yes, they would and glad of it, too.' Wilf hesitated. 'But if you could ask Lily at the shop to save the loaves and give them to the wives with their day's shopping tomorrow, Judson won't know what you're doing. He'd dob people in with the means test man just for spite, that one would. Though the new chap hasn't started work yet.'

'Is he really so bad?'

'Who knows? A lot of them are.'

'It was the same in Manchester. Everyone frightened of getting on the wrong side of one.'

'Well, Judson will go too far one of these days and then we'll throw him out of the village. But he was born here and his mother was a nice woman. What no one can figure out is why his landlord doesn't throw him out of his house, even when he gets behind with the rent. Worst of all to me, though, is that he treats his wife and children shamefully. Eh, if I had children I'd do my best for them.'

There was such longing in Wilf's voice that Harry ached for him.

'Any road, I usually manage to stay away from the dole, so he won't be able to dob me in.'

'I'll explain to Lily at the shop about the loaves, then, and pay her in advance.'

'Right, then. Now, let's get this room sorted out.'

Todd had wandered across to chat to the two men still digging, but he joined Harry and Wilf in bringing in the furniture and arranging it in the shelter.

Some pieces had to go back to be stored, but the one thing Harry insisted on keeping was the fireguard. It took up a lot of space, but he wasn't risking his daughter stumbling and falling into the fire. A lot of children got burned in accidents. And fireguards were useful for drying clothing on in wet weather as well. It was as if that thought had summoned the rain that had been threatening. As they were bringing in the last bundles it started to pour down suddenly.

The men looked up at the sky.

'It's setting in,' Wilf said. 'We might as well finish for the day, lads.' He turned to Harry. 'We can give you an hour or two's digging every now and then.'

'Thank you. I'll make sure you benefit by it somehow.'

Todd also said farewell, got into his truck and drove up the hill.

*

Harry hesitated then called, 'Wilf? Have you got a minute? There's something I want to ask you.'

'Yes, of course.' Wilf turned back and came across to join him.

'I've been wondering if you've thought any more about how to get my railway carriage up here. It's being delivered to Rivenshaw station in a few days. The chap who sold it to me said I should get some trolleys made to put under each end. Could you do that? I'll pay you.'

Wilf's face lit up. 'You still want me to do it?'

'Yes. How much do you think it'll cost?'

'I'll have to think it out. I might nip down to the station and have a look at the carriages on some of the trains, see how they're put together underneath. And we might be able to get hold of old railway sleepers to make the trolleys from.'

'They were going to deliver the carriage for a few quid till they found out where I'd be living, then they said they didn't deliver so far up the valleys because the carriage might get stuck. So you'd better bear that in mind.'

Wilf stood staring into space for a minute or two, then seemed to jerk out of his thoughts and focus on Harry again. 'I reckon I can do it, but I might need help. We need to find someone with a tractor. If I make two strong trolleys, and we pay a few men a bob or two to help out . . .' His voice trailed away. 'It's the tractor we need, though. Can't do it with horses.'

There was silence for a few moments and he seemed to be thinking, so Harry didn't say anything.

'I think I've heard Ben talk about a relative who's a farmer. Maybe he can put us in the way of hiring a tractor. I'll nip up and ask him.'

Harry had seen his companion's work and felt if anyone could do this, it was Wilf, who would do a far better job than he ever could. He'd always dealt in small machinery, but Wilf seemed to find it easy to think in terms of spaces and bigger objects as well.

'I'll be there too, of course, as an extra pair of hands, but you'll be in charge and if you have to hire some other people to help, well, I know you'll only do what's necessary. How does five pounds plus expenses to manage the job sound to you?' It was a lot of money, but there'd be a lot of work involved.

Wilf closed his eyes for a moment and let out a long shuddering sigh, then opened his eyes again and stuck out his hand. 'You're on. And what's more, I shall enjoy doing it.'

'Good. Now I'd better feed that girl of mine and get her to bed.'

'Just a minute. We're going to need axles and wheels to run the trolleys on. I know a junkyard where they dump cars that have been in accidents. Eh, there must be some careless drivers around. Anyhow, I reckon I can get what we need from there for a few bob each.'

'Wilf, you're a magician.'

He shrugged. 'I've had to manage on just about nothing for a long time. You can sometimes get real bargains if you keep your eyes open.'

Harry went to join Cathie in the shelter. 'Well, loviekins, here we are. Do you like your new home?'

She nodded several times. 'Yes, I do, even when it's raining. I like to watch the cloud shadows dancing over the moors and the people going past up to our village. You can see for miles and miles. I love that.'

'Aye. I like it too.'

She yawned suddenly. 'I'm tired now. But I'm hungry as well.'

'So am I. Let's have something to eat, then snuggle down in our beds. I know it's early but it's been a hard day.'

Cathie was peacefully asleep within minutes of finishing off her bread and jam. He'd have to get her better food than this tomorrow. She seemed to have regained her appetite, thank goodness.

He lay awake for a while, thinking over all that had happened today and listening to her peaceful breathing. The memory of his narrow escape from the police made him shudder. All because of Trowton, who was famous for not letting anyone best him. He hoped he'd never see that miserable sod again. Even he wouldn't come this far to get his own back, surely?

So much accomplished, but he still had a lot to do before he could provide Cathie with a proper home. He looked round the shelter and shook his head. He felt ashamed to have to lodge her like this. And yet she seemed happy here.

Then he reminded himself sternly that this was only temporary. And the shelter had already proved that it was weatherproof, hadn't it?

On that thought he yawned and snuggled down, his eyes going for one last time to the peacefully sleeping child. She hadn't had any difficulty breathing today. Surely that was the best sign of all that this was the right thing to do?

# 22

Todd felt happy to leave Harry settling in, confident he'd be all right, because it was clear that he'd already fitted in well with the other men from the village. It took some courage to do what he was doing and Todd admired him for putting his daughter's welfare first.

He couldn't help feeling partly responsible for the move, because he'd seen that his offer of a day a week's work had made a difference to the decision. But the work was there and coming in regularly because those who could afford to buy and run a motor car could usually afford to pay for repairs and maintenance.

The sale of used cars was a more chancy area. He found a car now and then and risked buying it. Or someone came to ask him to find them a car and he went into Manchester to visit a couple of chaps in the same business. Sales were usually profitable, but not frequent enough to count on for a living. *Yet*, he told himself. *Not yet.*

He turned into the yard of Spring Cottage at the top end of the lane, not sure whether he was doing the right thing in coming here today, but wanting to make sure Leah was getting on as well as could be expected of a recent widow.

When he knocked on the door, he heard a faint sound he couldn't place and no one came to see who was there. He listened carefully and as the sound came again, he realised what it was, so pushed open the door and called, 'It's just me, Todd.'

Leah turned from the sink, wiping her mouth and looking chalk white. She'd obviously been vomiting, poor thing.

She fumbled for a towel, knocked it to the floor and swayed dizzily as she started to bend down to get it. She had to abandon the attempt and grab the edge of the sink to steady herself, so he hurried across to pick up the towel and pass it to her.

With a sigh, she splashed more water across her mouth and used the towel to pat herself dry. But as she turned he could see that she was still dizzy so put an arm round her waist and supported her across to an armchair.

She pressed one hand to her forehead as if it was aching. 'Thank you.'

'Shall I get you a glass of water to sip? It sometimes helps.'

'Please.'

He saw some glasses on a shelf and ran water into one, taking it across to her, then standing back.

She took a couple of sips and a few moments later, drank the rest of the water thirstily then held the empty glass out to him. 'I'm sorry. Would you mind getting me another one?'

'My pleasure to help. And no need to be sorry. A lot of women are sick when they're expecting.' He'd found women's stoic endurance of the problems of pregnancy the same in all the other countries he'd visited during his post-war travels, and he admired them for it. 'Some pay a high price for their children.'

A faint smile crossed her face. 'But it'll be worth it, I'm sure. I just wish—'

He wondered if she was aware that she was cradling her belly as if to protect her unborn child. It was something all pregnant women seemed to do instinctively, even though her bump scarcely showed yet. He finished the sentence for her. 'You wish Jonah had known. We all do.'

She nodded and after a moment changed the subject. 'How's Charlie getting on?'

'Not his usual self. Grieving deeply for his brother, as you'd expect. The two were very close. I envied them that. I'm glad you've got Rosa to comfort you.'

She nodded and visibly pulled herself together. 'What can I do for you, Todd?'

'It's whether I can do anything for you. I was up in Ellindale and thought I'd pop in to see how you were going on. Do you need anything?'

'No. But thank you for asking.'

'I also thought I'd tell you about your new neighbours.'

'The man who's going to live in a railway carriage? Ginny was telling me about progress.'

'Yes. He and his daughter have moved into the shelter today.'

'I thought he'd start off there on his own before bringing his family to join him.'

'No. His wife's dead and there's only the child. He's brought her with him for the fresh air. She has trouble with her breathing. Asthma they call it these days. The two of them have moved into the shelter till their new home arrives, so they'll get plenty of fresh air, that's for sure.'

'When is the carriage being delivered?'

'It's coming to Rivenshaw station next week. But then we have to get it up the hill to its new site so they've got somewhere decent to live.'

She looked at him, head on one side. '*We* have to get it up here?'

He shrugged. 'Me and some of the other men are helping. We can't leave Harry to do it on his own, can we? Besides, it gives the fellows something to fill the time.'

'I've been meaning to start a club for them. Somewhere to go, something to do. They get so downhearted, and who can blame them?'

'Good idea. I heard Lady Terryng was going to start one in Wemsworth. If I can help in any way with that, let me know.'

She looked down at herself and sighed. 'It'll have to wait till I get some energy back.'

'In the meantime some of the men will probably help him install and fit out the carriage, so you'll have something to go and watch without tiring yourself too much.'

'It'd be rude to go and stare at him.'

Todd chuckled. 'Then most of the people in the village are rude, because I never saw so many of them taking a stroll down the hill.'

'Next time I go to the shop, I'll call in on Mr Makepeace. Is he going to be without work all this time? How will he manage?'

'He's got some savings and I'm able to give him a day or so's work every week if he can find someone to look after his daughter. He's very good with machinery of all sorts, especially the electrical stuff. He trained in the army as an electrician.'

'That's good. He should be able to find other work here and there, even if it's only little repair jobs to kettles and such. What's the girl's name, did you say?'

'Cathie. She's nine. I wondered—' He hesitated.

'Wondered what?'

'Whether you might keep an eye on her. The little lass is at an age where she might need a woman's help. They don't sound to have any close relatives. But if you're not up to it, I'll ask someone else from the village to look in from time to time.'

'No, don't. I'd like to help. And I'm only sick in the afternoons, just for an hour or so. Strange how it takes some people, isn't it? Most women feel worse in the mornings. Still, it's going to be worth it.'

As she smiled down at her belly, he saw that she was already starting to get a little colour back in her cheeks. He didn't break the silence because her smile was so beautiful, it took his breath away. He'd seen paintings of the Madonna and child but none of them had been as glowingly lovely as she was at this moment. Well, not to his mind anyway.

She looked across at him. 'You've taken my mind off my woes, Todd, reminded me that there are other people worse off than me. I'll call on Mr Makepeace and his daughter tomorrow. I doubt they'll want visitors tonight. They must be exhausted.'

'Yes, they are. And you look tired too. I'd better leave you in peace.'

'No need to go yet. I wanted to ask you something. How do you think Charlie's doing with the electrical goods shop?'

'Ah.'

'That sounds ominous.'

He hesitated because she didn't need any more worries. She'd have enough on her plate making a new life without Jonah.

'Tell me,' she insisted. 'I can sense that something's wrong.'

'I think Charlie's finding the electrical goods shop a bigger drain on his resources than he'd expected. Why do you ask?'

'Marion was telling me that he's had a few shocks. The stock was mainly older gadgets and Mr Flewett had left quite a few empty boxes in the storeroom that looked as if they contained goods. Only they didn't.'

'Charlie never said!'

'No. He doesn't like people to see his weaknesses.'

'Can't he set a lawyer on to Mr Flewett?'

'That's what Marion wanted him to do, but he won't. He says a lawyer's fees would be more expensive than anything he could win back, especially with the man having gone to settle in Blackpool.'

'Oh, dear. I already knew he had a useless repairman, but it's worse than I'd realised. I'd better have a word with Charlie.'

'Don't let him know I told you about the empty boxes.'

'No. I'll find a way to do it without involving you or Marion, who's also worried about him.'

They sat in comfortable silence for a while, then she said suddenly, 'It's good to have someone to chat to. I'm not used to silence in the evenings after the workers have gone home. Rosa's got her own life to lead. She's studying hard and she vanishes up into her room as often as not. Jonah and I never talked for talking's sake, but we always found something interesting to discuss. I can switch on the radio, but it isn't the same.' She paused to swallow hard, looking close to tears now.

'I get lonely in the evenings too,' Todd confided. 'There's just me in that tumbledown little house and I've never been the sort to go out to the pub boozing.'

'Well, if you're visiting Mr Makepeace, you're welcome to call on me afterwards, or even to bring them up to visit me. The little girl might enjoy a glass of lemonade.'

He decided to be open about the situation. 'I don't know whether he told you, but Jonah asked me to keep an eye on you if – well, if anything happened to him.'

Her voice grew sharper. 'I can manage perfectly well, thank you.'

'I'm sure you can. But I'll do as he asked nonetheless, because I gave him my word. I won't interfere, but if you do need help . . . with anything, big or small, please ask. Or even just a bit of company. We'd both benefit from that, by the sounds of it.'

She looked as if she didn't know how to respond. Luckily she was distracted by the sound of a car stopping outside, a voice calling goodbye and footsteps crunching on the gravel in the yard. But the sound stopped and although the car had driven off immediately, voices could be heard.

'That'll be Rosa and Ben. She often stops to say hello to him when she comes home. She's been having tea at a schoolmate's house. She and Evelyn Carpenter are great friends, and the family has an encyclopaedia, which is an added attraction. Both girls are studying hard and want to go to university or college.'

'So I gather. Rosa tells everyone she intends to become a doctor, and good luck to her. Your sister has a clever face. I hope she manages it. It's always harder for women to get into university from what I've read in the papers. What about her friend? Does Evelyn want to be a doctor too?'

'No. She says she wants to go to training college and become a teacher but I think she'll get married and have a large family. She's that sort of person, motherly, stops to look into every pram she passes in the street. I don't think Rosa even notices babies.'

The door banged open and her sister came in, her school hat in her hand, her hair in a tangle as usual by this time of day. 'They've moved in! We stopped the car to have a look. They've done a lot of digging and—' She stopped abruptly when she saw the visitor.

'If you mean Harry Makepeace and his daughter Cathie, yes, they have moved in. Todd's just been telling me about them.'

He stood up. 'I'll be going now, Leah. I'll call in another time.'

'Please do. And thank you for your help today.'

'My pleasure. 'Bye.'

Rosa gave her sister a strange look. 'I think he likes you.'

Leah wasn't going to let her follow that line of thought, so said cheerfully, 'And I like him, too. Don't you? He's helping the new family to settle in. He came to ask me to keep an eye on the little girl. She's rather frail, which is why they moved away from the smoky city, and there's only the father to care for her because her mother's dead.'

'I met her, remember.'

'So you did. She's a few years younger than you or I'd ask you to make friends with her.'

The suspicious look left Rosa's face. 'I saw a motorbike parked outside the shelter, and there was a light shining out from that old window you gave them. Fancy living there!'

'As long as it's weatherproof, they'll be all right for the summer. It's better than a tent. And the railway carriage should be nearly as good as a house, Todd says.'

Her sister didn't say anything else about Todd's visit to Spring Cottage, but the look on her face at the sight of him had made Leah feel a little strange. And worried. She was a recent widow. She didn't want anyone thinking she was encouraging men to come calling in *that* way so soon after Jonah's death, especially not her little sister.

Todd had been a friend of both her and Jonah for some time and he'd said he was lonely too in the evenings. There was a sad expression on his face sometimes when he thought no one was looking at him. It was strange how he'd set off to travel the world after the war, and stayed away for so many years. He had some incredible tales to tell of his travels.

She wouldn't like to be on her own among people who didn't speak English. No, she definitely couldn't have done what he had. But maybe he'd needed to get away. The war had changed the men who'd fought in it. Some of them had taken a long time to recover; some would never recover mentally, from what she'd read, even though their bodies weren't badly damaged. Todd had got better, though, and she hoped he would make a happy life for himself in the valley, settle down here, find another wife even.

That last thought made her frown, she didn't know why. It'd have to be someone special, because he wouldn't be happy married to a stupid woman, however good she was at running a home. He had a fine mind and always had something of interest to say.

Oh, why was she thinking like that? She was being silly. It was probably the effect of carrying a baby. People said women didn't always think clearly when they were expecting, and it was so hard when the father-to-be was dead.

If her child was a boy, she'd call him Jonah. She'd decided that as soon as she found out. But she hadn't thought of a girl's name yet. Johanna seemed to be the closest girl's name to Jonah, but she wasn't sure she really liked it.

Rosa nudged her. 'Wake up, dopey. You're standing staring into space. What's for supper? I'm still hungry. Mrs Carpenter doesn't set as good a table as you do. It's all fiddly food that looks pretty but doesn't fill you up.'

Leah pushed the silly thoughts aside and got on with the rest of her evening, listening to her sister's tale of what she'd been reading about in the encyclopaedia and suppressing a shudder at some of the descriptions.

Goodness, did nothing about the human body ever upset Rosa? As far as Leah was concerned, what was underneath the skin could stay underneath the skin – unless it was a baby. She couldn't wait to meet hers – in late August or early September, the doctor thought.

# 23

Harry woke in the grey light of early dawn to hear faint clunking sounds outside. It sounded as if someone was moving rocks. Surely Wilf hadn't started work this early?

He got up from his mattress and took the two steps necessary to peer out of the window. To his astonishment he saw a man bend to pick up another rock then start to walk off with a few of them in his arms.

He flung open the door and yelled, 'Hoy, you! Put them back!'

The man cast a startled glance over his shoulder and dropped the rocks, running off up the road into the village. He didn't run fast enough to prevent Harry from recognising him, though. No wonder Wilf had warned him about Judson.

His daughter's sleepy voice made him turn round.

'What's wrong, Dad? Why were you shouting?'

'A man was trying to steal our rocks.'

She sat up in bed. 'Why would anyone want to steal rocks? You can pick them up by the side of the road any time.'

'How would I know? To fill a broken bit of wall, to edge a garden. Things like that. Ours are smooth ones that would fit in anywhere without any work being needed on them.'

'We'll have to keep watch over our things from now on, won't we?'

'Yes, we will, love. But it's only a few people who do things like that. Most people are kind and helpful, as we've found out. And our life will be a lot easier after we get the railway carriage in place. We'll be closer to the road and the rocks that support the lower end of our new home will be cemented in place so no one will be able to pinch them. Anyway, the man's gone now. You can go back to sleep.'

She snuggled down. 'I like sleeping in here. It feels cosy.'

'Well, turn your back. I'm going to have a bit of a wash and get dressed. I'll never get back to sleep now.'

When he was dressed, he left his daughter to get up in privacy and went out to watch dawn lighten the sky still further, taking pleasure in sitting on his very own wall to do so. He gave it a fond slap with the flat of one hand to emphasise that.

Cathie joined him when she was dressed, sitting beside him and slipping her hand into his. She had her mother's old grey shawl round her shoulders and her dark brown hair was streaming down her back. She was always losing her hair ribbons. He tried not to show that he was listening to her breathing, but she could tell.

'It's all right, Dad. I'm not wheezing.'

'Good. That's what we want. Are you hungry yet?'

'No. It's my eyes that are hungry. I'd like to sit here with you and watch the sun rise over the moors. The sky's so pretty.'

What a fanciful child she was! 'All right. We'll watch till the sun's above the horizon then we'll have our breakfast. I reckon I'll do some digging this morning. The sooner we get the ground levelled, the better.'

To his surprise one or two people passed by even at that early hour, calling a greeting as they went down the road towards Birch End and Rivenshaw. These were probably the lucky ones who had a job to go to. Or men going off to tramp round the countryside, just in case there was work of any sort to be found in a nearby town or village.

A short time later a baker's van drove up the hill and he

watched it stop outside the village shop, delivering today's bread from the looks of it.

His mouth watered suddenly at the thought of fresh bread, warm from the oven. 'I'm going to nip up to the shop to buy a couple of loaves. Want to come with me, love?'

'Can I stay here and watch the sky? The colours are still changing.'

Dare he leave her? Surely it'd be all right? Ellindale was a quiet place and she'd be in his sight until he was in the shop. 'If you promise to stay out here on the wall and to yell for me if you need help.'

'Help for what?'

'Who knows? Anything. I won't be long. I'll fetch a shopping bag.'

She was still sitting on the wall when he came out of the shop with the loaves, jam, butter and a couple of tins of soup in the hessian bag, but this time a man was standing chatting to her. Harry began to walk faster, then saw who it was – Mr Carlisle from the big house on the other side of the village – so slowed down with a sigh of relief.

The man turned to smile at him. 'Good morning, Mr Makepeace. I'm having my usual morning stroll with my dog.'

'She's called Tippy and she likes me to stroke her.' Cathie touched the animal gently again and she swiped her tongue over the child's hand before going off to explore.

'I've been chatting to your little lass. She was saying she likes to read, so I've invited her to borrow some of our books. We have a whole room of them and quite a few are children's books, though they're a bit old-fashioned. Some of the people in the village borrow books because it's a long way down to the library in Rivenshaw and they can't all afford the bus fares.'

'It'd be good to have something to read. I'll bring her up later to choose a book.'

The knowing smile on Mr Carlisle's face said he knew exactly why Harry was coming too. Well, Harry wasn't ashamed of looking after his daughter. She was the most precious thing in his life. Not that he thought he had anything to fear from this man.

'You can borrow books too, if you're a reader.'

'I am. And I'd appreciate that, Mr Carlisle. Thank you very much.'

'Everyone in the village calls me Finn. I'm not one to stand on ceremony. And you're Harry, aren't you?'

'Yes. If you're sure it's all right to use first names.'

'I am. The other thing I wanted to tell you about is that Cathie can get a glass of milk with the other older children when they come home from school in the afternoons or at the same time at weekends. Gillian serves it in the back room of the pub. All the children in the village receive a glass.'

'What does that cost?'

'Nothing. I provide it because milk is really good for growing children. It doesn't cost much and me buying the milk also helps one of our local smallholders, saves him traipsing into Rivenshaw to sell his milk. All right?' He gave Harry a challenging look as if daring him to stand on his pride and refuse the offer.

As if he was so stupid as to deprive Cathie of fresh milk when all the other children were having it! 'Thank you. That's very kind of you. I'll bring her up.'

Mr Carlisle whistled and the dog came running across from her investigation of the land at the other side of the road. She trotted up the hill by his side, an ugly mutt with part of one ear missing and a long pink tongue hanging out of her mouth which made her look as if she was grinning at the world.

'Mr Carlisle's nice,' Cathie said even before he was out of earshot. 'He says his nephew stays with him sometimes but

Reggie's older than me. Do you think there'll be anyone of my own age to play with in Ellindale, Dad?'

'I should think so. You'll meet other children when you go for your milk.'

She bent over the shopping bag and sniffed appreciatively. 'That bread smells good. There's nothing like fresh bread, is there? I'm getting really hungry now.'

'Then we'd better go in and have a slice or two. I got a jar of jam as well.'

At the top end of Ellindale village, Nina woke up with a start, wondering for a moment where she was.

Oh yes! She was at the youth hostel. She slipped out of bed and went to stare through the window at the big yard around which the buildings clustered. Ben was out there already, loading something onto the back of his truck. Ginny Dutton was just arriving from the village, carrying a shopping bag with a loaf sticking out of it. She clearly started work early at Spring Cottage. But there was no sign of life from inside the house. Perhaps Mrs Willcox was still sleeping? She'd looked utterly worn out last night, poor thing.

Nina got up, stretching happily. She'd slept so well, more soundly than she had for a long time. She'd better get dressed now and start earning her keep.

As she walked into the little kitchen to get her breakfast, she looked round possessively. The hostel was already very clean, so she needn't do any housework today other than a bit of dusting. It might be useful to take an inventory of every single thing there was in the various rooms, including the food.

Before she had even filled the kettle, someone knocked on the door and she opened it to Ginny's smiling face.

'Leah wondered if you'd like to have breakfast with us at

the house. I brought a fresh loaf up with me and they'll deliver the others later.'

'I'd love to join you.'

'Well, you look as if you're ready, so why don't you come across with me now? No need to lock the door.'

Inside the house Leah was sitting by the fire, staring into the flames.

There was a smell of toast and Nina saw an electric toaster with gold-brown bread sticking out of it.

'Are you with us, Leah love?' Ginny teased.

'Sorry. I was just thinking about something. I thought you might enjoy eating your breakfast here when we don't have anyone staying at the hostel, Nina. Unless you prefer to have some quiet time on your own, of course. Ginny brings up fresh bread from the shop when she comes in the morning, so we usually toast yesterday's bread. It's as easy to feed three as two.'

Nina had had years of her own company while she was caring for her father, so said immediately, 'That's very kind of you. I'll be glad of a bit of company to start my day.'

A timer rang just then and Ginny bustled across to the pan on the gas stove. 'I'll get them.' She pulled out three eggs and set them in carved wooden egg cups, putting one in each place and joining the others at table.

'We're having eggs today in your honour,' Leah said. 'We usually make do with toast and honey.'

Nina cracked open the top of the boiled egg and since the others were dunking pieces of toast in the soft yoke, she followed suit. It seemed to taste better than the eggs she'd bought from the little shop near her old home. 'Is this egg newly laid? It tastes wonderful.'

'Yes. Mrs Kerkham sells them to us. They have a farm at the other side of the village.'

'Would she sell me a couple of eggs occasionally, do you think?'

'If she has them. She doesn't always have any to spare in winter, but the hens are starting to lay better now the weather is warming up.'

'I can show you where to go for them if you walk back with me this afternoon,' Ginny offered.

'That'll be lovely. I wouldn't want to go knocking on the wrong door.'

Leah gave Nina an understanding smile. 'There's a lot to learn, so don't worry if you make mistakes at first. We all do in a new place and people round here won't get angry at you for going to the wrong door. And if you come across to the house in the afternoon when you know how many hikers you've got staying, I can phone the baker to deliver extra loaves with his second delivery of bread.'

There wasn't time for Nina to learn much more about the village and its surroundings that day, however, because a couple of hikers turned up in the early afternoon. The two young men registered and paid a shilling each for a night's lodging, then decided to leave their rucksacks at the hostel and go off for a walk across the nearby moors.

'Do you need a meal tonight?' she asked them before they left. 'It's only sixpence for a sandwich and a pot of tea.'

'Thanks, missus. That'll be grand.' One young man couldn't seem to stop staring out at the countryside and she realised why when he added, 'I hadn't realised it was so pretty up here on the tops.' He smiled ruefully at her. 'The lady my mam cleans for give me an' my brother the money to come here for a holiday. We've never had a holiday before but she read about youth hostels and told us what to do. She said we were looking peaky.'

They were very thin, that was sure. 'And do you want breakfast as well? If you do, I'll have to order extra bread.'

'How much is that?'

'Threepence each. As much toast, butter and jam as you

can eat and a pot of tea.' Leah had said not to skimp on food, especially with those who looked poor and hungry. Nina could see for herself now why she'd said that. These two looked as if they hadn't had many square meals lately.

'Yes, please. She give us the money for that, too. She said we weren't to bring any money back, just rosy cheeks and lungs full of fresh air.'

Nina watched them go, thinking what a good idea youth hostels were for ordinary folk. The two young men had been glowing with happiness at this simple treat.

Three young women turned up later in the afternoon just as she was about to go into the village with Ginny, and they too wanted tea and breakfast. After they'd been settled in, Nina went across to tell Leah her numbers. Luckily the village shop had a couple of loaves to spare. She'd have had to throw together some scones if they hadn't had any left. She must make sure always to have plenty of flour on hand.

'Shall I ask her to have them delivered?' Leah asked.

'I think I'd rather stroll down to the shop myself. I need some butter and jam as well, and a couple of things for myself. And it'll be good to meet the shopkeeper again.'

At the shop Lily brought out the loaves she'd been saving, then Nina ordered a whole pound of butter, more than she'd ever bought at once in her whole life before. But with five hungry young folk to feed, she doubted there'd be much left.

She watched Lily take off the muslin cover and hack some butter from the big block on its marble tray, which stood on the lowest shelf of the wall behind the counter. Lily then expertly shaped it with her wooden paddles to form an oblong pat, using a carved piece of wood to press a little flower shape into the top to finish it off.

'Wilf Pollard made me this,' she said proudly. 'My own little mark. He can carve anything, that one, figures, animals, you name it.'

'It looks too pretty to eat now.'

'I'll need to order some more from the farmer soon. Most people round here can only afford to buy marge, not always that even, but we have a few people who can afford butter. And now there's you and the youth hostel.' She finished wrapping the butter in greaseproof paper, folded the ends neatly and passed it across the counter. 'There you are.'

On the way back Nina called at the farm and was able to buy six eggs for the youth hostellers' tea, so that she didn't have to open tins of corned beef. She had been going to explain to Mrs Kerkham what she was doing, but the farmer's wife laughed and said everyone already knew about her taking over at the hostel.

'Will there be enough eggs to spare for me to buy a few now and then?'

'There will in warmer weather, which is when you'll need them most. In fact, it'll be a godsend to sell a few more,' the farmer's wife said frankly. 'The hens are laying well again now after the winter. Eh, I don't know how we'd go on without my egg money.'

On her way back to the road, Nina saw a man digging and when she called a greeting, he stopped to smile at her.

Greatly daring, she opened up a conversation. Her father had always forbidden her to talk to strangers in the street, but she thought it only civil to speak, especially in such a small village. 'Looks as if you've been working hard,' she said. 'Are you going to build something here?'

'I'm putting in an old railway carriage for me and my daughter to live in.' He gestured to the child perched on the wall nearby. 'We can't afford to build a house.'

Nina turned to look at the view. 'What a lovely place to live! I'm new to Ellindale too.'

'The matron of the hostel,' he said.

'Everyone knows about me but I've not been here long enough to pick up the gossip about you yet.' She didn't like to ask about his wife, but the child looked as if she needed a bit of care. Even as Nina watched, she jumped down and caught a button between two rocks. When it came off she picked it up and stared at it in dismay.

'I'll see if I can find time to sew it on tonight,' the man said. 'After I've cooked tea.'

'I could sew it on for you in a minute,' Nina offered without thinking. 'I enjoy sewing. Do you have a needle and the right colour of thread?'

'I know where they are,' the child said and ran into the house before her father could stop her.

'I don't like to impose,' the man said stiffly.

'I'm sorry. Am I interfering? Only everyone's been so kind to me here it's good to do something for someone else.'

His expression softened. 'They are kind folk here, aren't they? I'm Harry Makepeace, by the way, and that's Cathie. I'm a widower.'

'I'm Nina Halshall. I used to live with my father but he died.'

'I'm sorry.'

Again she spoke without thinking. 'I'm not. He was a mean old devil and made my life a misery.' She clapped her hand to her mouth. 'Sorry. You don't want to know my business.'

He gave her a rueful look. 'Everyone in the village will want to know your business, I think. And it's kind of you to sew on a button. As a widower, there are some jobs I haven't taken to. And since Cathie's been ill a lot, she hasn't had a chance to learn to sew.'

'I'd be happy to teach her.'

'You're going to fit in well here,' he said. 'You're generous with your help.'

She smiled and when Cathie brought a mess of sewing materials in a battered workbox, she fished out a thread and had the button firmly secured in a short time. Then she handed back the box and stood up from the stone she'd been sitting on. 'I'd better get back now. I have five hungry young hikers to feed.'

'Thank you for sewing on the button,' Cathie said.

'I'll teach you to do it, if you like,' Nina offered.

'That'd be good. I could sew Dad's buttons back on for him then.'

Her father rolled his eyes at this revealing statement and Nina smiled then set off back.

She didn't know what had made her speak so frankly to him, except that he had an honest face and she was so very tired of living shut off from other people. It'd be a pleasure to teach that nice little girl to sew.

All in all, it had been a very pleasant first day in her new job, Nina decided. She was going to enjoy working and living in Ellindale, she was sure. And Leah had lent her a book to read that evening as she kept an eye on the hikers.

Harry watched the woman walk back up the hill with her big shopping basket. He hadn't liked to offer to carry it for her, because he was in such a mucky state, and anyway, she didn't seem to be worried by its weight.

'Miss Halshall is nice, isn't she?' Cathie said. 'Do you think she'll keep her promise and teach me to sew?'

'Yes. But give her time to settle in. She's like us, new to the village.'

He didn't know why he felt so certain Miss Halshall would keep her word, but he did. She had a nice open face, not beautiful, not even pretty, but honest and open, which was much more important, he always felt.

Good heavens! Why was he thinking about her? He'd better not get fanciful about her after one meeting. He missed having a wife, but he couldn't afford to keep one at the moment, let alone risk having more children. He'd decided that after Dora died and other women made it obvious they were interested. No, he had enough on his plate.

Besides, he'd married Dora because he loved her and enjoyed her company, not just to get a housekeeper. If he ever married again, which he probably wouldn't, it'd be for the same reason.

# 24

Wilf turned up in the early afternoon, beaming at Harry and holding out his foot to show the new sole on his shoe. 'That's good strong leather, that is, and who cares if it's green? I shall have dry feet for a while and so will my wife and my brother's family.'

Harry leaned on his shovel, panting slightly, ready to take a breather. 'I'm glad to hear it came in useful. It was just lying around and I still have more than enough for my own needs.'

Wilf took the shovel out of his hands and moved him gently to one side. 'I'll spell you till it's time for me to catch the bus into Rivenshaw and sort out those railway sleepers for the trolleys, then you can take over again. I'll see the bus pass from here and catch it on its way down.'

He dug steadily for a while, taking care not to dirty his shoes, then the bus passed on its way up and he put down the shovel and clapped his hands to get most of the dirt off them.

'It won't take much more to finish the digging, then we can set the stones in place round the edges – Ben said he'd help us do that – and trample earth down inside, while putting in some of the smaller rocks that are lying about. Moving them will help clear the space to put in a garden as well, though there are some clumps of rock you won't easily be able to move. You chose the right place to put your carriage.'

After Wilf had caught the bus, Harry busied himself making

piles of some of the bigger stones that had been in the outer wall, ready to cement them together to form a small retaining wall all round and a bigger one about two foot high at the bottom end to make level ground for the railway carriage.

He didn't allow himself to start worrying about how they'd get the carriage up here to Ellindale, didn't dare. Wilf had said he could organise it and somehow, he believed him.

Eh, it was a long time since he'd felt this good. He kept waiting for something to go wrong, but it hadn't so far.

When he saw the next bus chug up the hill, bringing the other village children home from the elementary school in Birch End, Harry was ready for another break, so walked up with Cathie to collect her glass of milk.

As soon as they got off the bus, the children went straight to the rear of The Shepherd's Rest. He'd expected them to jostle one another, but they formed an orderly queue so he and Cathie joined the end of it.

When they got inside he noticed one girl giving Cathie a shy smile and nudged his daughter, whispering, 'That girl looks about your age.'

Dilys must have heard and beckoned to the other child. 'Alice, this is Cathie. She's come to live in the village but she's been ill so she's not back at school yet. I'm counting on you to look after her and tell her where to go when she starts school. Now, come and get a glass of milk, both of you.'

'We can play out together afterwards too, if you like,' Alice volunteered.

'I've got a skipping rope,' Cathie said.

'Oh, good. Mam had to use mine for a clothes line when ours got too frayed.'

'I can't play rough games yet till I'm better.'

'What's wrong with you?'

'I can't catch my breath sometimes. But I can breathe better up here.'

'That's all right. I don't like rough games. Can I come and see your home when it arrives?'

Cathie nodded and the two girls smiled tentatively at each other, then stayed side by side as they drank their milk.

Harry waited a few moments but he couldn't spare much time so had to interrupt the budding friendship as soon as their glasses were empty. 'We have to go back now because we're getting the ground ready for the railway carriage.'

'I can walk down with Cathie,' Alice offered.

He hesitated then nodded. Mrs Pyne had told him a few times that he was too protective. His daughter would be quite safe with the other children. He noticed several children listening and thought ruefully that he'd have an audience watching what he was doing as soon as they got to know Cathie. Still, if it helped her make friends, he'd put up with as many spectators as necessary – well, he would as long as they kept well back from the work. He didn't want any child getting injured.

It was only natural that people would want to find out about newcomers. He'd already noticed how people slowed down and stared at the progress he'd made as they walked past.

Best of all, though, this was yet another day when Cathie hadn't panted for breath. As he walked down the hill to their home, leaving the two little girls to follow at their own pace, he prayed the fresh air would continue to work its magic on his child.

When Harry got back home, he saw a lorry driving up the hill and it stopped outside his new home. When he saw the huge pile of wood on it, he ran to see if they needed help unloading.

Wilf got out of it and gestured proudly to the pile of wood in the back. 'I hope it's all right but I bought enough to make the trolleys and to stand the carriage on.'

'I didn't think you'd manage to get it here tonight,' Harry called.

The driver jumped down. 'It was Wilf saying you two would help unload it that made the difference. I'll need paying first, though.'

Harry saw to that while Wilf began tugging planks and old railway sleepers off the back of the lorry. The driver shoved the money in his back pocket and joined them. Once again, it cost less than Harry had expected. It seemed his new friend was good at finding bargains.

'We need to carry the wood further on to the block,' Wilf said. 'There's a chap with sticky fingers lives in the village, and though he'd not be strong enough to take any of this, I've heard he has friends with thieving habits who pay him to spot things worth stealing and then drive out to take them.'

The driver made a disgusted noise. 'I'd only need to catch him stealing from me once and he'd not know what day of the week it was by the time I'd taught him a lesson.'

'He's cunning with it,' Wilf said. 'You're never quite sure it's him or we'd have done something about it.'

'A pile of wood like this would attract people if it was left for long.'

'I'm a light sleeper,' Harry said grimly.

When the driver had left, Wilf stood looking at the wood. 'There's not much time to make those trolleys. I think I'll make a start tonight. There's a couple of hours of daylight left yet.'

'I'll help you and send Cathie to the shop for something for us all to eat.'

'All right. Can you nip up to my house, Cathie love, to let

my wife know what I'm doing? It's just opposite the shop, the one with the red door.'

She took the money her father gave her and went off to see what the shop could let them have. Harry watched her go a bit anxiously.

'She'll be all right in Ellindale,' Wilf said. 'She'll not be out of the sight of people at any time when she's going to the shop.'

'You're right. I know I fuss too much, but I've nearly lost her a couple of times.'

The two men were so involved in sorting and stacking the pieces of wood that when Cathie returned, they told her they'd not bother to stop and eat till they'd finished.

'You get yours, love.'

Cathie nodded and went into the shelter.

By the time dusk crept up on them, the two men had the heavy pieces of wood sorted into piles and had stacked some smaller pieces near the house. The seller had thrown these in free because they were only good for firewood.

Harry stood frowning at the piles. 'I think I'd better sleep out here tonight.'

'You'll need your strength tomorrow. Look, there's a lad who lives near us and he'd stand guard all night for two shillings, and you could trust him, too. Ray, he's called.'

'Can you send him along?'

'Aye.'

'But first, you need something to eat. Here, take this with you.' He went across to the shelter and took a tin of corned beef off the shelf and cut off half the extra loaf to go with it. 'It's a thank you for your help.'

Wilf hesitated, looking as if he was going to refuse, then nodded his thanks, mouth set in a tight line of unhappiness.

Eh, the man was proud, Harry thought, but then no one

liked taking charity. 'I can't thank you enough,' he said. 'Nor can I pay you what you deserve. But I'll make it up to you properly one day, I promise.'

His companion merely shrugged. 'No jobs to be found this week, so I prefer to do something useful while I wait for the wood to be delivered. Me and my wife are eating better, thanks to you.'

A few minutes later Ben turned up and stopped his truck to check progress. As the two men started examining the site that had been dug out for the railway carriage, Todd arrived in a vehicle Harry hadn't seen before. He walked over to the road to greet him. 'Got a new car?'

'Nah. Been repairing this one, just giving it a test run.' He gestured towards the piles of earth. 'Someone's been working hard.'

'Only way I know to get things done,' Harry said but the comment pleased him. 'And Wilf's helped me a lot.'

Ben came up to join them. 'You'll need to get some cement and sand before you build your retaining wall.'

'I was going to drive into Rivenshaw first thing in the morning to get some.'

'If I go home and unload my truck, we might just have time to nip down to the hardware shop tonight so that we can make an early start on that wall in the morning. They stay open quite late, and I can carry a lot more on my truck than you can.'

Ben had said 'we', Harry thought, trying not to look too hopeful.

'I can give you a morning's help tomorrow as I only have a small job to do in the afternoon.' Ben sighed. 'Folk aren't building many new places at the moment so it's mostly small-scale repair work. Thank goodness for the phone at Spring Cottage. Leah letting me use it makes a big difference to getting jobs. I should think things were done much more slowly in the days before telephones.'

'That's progress,' Wilf agreed. 'There's some as don't let others use their phones, but the Willcoxes have allus been generous. I've had a few jobs called in there or at the shop, and Mrs Willcox sometimes sends Ginny down to the village to let me know straight away. Kind, that is.'

Ben nodded. 'She makes a big difference to me too, letting me have that place rent free. I'm earning enough to get by, if I'm careful, so I'm luckier than most. Anyway, what am I doing standing here nattering? I'll just drop my tools off at home and come back for you, Harry.'

'We'll have to take Cathie with us. I can't leave her here on her own.'

'Or she can drive up to Spring Cottage with me and you can pick her up from there,' Todd suggested.

'I don't like to trouble Mrs Willcox.'

'It'll do her good to have a visitor, take her out of herself,' Todd said. 'It's always like that once the funeral is over. People haven't settled into a new way of living yet an' they're a bit lost.'

Harry nodded, remembering how hard it had been for him after Dora died. He turned to his daughter. 'How about that, Cathie, love? Would you like to go up to Spring Cottage with Todd?'

'Yes, please.' She smiled at Todd. 'If I go with Dad he'll just talk on and on about the cement and sand.'

Everyone laughed and Harry put away his tools, locking the shelter door behind him.

'I'll get young Ray to come round straight away to keep watch,' Wilf said.

'How about I leave my truck here as well?' Todd suggested. 'Cathie and I can walk up to see Leah and if you leave an oil lamp burning low in the shelter, it'll look as if there's someone still here. We don't want Judson coming poking about again, do we? And there'll be no one within earshot till you get back if Ray wants to call for help.'

'Judson was here in the early morning trying to pinch some dressed stones.'

'What the hell for? He doesn't have a garden, let alone one that needs walls.'

'Maybe he's arranged to sell the stones to someone, or it's a sample of what they could pinch.' Wilf scowled at the thought. 'It'd better not be someone here in Ellindale who's plotting with him. We'd not put up with another thief. And we've had more than enough from Judson. Folk feel sorry for his wife, but she's a lazy bitch and a bad mother. It upsets me to see children so thin and with bruises that don't come from falling.'

There it was again, Harry thought. The people of this village seemed more like a big family. It wasn't that they got on perfectly. He'd already heard a few grumbles about this and that. But they 'rubbed along together' as the saying went. Well, most of them had grown up together here, hadn't they?

There was something to be said for living in the place where you were born. He really envied them their friendships and families.

## 25

For the second day running Todd knocked on the door of Spring Cottage. When Leah came to answer it, she looked pale and strained and he wondered if he should have come today. But it was too late to change that.

'Hello. We came to see how you were feeling.'

She shrugged and smiled at his young companion. 'Hello, Cathie. How are you enjoying living in our village?'

'I love it here. It's so beautiful looking out over the moors.'

Todd was happy to see this display of good manners. It was only what he'd expected from Harry's child or he'd not have invited her here today. He'd hoped Leah would be over her sickness by this time of day. He couldn't help feeling protective of her and wondered whether her husband had noticed that he found her attractive. Was that why Jonah had asked him to keep an eye on her when the inevitable happened?

There was no one else close to her except her much younger sister. Her brother-in-law had his own worries at the moment with that run-down shop and that was another thing Todd was keeping an eye on. Charlie had been looking more and more worried.

'Do come in and sit down. I need to rest for another ten minutes or so then I'll be fine.'

He followed her across the room and took the seat she indicated, which was the one where Jonah had usually sat. 'I'm keeping an eye on Cathie for an hour or two while her father and Ben buy some sand and cement in Rivenshaw. I don't know whether you've been past their block of land lately, but they've levelled the ground nicely for the railway carriage and now need to build a wall to support the lower end of it.'

'It all sounds very exciting. I must go and have another look.' She gave him a faint smile. 'It's time I started getting out and about again.'

'There's no hurry, surely?'

'I'm not one to sit idle. Actually, I was just going to have a glass of ginger beer. Would you like one, Cathie?'

The girl beamed at her. 'Thank you very much. I'd love one. Dad and I have to be careful with our money, you see, till he's found proper work again.'

Trust a child to come straight out with that information, Todd thought. 'I'll be employing your father for a day a week, at least. He's very good with machinery.'

She nodded. 'My dad can mend anything.'

Leah went across to a cupboard and pulled out a bottle, pouring three glasses of ginger beer then setting hers down again after one sip while her visitors drank theirs with appreciative murmurs. 'Tell me about your new home, Cathie. What's the carriage like?'

'I haven't seen it yet, though I'm the one who saw the advert saying they were for sale. Dad says it's got a bit of damage but it's a first-class carriage and there's a window along the top. I can't imagine how that looks. I haven't ridden in a train since I was very little so I don't really remember what they're like inside.'

'Then it'll be all the more exciting for you when it arrives, won't it?'

Todd admired the way Leah got Cathie talking. Later she called her sister down from doing her homework in her bedroom to join them in the kitchen. Leah was a quiet woman, yet she was good with people of all sorts. It was another thing he liked about her.

He liked her too much for his own good.

The two girls got talking and he was surprised at the questions Cathie asked about Rosa's plans to become a doctor. She seemed a clever child. Perhaps she'd win a scholarship to the girls' grammar school in Rivenshaw, as Rosa had. The Esherwood Bequest covered all the fees, and the books and uniform too. He was sure that even if she passed the entrance examination for the Girls' Grammar, which she'd be taking next year probably, Harry wouldn't be able to pay the fees, or even buy the uniform at the moment.

As he sat beside Ben on the way down the gentle hill into Rivenshaw, Harry felt freer than he had for ages. He hadn't realised what a strain working for Trowton had been till he got away. Moving to Ellindale seemed to be working out very well. He'd not have dared stay anywhere near the factory after quitting his job, because he suspected that if he had done, his former employer would have found a way to get back at him for leaving. Well, Trowton had already tried to have him arrested, hadn't he? That memory still made Harry shudder.

'Are you cold?' Ben asked.

'No. Just someone walking over my grave.'

'I don't like that saying. I try to stay optimistic about the future.'

'I don't usually say it. I don't know what made me use that phrase just now – thinking about my former employer, I suppose. He's a nasty devil and to tell you the truth, I'm glad to be out of the area, away from his spite.'

'He won't come after you now, surely?'

'I hope not.'

They arrived at the hardware store just then and Ben drove

round to the back where building supplies were sold from a big yard. In the end Harry ordered more than he needed for building the retaining wall, because it was much cheaper than buying it in sacks. He'd need it to build other walls in the near future anyway. He'd have to build a covered privy as soon as possible. He'd dug out a temporary hole, but some things wouldn't wait because it was a bit hard to go to the lavvy in the rain.

Also of course, when the railway carriage was in place, he'd need some sort of connection between it and the shelter. He still thought the shelter would make a good permanent kitchen. That task wasn't as urgent, thank goodness, and they could manage without a passage between the two till he found a proper job.

The obliging owner of the hardware store promised he'd arrange for a load of sand to be delivered the next morning as early as possible, and they took the bags of cement with them.

'Would you mind if I did a quick bit of grocery shopping before we go back?' Harry asked Ben. 'I can't feed Cathie bread for every meal and there are some things Lily doesn't sell yet.'

'Good idea. I could do with a few things myself so I'll come with you. I eat my main meal at teatime with Leah, because I'm living in a converted stable. But I get my own breakfast and I like to have some food available in my own place. We can take as much time as you need. I've nothing urgent to do this evening and your Cathie will be safe with Todd and Leah.'

So Harry went into a butcher's and bought some stewing beef to put a stew on to cook slowly by the fire the next day. He also got some Oxo cubes to flavour it, then some onions, carrots, parsnips and potatoes from a nearby green-grocer's. He hoped he'd got everything. He was a bit worried about cooking on an open fire, because he'd never tried it before.

That made him suddenly think of another way he could repay Wilf for all the help without hurting his pride. He'd ask if Wilf's wife could come over and show him how to cook the stew, then give her some of the finished product to say thank you. He nipped back to the butcher's to buy another half pound of meat.

It wasn't just a pretence, either, asking for her help. He wasn't a good cook even with a proper kitchen. He'd made stews on the gas cooker in his old home occasionally, and they'd been edible, but they'd never been particularly appetising.

The shops were all getting ready to close down now and he noticed a couple of women hovering nearby to see if any damaged fruit or vegetables were being sold more cheaply. They looked desperate and hungry. One had a small child clinging to her skirts and the other was carrying a baby in a ragged sling. The baby had a face like that of a gaunt old man, which said something about how hungry the mother must be.

He couldn't bear to see such pinched faces on children, so gave in to impulse and slipped the women a threepenny bit each, telling them to buy something for the children's tea. He wished he could afford to be more generous, and their gratitude and the tears of relief in their eyes brought a lump to his throat.

He didn't think Ben had noticed but when he looked, Ben was doing the same thing to an older woman.

'It's the lame helping the lame, really,' Ben said. 'Like you, I have to watch my pennies but that old woman reminded me of my grandma.'

Shopping finished, the two men took a stroll round the town centre so that Ben could point out the main features.

As they passed the railway station, he asked, 'When exactly is the railway carriage coming?'

'In three days' time but they haven't said what time of day. I was going to ask next time I came into Rivenshaw.'

'Well, you're here now so why don't you nip in now and see if someone can tell you?'

'I've taken up too much of your time tonight, and anyway, the stationmaster will probably have gone home for the day.'

'There's still time and enough light to see by. I've plenty of time to spare in the evenings, too much sometimes.'

They were lucky and the stationmaster was still on duty, so he was able to tell them they could pick up the carriage at noon in three days' time. 'Sorry if you were expecting it sooner, gentlemen, but they couldn't get it out of the railway yard till they'd taken the other old carriages away.'

'It works out better for us,' Harry said. 'We still have to build the trolleys to get it up the hill.'

'Rather you than me. Those carriages are damned heavy and hard to move once they come off the rails. We have some specialist equipment.'

The thought of that lack didn't raise Harry's spirits at all.

As they walked back to the lorry, Ben said, 'You can trust Wilf to plan carefully how to move that carriage. He's building your trolleys, but you'll need quite a few people to guide the carriage up the hill, even with a tractor pulling it. Um, I wouldn't mind buying one of the trolleys off you afterwards. With a few alterations, I could use it as a trailer when I have bigger loads to move around.'

Harry looked at him, suspicious that he too was being offered charity. 'Would you have done this if I hadn't been needing the trolleys?'

'Perhaps not yet. But it'll be a cheap way to get hold of a trailer and I'm definitely going to need one as work picks up. If Wilf's making the trolleys, he'll do a fine job, I'm sure.'

'He's very capable about anything to do with wood.'

Ben waited a moment then prompted, 'So? Will the trailer be for sale? I'll pay whatever you and Wilf think fair.'

'All right.' They shook hands on it.

'There you are, then. We'll both benefit from this. You may be able to sell the other trailer once you've finished with it, as well.'

Harry went back to Spring Cottage with Ben, thanking him again for his help, then Ben went into his own dwelling to wash off the day's dirt and Harry went across the yard to pick up his daughter.

It had been one of the most satisfying days he'd spent in a long time – since his wife died, in fact. He'd been lucky finding Ellindale. He prayed his luck would continue. There were so many things that could go wrong in getting a railway carriage up the hill to the village that his heart lurched in anxiety every time he thought about it. It might not be steep but it was long and narrow in places.

He'd rushed into all this without proper planning, desperate to get his daughter away from the smoky air, and he was paying the price for it now. He could only hope Wilf and Ben would continue to help him out of the mess.

Yet he still worried a little about Trowton causing mischief, he didn't know why.

He knew where his daughter got her lively imagination from – him. He should push all thoughts of that nasty old man aside and get on with his new life. But could you ever stop worrying about something or other? Life didn't run smoothly for anyone and what you worried about you prepared for, as best you could, which sometimes helped.

It didn't take long to unload the bags of cement and Harry left Ray keeping guard over them, while he went up the hill with Ben to pick up his daughter.

He found that Leah had given Cathie a meal and had one waiting for him as well. How kind that in her grieving time she'd think of others like that!

He ate the food quickly, enjoying the ham and eggs, then they thanked their kind hostess and left because Cathie was looking sleepy. She held his hand as they walked back, chattering away.

Her voice faded into a yawn the minute she lay down to sleep and he stood for a few moments looking down at her sleeping face by firelight. She already looked better for the fresh air. Surely he wasn't fooling himself about that?

He left the oil lamp burning low, in case anything happened during the night, then he followed Cathie's example, pulling his mattress down from the wall to where it just fitted on the flat paving slabs, which formed the floor, if he put one end under the table.

He was aching from the physical work, which was harder than he was used to, but it was a good ache. It reminded him of how much had been accomplished that day.

# 26

To Harry's relief, Wilf's wife walked over that morning to look at their progress and when she heard from her husband how worried Harry was about cooking on an open fire, she immediately offered to come and teach him how to cook a stew from the ingredients he'd purchased.

Enid Pollard was a tall, thin woman, who might have been pretty if she were better fed, but now only looked gaunt and careworn. Her hands were reddened and cracked by the washing she took in, and looked sore.

She came to the shelter, stopping in the doorway to study the interior. 'It's small, but I'd sell my soul to own our own home like you do. How are you getting on, Cathie?'

'I feel a lot better here. Can I watch what you do, Mrs Pollard? I want to learn to cook too.'

Enid's whole face softened when she spoke to the child. 'Of course you can, love, and you can come over to my house for a chat any time you like if you get fed up of the men. If we had more food, I could teach you how to cook all sorts of things.'

It seemed obvious to Harry that she loved youngsters, as childless women often did, and he felt sad that she and Wilf hadn't produced any of their own. Sometimes, when Cathie slipped her hand in his and smiled up at him, he felt like king of the world. There was no feeling like it.

'Why don't you get out your ingredients, Mr Makepeace?' Enid suggested.

'Why don't you call me Harry, like your husband does?'

'Harry, then, and I'm Enid to my friends. So . . . the ingredients?'

He went outside to the tin with meat in it that he'd left in the old mesh-walled meat safe. He'd put it on rocks in the shade at the back of the shelter because that seemed the coolest place. In warmer weather he put a damp cloth over it and the evaporation kept the inside cooler.

Harry took the meat and vegetables into the shelter and spread them out on the stone slab that served as their table. There was only just room for the three of them to stand round it. 'Did I forget anything?'

'No, you've catered well. Eh, look at all that meat. But it would help to thicken the gravy and it'd make the stew go further if you put some pearl barley in. Now, where do you keep your salt?'

He looked round in consternation. 'I should have bought a new packet when I was shopping. There's only what's left in the salt cellar and I think that's with our other things in Rivenshaw. I can send Cathie up to the shop for some salt and pearl barley, but will you put the stew together for us later? And you must take half of it home with you in return for your help.'

Her voice was sharp. 'There's no need for that.'

'I bought extra meat on purpose, because your Wilf's helped me so much, and the stew will go off before me and Cathie can eat it all.' Which was a lie, because he could eat heartily when food was available, but this pretence might ease her stiffness. 'I don't know what I'd have done without your husband, and now you're helping me and Cathie as well.'

She said nothing, looking longingly at the meat. 'It's just what neighbours do.'

'Well, Wilf's done far more than most neighbours would even think of doing. I can't afford to pay him wages, but if

I give you a bit of food now and then, I shan't feel as guilty. I'd appreciate your help as well as Wilf's because there are times when a lass needs a woman. Cathie's been ill so often she hasn't been able to help in the house like other girls do. You could teach her how to do all sorts of things.'

Enid sniffed and tried to wipe away a tear without him seeing it. 'Well, all right then, and thank you very much. I'll come round and put the stew on for you just before lunch, and show Cathie how to do it. Then I'll come down the hill and check on it a couple of times. But I've some washing to do for a lady today – the whites are soaking now – so it'll be up to you to make sure the fire doesn't burn too low or too high, and you must stir the stew now and then as well. Burned stew doesn't taste good.'

'I could do the stirring,' Cathie said.

'I don't want you playing around with a heavy pan balanced on the edge of an open fire,' Harry said firmly. 'Promise me you won't even try.'

'But Dad—'

'Promise!'

She sighed. 'I promise. But it's not fair. Other girls my age do all the cooking.'

'And so can you when we have a proper gas cooker and can use the lighter pans again, not to mention you getting your strength back.'

Enid put in tactfully, 'You could keep an eye on it, though, and fetch your father or some other grown-up if you think it needs attention. I'm sure he won't mind you using the end of the poker to lift the lid and peep in.'

Cathie looked at her father and when he nodded, she sighed and said, 'All right. I'll do that.'

When Enid had gone home, Harry got out some coins and handed them to his daughter. 'That should be enough for a packet of salt and one of pearl barley.'

He went outside and watched her set off up the hill. He was too protective, he knew, but if he lost her now, he'd never get over it.

Setting his worries aside, he turned back to wall building. They'd arranged that he'd help Ben with that for the rest of the morning, leaving Wilf to start building the trolleys nearer the road. He'd work with Wilf in the afternoon.

There were several piles of railway sleepers to one side of the flat space near the road. They looked mucky and splintered but Wilf said they were still very strong.

Eh, he'd rushed into this like a mad fool. Thank goodness for his new friends.

What they were doing was attracting a lot of attention from people in the village but Harry ignored them. One thing he couldn't ignore, though, was that Judson came and hovered nearby more than once. The man was always on his own, and no one so much as said good day to him.

Before Harry could comment on this, Wilf came to join him. 'What's that sod doing here? It's the third time he's come to have a look this morning.' He glared across at Judson and the man turned away and walked off slowly up the hill, stopping twice on the way up as if to check that he was still being watched, then turning into one of the little back alleys between the groups of houses that led sideways off the road.

Half an hour later Judson turned up yet again. Wilf threw down his hammer, set one hand on the wall and jumped over it on to the road. 'Get away from here, Judson! I know what you're doing, looking to see what you can steal later. Well, if even one screw goes missing, I'll know it, because I count them and I'll come after you.'

'I've a right to use the road like anyone else,' the sour-faced little man said defiantly, though he'd backed away and looked poised for flight when Wilf jumped over the wall.

'Oh, have you? Then I've a right to come and join you.' Wilf took a couple of steps towards him and he ran into the nearest alley.

Wilf didn't come back to work till Judson was out of sight. 'Never have anything to do with that thieving sod, Harry lad.'

But they all saw Judson a few times more, though this time he stayed further up the hill near the shop to watch, as if he was trying to keep out of sight.

'That sod's there again. Does he think we're going to leave our tools lying around for him to pinch?' Wilf said at one point as he walked past the others on his way to get a drink of water from the spring.

Ben stopped work to stare at Judson. 'You'd better watch out for him coming back after dark, Harry lad, and be sure to lock away all your tools inside the shelter with you. He's probably telling some of his nasty friends from down the valley about everything you own, not to mention your wood. He'll be planning how to lay his hands on a few of the sleepers.'

'You'd hear a car or a handcart.'

'If it's a handcart, they could muffle the wheels by running them over old sacks when they got close.'

'I'd better hire Ray to keep watch every single night, then, till we get the railway carriage here. I'll be nearer the road once I'm able to sleep in it.'

'Aye. Well worth paying him. And hire him and a friend during the day we pick up the railway carriage, as well. A lot of people are planning to go into Rivenshaw to watch, so there'll be fewer people around in the village.'

'Have folk nothing better to do than gape at what we're doing?'

'Not really. Especially the men. Time can hang heavy.'

'I never thought to have this sort of trouble in Ellindale,' Harry exclaimed.

'There are thieves everywhere, but if Judson doesn't watch out, we'll be chasing him out of the village for good. He pinched a kid's butty the other day. Said the kid dropped it and the bread fell buttered side down, which is a lie. The father gave him a thump when he found out.'

'Mean sod.'

'I did hear his landlord had given him a warning to pay some of the rent that's owing by the end of the week or he'll be thrown out of the house, so Judson may be more desperate than usual to get hold of something to sell.'

'Well, he's not getting it from me.'

By lunchtime, Ben had finished the retaining wall. The three men stood together studying it.

'Looks nice and strong,' Wilf said.

'It'll do,' Ben allowed. 'I could have put it together more neatly if I hadn't had to work so quickly. Now, I'd better get off to my next job. Leave that mortar to settle in the wall for a few hours.'

Once Ben had left, Wilf grinned at Harry. 'The stonework looks neat enough to me.'

'Aye. But I respect a man who takes pride in his work. You're like him, care about what you do, always try to make a good fist of things.'

Wilf flushed slightly and shrugged his shoulders.

'Let's have something to eat an' then we'll work on the trolleys.'

'After we've eaten, could you nip down into Rivenshaw and fetch me some bolts?'

'Better if I go now while you eat the sandwich your wife made you.' He guessed there'd be nothing in it but a scrape of margarine and that'd give Wilf a chance to conceal that.

'All right. Have you got something to write on? Good. You set down what I tell you then go and buy it all. I didn't want to risk buying too much the first time, but now I've got a good bit done, I have a better idea of what I'm going to need. I don't want to risk any weaknesses in them trolleys. They'll have a heavy load to bear.'

Enid had come back, so Harry left Cathie helping her prepare the stew and drove down into Rivenshaw. He knew this road by heart now, every twist and turn of it, and for all Wilf's reassurances, he couldn't help thinking about the size of the railway carriage and worrying about whether they'd get it safely up the hill on two home-made trolleys.

By late afternoon the stew was sending delicious smells out to tempt the two men to stop work for the day. And anyway, it was looking like rain.

Enid brought a saucepan with her on her final visit to check the stew, but hesitated when Harry told her to take half of it.

'Here. Let me do it.' He took the battered old saucepan from her.

The amount he ladled into it brought tears to her eyes and she whispered her thanks in a choked voice, then clutched it to her bosom as she set off back up the hill.

Harry was putting away all his tools before serving up the meal to Cathie when a great wail of anguish rang out.

He looked up the road and saw Enid sprawled on the ground with the stew spilled in front of her. Another woman was running down the hill towards her and Wilf had abandoned his tools to go to his wife's help.

Harry set off after him, yelling at Cathie to stay where she was.

Wilf bent over his wife. 'Are you all right, love? How did you fall?'

She didn't attempt to take the hand he was offering to pull

her up. 'Someone pushed me. On purpose. They must have been hiding in the alley.'

'What? Who the hell would do that?'

She was sobbing, her words coming out in short bursts. 'I don't know. I didn't see anyone – I just felt someone give me a shove. Next thing I knew, I was on the ground face down and all our lovely stew was spilled. Oh, Wilf, just look at it!'

He patted her back as the sobs continued. 'Nay, then, nay. It *must* have been an accident.'

The other woman had joined them by then and Harry saw that it was Nina Halshall.

'It wasn't an accident,' she said. 'The man did it on purpose. I was standing in the shop doorway and I saw him dart out of that alley, shove her over then run away.'

Then Cathie yelled, 'Dad! Dad! There's a man. Dad, come quickly!'

'I'm coming.'

As he started to run back Harry saw a man run down the block to the lower end. Something made the man jerk and yelp in pain, then he speeded up again and jumped over the wall before racing off down the hill. It looked like Judson but Harry's eyesight wasn't good enough to be sure at that distance. He didn't even try to go after the fugitive, more concerned to make sure his daughter was all right.

He stopped next to her. 'He didn't hurt you?'

'No.'

'What happened?'

'It was that man who kept coming to stare at us, Judson. He crept along by the wall, bending down, but I saw him. He didn't see me, though, and picked up Wilf's hammer, so I yelled for you and threw a stone at him. It hit him on the shoulder and he let out a yell and dropped the hammer. I threw another stone, but that only hit the edge of his leg then you started running back so he ran away. I got him in the back with my third stone, though.'

'Well done, love! Well done indeed.'

Mrs Kerkham yelled from the back wall, 'Is everything all right, Mr Makepeace?'

'It is now. Judson tried to steal a hammer and Cathie threw stones at him. She hit him too, made him drop it.'

'Clever lass!'

'Look, can you keep an eye on her and Wilf's tools for a few minutes? Judson knocked Enid over and I think she must be hurt because she was screaming.'

'Yes, of course. Eh, the cheek of it, trying to steal things in broad daylight. If my Peter had caught him, he'd have flattened him good and proper.'

Harry turned to his daughter. 'Cathie love, stay here with Mrs Kerkham while I see if Enid and Wilf need help.' He could still hear Enid sobbing, such a despairing sound.

'All right. But I'm going to find some more stones in case he comes back. I'm good at throwing balls after throwing them against our wall at school, and stones aren't much different.'

But her father had already run back up the road.

Mrs Kerkham clambered over the wall and came to stand with her, both of them watching what was going on up the road as well as keeping an eye on the tools.

By the time Harry rejoined the others, Enid was scrubbing her eyes and her sobs had more or less stopped.

Her voice broke, though, as she muttered, 'I was that shocked, Wilf. I could only think I'd lost all that good food. It broke my heart to see the gravy soak away. Took me a minute to pull myself together and I never even saw who it was. But it was done on purpose. I didn't trip or bump into anyone, and I *felt* the hand on my back.'

'Why would anyone deliberately waste good food like that?' Wilf asked angrily.

'I reckon he did it to draw us away from the building work so that he could pinch the tools.' Harry explained what had happened.

'Was it definitely Judson?' Wilf asked. 'Because if so . . .'

Miss Halshall had joined them by then. 'I saw the man who did it. He might have thought I was too far away to recognise him again, but I've got good eyesight.'

It spoke in her favour that she'd come running to help, Harry thought.

'I don't know his name, but I'd recognise his face if I saw him again.'

'Cathie said it was Judson and he was trying to steal your hammer.' Harry told Wilf how his daughter had driven the thief away.

'No one else would set about it so stupidly, let alone try to steal things in broad daylight. He's always been one to act first and think later.'

Enid dropped to her knees and began fumbling with the pieces of food, trying to separate the larger pieces of meat and potato from the grit and dirt, and dropping them on to her frayed handkerchief. 'I can wash these carefully. They won't taste as good but I can get them clean, at least. We can't afford to waste such good food.' Tears of shame were trickling down her cheeks but she picked up even the smallest pieces.

Without speaking or commenting, Nina bent down and helped her pick up anything that might be worth retrieving.

'Judson's not going to get away with this,' Wilf growled, his hands clenched into fists. 'I'm going to shovel some of this dirt into his mouth. That's after I've thumped him sense- less. I'll—'

Enid lunged for his ankle as he turned to leave them. 'No,

don't attack him, Wilf. The police will lock you both away for fighting if you do, no matter why you did it.'

Nina stood up. 'I'd be happy to go with you and report it to the police. I'd recognise the man again. He was small and thin, with a ragged grey jacket and a dirty orange scarf knotted round his neck. He hadn't shaved for a day or two, either.'

'That's Judson all right but what can the police charge him with? *Spilling a stew on purpose? Bumping into someone?* The best they can do is caution him. And only Cathie saw him take the hammer. They won't take a child's word about that. No, we have to deal with this ourselves. He's getting worse. He doesn't usually steal from folk in Ellindale.'

As she stepped back to give Enid room to stand up, Nina stumbled on the edge of a rut and Harry instinctively reached out to steady her and stop her falling. For a moment he was holding her close and could smell the soap on her soft rosy skin, see how shiny her hair was, see her lovely blue eyes.

She pulled back, flushing slightly and he knew she was as aware of him as he was of her. What a time to find a woman attractive!

She was looking worried as she asked, 'Do you often get attacks like this in Ellindale?'

It was Wilf who answered, because Harry was still staring at her. 'No, we don't. And I'm going to make sure it doesn't happen again.' He squatted beside his wife. 'Don't pick any more of it up, love.'

But when he tried to pull her to her feet, she tugged her arm away and continued to pick even the vegetables. 'I can wash out all the grit off them. We can't *afford* to waste good food, love, and there's such a lot of *meat* in it.'

Wilf stood up again, looking at Nina in embarrassment, not knowing what to say.

'Your wife's right. In times like this every mouthful of meat is hard won. That was a horrible thing to do, but the food isn't rotten, just dirty, so it can be washed. Here, that handkerchief is full, use mine. It's quite clean.'

Wilf sighed. 'They should have thrown away the key last time they locked Judson away. Anyway I'm going to look for him. He lives at the back of the village.'

As the two women were finishing picking up the pieces, Harry had had an idea. He hurried up the hill into the shop and bought a tin of Oxo cubes for Enid.

When he came back he held it out to her. 'This is to make some more gravy.' When she didn't take it from his hand, he slipped it into her apron pocket.

'Thanks. I'd better get this home.' Enid walked away, clutching her battered pan carefully because it had some food and gravy still sticking to the bottom of the inside. She was carrying the soggy handkerchieves full of dirty food in her other hand.

Harry felt sorry for Wilf, who was obviously humiliated that she'd retrieved it, even though she was right about not wasting food.

'I'll be back after I've seen if we can find Judson,' Wilf called after his wife.

'He'll not go home,' she called back without turning her head.

'He usually does.'

'What, after being caught thieving in daylight? Even he isn't that stupid.'

Harry watched Nina walk away. She'd been so kind to Enid, as she'd been kind to Cathie, sewing her button on. What a nice woman she was – and a cosy armful too.

He went home, and explained to Cathie and Mrs Kerkham exactly what had happened. After their neighbour left, he warned his daughter never to let Judson into their home, or to be alone with him anywhere.

'I've seen his children walk up to get milk in the mornings,' she said. 'They're only little and they're always the hungriest, Gillian says. Alice says they come back in the afternoon after the bigger children have finished and Gillian gives them extra milk, but Alice's mum told her not to tell anyone.'

'Heaven help those children with parents like that! They'll be lucky to live to grow up. We'll wait to have our tea, shall we? In case Wilf needs my help with anything.'

But when his friend came back to pick up his tools about half an hour later, he still looked angry.

'Did you find him?' Harry could guess the answer.

'No. Not a sign of him anywhere. And his wife was no help, just screeched at me to leave her alone. She was coughing and looked terrible. But I pushed into the house and searched it, just in case he'd dared to go back.'

He made a disgusted sound. 'Filthy, the place is, and the way those children were scratching I should think they've got lice.'

'Don't go near them when you're getting your milk,' Harry warned his daughter.

'No, Dad. I wouldn't anyway. They smell awful.'

Wilf was still focused on Judson. 'He'll be hiding somewhere till it's dark, I suppose. But he won't manage to hide from me forever. I'm going to wait near his house after it gets dark. If he goes back there tonight, I'll catch him.'

He picked up his tools and walked off, still radiating anger.

'Let's go and get our tea,' Harry said, so he and Cathie went back into the shelter. He wasn't really hungry for he kept thinking of Wilf and Enid, washing the food and having it in thin, watery gravy made of Oxo, instead of the lovely gravy they were enjoying.

By the time Ray turned up to keep watch during the night,

it was getting dark and raining steadily. Harry found an old tarpaulin and spread it between the frame of one of the trolleys and the wall, weighted down with stones. That'd keep the lad more or less dry.

'I heard about what Judson did,' Ray said. 'My mam was furious about him ruining good food like that, said it was worse than pinching the hammer.'

'Well, he'd better not come back to Ellindale because Wilf will be waiting for him.'

He went back to the shelter and chatted to Cathie for a while, then settled down to go over his accounts and add the screws and other hardware he'd purchased today to the expenses. Money was still going out faster than he'd expected, but what could he do? He had to finish what he'd started and get a roof over Cathie's head. He'd be able to last a few months, with a day a week working for Todd, if he was very careful. And surely he'd find something else as well? He was a skilled electrician, after all.

# 27

Barry Judson didn't dare go back to Ellindale and hid in the fields till it was fully dark. When he crept back to his house, he saw a figure hiding nearby. He waited a while, but the man stayed where he was and as he paced up and down, Barry saw it was Wilf.

He gave up the idea of sleeping in his own bed, if you could call it sleeping with his wife coughing all the time. Cursing intermittently, he began the long walk down the hill into Rivenshaw. He spent the night there, huddled on the bare flagstones in the corner of a room where a chap lived who was as close to a friend as Barry had. They did each other favours when they could, anyway, and drank a pint together when they could afford it.

Patrick's wife complained about Barry staying there, but his friend gave her a clout on the ear and she shut up. Serve her right.

Knocking Enid over and spilling the stew had been a stupid thing to do, Barry thought glumly as he shivered the night away. But what was in the pan had smelled so good, he'd been near sick with hunger and jealousy, and he hadn't been able to resist giving her a shove. Why should a scrawny biddy like her have a good meal when he was scratching to find even a piece of dry bread?

Well, that decided it. He had to get enough money from somewhere to move right away from Ellindale. He intended to move away from his wife while he was at it. She was no use in bed any more, and she'd never been a good housewife, even when they were first wed.

She'd also told him she was expecting again. As if he needed yet another mouth to feed.

He'd had an offer of a job and he hadn't been going to take it at first, but he would now.

That same day Charlie Willcox had to face the fact that he'd not only bought a business that was in a far worse condition than he'd expected, but had been cheated.

The stock in the back room contained a lot of empty boxes that might once have held smaller items like toasters and kettles, but were now empty. How could he not have noticed? He should have checked every single item on the stock list before paying good money out for a bad shop.

The door opened and Bexley came in, late as usual.

'What time do you call this?'

'Sorry. My wife isn't well.'

'You used that excuse last week. Get to work now and don't be late again. There are five items waiting for repairs and you didn't finish any of them yesterday, as you said you would.'

Gordon shrugged. 'Sometimes they're tricky.'

'So get on with it!'

But when Charlie looked into the back later, after serving a customer, there was no sign of Bexley. The man hadn't left via the shop. He heard the back gate creak and looked out of the window. It was swinging open, when it was usually kept locked.

He went out to look in the back alley, but there was no sign of anyone. As he came back in, he locked the gate and put the big iron key in a new hiding place in the workshop.

Something was different. He looked round. Oh, hell! Some

of the tools were missing, tools that belonged to the shop not Bexley, according to the items on the inventory given to him. And they'd been on the rack this morning.

He'd been too kind, feeling sorry for Flewett when he bought the shop, because it was obvious that his wife was very frail.

First things first. He locked up the shop, putting a card saying 'Back in 10 minutes' in the slot on the door, then walked along the street to the police station.

Fortunately, Sergeant Deemer was in. Charlie could see him from the counter. 'I need to speak to the sergeant privately?'

'Could I ask what for, sir?' the young constable asked.

'No, you can't. It's private.' He raised his voice. 'Gilbert? I need to see you.'

The sergeant came to the door of his office, took one look at Charlie's face and gestured to him to come in.

'Not to be disturbed, Catterby,' he told his constable, then turned to his visitor. 'Sit down and tell me what's wrong, Charlie. I can see by your face it's serious.'

'I've been diddled and robbed.'

There was dead silence as Gilbert gaped at a man he'd have considered the last to be cheated. 'Who by?'

'First Flewett then Gordon Bexley, the so-called repairman.' Charlie explained exactly what had happened, feeling a fool, but not such a fool as to let them get away with what they'd done.

'Let's go and have a look round your shop.'

Charlie let them in but left the closed sign in place.

'The place needs brightening up a bit,' Deemer said.

'Yes. I was getting round to that. But I stretched myself a bit buying it.'

'Not like you to get taken for a ride.'

'No.' Charlie sighed. 'I was a bit over-enthusiastic about the prospects for selling electrical appliances. And I still think it's one of the coming things.' He reached for one of the rear boxes and thrust it into his companion's arms.

Deemer braced himself then started down in surprise at how light the box was.

'Empty. And yet it was listed as one of the items I paid for.'

'You'll need to make a list of everything that's not there.'

'I will. Then today I told Bexley off for being late and not getting on with the work. When I came back he'd legged it, and taken all the best tools with him. He was no good at his job anyway. I have a queue of customers wanting items repaired.' He let out a heavy sigh and looked at Deemer. 'What must I do?'

'Make your list. I'll contact the area inspector and get some detectives on the job but do you have Bexley's address?'

'Yes.' Charlie went to a box and took out a card, handing it to the sergeant.

'There isn't a Number Thirty on that street.'

'What?'

'This seems to have been well planned. I wonder—' He frowned then said, 'Maybe it wasn't Flewett but Bexley who did all the stealing of stock? I've known Flewett for years. He's never seemed like a thief. It could be that Bexley has been stealing from him for years. I'll get one of our regional detectives over to look into it. And in the meantime I'll ask around. I'm sorry, Charlie.'

'You'll not tell people? I'd look such a fool.'

'I won't be able to avoid telling the regional inspector and word will get out, but I'll keep it as quiet as I can.'

When Deemer had left, Charlie got out the list of goods, intending to make a start. But he found it hard to concentrate. He'd used the fizzy drinks company as part security. If he didn't get this sorted out, Leah could end up losing a lot of money, maybe even her home.

He'd expanded too fast, that was the trouble. He'd expected everything to go well, as his pawnshops had, and that wasn't realistic.

He had other assets, of course he did. And he'd sell them all rather than see his brother's widow suffer. Only, some of them would make a big loss if he sold them now. And besides, he had a wife and child to support. He didn't want them to suffer.

He felt like weeping, and might even have shed a tear or two had someone not knocked on the shop door just then. He served the customer and managed to sell the woman an electric iron. But it was the only sale that day.

By the end of the afternoon he'd decided to wait a day or two before telling Leah. But he'd have to tell his wife. Marion could read him like a book and she'd know that something was wrong the minute she saw him.

He was right. The minute he walked through the door she demanded to know what was wrong now.

When he'd finished telling her, she sat thinking it over, then asked, 'What does Finn say about it?'

He frowned. 'I haven't told him.'

'Why not? He used to be a policeman. He's your friend. Go and ask his advice tomorrow morning.'

'I can't. There's no one else to mind the shop now. I need to hire someone. There'd be a queue for the job, only they'll have to know about electrical appliances and not a lot of people do yet.'

'I'll come in and mind the shop. And I'll get Vi in to help me find someone permanent. You, my lad, have to sort out this problem, not to mention running your other businesses, the ones that do make money.'

'I don't see how.'

'It's not like you to despair before you start, love.' She put her arms round him. 'We'll work through it, you'll see.'

# 28

The next morning Harry began taking down some of the garden wall and levelling the ground to make a big enough entrance for the railway carriage to be brought on to the site. Hard work, but necessary.

When he paused to ease his shoulders, he saw Mrs Willcox and Miss Halshall walking slowly down the hill chatting. He stopped work for a moment to watch them.

He was glad to see Mrs Willcox looking a bit better today. When he'd glimpsed her at her husband's funeral, she'd seemed ill. He'd found out afterwards that she was expecting. It must be hard on a woman to have a child after losing its father but at least her child wouldn't go hungry. From what people said, she wasn't going to be short of money. Well, good luck to her.

The two women stopped near him to say hello, and he was happy to continue resting a little longer. The ground was muddy after the night's rain, and he must look a right old mess, while they both looked clean and fresh.

Mrs Willcox spoke first. 'I thought I'd get a breath of fresh air and satisfy my curiosity at the same time. My goodness, you must have worked hard to do so much in a few days, Mr Makepeace.'

'We have. I've met some grand chaps here who're lending me a hand. We're collecting the railway carriage from Rivenshaw the day after tomorrow.'

'It'll be a big job getting it up the hill.'

'Yes, but Wilf thinks he can do it.'

'If anyone can, it'll be him. He ought to have become an engineer.'

Harry had thought that himself, but poor lads rarely got into such interesting and well-paid jobs. They had to go out to work as soon as possible, not waste years training. He'd been lucky to be trained by the army.

'Did you catch the man who knocked Mrs Pollard over?' Miss Halshall asked.

'No. Wilf kept watch on his house for an hour or two last night, he was so angry, but Judson didn't come home. Eh, that was a stupid thing to do, unkind as well.'

Miss Halshall hesitated. 'I was wondering if your daughter would like a sewing lesson this morning? It can't be much fun for her sitting around watching you dig.'

He'd thought that himself, but had nowhere else to send Cathie. He missed having Mrs Pyne next door. 'Are you sure? We don't want to impose.'

'I'd enjoy it. I like children.' She smiled at something beyond him and once again, her rather plain face became attractive.

He turned to see what she was smiling at and it was Cathie, who had overheard the offer and was looking at him expectantly. 'Would you like a sewing lesson, lovie?'

'Yes, please. I've got my mum's old sewing box but it's with our other things in Rivenshaw till we get our new home.'

'That's all right. I've got plenty of thread and needles, and Mrs Willcox has given me some scraps of material because I like doing patchwork.' Nina had learned to do patchwork to make something out of nothing thanks to her father's stinginess and was quite good at it now, if she said so herself. 'Maybe you'd like to make yourself a patchwork apron?'

He watched in surprise as Cathie, who was often shy with strangers, went off up the hill with Miss Halshall, chattering away. For some reason he was quite sure he could trust the matron to look after his daughter.

Mrs Willcox lingered. 'When I heard about your big day tomorrow, I wondered if it would help for Cathie to come up to Spring Cottage and spend the day with Nina and me while you're bringing up the railway carriage? When it gets near its new home, Lily will see it and she can phone us from the shop so that Nina and I can bring Cathie down to watch it put into place.'

'That's very kind of you. It'd definitely be a help.'

'We both love children, so we'll enjoy her company. I'll let you get on with your work now.'

She walked up the hill and into the shop. He bent his back to the digging again.

Two lonely women, he guessed. He knew what it was like to be lonely, even though he had Cathie to comfort him.

He seemed to have met with such kindness from nearly everyone in Ellindale. What a special place it was.

Cathie had a wonderful time with Miss Halshall. She was given a choice of materials, and found some pieces with red in them in various patterns. When she held them together they looked bright and fresh. She concentrated hard, listening carefully and practising her stitches on a spare scrap of material till she could sew a neat row.

'You've taken to it well, dear.'

'Thank you, Miss Halshall.'

'It'd be easier with a sewing machine. I had my mother's old one, but I had to leave it behind when my father died and my brother inherited everything.'

'Didn't you get a share?'

'No. My brother's wife is rather . . . um, greedy. I'm going to save up for another machine. I like sewing.'

They smiled at one another and Miss Halshall said, 'Why don't you call me Auntie Nina? It's much friendlier.'

'I'd like that. I don't have any real aunties but I called our neighbour Auntie Janey. She was lovely and I miss her, but we can't go back to see her because Mr Trowton will try to hurt my dad.' She told her new friend about the police coming round to their house just before they left Manchester and they both agreed that her dad was well out of it.

When the clock began to strike the hour, Cathie looked round in surprise. 'Is it twelve o'clock already? I'd better get back. You'll be wanting to have your meal.'

'Why don't you have a sandwich with me? I have plenty. And we could open a tin of soup to go with it. I have tomato or oxtail. You can choose.'

'Are you sure you have enough to spare?'

'I have plenty. And I haven't had a guest here yet, so you can be my first.'

Just as they were finishing the meal, there was a knock on the door and when Nina opened it, Cathie saw her father standing there.

'Why don't you come in, Mr Makepeace?'

'I'd better not. I'm all mucky from the digging. I came to get this scamp here back for her dinner.'

'Auntie Nina gave me something to eat. She said she had plenty to spare.'

'I hope you don't mind, Mr Makepeace? I was enjoying Cathie's company and I thought it'd save you some trouble. But I should have asked you first. You must have been worried about her.'

'I knew she was safe with you. You'd better thank Miss Halshall and come back with me now, Cathie love. I don't want you wandering round on your own till that Judson's been caught.'

Nina watched them leave, the girl chattering away to her

father and him bending his head slightly to listen to her. He was a good father, you could tell. He'd probably been a good husband too.

She blushed at the thought that crept into her mind at that idea, but it wouldn't go away. Well, she was only human and everyone had their dreams, didn't they? Even if they had to keep them secret.

# 29

Harry slept badly the night before they were due to collect the carriage, in spite of being tired from the hard work. Everything was ready. Ray and a friend were keeping watch because he needed his sleep. But still it eluded him.

His mind bounced from one thought to another, coming back always to the railway carriage and its perilous trip up the hill. He'd be glad when the sky began to lighten. No use getting up till it was light enough to see what he was doing.

He woke with a start after an uneasy doze to find the shelter filled with grey light. Sighing in relief that he didn't have to lie there any longer, he reached out to shake Cathie's shoulder gently. 'Time for us to get up, love.'

She was awake instantly. 'Hurrah! The railway carriage is coming today.'

'Yes. Turn your back while I get dressed.' He got up and pushed some fresh splinters of wood into the embers before getting into his clothes. He'd had a wash the night before – just a lick, spit and a promise because he'd be dirty again within minutes – so he could start work at once.

He opened the door and peered out while Cathie got dressed. It wasn't raining, thank goodness, and the ground had dried a lot yesterday. They had enough to face without mud adding to their problems.

'I'm ready now. Dad, *please* won't you let me come down with you and watch? I won't get in your way.'

'We went through this yesterday, love. I'd have to keep an eye on you and I need all my attention on the carriage today.'

'It's not fair. Everyone else will see my new home before I do.'

'Mrs Willcox won't, nor will Miss Halshall.'

'She said to call her Auntie Nina.'

'She's not *my* auntie, though.'

That drew a giggle from her. 'Silly. She couldn't be your auntie. She's old, like you.'

Old! He didn't feel old but he supposed he was to a child. And Miss Halshall was definitely not old. She seemed a woman in her prime to him. 'All right. I'll just have a word with the lads. Call me when the kettle boils and I'll brew us some tea.'

When he went outside he saw Wilf walking down the hill from the village, and his wife with him, so waved to his friend. The two lads who'd been keeping watch were sitting on one of the trolleys, yawning. He went across to them. 'Everything all right?'

'Heard something a couple of times,' Ray said. 'But when we called out to ask who was there, the noise stopped. We walked up and down a few times and Pete saw someone creeping away.'

'Did you recognise him?'

'No, Mr Makepeace. Sorry. It was too dark. I could only see a dark outline against the sky.'

'It happened again later, though,' Ray said.

'There was more than one of them the second time,' Pete added.

'You'd better keep careful watch today while we're away,' Harry warned. 'They might try to break into the shelter and steal our things. Are you sure you can stay awake?'

They both nodded vigorously and Ray said, 'We've asked a friend to join us. We'll share the money with him and he'll make sure we don't fall asleep.'

'Good, lads. But I can spare another shilling for him, as long as he really does keep you awake.'

They smiled happily at that.

As Wilf and Enid joined them, they heard the sound of a truck chugging down the hill.

'Ben's up early as well,' Harry commented.

His friend stopped and jumped down from the truck. 'Excited?'

Harry shrugged. He was more anxious than excited, just wanting to get on and do it, do anything rather than stand around waiting and worrying.

'It'll be all right,' Wilf said gently. 'That's why I've brought Enid with me. Tell them, love.'

'A friend of mine overheard Judson's wife hinting to Lily at the shop yesterday afternoon that her husband was going to get his own back on you today. Lily tried to get Minnie to tell her the details, but she clammed up.'

'Damnation! What's that fool planning to do now? Is there anyone else I can hire to guard the site?' Harry asked. 'I don't feel good about leaving it with just three lads to keep watch.'

'That's why I'm here,' Enid said. 'I'm going to keep an eye on things for you.'

'No offence, love, but what can a woman do against Judson and his little gang?'

'You don't know my Enid,' Wilf said. 'Anyway, she won't be the only person left in the village, will she?'

'Anyone who's fit enough to walk is planning to get down into Rivenshaw to watch the show,' Harry said. 'There won't be many men left here.'

'Not the women,' Enid said. 'Some of them will be staying. Not everyone is interested in watching a carriage come slowly up a hill.

'Leave it to Enid and her friends,' Wilf said.

What else could he do? Harry wondered. 'You and Mrs

Willcox will keep Cathie safe? She's more important than anything.'

Enid nodded. 'Of course we will.'

Ben gave Harry a nudge. 'Come on, lad. We need to make a start. We have to get that tractor from my friend at the farm and attach the trolleys to it. We're lucky someone down the valley has a motorised tractor. They still use horses on the smaller farms round here.'

'Let's get the trolleys up on the back of the truck, then.'

The trolleys were heavy and only just fitted, so the three men had to squash into the cab of the truck.

Harry waved to Cathie and they were off.

The lads turned to Enid. 'Do you think there's going to be trouble, missus?' one of them asked eagerly.

'Might be. But we'll be ready for it and you won't be on your own. I've got some friends coming to join us.' She turned to Cathie. 'Have you had your breakfast, love?'

'No. We boiled the kettle but Dad didn't even wait for a cup of tea this morning.'

'Then we'll have one now,' Enid said. 'Do you lads want a cup as well?'

'If you can spare one, missus.'

While the tea was brewing she gave Cathie some bread and jam.

'I'm not eating it if you don't have some as well.'

Enid hesitated, then cut a slice herself.

'I think the lads should have one too.'

'And what would your dad say to that?'

'He'd agree. They haven't had anything to eat, either.'

'All right, love. I'll make us all a jam butty.'

After they'd cleared the breakfast things, Enid and Cathie walked up the hill to Spring Cottage.

*

Leah came to greet them at the door. 'Ginny started work early today so that she can catch the bus down to watch the railway carriage being put on the trolleys, and I've closed down the factory for the day. No one's got their mind on their work. The men all want to see the railway carriage brought up, and some of the women do too.'

'We might need a change of plans,' Enid said when they were sitting round the table. 'Ginny, you should listen to this. A friend of mine heard Judson's wife boasting in the village shop that Harry was going to get his comeuppance today. Minnie Judson's a fool who can't keep her mouth shut about anything. And there were people prowling round Harry's site during the night, the lads keeping watch told me.'

There was silence.

'Dad's worried someone will come and try to steal things while he's away,' Cathie said. 'But he's left three lads keeping watch.'

'Will they be enough, though?' Enid asked. 'Wilf and I talked about it. He thinks some of us women should stay on the block or nearby as well. But I think we should go further than that, maybe plan a few surprises, just in case someone comes thieving. So if I leave Cathie here with you, can you let Nina come down to keep watch with me?'

'You're not leaving me out of this,' Leah said at once. 'It's my village too.'

'In your condition . . .' Nina began.

'I'm not planning to get into any fist fights, but I've still got Jonah's gun. I don't like the horrible thing, but this is an isolated place and there won't be any younger men left in the village. So I'll load it and bring it along.'

Enid threw her hands wide. 'All right, then. But you two have to stay in the shelter. Let's work out what to do and who'll come and help us. If Judson brings those chaps he hangs around with in Rivenshaw to loot the place, which is what he sounds to be planning, he'll find us waiting.'

'They're rough devils.'

'I can be rough too when it's needed,' said Enid. 'But we'll make sure we outnumber them.'

'Judson hasn't been seen in Ellindale since he pushed you over, Enid.'

'No. And he knows he'll not be able to come back and live in the village. My Wilf is determined about that and he's made sure people spread the word about it. He told Minnie to her face when he saw her in the street that she should start packing. So we think if Judson does come, he'll be trying to get away with as much stuff as he can steal in one last raid.'

Ginny frowned, trying to think it through. 'But how will he get here without anyone seeing him lower down the hill? He'd have to pass them on the road. Don't you think you're seeing more trouble than he's capable of?'

'Those new friends Judson's made since he came out of jail are nasty brutes. I heard that the police in Rivenshaw are keeping an eye on them.'

'But they still have to get here with a car to carry stuff away in.'

Leah considered this, head on one side. 'Well, there are tracks across the moors you can drive a vehicle along. I see cars sometimes when I'm looking out. It's a bumpy ride, but I've not seen any get stuck.'

'So they could be up here already?'

They were all silent, thinking this over.

Enid broke the silence. 'Let's work out what to do. I'm still mad enough about that stew to thump Judson if I so much as catch sight of him.'

She smiled, and it wasn't a nice smile. 'In fact, if I don't get a chance to thump him today, I'll be sadly disappointed. He made me cry, and I don't usually let myself cry, not about anything.' Not in public, anyway, she thought.

# 30

Ben drove to a distant cousin's farm, which was a mile or so out of Rivenshaw to the south, and they found the tractor and its owner waiting for them in the yard.

Lenny, who was older than Ben by about twenty years, greeted them cheerfully. 'How do, lad? I'm looking forward to today. I've a job or two that might be easier if I can pull a trolley behind the tractor without it dragging me all over the place.'

'This one won't pull, and I can build you an even better one, if you like,' Wilf said at once.

'I'm not promising owt afore I see how them trolleys go today.' He stepped back, arms folded, eyes shrewd and watchful for all his joviality.

They'd decided it'd be easier to attach the trolleys to the tractor at the farm, rather than trying to do it in the town square outside the railway station in case there were adjustments to be made. They lifted the trolleys down from the truck but after studying the tractor, Wilf immediately decided on a small modification, which he said would make the link more secure.

Ben paced to and fro, fretting at having nothing to do but not liking to go inside the farm in case he could help.

'It's a good thing we started early,' he muttered to Harry, but the latter had hardly said a word today.

'We'll be all right,' Ben said softly.

Harry nodded.

He was given a couple of small tasks when Wilf needed another pair of hands, otherwise he too could only stand and watch. And worry.

The farmer's wife came out about half an hour after their arrival with some tin mugs of tea on a tray, and a plate of her best parkin.

It was only when he saw the food that Harry realised. 'Eh, I forgot to eat this morning. I haven't even had a cup of tea, only a slurp of water.'

Wilf gave him a quick sideways look. 'Worry can do that, take away your appetite. I won't let you down today, lad.'

Harry knew his friend would do his best, but however much anyone tried to reassure him, it now seemed an impossible task. Why, even the railway company refused to try to deliver old carriages up into the more remote moorland villages.

At last, after two hours' solid work, the adjustments on both trolleys were finished and Wilf gave the last one an affectionate slap. 'That'll do.'

One trolley was chained behind the other and when Lenny tried driving them out of his yard, they bobbed along behind him more smoothly than anyone had expected. They were both topped with heavy duty clamping systems ready to attach them underneath the two bogies that supported the bottom of the railway carriage, and there were spare chains and ropes if required.

Wilf stood back, rolling his shoulders to ease the stiffness. 'We can set off now, lads. If we need anything else to secure the trolleys to the railway carriage, we can surely find it in the hardware store in Rivenshaw. They keep a good stock. You'll be all right driving the tractor into town now, eh, Lenny?'

Ben's cousin nodded. 'I'm looking forward to it. But we'll go carefully. This damned machine cost me a fortune, so it has to earn its keep in every way possible, like me hiring it out to you today.'

They set off, with Ben driving the truck very slowly behind the big slow vehicle and Wilf hanging on it at the side of the driver, keeping an eye on his trolleys.

Ben didn't try to chat to Harry. Nothing they could say or do would ease his friend's anxiety except getting the job done. And who wouldn't be worried when his home had to be transported up a twisting road that was narrow in parts?

To Harry's dismay there were a lot of people standing around in the town square in Rivenshaw, most of them near the railway station. They pressed forward to stare at the tractor and trolleys, and Lenny had to wave them out of the way.

'Do they think this is a damned raree show?' Harry exclaimed.

'They could come in useful,' Ben said, his easy tone a contrast to Harry's terse speech. 'If we need extra muscles to shove something, I bet some of the younger ones would love to help.'

Harry shrugged. 'I suppose so.'

The stationmaster came out to greet him. 'It's not here yet.'

'Why not?'

'They're running a bit late. They managed to find a telephone and let us know. There was an accident on the road here.'

Harry looked at him in surprise. 'Road? I thought it'd be coming by rail.'

'Not this one. It'd have been more trouble to put it back on the rails in Manchester and then get it off again here than it was to tow it behind the specially made lorry they use.'

'If they have a special lorry I don't see why they couldn't deliver it to my home,' Harry grumbled.

'You'll understand why when it arrives.'

'How late will they be, then?'

'About twenty minutes or so, they think. You might as well get yourselves a cuppa in the tea room.' He pointed across the square.

Harry didn't even look across at it. He intended to stay put here till his carriage arrived.

Todd had turned up to join them at the entrance to the station while this conversation was going on. 'You could come to my house instead. I'm only two minutes' walk away and I could make us a quick pot of tea.'

But Harry shook his head a second time. 'No, thanks. I'd rather keep an eye on the trolleys. You know what lads are like. They can't help fiddling with things. We've got the tractor and the trolleys ready to go and we don't want to risk anything being tampered with.'

'I'll stay around in case you need another pair of hands, then.'

Harry saw Ben wink at Todd and knew why. Well, he couldn't help it. This was an anxious time for him. But he was never doing anything risky again for the rest of his life.

As if to prove Harry right about lads tampering, a few minutes later Wilf suddenly roared, 'Hoy, you! Get away from that!'

A lad ran out from behind the trolleys and a bystander grabbed him by the collar, bringing him up short, even though he kicked and struggled.

'What was he doing?' Harry asked.

'Fiddling about with the wheel on your trolley.'

'What were you trying to do?' Wilf crouched to look at the wheel and picked something up from the ground under it.

The lad didn't attempt to answer, but another man pushed

out of the crowd and grabbed him from the bystander. 'That's my son, so if he needs bringing into line, I'll do it.' He gave the lad a shake. 'Tell him what you were doing, Alf.'

'A man paid me a shilling to shove some nails into the hole where the chains go in.'

'Which man?'

The lad looked round. 'He's gone now.'

'What the hell did he want you to do that for?'

The lad shrugged. 'I don't know.'

Wilf was furious. 'Didn't you think these might damage it if you stuffed them inside the hole for the chain?' He picked up a nail from the ground and used it to poke a couple of other nails out of the hole.

'How can little nails like these damage a heavy trolley?' The lad pulled a few more nails out of his pocket and held them out.

'Where's the shilling he paid you?' his father demanded.

Alf looked at him pleadingly.

'Give it to me.'

Scowling the lad fished in his pocket and handed over the coin.

The man held it out to Wilf. 'I'm sorry if he's damaged anything. Maybe this'll help. He wasn't brought up to do that sort of thing, but these lads who haven't got jobs to occupy their time have to use up their energy somehow. This one spends half his life getting into mischief. And *I – have – had – enough – Alfred Marton!*'

More shaking of his son emphasised this point, then he frowned and asked, 'Were you the only one doing it?'

'I don't know.'

The father clouted him. 'I can allus tell when you're lying. What else have they arranged?'

'I don't know what else, do I? But one of the men was talking to two other lads.'

'Men?' Harry asked sharply. 'There were more than one of them?'

'Three of them, an old one and two younger ones.'

'Tell me what the older one looked like.'

The lad shrugged. 'Bald on top with a fringe of hair, and a big nose. Oh, and a ginger moustache. Looked silly, that did.'

Harry stared at him. That was a recognisable description of Trowton. Was it possible he was here to create more trouble? He stared round the square, but couldn't see anyone remotely like his former boss. First things first. He watched Wilf checking that no damage had been done to any of the other trolleys.

The father of the lad let out a growl of disgust. 'Stay right next to me from now on.' He turned to Wilf. 'Has he damaged it?'

'No. He was stopped in time and he didn't shove the nails in deeply enough anyway.'

'If you need someone else to keep watch on those trolleys, I'll help you.' The man turned round to shout, 'Martha, keep our Alf by your side from now on. He's in trouble again.'

A weary looking woman nodded and beckoned the son, who got another clout when he reached her and a shrill demand to know how he found all this trouble to get into.

Wilf frowned at him. 'Do you have any enemies, Harry?'

'Only Trowton, the chap I used to work for, and he's in Manchester. He'd not go to all this trouble, surely? Only . . .' His words trailed away.

'Only what?'

'The lad described a bald man and it sounded just like Trowton. Bit of ginger hair in a fringe and a big nose.'

'Here in Rivenshaw?'

'If it is him. Oh, hell! I thought I'd got away from him.'

'We won't let him damage your new home.' Wilf beckoned to two burly men standing on the corner and they strolled over to join them. 'These are friends of mine. I asked them to come along in case we need help. Don't let anyone else touch the trolleys, or even go too close to them.'

They nodded to Harry as if to assure him that they'd do that.

He nodded back, but his mind was spinning. Surely Trowton wouldn't go to these lengths to get back at him? Only who else could it be with that description? The man had been acting strangely for a while now, but coming so far to get back at an employee who gave notice was beyond reason.

Perhaps the machinery was giving Trowton trouble again. But how could he blame that on Harry? If there were any problems they were likely due to Trowton skimping on the maintenance.

He turned to Wilf. 'Trowton wouldn't have come all this way just to pay lads to stuff nails into the wheels. He must be planning something else. But what?'

Wilf was looking grim. 'We'll keep a careful watch. Very careful.'

'Well, if you need to hire more men, do it.'

But with a crowd of people gathered round, it was hard to watch everything that was going on. Harry felt sick with worry, sick and helpless.

A police constable came across the square to join them shortly afterwards. 'Sergeant Deemer saw the crowds and sent me to keep an eye on things. What's going on?'

Harry was still staring anxiously round so Ben explained why they were waiting. 'Until the carriage arrives we can do nothing.'

'Ah. I see.'

He looked so young, and Harry wondered how he could keep order.

The constable was looking round but making no attempt to move among the crowd or talk to people.

Todd grinned at Harry and jerked his head in the constable's direction, rolling his eyes, clearly feeling the same.

What next? Harry thought. Perhaps the king would be coming to watch the show.

# 31

Just before midday a man walked up the hill towards Ellindale, slowing down when he came to the piece of land. There was no one in sight in the village, no one working on the empty block.

He waited, staring to and fro across it as if searching for something, then looking up towards the village and down towards Birch End. He did this several times, not moving.

No one came into sight and after waiting a few more minutes he went back down the hill, whistling cheerfully.

Once he'd disappeared round the first curve below the village, two lads crept out from under an old tarpaulin. One ran down the road, stopping where it curved to see where the man had gone without showing himself. His companion stayed near the tarpaulin, watching him. When the lad made the signal they'd arranged to indicate that the stranger had gone further down the hill, the one by the wall called, 'Tim's gone further on, missus, still following that fellow.'

Enid came out from behind the shelter.

'He didn't see us,' the lad said jubilantly.

'Well, there are bound to be others with him and they'd better not see you either till we find out what they want.' She turned round quickly as she heard the other lad come running up the hill.

'That fellow turned off the road towards Crag Hey Farm, missus, an' went right along towards it. I didn't think anyone was living there now.'

'Nor did I. They must have come up last night and stayed in the old farmhouse,' Enid said. 'Judson probably told them about it. They'll feel at home there, because it used to house a nest of villains.'

'If they come and steal things, how are they going to get away afterwards, though?' one lad asked. 'Mr Makepeace will be bringing the carriage up the hill and he'll see them coming down. And there's parts where they won't have room to go past the carriage.'

'They could hide somewhere in Birch End till he's past, you dafthead,' the other said.

'Only if they can get that far in time. The railway carriage might be blocking the road by then. It's after midday now, I should think.'

They started pushing and shoving one another, arguing about that till Enid told them to stop this minute.

They obeyed her immediately.

Leah smiled as she watched them. She'd come to stand in the doorway of the shelter, with Nina and Cathie just behind her. Now all three came across to join the others.

'What do you think they're going to do?' Nina asked.

'Obviously they're planning to rob us, after which they could get away along the track that leads from Crag Hey Farm across the moors,' Leah said thoughtfully. 'I've walked along it quite a few times.'

'Could a car get along it?'

'A modern car or van might manage to drive along it, if it's a sturdy vehicle. The track meets another one about a mile away from the valley, a wider one, but still not tarmacked, and I've seen cars go along that, though I don't know exactly where it leads.'

'I bet they *are* planning to escape across the moors,' Enid said. 'Only we'll make sure they don't get away with it.' She turned to Cathie. 'Right, love. You go up to the shop and tell the women waiting there to come down to their hiding places here. Then you stay at the shop with Lily. I think they'll come here first because that man didn't go up to the shop at all.'

As Cathie opened her mouth to protest about being left out, Enid added, 'No arguing, young lady. You promised to do as we told you.'

'Oh, all right. But it's not fair.' The girl ran off up the hill.

Nina had been watching Enid, and the other woman seemed to be almost sparkling with determination and excitement. She was more like her husband than people realised. Look how the lads had obeyed her just now. She and Wilf would both have been leaders if they'd come from a more affluent background. They were the salt of the earth, people you could depend on in a crisis, even in these hard times, when they had little to offer but friendship and a helping hand.

Nina would give anything to have a husband to love and be loved by, and she'd longed for children for years. Enid didn't have any children, but she did seem to have a happy marriage. The way she and Wilf looked at one another showed how close they were.

Harry was much gentler in nature and he—

Nina told herself sternly to stop these silly fancies and concentrate on what was going on. Some of the younger, stronger village women were hurrying down from the shop, looking excited, each carrying some form of weapon, even if it was only a poker or rolling pin. They'd left the older women to look after the children.

Enid was standing by the road waiting for them, when she spun round suddenly and stared down the hill. 'Shh! Listen.'

There was the sound of a car engine in the distance.

'Get out of sight quickly!'

As the women slipped over the back wall on to Kerkham

land or into the shelter, the lads got back under the tarpaulin and silence settled on the plot of land once again.

Nina had been told to go inside the shelter with Leah, and had firm instructions from Enid to keep her from joining in any trouble. That baby she carried was too important to risk.

It was a good thing young Cathie was up at the shop now, Nina thought. This could get nasty, but she'd never met such a determined group of women and she didn't think whoever was coming here expecting a thieving spree would get the better of them.

She fully intended to play her part in defeating the thieves. A man like Harry, so hard-working and caring about his child deserved all the help his neighbours could give him.

A small open-backed truck came into sight, with the name of a business on the side *ENTWISTLE* and under it in big letters *DELIVERIES*.

It wasn't a local firm, so they must have stolen it from somewhere outside the valley, Enid thought. If so, they'd not only have stolen a vehicle but a man's livelihood and that only made her more determined to stop them.

Two men were riding in the back of the truck, heedless of whether anyone saw them, and she could see two other figures in the cabin. She drew right back behind the shelter as the truck drew up at Harry's land, but she could still see what was going on by looking between two of the larger, uneven stones that formed the corner of the wall.

It didn't surprise her when Judson got out of the passenger side. Ha! This would be the last time he'd cause trouble in the village.

The two men let down the back panel of the truck and jumped out. Rough looking pair, they were, and younger than the others, the sort who didn't have steady jobs even in better times. She'd never seen them before.

She knew the driver by sight and vaguely remembered seeing him in Rivenshaw. He stayed in the driving seat and reversed the truck on to the cleared area as soon as the others were out of his way. The engine stopped and he jumped down from the cab, grinning. 'Nice of these folk to make room for us to carry things out to the truck, isn't it? I reckon we'll clear this place quickly, so we might as well see what the shop has to offer afterwards.'

'A tasty young woman for a start,' another said loudly. 'I've seen her a couple of times. Quite a looker. We've time for a bit of fun as well, eh?'

They all laughed.

Enid felt outraged. What sort of creatures were these? Filth, that's what. And even that word wasn't bad enough to describe them.

The driver continued to order the others around. 'Let's look inside the shelter first. Makepeace will have locked anything worth stealing in there. Judson says he has some good tools, for a start.' He looked at the preparations for the carriage. 'And before we go we'll see how much of that wall we can knock down.'

Judson was at his elbow, fairly jigging about with excitement. 'That'll show him!' he yelled. 'Serve him right, the arrogant sod.'

'We've work to do first, so calm down, Barry lad.'

They moved purposefully up the slope but just before they got to the shelter, Enid yelled, 'Now!'

Stones of a size to fit in the hand, which had been stored in piles here and there earlier that day, whizzed across, hitting the men from several directions. The intruders cursed as they tried to duck them. Some missed completely but there were a few hits and then one hit the leader on the temple and felled him.

A woman's voice shrilled in triumph as he lay where he'd fallen. 'Told you I could hit him once I got my aim in.'

Another woman called, 'Tie him up quickly before he comes to.'

Two of her companions cheered and moved towards him, others ran to Judson, taking him by surprise and grabbing him before he could run away. He began kicking and punching, calling to his companions to help. But they were too busy dodging other stones that were still curving through the air towards them, occasionally scoring hits. By the time they turned to flee towards the lorry, the remaining women had caught up with them. Brandishing their impromptu weapons, a couple barred the doors of the lorry.

The intruders stopped, looking back to their leader for instructions but he was still lying groaning on the ground, only semi-conscious. Two women were tying him up.

A woman with a cudgel clouted the nearer of the two men, aiming at the back of his head. He ducked but she still hit his shoulder hard enough to make him yell out in pain and stagger.

There were three times as many women as intruders and every single one had grim determination on her face.

'This is Ellindale!' Enid yelled. 'We stick together in our village and we don't let thieves get away scot free.'

The men hesitated not seeming to know what to do.

She looked at Judson and felt fury run through her, couldn't help giving in to the temptation to push one woman aside and slap him good and hard on the face.

He tried to get away from her but she was taller than him and grabbed him by the jacket. The two women who'd been holding him let go, standing at each side ready to grab him again. They knew what this was about.

'Waste good food, would you?' she yelled and gave him another slap that jerked him sideways.

He raised his hands, trying to cover his head and stepping back, but he fell over on the uneven ground. When he was down Enid kicked him in the ribs a couple of times then stood back and nodded to the other women to show that she'd finished. 'Get up, you.'

But he didn't. 'How the hell did you know to expect us?' he asked, wriggling backwards along the ground.

'Your wife let it slip.'

'She never!'

'Oh, but she did, an' that gave us plenty of time to prepare.'

'I'll kill the bitch.' The fury at what his wife had done lent him a sudden burst of strength, and he jerked backwards so rapidly he was able to get up before any of the women could grab him. He took them by surprise by not heading towards the road but running diagonally across to the back wall. He was over it before anyone could stop him, running across Kerkham's land now.

'I should have resisted the temptation to thump him,' Enid muttered. 'He'll have gone home to thump Minnie now. Make sure these rats are all tied up securely. Alice and Jane, come with me. We'd better go after Judson. He might really hurt her this time.'

'She's used to him thumping her, deserves it boasting about what he was going to do to you.'

'Well, I don't like men beating women, even her,' Enid said fiercely, 'and Minnie hasn't been well for a while now. I know she's lazy and stupid, but I've often felt sorry for the poor creature, married to *him*. Just think about it.'

They both shuddered involuntarily.

'Lately Minnie's been walking slowly, like an old woman, and her not even thirty,' Enid added. 'So I'm going after him. Anyway, it's my fault he escaped. I gave in to my temper. My job to fetch him back.'

She set off running, taking the road up the hill, outdistancing her two companions easily.

# 32

When Judson burst into his house, he found Minnie slumped in the old rocking chair, coughing into a blood-stained rag.

'You stupid bitch!' he yelled. 'What did you say to warn them?'

'I never . . . said . . . nothing.'

'Liar!' He dragged her up by the front of her bodice and slapped her face hard, which set her off coughing even more violently. 'You must have said something.'

'I didn't. Stop it, Barry. I didn't.' She scrabbled at him, trying to make him let her go, wheezing for breath in between racking bouts of coughing.

'Ah, you're worthless, you are.' This time he punched her in the face. She screamed and choked, suddenly clutching her chest and vomiting up bloody fluid all over him.

He hurled her away from him in disgust but as she stumbled backwards, she tripped over the foot of the rocking chair and fell sideways towards the hearth, arms flailing. She hit her head against the wall next to it with a dull thump and the sound cut off as she fell sideways into the fire itself.

When she didn't get up, even though the embers must have been burning her face, he dragged her away, but it was like dragging a rag doll. She was limp and when he dropped her on the rug, she lay in a tangle exactly as she'd fallen. One of her cheeks had been scorched and blackened by the fire, but she hadn't cried out when she fell into it.

He kicked her. 'Get up!' He looked more closely and said in a voice which wobbled, 'Stop pretending you're unconscious. I'm sorry you're burned.'

But she didn't react.

He froze, looking down at her in horror, letting the hand that had been outstretched to pull her up drop to his side, then clamping it to his mouth.

The door banged open and Enid rushed inside. 'Get away from her, you brute.'

He tried to push past her to get out of the house but behind Enid were two other women and they held him fast as he struggled and sobbed incoherently.

Enid knelt beside the still figure on the floor and drew in a breath of shock. 'Eh, no. *No!*' She placed her fingers against Minnie's throat but found no pulse. 'She's dead!'

He stared at her aghast as his fears were confirmed. 'She can't be. She was just screeching at me a minute ago.'

'Well, she'll never screech again. You said you were going to kill her and you have.'

'I didn't kill her – she fell.'

Enid stood up. 'You've her blood all over you and the cheek that didn't get burned looks red, so you must have thumped her.'

Judson looked down at his wife, then looked away again, horror twisting his narrow face into a gargoyle. 'It was an accident, I tell you. I pushed her, but she tripped and stumbled into the fire. I didn't do it.'

'Tell that to the police.' Enid closed the staring eyes, her fingers gentle. 'Poor creature. She led a terrible hard life with you, Barry Judson, her and your kids. You're a poor excuse for a man and—' She broke off, then asked, 'Where are the children?'

'How the hell should I know? I've only just come back.'

Enid looked round. There was nowhere to hide in the kitchen. She went into the front room, which was empty of furniture, but had a pile of ragged bedding on the floor. She wrinkled her nose in disgust at the foul-smelling mess in a chamber pot in one corner.

She went upstairs and found the children in the back bedroom, which was also bare of furniture. They shrank away to the far corner as she went in, pressing against the wall.

'Don't hit us, missus. We didn't do nothing,' the older one, a little girl, pleaded. She could only be four or five, Enid couldn't remember which. Either way, she was small for her age.

Enid's voice softened and she knelt down to bring herself to their level. 'I won't hit you. Your mammy's fallen over and hurt herself. She wants you to come to my house with me. You'll be safe there.'

The girl shook her head. '*He's* still downstairs. I was watching out of the window for him to go.'

Enid heard rumbling from the little boy's stomach and wondered when they'd last eaten.

'I've got some bread and jam at my house. Would you like a slice?'

They both nodded and the boy licked his lips involuntarily.

She gestured towards the door. 'Come on downstairs, then. I won't let him hurt you again. I'll take you to my house and get you something to eat.'

At the bottom of the stairs which led down between the two rooms, both stopped moving at the sight of their father in the kitchen at the rear. But Judson hardly even glanced in their direction.

Enid turned towards the back of the house as they stood behind her on the two lowest steps. She had been shocked by the sight of their poor little bodies clothed in near rags, even more shocked at how thin their arms and legs were.

And both of them bore several bruises. Her heart clenched. How could anyone treat children so young this badly?

They were holding each other's hands again, looking at her uncertainly, so she spoke softly. 'Do you know where I live?'

They shook their heads.

'The house with the red door opposite the shop.'

The little girl nodded at that.

'Let's go and get that bread and jam.'

They both nodded vigorously. Enid held out her hands and after studying her anxiously for a moment longer, they came down the final step. The little girl took one of her hands and her brother took the other. Such little hands they had, Enid thought as she held them and smiled down reassuringly at the faces lifted to hers.

Judson suddenly seemed to notice them and stared down the hall towards the front door. 'Where are you taking my kids?'

'Away from you.' She looked at the other two women. 'Keep him here. I'll get someone to phone for the police. Don't let him get away.'

Their grimly determined expressions said they didn't need reminding of that.

But Judson was making no attempt to escape. He'd turned back to the hearth and was staring down at his wife's body.

Were those tears trickling down his cheeks? Enid wondered. Was it possible?

The last thing she heard as she took the children away was him saying, 'It was an accident. I'd never have *killed* Minnie.'

When the leader of the thieves regained consciousness he began struggling against the clothes line fastening his hands behind his back and cursing the women surrounding him, and all the sodding bitches in the world with them.

'Shut your mouth or I'll fill it with dirt to match the words coming out of it,' one said.

After struggling in vain, he lay still, scowling.

'You were too confident,' another woman said scornfully.

'Look, I'll give you a pound to let me go.'

The first speaker laughed at him. 'I'd not do it for five pound. I'd rather see thieves like you locked away in jail.'

'We've not stolen anything.'

'What about the truck? I bet your name isn't Entwistle.'

He glared at them. 'Ten pound then.'

'I'd never take dirty money.'

After staring from one to the other and meeting similar disgusted gazes, he said nothing more.

'Do you think Enid's found Judson?' Nina wondered aloud.

'If anyone can catch him, it's her.'

A few minutes later they saw her appear from the alley further up the road with two children holding her hands.

'Those are Judson's children,' one woman said. 'Look! She's taking them into her house.'

'Poor little things,' another woman said. 'If it weren't for Mr Carlisle's milk, bless him, and people slipping them food now and then, those two would've died of neglect years ago. Well, I've give 'em a bite now an' then myself. It's not their fault their parents are thieves. How old are they, three and four? No, the lass must be five now. She was born just after my Ada.'

'They look younger,' Nina said.

Enid came back to her front door and beckoned to them.

Leah took charge. 'Why don't you go and see what she wants, Nina? We'll keep an eye on these thieves.'

Nina looked at her doubtfully, remembering Enid's instructions about taking care of her.

Leah smiled. 'They won't be able to hurt me. They're well and truly tied up now.'

As if to prove her wrong, the leader lashed out with his bound feet, only just missing her. One of the women kicked him where it'd hurt most. He yelped and writhed around.

'I enjoyed doing that,' she told him. 'Please try to escape and give me a reason for another go at you.'

He lay completely still after that.

Nina hurried up the hill and found the door of Wilf and Enid's house standing wide open. She tapped on it.

'Come in!'

She found Enid in the kitchen, cutting slices of bread. The two children were standing next to the table, with eyes for nothing but the food.

'Sit down at the table to eat,' Enid said gently as she scraped a thin layer of margarine on the bread. 'Here's a plate for each of you. No, don't grab and there's no need to stuff it in your mouths like that, either. No one's going to take it away from you. Eat it slowly.'

But they continued to take the biggest bites they could cram in, watching her all the time, clearly afraid of the food being taken away from them again. Eh, what sort of lives had they led?

She gestured to Nina to come out into the hall and said in a low voice, 'Judson's killed his wife. I don't think it was on purpose but she fell and smacked her head on the hearth, so I reckon he must have thumped her.'

'No!'

'Could you go to the shop and ask Lily to call the police? The others will make sure Judson doesn't escape, but I thought it best to get these poor little creatures away. And when you come back from the shop, bring some milk and another loaf. Here's my jug. Tell Lily I'll pay her later. She knows she can trust me.'

Nina gaped at her for a moment as she took in this

information, then picked up the jug and hurried across the road.

There were no customers in the shop, so when Nina had told Lily what had happened, she stood next to the counter and listened to the shopkeeper speaking to someone at the police station from the back room.

Lily poked her head into the shop. 'They're coming as soon as they can get up the hill. The carriage is on its way up but they won't be able to get past it because it takes up most of the road. They want to know if we can keep the men from getting away.'

'Oh, yes. We've got them all tied up.'

Lily passed this information on, then there was the sound of the phone being put down and she came back into the shop. This time she was followed by Cathie and two older women.

It was the child Nina looked at first. 'Are you all right, love?'

'Yes. I can't wait to see my new home, though. I wish Dad had let me go with him.'

'I don't suppose he'll be long.' Nina turned back to pass on her second message to Lily. 'Enid needs some milk for Judson's children and another loaf. She says she'll pay you later. The poor little things are starving.'

'No need to pay for that. I feel sad every time I see those two.' Lily took the ladle from the big milk churn and filled the jug, adding a bag with two buns in it and saying airily, 'They're broken so no use for selling. You might as well take these too.'

'That's kind of you.'

When Enid went back into the kitchen after speaking to Nina, she found the children's plates empty. Judging by the complete lack of crumbs and the faint smears, she suspected they'd licked them clean.

'My friend's bringing you some milk,' she said.

The little girl nodded. 'Thank you, missus.'

The little boy looked weary and after blinking a few times, he put his head down on the table and fell instantly asleep.

The little girl looked at Enid anxiously. 'Sorry, missus. But Mam kept us awake all night coughing, an' we was so hungry Ronnie kept crying.'

It took Enid a minute to remember the girl's name. 'It's all right, Peggy love. You can have a rest too, if you like.'

With a sigh, Peggy put her head down and followed her little brother's example.

As she stared down at the two heads resting on her table, Enid knew exactly what she intended to do once this mess was sorted out.

# 33

Wilf lifted his head. 'What's that noise?'

Harry listened and heard the heavy chugging sound of a large vehicle somewhere nearby. 'I think – surely it's the carriage arriving?'

The stationmaster came to the entrance and beckoned to them.

'They're here, Mr Makepeace. That must be the special lorry. It's much louder than the others. Once they've got the carriage in place, you'll have to take your trolleys round to the side yard. I'm told they have special equipment to get the carriages on and off the lorry. Eh, the driver will have to be good at it to do that job all over the county.'

Harry nodded and asked Todd to help the young constable clear a way through the crowd for their two vehicles.

Todd grinned. 'Happy to. That one will never manage it on his own. Look at him, just standing there like a living lamp post.'

Lenny was already climbing into his tractor and Ben was striding towards his truck. Todd quickly took over clearing their way, asking the policeman to help him, then giving the necessary orders himself.

The younger man seemed happy to do as he was told and was more interested in chatting than doing his job properly. 'That Makepeace chap's rare het up about this, isn't he?'

'Wouldn't you be on edge if this were your home and someone was trying to sabotage it?' Todd asked.

'Sabotage it? What do you mean?'

He explained about the attempt. 'Not very well thought out, but it could have done some harm.'

'Good thing I'm here, then. They won't dare try anything now.' The policeman stood straighter, his eyes raking the crowd.

He looked like a film star from the silent movies over-acting, Todd thought, and stifled a sigh at such youthful optimism. He wished the sergeant were here. Gilbert Deemer could keep order in a madhouse. He was one of the best policemen Todd had ever met.

'I'd never want to live in a railway carriage, though,' the young constable said as they walked forward together waving people back from the entrance to the side street that led to the railway yard. 'Give me a proper house any day.'

Todd didn't bother to tell him that Harry hadn't had much choice about where he lived. He doubted this chap would understand how far desperation to keep a child well and healthy could drive a man. The constable looked to be about twenty and, judging by his plump face, was far too well-fed to comprehend how hard many folk were finding it to keep bread on the table.

It'd be fun to tell Leah about this incident. She'd quickly see the humorous side of it. Then he sighed. He thought about her all too often and he had no right when she wouldn't even have Jonah's child until September.

But he wasn't fooling himself. He was quite sure about that. You could tell when a woman enjoyed your company, just as you could tell when a woman was special and worth courting. Well, you could if you bothered to open your eyes to what the world was like.

Wilf and Harry followed the tractor and the bobbing trolleys round to the far side of the square and down the short street lined only by warehouses and workshops, which led to the railway yard. It had a big turning circle for vehicles at the inner end.

The gates were standing wide open and the lorry that had brought the carriage had already been driven into the yard. It was neatly positioned, leaving the rear end with the carriage on it just outside the entrance.

Wilf was already examining it. 'By hell, that's a big lorry! How did he get it into place so quickly? It's exactly in the centre of the open part, just as you'd want.'

He bent to study the long rear underbelly of the lorry. 'It's an old vehicle, this, and was built in one rigid piece. They design them better these days. If we had one of those newer articulated lorries made by Scammell, we'd be able to get your carriage right up the hill with no worries.'

He considered the lorry again and shook his head sadly. 'They're right, though, not to try to deliver your carriage on this one. It'd not get round the tighter corners on the road at the top end.'

'How the heck can you tell that?' Harry asked.

'I don't know. I just sort of measure it in my head. I can *see* it.' Wilf's hands moved to and fro as if framing something.

A man climbed down from the cab of the huge truck and waited for his companion to join him, then walked back along the side of the railway carriage towards them. 'Mr Makepeace?'

Harry stepped forward. 'That's me.'

'I'm Dan Oakham and this is Ralph, who's helping me. We've brought your little home to you.'

*Little!* Harry thought. If they'd had to live in the shepherd's shelter for a couple of weeks, they'd not even joke about the carriage being small. But he didn't say so. No point in antagonising them.

Dan offered his hand. 'Nice to meet you. There are quite a few people buying these old railway carriages these days, you know. Fortunately for us, people mostly put them in a field at the seaside and use them for holidays or weekends away. Those are easy to deliver. What will you be using yours for up near the moors – country holidays or renting out to hikers? It's all the rage, hiking is. My nephew goes out walking in the countryside every chance he gets.'

When Harry could get a word in edgeways, he answered the main question, 'I'm going to be making a permanent home in this one and it'll be plenty big enough for me and my daughter, I'm sure. I've bought a piece of land to put it on.'

'So no rent to pay. Good thinking.'

Harry introduced Wilf, Ben and Lenny, and they all stood looking up at the carriage. From this close it seemed bigger than he'd remembered. Especially when you thought of getting it all the way up to Ellindale.

'Are you in charge of moving the carriage?' Dan asked.

'No, Wilf here is managing that for me.'

The two men discussed how to set about it and Harry stayed out of their way. He watched his friend go all round the lorry with Dan, examining how the carriage had been built and secured in place. Wilf even got down to lie on the ground under it a couple of times, muttering to himself.

'What I'm not certain of,' he said at last, 'is the *best* way to get the carriage on to my two trolleys. You've had experience of doing this, Dan. I'd really value your advice, if you don't mind.'

'I don't mind at all. I have more respect for people who ask about things they're not familiar with than I have for those who just rush in. We've got four special jacks, if you can call them jacks. They're much bigger than normal with a few extra bits and they do the job pretty well normally. Ralph's getting them set up now. Come and look at them.'

And so it became a quartet walking round the carriage,

gesticulating and working out exactly how to get it off the lorry and on to the first trolley before edging the second trolley in at the rear.

Harry didn't understand half of what they were saying.

When they paused Dan looked at Wilf with respect evident in his expression. 'You seem a capable chap and you've done well with those trolleys for someone without any experience of this sort of activity. There aren't many chaps outside the railways that have your grasp of the problems involved.'

Wilf couldn't hide his pleasure at this compliment. 'I enjoy working out how to fit things together.'

'I can see you do. It's a gift, that is. There are a lot of cack-handed idiots around who couldn't set a cup straight on a saucer. Your trolleys will be fine as long as they hold the weight, and I reckon they ought to, from the looks of them.'

He studied them again. 'In fact, you've probably made them stronger than you need, but I'd do the same. Can't be too careful. And they're neatly put together too.'

'I just followed the old rule: measure twice, cut once.'

'Well, we can help you get the carriage transferred on to the trolleys. I'd have had to refuse to hand it over if you hadn't had something suitable to put it on. It'll probably take us about an hour.'

Harry had been standing to one side, but he was surprised by this and couldn't help asking, 'You can do it that quickly?'

'Unless anything goes wrong. And it doesn't usually. We've had a bit of practice at this.'

Dan and Ralph set to work, including Wilf in what they were doing as smoothly as if the three of them were used to working as a team.

Harry found himself relegated to the job of occasional labourer or spare pair of hands.

Lenny stood near his tractor, fidgeting around for a while,

but grew tired of waiting so called out that he was going to the café to buy a pot of tea and something to eat and he'd be back in half an hour.

Todd came along the street to help at one stage, leaving the constable on his own. But without Todd's presence, the spectators gradually crept forward, and after a few minutes Dan yelled to the observers to 'keep those ruddy spectators away', so Todd had to take over the job of keeping people back again.

Ben joined him and they patrolled the end of the short street, doing far more to keep nosey-parkers at bay than the young policeman, who merely moved to and fro, from time to time calling out nervously, 'Now, now. Do keep back, *if* you please!'

'He must be very new to the job,' Todd muttered.

'Still wet behind the ears,' Ben agreed.

Gradually, the end of the carriage was moved from the lorry on to the first trolley, using makeshift rollers on the bed of the lorry. Then the vehicle was driven very slowly forward into the yard, again using the rollers to get the carriage off it and on to the jacks. Once the carriage was stable, the second trolley was rolled into place at the end and the jacks were removed.

After that the three men stood back, smiling and nodding at one another.

'How's that, Harry lad?' Wilf called over his shoulder.

'Marvellous.' Harry walked round the carriage, jumping up and down a couple of times to try to peer through the windows, but they were too high as well as dirty and he was unable to see anything inside it clearly. He wondered how he could make sure everything was in the same condition as when he'd bought it.

Dan guessed what he was thinking. 'Better not climb inside

while it's on those trolleys.' He looked at the jacks lying against a wall now. 'You know what? We aren't due to move on from Rivenshaw till morning, because we had to start work before dawn today to fit in another job and we're part way to our next job here. So if you can promise to get the jacks back to us by seven o'clock tomorrow morning at the latest, Wilf, I'll lend them to you.'

'You're sure? It won't get you in trouble?'

'He's the—' Ralph started, but Dan elbowed him in the ribs.

'Eh, that'll make a big difference. I can't thank you enough.'

Harry watched Dan and Wilf shake hands to seal the bargain. The two of them seemed to have got on particularly well, as if they spoke a language others didn't, a language that involved a lot of gesticulating and estimating things visually 'by rack o'th'eye' before they confirmed details by actual measuring.

Harry felt more hopeful as he looked at the carriage and Wilf's smiling face.

Perhaps things were going to work out all right.

While they were completing the transfer of the carriage to the trolleys, Charlie Willcox came to join Todd. 'Is everything going well?' He looked and sounded subdued, not at all like his usual ebullient self.

'Yes. Those chaps know what they're doing.' Todd frowned at him. '*You* don't look so spry, though. What's up?'

'I'll explain later. I just wanted to see Harry about something, but he's busy, so could you tell him that I'd appreciate his help with something urgent.'

'What with?'

There was a shout and Todd spun round. 'Look, I'll come round later and you can tell me all about it. This next part of the job is going to need all hands on deck, so to speak.'

'Yes. Yes, of course. I might drive up and talk to Leah about . . . things. It involves her and the fizzy drinks factory.'

'Don't go today. We're taking the carriage up the hill and we'll be travelling along very slowly. There won't be room for another vehicle to pass us up near Ellindale.'

'Oh. I see. Well, I'll leave you to it and you won't forget to come round tonight, will you, and you will ask Harry to get in touch with me? I need a few electrical repair jobs doing and it really is urgent. I'll pay him well for some help.'

'I'll tell him. He'll be interested in that. What happened to the other fellow?'

'He left suddenly.'

Todd watched his friend walk away. He had never seen Charlie look so strained. Then Wilf called out and he pushed that worry to the back of his mind and went to help. First things first.

It took a surprising number of men to help manoeuvre the carriage out of the street and guide it through the town centre.

Now definitely wasn't the time to tell Harry about the job offer. There might be a good chance of regular work for him if Todd had guessed correctly. But his friend had other things on his mind at the moment and could hardly string two words together for worrying about today's job.

The tractor made its ponderous way through the centre of Rivenshaw, pulling its load, sometimes guided or braced by helpers as it went round corners. Men with nothing better to occupy their time actually jostled one another to do something useful.

At first most of the crowd followed them, oohing and aahing, pointing out details on the carriage to one another. But gradually, once they'd seen as much as they wanted, most of them dropped back. If the slopes up the valley hadn't been so gentle and the day pleasantly sunny, Wilf reckoned more of the others would have dropped back too.

The tractor moved slowly but seemed to have no difficulty pulling the load. For a while Harry and Wilf walked beside it, watching every sway of the carriage at bumpy places on the road, listening to every rattle and clank of the trolleys and their chains.

'I'll carry on walking next to it,' Wilf said after the first mile. 'You ride with Ben.'

'Are you sure?' Harry asked.

'Yes. You look exhausted. I bet you didn't sleep last night.'

'Not much.'

Wilf patted his shoulder. 'We'll get it there for you, lad.'

Harry was weary so he fell back and climbed into the cab of the small lorry.

'I'm a bit tired,' he said. 'Do you mind if I ride with you for a while, Ben?'

'Not at all.'

'I didn't expect Todd to stay with us so far.'

'He's going to follow us right up to Ellindale. He'll probably enjoy a chat with Leah and he wants to join in the fun.'

*Fun!* Harry thought. He'd never had less fun in his life.

# 34

It surprised Harry how many people, mostly men and youths, continued to follow the carriage up the hill. It seemed to take forever to reach Birch End and he groaned as he found locals lining the route there as well. This was going to be hard enough without spectators, who were bound to call out and interfere.

He knew Charlie Willcox lived in this village, but somewhere further back from the road, among the posher houses. He'd not had time to explore that end yet. To his surprise, Charlie's wife was among the spectators and beckoned to him.

'Go on. Jump down and have a quick word with her,' Ben said. 'I'll drive more slowly till you get back. Don't be too long, though.'

Harry didn't waste his time on greetings. 'What is it?'

'I know you need to keep an eye on the carriage but there are two things you ought to know. Look, I'll walk along with you as I explain.'

'Go on.'

'First, my Charlie's in desperate trouble at the new shop and he needs your help with the electrical side of things. After today, do you think you could nip down to see him, set his mind at rest? Even before you start work on your carriage? I know it's asking a lot but he'll pay you well.'

'I will if I can. If nothing goes wrong with this.'

'Well, the railway carriage is the other thing. Early this

morning my maid's younger brother saw some men in a big car driving up the hill, followed by a van, but he couldn't see who was in that. He didn't like the looks of them. He reads a lot of spy stories, and that makes him very fanciful but this time it's a good thing he followed them. He managed to get quite close without them seeing him. He says a group of men got out of the van as well as those in the car. There was an old man sitting in the car, who didn't get out but gave the orders.'

'Go on.' Harry didn't like the sound of this.

'My brother could hear them clearly and told me they were talking about being paid by the old man to lie in wait for you and damage the carriage so that it couldn't be used as a home. They were laughing about it too, saying it'd be easy money.'

'Did he say what the old man looked like?'

'Bald, with a big nose.'

'*What?* Thanks for that. I'd better tell Wilf.' He started to move forward, but she pulled him back.

'I know you'll need to sort that out first and get the carriage in place, but please, Harry, can you go and see Charlie tomorrow? I've never seen him so upset as he's been lately.'

He wasn't going to turn down the chance of a job. 'I'll go and see Mr Willcox as soon as the carriage is in place, I promise. Thanks again for the warning.'

'It may not be anything – lads invent tales or exaggerate what they've seen – but you'd best make sure.'

It didn't sound like a made-up tale to Harry. Old man, she'd said. From the description it could be Trowton. Well, who else hated him? The man must have gone mad to go to such extremes to get him back to work in the factory, if that was what this was about.

He ran on and clambered back up into the cabin of Ben's truck. He didn't settle, but told him quickly what Mrs Willcox had said, then got out again and ran forward to speak to Wilf, who was still walking near the lumbering, slow-moving tractor and its load, sometimes at the side of it, other times behind it, keeping an eye on the trolleys.

When he heard what Marion Willcox had found out, Wilf's face grew grim. 'We're getting to the most difficult part of the journey, where the road narrows and there's a steep drop on the right. If anyone is going to try to stop us, that's where they'll do it, or at least it's where I'd choose if I were that sort of rogue. I'd better go ahead and see if they're there and if so, whether they've done any damage.'

'You're not going on your own,' Harry said.

'No. I'll be taking some of the lads with me. I won't let anyone spoil this for you, or for me either. I'm proud of how it's gone so far, and I'm not letting anyone take that away from me. You don't get much to be proud of in times like these.'

The men who came forward to join them when Wilf beckoned included the ones who'd been helping keep order in the square. He began to give them low-voiced orders. After a few moments one of the younger chaps ran back to collect a couple of his friends and beckon to a lad near the rear of the procession. The lad listened intently to Wilf and scrambled up some rough sloping ground at the left side of the road, disappearing from sight among the low vegetation and rocks.

A horn tooted from behind the group and people moved to the sides of the road to allow a car through, which pulled up behind Todd's van.

'That's Sergeant Deemer!' Wilf exclaimed in relief. 'Eh, I'm glad to see him. It'll be good to have a policeman with us if there's trouble, and he's one of the best. Go and tell him what Marion said.'

When Harry brought Deemer up to date, the sergeant

grew loudly indignant. 'They're not going to cause trouble like that on *my* patch.'

'Were you wanting to see someone in Ellindale?'

'The women there seem to have captured some thieves.'

'No one's hurt?'

'None of the women anyway. Oh look. We'd better move on. I'll have to follow your carriage.'

'It's turning into a right old circus, isn't it?' Wilf murmured when Harry moved to join him at the front and tell him what Deemer was doing there instead of getting back in the truck with Ben.

'Mmm.' Harry was beyond words, but not beyond readiness to act.

It seemed an anti-climax when they started again and kept moving as slowly as ever. It really fretted him to be going so slowly. If something bad was going to happen, he wanted to get it faced and defeated.

The lad came scrambling down the hillside to their left and ran to tell Wilf what he'd seen from above the road ahead. 'They've dug out the ground round the second bend from here. They've made the road narrower.' He frowned. 'Why have they done that? What if the carriage can't get through? What if it falls over the edge?'

'That'll be what they're after,' Wilf said. 'Some folk are born bad and some of the bad ones are rich enough to pay others to commit crimes that benefit them. Always keep your eyes open for bad folk, young fellow, and keep away from them.'

The boy listened to this advice and nodded solemnly.

'Notice owt else?'

'There's a chap on watch nearer to us.'

'He'll be to let them know when we're nearly there, I should think.'

'Yes. But there's something strange: an old fellow is sitting in a car watching them. He's not doing anything, just watching. He isn't moving at all.'

'Isn't he now?'

Wilf went to ask Lenny to stop the tractor and pretend to be fixing something, then he beckoned the sergeant, Harry, Ben and Todd across to join him and made a suggestion as to how they should tackle this problem.

The lad keeping watch on the road from the southern end of Ellindale village, in order to let Leah know when the railway carriage was in sight, didn't see the man approaching because he felt safe behind a dry stone wall. The first thing he knew was when he was grabbed from behind and thumped a couple of times as the man questioned him.

He couldn't understand what this stranger was doing here, but the man had thumped him for nothing, so he wasn't going to tell him anything. He insisted he was on his own, watching for the tractor pulling the carriage to come into sight because he wanted to be the first person from Ellindale to see it. The man thumped him a couple more times but that only made him more stubborn and he didn't change his story.

They tied him up and dumped him a short way up from the road. He was furious with himself at being caught like that. Alf Tupper wouldn't have been so stupid. Alf was his favourite hero in the magazine *The Boy's Own Paper*, which he sometimes managed to read at the library.

He waited but the men didn't come back, so he started wriggling about. It took longer than he'd expected but he managed to get his arms free. They didn't know as much about knots as he did and had tied him up sloppily. It took him a while longer to untie the rope round his ankles because they'd taken his penknife.

He was terrified they'd come back and catch him trying to escape. They might not be content to thump him next time; they might kill him. But he wasn't letting Mrs Willcox down. She was relying on him to keep watch.

When he got free, he checked that no one was in sight and crawled carefully along the ground at the top, keeping out of sight as much as he could.

No shouts followed him and when he'd got far enough away from the men still working on the verge at the lower side of the road, he risked standing up and ran as fast as he could to Farmer Kerkham's house, which was the nearest.

He was even glad when Mr Kerkham stepped out from behind a building, caught hold of him and threatened to give him a good thumping for trespassing.

'What are you doing here, lad?' he roared

'There's some men down the road planning to stop the carriage and push it down the hill! Honest, Mr Kerkham. I'm not fibbing.'

The farmer studied his face, frowning.

'I'm not lying, honest I'm not. There's a lot of them, about eight I think.'

'I'll come with you and heaven help you if you're telling me lies.'

Enid came down the hill just before the boy reached the plot of land. She'd left the two Judson children in the kitchen under the watchful eye of an elderly neighbour. A promise of more bread and jam for dinner would keep them there, she was sure.

Some of the other younger women asked where she was going and decided to join her to 'watch the fun', as they put it, and before they'd gone far, Leah caught up with them, followed two minutes later by Nina and Cathie. The group stopped just below the village when they saw Mr Kerkham coming across his field towards the road, with his hand firmly on the shoulder of a lad.

'Something wrong, Mr Kerkham?' Enid asked.

'This lad says he's seen some mischief being planned, says some fellows are trying to stop your menfolk from bringing that carriage up here.'

After the lad had told his story again, the women looked at one another.

'Who are they?' Leah asked. 'Did you recognise any of them?'

The lad shook his head. 'They're not from round here and the old man is dressed posh. He was sitting in a big car, watching. It's an ambush just like in the cowboy films an' I reckon they're going to push the carriage down the hill. They've dug up some of the wall and the side of the road already.'

Nina frowned. 'What does the man in the car look like?'

'Bald, bit of scraggy ginger hair round by his ears, an' a great big nose.'

'How could you tell all that from a distance?'

He shrugged. 'I got good eyesight an' I was looking at him from the side so you couldn't miss the nose.'

Cathie said at once, 'That sounds like Mr Trowton. My dad used to work for him and he's a horrible man.'

The lad nodded. 'I heard one of them call him Mr Trowton.'

Enid smiled, looking rather like a cat about to play with a mouse. 'I reckon we should go and join in the fun, give them devils a shock. What do you say, girls?'

The other women all nodded or said yes.

'Not you, Leah,' Enid patted her stomach suggestively.

'I know.'

'We can't leave you on your own, though.'

'Cathie will stay with me, won't you, love?'

'I want to help Dad.'

'You might get in his way.'

After a short silence, Cathie sighed and agreed to go back with Mrs Willcox.

Peter Kerkham looked at the men still lying on the ground on Harry's land. They might have been tied up but that didn't stop them wriggling about when they thought no one was looking or glaring at the group of women.

'I never was any good at fighting.' He raised his voice so that the men could hear him clearly. 'What I'll do instead is get my shotgun and stay with Mrs Willcox and Cathie. I can pepper them thieving sods good and proper if they try to escape. Or I could hit them over the head if they looked like getting free of the ropes. That'd teach them a lesson. I'll bring my cudgel as well, *and* my wife can join us with the poker.'

He turned and tramped off towards his farm without waiting for an answer.

Enid hid a smile. 'Right then, girls. That's settled. We'll put a couple of rocks in our pockets just in case we get attacked on the way.'

'Can I come with you, missus?' the lad pleaded.

'No. I want you to help look after these men. Find a big stick and if any of them try to escape, hit them good and hard.'

He cheered up visibly. 'Yes, missus. I can do that.'

'Come on,' Enid ordered. 'There's no time to waste. You and me will go down the road openly, Gladys, then they may not notice the others at first.'

The group of shabbily dressed young women set off, striding down the road to the bend. Before they got there all of them except Enid and Gladys slipped up the hillside.

The two remaining women walked boldly down the centre of the road, pretending to chat to one another. But their apron pockets were weighed down by stones and they each held one rock in their hand, hidden by the folds of their skirts.

'They'd better not mess with me,' Enid muttered. 'I've had enough of this.'

'I agree,' Gladys echoed. 'The women in the town may be softies but we aren't. If I can wrestle a sheep down to shear it, I reckon I can deal with any man attacking me.'

# 35

Wilf kept his eyes open as he led four of the valley men further up the hill to seek out the strangers. But even though they were watchful, an attack seemed to erupt suddenly from each side as they got to the bend and they could do nothing but try to fight the others off. The melee quickly turned vicious.

His observers had seen only a couple of strangers and the leader, so he hoped to outnumber them and end the fight quickly, but there were more than that.

Then he heard someone yell in a deep, hoarse voice, 'Get the carriage!'

Other men appeared from behind the van and Wilf cursed under his breath as they ran on down the hill past him and his companions. It was impossible to follow them until they'd fought off the others, so he could only hope his friends would cope.

Anger seemed to lend him strength and he knocked down his opponent and turned to follow the second group of attackers. The latter were using any dirty trick to kick and punch their way through to the carriage and one man was doubled up holding his groin.

Sergeant Deemer blew his whistle hard, and yelled at the top of his voice to stop in the name of the law, but the strangers ignored that. Two managed to get to the side of the carriage nearest the drop down the hill. Before anyone could stop them, they began yanking and slashing at the ropes holding it in place, trying to rock it so that it would fall off and roll down the hill at the side.

When the carriage began to sway, Wilf redoubled his efforts to reach those men but couldn't get round to that side. But to his relief there weren't enough of them to dislodge it from the trolleys and the rest of the valley men were managing to keep the other strangers away from that side.

Then someone fired a rifle. Men who'd fought in the Great War would never mistake the sound of a shot. As the bullet hit the carriage, the valley men froze briefly, because this was taking the fight to another level and none of them was armed. They dived instinctively for the nearest cover as most of them had throughout the Great War, and the attackers yelled in triumph.

Harry bent and picked up a stone, hurling it at the man who was raising the gun and taking aim again. As the stone hit his shoulder, the man swung round, aiming the weapon at Harry now.

It was Todd who saved Harry's life, by diving at his legs and dragging him down on the ground out of the way. The second shot missed, but whizzed too close above them for comfort. That was another sound you couldn't mistake.

Another shot missed them by an even narrower margin as they wriggled hastily backwards.

'I reckon that sod must have been a marksman in the war,' Todd muttered. 'Let's see if we can take cover below the edge of the road.'

But suddenly a stone arced through the air from the other side of the fray and hit the man with the gun on the back, making him jerk round in shock. He covered a potential enemy with a sweep of his rifle but there was no one in sight.

'Who the hell threw that?' Harry exclaimed. 'We've no one up there.'

Whoever had thrown the stone must have ducked out of sight again.

Then a woman yelled, 'Now!' and several stones rained down on the strangers at once, again from the upper side of the group.

'It's the women.' Todd watched another stone hit an attacker on the back of his head. 'Eh, well thrown!'

That voice sounded like my Enid, Wilf thought, taking advantage of the distraction to run up to the leader and punch him in the face. The marksman tried to raise his gun again, but another defender was there with a stick, knocking it out of his hand. Fortunately none of the other strangers seemed to be armed with guns, only the leader.

Gradually, with the help of the women, the attackers were driven back to their van and car by sheer weight of numbers. One of them tried to start the van but was dragged out of the driving seat by two screeching women.

Another attacker opened the door of the big car and tried to get into the driving seat, but Enid rushed up behind him and dragged him back by the hair, thrusting him face down on the ground with the help of Gladys and Nina.

Two of the men got away by hurling themselves down the steep hill, somehow managing not to fall, and then running off across the moors. Surprise gave them enough of a start to allow them to get away.

The rest were captured and then formally arrested by Deemer.

All this time the old man in the big car had sat staring vacantly ahead of him.

It was Enid who crept round the car to look at him more closely and guessed what had happened.

When her husband came rushing to her aid, she said sharply, 'I'm all right. I think this one's had a seizure and that's why he's just sitting there. Look at the way one side of his mouth's drooping and he doesn't seem aware of what's happening.'

As Harry came up to join them, Wilf snapped his fingers in front of the man's face. 'It must be a massive seizure. He's not reacting to anything.'

'It's Trowton,' Harry said. 'The man I used to work for. Serve him damned well right. He always was a nasty sod. He was doing this to get back at me for not working for him, I reckon. He threatened several times that he would make me regret it if I stopped looking after his machinery.'

'Well, he didn't succeed,' Wilf said. 'How the hell much did the idiot spend on it? He must have been insane. As if he couldn't find other men to repair his machines. There are dozens of engineers out of work. And in the end, I doubt he even saw what happened.'

Deemer came up to find out what was going on and looked at the motionless figure. 'I've seen it before: old people acting strangely for a while, then having a seizure of some sort, and either dying or losing their wits entirely. I suppose we'll have to take him to the hospital in Rivenshaw, but they'll not be able to do anything for him. As he can't even move, I'll make sure the remaining men are secured and carted away first.'

He turned to Wilf. 'By heaven, they're a rough lot. Give them the slightest opportunity and they start struggling to escape. I recognise one or two of them. They're from Backshaw Moss.'

'Those streets should have been knocked down years ago. They're a breeding ground for criminals and disease.'

'You don't have to tell me that; tell the Rivenshaw Town Council.' He studied the prisoners again. 'Others are complete strangers to me. Someone's brought them in.'

Wilf pointed. 'That one seemed to be the leader.'

Deemer turned to study the man. 'He refuses to say a

word. Oh well, he can't keep quiet for ever. Ben's lending me his truck to take them down to the police station, but I'll have to phone for help from the regional inspector. There are too many for me and my constable to manage. Ben's going to stay here with you and let another fellow drive the truck for me, in case you need his help. I've co-opted a couple of locals as special constables, who're happy to earn a few shillings.'

'Right, then. I'd better have a careful look at that carriage now,' Wilf said. 'They cut some of the ropes and tried to pull it out of balance. We don't want it falling off the trolley when we start moving it again.'

'I'll be back to pick up the old fellow and drive their vehicles away. Can you move them out of your way?'

'Oh, yes. We've enough men who can drive. We'll park them in the village square once you've taken the old fellow away.'

Lenny had locked himself in the tractor cab as soon as the fighting started and only got down when he was sure it was over.

After Deemer had left, Wilf and Harry went across to join him and they all studied the edge of the road at the lower side. The attackers had knocked down part of the retaining wall and dug some of the soft ground of the verge away, making the road too narrow for the carriage to pass that point safely. As there was quite a steep drop on the lower side, any vehicle slipping over the edge, or pushed over it, would go bouncing down the hill.

'I'm not even trying to move the carriage till the road's fixed up,' Lenny said. 'If that edge gives way, my tractor would go over as well.'

Men came forward and women too, gathering round and staring down the slope, then turning to call out to Wilf and Harry.

'Tell us what to do.'

'How can we help?'

'What should we move first?'

Harry was deeply touched by this.

'Give me a minute or two to work it all out. Someone find Ben and tell him he's needed here,' Wilf said and they fell silent, waiting.

He moved to and fro, studying the ground that had been disturbed, then rolled his sleeves up, ignoring his bruises and grazes, just as others were ignoring black eyes or split lips. He moved carefully along the damaged wall, studying it and the soft, scattered earth that had been dug out of the verge.

Ben joined him at the edge and the two conferred about the damage.

After a few moments Wilf called loudly, 'If a few of you can collect the stones knocked out of the wall from down the slope, or other stones that might fit, Ben's going to build up the retaining wall at the edge of the road again. Do what he tells you.'

There was nodding and then some of the nimbler ones clambered down the slope while others waited patiently.

'We'll need to brace the land along the edge of the road with some smaller rocks and earth as well as rebuilding the retaining wall,' Ben said. 'Look out for some bigger, smoother stones, and smaller ones for filling gaps as well. And we'll need some shovels.'

'Does tha' know how to build a dry stone wall?' an older man asked.

'I helped wallers build them for farmers when I was a lad, and I know how to fit rocks together solidly without mortar. It'll take me longer than it would a real waller, though.'

He began to move the fallen stones and the others followed suit.

Enid and another woman carried some shovels across. She

too was displaying a couple of bruises on her arm and face. 'Well, at least those fellows have left us some shovels. Me and the other women have collected them and we can help dig as well. We were none of us brought up soft.'

Wilf gave her a quick hug. 'I can always rely on you, lass.'

For a moment Harry had to fight not to give way to his emotions, he was so grateful, then he managed to steady his voice and say, 'Just tell me what to do.'

Wilf slung his free arm round Harry's shoulders as well as keeping hold of Enid. 'Let's move back a bit and let Ben manage this. Cheer up, lad. I think your main troubles are over now. I doubt there's another bunch of lunatics running round attacking people.'

'Thank goodness!'

'How about you go up to the village and tell folk what's happened, Harry, then go to The Shepherd's Rest and ask Don and Izzy if they can supply us with food when we've finished. There are enough people willing to use their muscles here. It'd be only fair to feed them afterwards, don't you think? Anything will do. They're not fussy.'

'Good idea. I'm happy to pay for that. They're a grand bunch.'

'They are that!'

'Take Nina with you,' Enid said. 'She copped a nasty thump on her left arm and she's moving it carefully. We don't need her to dig, because there are plenty of others. It'd be good to have someone to keep an eye on the village, though, and on Mrs Willcox especially. We tried to keep her away from the fighting but who knows what she'll do now? She's quiet but as stubborn as they come when she wants to do something. She won't like being left out of this.'

Harry didn't quibble. He knew Wilf and the other men were stronger than him physically, and besides, this was something only he could do, pay for a meal. The helpers would find good solid food waiting for them when they finished for the day, he vowed. Surely the baker could send up enough bread by his delivery lad on a bicycle till cars could get through to the village again?

'I'll be back in time to see you move the carriage,' he called as he set off. 'Send someone to fetch me if I'm still up there.'

Ben lifted up another larger stone, hefting it in his hands. 'Before you go, Harry, you should know that the wall might not be finished till tomorrow. I need to get it right. That carriage is a heavy load and the road is at its narrowest here.'

Harry hadn't expected that long a delay and couldn't help muttering, 'Oh, hell. What next?' under his breath as he walked up the hill.

At The Shepherd's Rest Harry made arrangements for the people working on the retaining wall to be fed. This sent Don hurrying across to the shop to phone the baker to send him up some loaves and cakes, and then he bought some corned beef for sandwiches from Lily.

Nina collected Cathie as they reached Mr Kerkham, who was still watching the prisoners on Harry's plot of land. 'Sergeant Deemer says he'll come back for them next. He'll have to bring enough men to march them down, because he won't be able to get Ben's truck through this far yet.'

'I thought we'd be going back to the railway carriage now it's safe, Dad,' Cathie said. 'I haven't even seen it yet.'

Harry didn't really want her near it, in case things went wrong, but he could hardly deny her the chance to look at it when most of the village had already seen the outside of it at least.

'You go back to the carriage, Harry. I know you're itching to help with the work. I'll walk down with Cathie in a little while,' Nina said. 'I'll just have to get something to drink, love, and put some sticking plaster on this cut. It keeps opening up again and bleeding all over me. After that we'll follow your dad back down.'

Harry took her arm without thinking and studied the cut. 'You need to bind it together tightly.' His eyes met hers and for a moment he found it hard to breathe, then Cathie brought him back down to earth.

'Aww! I want to see inside my new home.'

'You won't be able to get inside the carriage yet, love, even if you do go down there,' Harry warned. 'No one will till everything is secure.'

She let out an aggrieved sigh.

He exchanged smiles with Nina at the expression on his daughter's face. 'Thank you, lass. I don't know what I'd have done without your help.'

She blushed so fiercely he couldn't think what to say next, so muttered something about 'getting back to it' and strode off down the hill.

# 36

When he reached the carriage, Harry found people still working hard, both men and women, following orders from Wilf and Ben. The wall was taking shape but not as quickly as he'd hoped. He took his turn at shovelling dirt behind what was left of the lower part of the wall, obeying Wilf or Ben's orders. They got a layer of earth in the gap and trampled it down, but more would be needed as the wall grew higher.

Unfortunately daylight was starting to fade. Ben was right. There was too much to make good again, and they couldn't possibly finish it before night fell.

When he looked round, Harry was surprised to see how many other people from the village had come out to have a look now the danger was over. It was mostly the older or very young ones who strolled down the road and often lingered to watch. He went across to Wilf to ask whether to ask them to move further back.

'No. They're doing no harm and they don't have much excitement in their lives these days.'

*Excitement!* Harry thought glumly.

He saw one of the older men coming towards them. 'Sorry, but we need to keep this space clear,' he said apologetically.

'Not from me, tha doesn't. I'm a waller.'

There was a shout from Wilf. 'Clarry Braddon! I thought you'd gone to live with your daughter in Rochdale.'

'I couldn't thole living in a town, felt as if I was suffocating, so I came back to live with my cousins instead. I can still do enough to earn my keep an' I get the old age pension so I'm not a burden. I've only been here a few days. Eh, what a thing to happen!' He jerked his head in the direction of the wall. 'Need any help?'

'Help like yours? I can't think of anything we need more at the moment than your advice and guidance. Ben! Come and meet Clarry Braddon, best waller we've ever had in the valley. He moved away before you came to live here.'

'I've heard you mentioned, Mr Braddon.' Ben jumped up and came to shake hands.

'Nay, just call me Clarry.'

In no time the two men were chatting, then the old man took off his jacket and rolled up his sleeves. 'I'm not just here to talk. Th'art not doing badly considering, lad, but I can do better. It'll want to be good and strong, that wall will, and retaining walls are a bit different from free-standing ones. We'll lean the copestones inwards, like they do in Cornwall, so that the grass roots can grow between and over them, and make it all stronger. A good wall should be built to *last*, tha knows.'

The old man's smile said how happy he was to be needed.

There was the sound of a vehicle approaching and Harry saw that Sergeant Deemer had returned for the rest of the prisoners. As he walked towards him, he caught sight of the special heavy-duty railway jacks lashed to the back of the tractor. Oh, no! He was supposed to get them back to Dan by seven o'clock in the morning.

He turned to Wilf. 'What are we going to do about returning the jacks to Dan?'

'Hell fire! I'd forgotten them. We definitely won't be finished with them by then. We'll still be building the wall.'

They fell silent for a moment or two, then Harry said, 'I'll ask Sergeant Deemer if he can get word to Dan about what's happened. I'm not even going to try to return them. We need them desperately.'

He went across to explain to the sergeant what the problem was and Deemer promised to tell Dan about it when he went back into Rivenshaw with the other group of prisoners from the village. 'Now, I need some special constables to help me take the prisoners in from Harry's land. A couple will need to be able to drive, and you'll get paid for it.'

There was no shortage of volunteers, so Deemer chose some men and went up to deal with the final group of villains.

Which left another worry sitting on Harry's shoulders. He felt guilty about forgetting the jacks, when Dan had been generous enough to lend them to him, but as Wilf said, their need was desperate so he wasn't going to return them yet, even if he got fined for keeping them too long.

A short time later Harry saw a small group coming down the road from the village, pushing something in an old wheel-barrow that creaked and groaned. The contents looked heavy but he couldn't at first make out what they were.

Nina and his daughter were walking behind the group and Mrs Willcox was walking at the side of the barrow. An older man and woman were wheeling it and struggling to keep it from running away from them on this steeper part of the road. He hurried forward to help them hold the thing steady. It was filled with bottles making a sloshing sound.

'We thought you'd all need something to drink, so we filled some of my bottles with spring water,' Mrs Willcox said.

'What a good idea!'

They stopped the wheelbarrow a few yards uphill from the tractor and waited for Wilf's attention.

How we all depend on him! Harry thought.

But at that moment Wilf was watching intently as Clarry

and Ben put some particularly large stones in place. There were already bigger ones laid to remake the foundation of the wall that had held the edge of the road back for as long as anyone could remember.

'My great-granfer laid these stones,' Clarry said. 'And it wasn't till my father was getting old that they needed more than a touch of maintenance. You can't beat a good stone wall. It'll outlast the man who builds it, give better shelter than a hedge and it won't burn if there are fires in a dry summer.'

From the way Wilf and some of the other men smiled, they must have heard Clarry say that more than once, but they all murmured agreement and let him continue talking.

It was a few minutes before they'd finished that section of the foundation to Clarry's satisfaction, and only then did Wilf come across to them.

'Mrs Willcox! I hope those bottles mean you've brought us a drink of water.'

'We have indeed.' She handed him a bottle and he took a big swallow of it.

'We won't be able to work much longer, I'm afraid.' He looked regretfully up at the setting sun.

'The carriage will still be here in the morning,' Clarry called. 'And so will the stones.'

Ben came across to get bottles of water for himself and the old waller. 'You can learn a lot from an old chap like Clarry. It's an ill wind . . . I'm glad for a chance to work with him.'

Clarry clapped his hands together to get the worst of the dirt off them before accepting the bottle. 'It's too dim for me to work. I need a good strong light to see things these days. I'll be back at first light tomorrow, lads.'

'Thank you, Clarry,' Harry called.

'We'll get your new home there tomorrow, lad, and I'll take

a look at your retaining walls for it as I go back. There'll still be enough light to make sure they're strong enough.'

With a final nod, he walked off up the hill and another old chap fell into place beside him. They walked slowly, backs bowed by age, white hair sticking out untidily below their cloth caps.

Wilf stared at them. 'I'd like to carve two figures like them. And I will one day.' Then he brought his mind back to the business at hand. 'We'll post some men to keep watch and start work again at dawn. I'll stay here overnight if you like.'

Harry shook his head. 'You've worked hard and we'll all be depending on you tomorrow. I'll stay here and you get a decent night's sleep.'

'All right. But wake me up if there's an urgent message to get those jacks back before morning.' He stood considering this, head on one side. 'I don't think he'll take them away from you, though. He's a decent chap, Dan is. He knows how desperately you need them. You can't find jacks like that anywhere else but on the railways.'

Harry looked round at the people who'd now stopped work and clapped his hands to get their attention. 'I've ordered some sandwiches from The Shepherd's Rest to thank you for your help. Wilf, can you send some sandwiches down to those who stay here with me? Good. Luckily, it doesn't look like rain.'

'I'll collect some blankets and send them down with the sandwiches,' Enid said.

He turned to Nina. 'Could you keep an eye on Cathie for me tonight?'

'Of course I can. We've plenty of spare beds in the hostel.'

'Can I just walk round the outside of the carriage now, Dad? I can at least see the outside closer,' Cathie pleaded.

'Of course you can, love. Come on.'

'Why did those men try to ruin it?'

'Mr Trowton hired them because he wanted to force me back, or else out of spite.'

'I don't want to go back, not ever. I saw his car, you know. He was sitting there not moving. Is he dead?'

'No, love. But he's had a seizure and I doubt he'll recover. Sergeant Deemer is taking him to hospital soon.'

'Mr Trowton was a bad man. Mrs Pyne hated him.'

'And she had good cause. He treated her badly when she worked for him and sacked her for no reason.'

Harry took his child slowly round the carriage, explaining what was inside and lifting her up to look in through a couple of the windows, though it was too dim to make out details. When he pointed out the small window of the toilet compartment, she brightened.

'Does that mean we'll have an inside lavvy?'

'Yes, love. Well, we will, once I've connected it and dug a connection to the sewage line from the village.'

'Ooh, goody.' At the front part of the carriage she stopped to ask, 'What's that little hole for?'

'It's where one of those men shot at us earlier on. That's why I couldn't risk you coming down here sooner.'

Her eyes grew big and round. 'Ooh! How exciting! A bullet hole! Can we leave it where it is, so I can show my friends? I've made one friend already in the village when we get our milk and Alice says there are other girls I'll get on with at school.'

'We're definitely not leaving the hole.'

'Awww.'

Harry walked up to the village with her and left her with Nina. Eh, it was lovely to hear his little Cathie talking like a normal child, looking rosy for the first time in ages, even pouting and disagreeing with him instead of being lethargic.

★

Before Harry went back down to the carriage, he called in at the shop. Lily came out from the back. 'Oh, good. There you are, Mr Makepeace. I have a message for you from Mr Oakham. Can you please phone him on this number? It's the place he's staying at. You'll have to come through to the back to phone.'

Harry's heart sank and he followed her into the living quarters. Dan must want the jacks back. 'I'm so sorry to disturb you.'

'I don't mind. I like to help people. I just charge them a bit more than what it costs me for a phone call usually. A halfpenny here and there mounts up.'

He got through to the number and then had to wait for the man who answered to bring Dan to the phone.

The booming voice made him jump. 'How's it going, Harry lad?'

'All right but it's taking much longer than we expected. Did Sergeant Deemer tell you about the attack?'

'Yes. And look, you can keep the jacks for another day and then take them to the stationmaster and he'll send them on to me.'

Relief made him sag for a moment. 'But won't you get into trouble about that?'

'No. Um, actually, I'm one of the company engineers and I'm mostly my own master. I like to work outside the office as often as I can to keep in touch with the men and how jobs are done, which is why I was delivering your carriage.'

'Oh, that's such a relief! I can't thank you enough.'

'One day you can show me round your carriage home and buy me a pint at your local pub. That'll be thanks enough. I'll be coming up to see your friend Wilf as well once things quieten down.'

When he put the phone down, it was a few moments before Harry could pull himself together and get going again.

'Everything all right?' Lily asked as he went through to the shop from her living room.

'Things are fine. Better than I could have expected, actually. How much do I owe you for the phone call?'

'Twopence.'

He fumbled in his pockets and realised he'd left his money at home because these were his ragged working clothes. 'I'll have to owe it you. I've not got my money on me because I've been digging.'

'That's all right. I know where you live *and* where you're going to live. You won't be running away after going to all this trouble to bring in your railway carriage. I'm dying to see it.'

They both smiled, then he added, 'Can you please get me six extra loaves tomorrow morning for their breakfast? And two jars of jam. No, make it three.'

'Butter?'

He shook his head. 'They'll have to make do with a scrape of jam. I don't have a lot of spare money. I'll make it up to them one day.'

Her voice was soft with understanding. 'They won't mind. It makes them feel good to help. I can ring the baker tonight.'

'Thanks.'

'Do you want me to slice the loaves and put the jam on them?'

'Would you mind?'

'Actually, I'd *like* to do something to help get your home here.'

The young shopkeeper was another generous inhabitant of Ellindale, Harry thought as he walked down the hill to where the carriage was still waiting to be delivered, perched on its trolleys. It was surrounded by the locals. Wonderful people, if a bit nosey. He grinned at the sight of them.

He was as glad as the other workers when today's sandwiches

from the pub arrived. He'd found his appetite again now that there was truly hope for his new home's safe delivery.

He slept down by the carriage that night with the other men on watch. It was cold with only one ragged blanket to wrap round his shoulders, but he didn't care. He couldn't bear to leave the carriage unattended. Not now, not when they were so close to making it his and Cathie's home.

They had two people keeping a lookout at all times, patrolling for two hours each by Harry's old turnip watch, which he fetched and hung on the outside of the railway carriage near an oil lamp, because no one else carried a timepiece. No need to worry about it being safe with men like these around.

Nothing disturbed the peace of the night and he even got a little sleep because he was too tired to care about the hard ground and he had a reasonably full belly.

# 37

When the day's work ended, Enid and Wilf walked up the hill to the pub through the long shadows of evening. She seemed a bit on edge and he wondered why, but he soon forgot about it in the pleasure of going into the pub and eating enough of the sandwiches to fill his belly comfortably for once.

He noticed Enid go across to Izzy and hand over a coin, then wrap two sandwiches in a piece of crumpled paper and put them into her pocket. That surprised him. As they left the pub he asked, 'What are you buying sandwiches for? We've only just eaten and we've got a bit of bread and marge left at home for breakfast, haven't we?'

'They're for the children.'

He stopped walking to frown at her. 'What children?'

'The Judsons' children.'

'What have they got to do with us?'

She hesitated then said in a rush, 'I'm looking after them.'

'Why you? We've got enough trouble feeding ourselves without adding two extra mouths that don't belong to us. Surely they can be sent to an orphanage? They'll think they're in heaven, because they'll be better treated there than they ever were at home.'

'But they won't be loved. No one will really care about them.'

'Nor do we. Those children are *not* our problem, Enid!'

More silence then she barred his way into their house. 'I

*want* to look after them, Wilf, maybe even adopt them too if things go well.'

'*What?* You want to adopt *his* children?'

'They're such sad little creatures, it hurts me to see how thin they are. If they were fed and brought up decently, at least they'd stand a chance in life. As things are, it's a wonder they've even survived this long.'

'Enid, I—' Then he saw the tears tracking down her cheeks and that stopped him. His Enid didn't let herself weep, and heaven knew, she'd had plenty to weep about during recent years. What's more this was the second time she'd wept in a week, what with that spilled stew. 'Oh, love, we can't—'

The weeping turned to hard sobbing that shook her whole body. He couldn't bear that and pulled her into his arms. 'Don't, love, don't. Shh, now. You know I can't stand to see you weep.'

'I d-don't normally. It's just so . . .' Her voice trailed away, then she said in a whisper, 'I've wanted to have children so much and we've not managed it the usual way. I haven't let you see me weeping about it, but I have cried many a time. I don't think we ever will manage it. It happens like that sometimes.'

She paused for a moment to dab at her eyes. 'No one wants these children, no one in the whole world. Except me. Please, Wilf. Think about it. Meet them properly. See how you get on with them, see how that little girl, who's only five, looks after her brother. Please, Wilf . . . give me a chance to become a mother, the only chance I've ever had.' She stared at him pleadingly for a moment, then led the way into the house.

He knew then that he was lost but wasn't ready to admit it yet. He followed her inside and they woke up the kind neighbour who'd been dozing in the rocking chair Wilf had made for his wife.

His eyes were drawn immediately to the rug in front of a low fire, where two tiny figures lay cuddled up to one another. The little girl had her arm round her much smaller brother, protective even in sleep. He'd seen them around, of course he had, but hadn't had anything to do with them. Now, he looked at them closely for the first time. They were so small, much smaller than the children down the street who must be about the same age.

Wilf closed his eyes for a moment to block out the sight, then opened them again as Enid came back from showing the neighbour out and thanking her for keeping an eye on the children.

She knelt down to brush a curl away from the little girl's forehead, such a tender gesture it made something ache inside Wilf's chest. His wife's longing for children showed more clearly today than ever before. How could he deny her this chance? They'd been married nearly ten years now – ten! – and not seen any sign of a baby. Sometimes women lost the infants they were carrying, but Enid had never even started one.

He pulled her to her feet and into his arms. 'Eh, lass, what are you getting me into now?'

She started weeping again, but this time it wasn't racking great sobs, it was happy tears, mingled with smiles and damp kisses on his cheeks and lips.

'You'll think about it seriously, Wilf, you really will?'

'Yes, love.'

'Oh, thank you, thank you!'

'Don't press me to jump straight in about adopting, though. Give me time to get used to the idea and to see how we all get on together.'

More kisses were dabbed on his face, then he held her close for a few moments. He loved holding her. She was the biggest treasure in his world.

The little girl woke up and stared at them in obvious fright, so he moved away from Enid and turned up the oil lamp so that he could see their faces more clearly.

The two of them didn't look like either of their parents, were just like any small children who'd cried themselves to sleep, eyes reddened, hair a messy tangle.

The little boy woke up and clutched his sister. When Wilf took a step closer, they shrank away from him, clutching one another.

Enid knelt down again. 'No need to be afraid. This is my husband Wilf. You've seen him in the street, haven't you? He's a kind man. He won't hurt you.'

They looked at him doubtfully, as if they didn't believe that possible.

'Let's go out to the lavvie now you've woken up,' she said. 'We don't do it in the house; we don't use chamber pots here.

'These are for you afterwards. They've got corned beef in.' She pulled the sandwiches out of her pocket and put them on the table before leading the two little ones out into the yard.

Wilf shook his head and admitted it to himself. He couldn't say no, not to Enid's deep, hungry longing for a child – nor to the sight of such fragile little creatures desperately in need of loving care.

When the three of them came back in, Enid made the children wash their hands before eating, which seemed to surprise them. They sat down at the table and she cut a sandwich in half and put it on a plate between them. They made no move to touch it, just stared at the two halves then looked at her as if asking permission to eat it.

'It's for you. Eat it slowly this time and chew it properly. There's no hurry. No one's going to take it away from you.'

'What about the mister?' the little girl whispered.

'He's already eaten his sandwiches at the pub and so have I. These are for you two.'

'Eh, thanks, missus.' She turned to nudge her little brother. 'Eat it slowly this time, Ronnie.'

But he couldn't help gulping it down quickly, his eyes darting from side to side as he watched for anyone who might try to take it away from him.

That upset Wilf, it really did. 'You'd better find them somewhere to sleep, love. And we can surely get them better clothes than those rags, don't you think? We don't want our children looking like paupers.'

Enid looked at him, hope slowly brightening her eyes. 'Does that mean—?'

He lowered his voice so that only Enid could hear him. 'Aye. I don't need to wait to decide. I can't bear to see kids so neglected any more than you can. But we'll do it properly, mind. Go to the authorities and offer to adopt them two. I'm not having *him* taking them away from us once we're started caring about them. In fact, I'm not having him coming near them again ever.'

She kept her own voice low. 'He'll be in jail for a long time, I reckon. He may not have killed Minnie on purpose but he did kill her.'

'He's scum, that one is.' He looked across at Peggy and spoke more normally. 'Finish off your sandwich, love.'

When he turned back to his wife, Enid flung herself into his arms. 'You're the best husband in the world, Wilf Pollard, and you're going to make the best father, too.'

'Am I? I hope so. I can't be worse than *him*, any road, can I?'

They turned together to smile at the children.

'We've got a place for you to sleep upstairs and if you want, you can live here with us from now on,' Enid said.

'What about Mum and Dad?' Peggy asked.

'You're mother's dead. Do you know what that means?'

Ronnie looked a bit bewildered but the little girl seemed to be thinking aloud. 'Yes. Like old Mrs Smales. She died and they carried her away in a box. Mum's been sick for a long time. Will they put her in a box, too?'

'Yes, dear. But she won't know. She can't feel anything now.'

There was silence. Ronnie didn't seem to understand the implications of this but Peggy was clearly still thinking it through.

'Did we do it?'

'What?'

'Kill Mam.'

'Why on earth would you think that?'

'She used to say we'd be the death of her.'

Enid felt furious at this. 'It wasn't your fault she died, not at all. Your father did it by accident so he's going to be locked up in prison.'

More thinking, then, 'Does that mean he won't be able to hit us any more?'

'He definitely won't. You can live here with us, and no one will hit you from now on. Me and Wilf don't hit children.'

Peggy moved closer to Enid and reached out hesitantly to take her hand. 'Eh, missus, it'll be grand, that will.' Then she shot a shy, smiling glance at Wilf but didn't seem confident enough to take his hand. 'We'll try to be good, mister. But our Ronnie's only little and he makes mistakes.'

'We all make mistakes, Peggy. He'll learn from them.'

The smile on the child's face finished Wilf off. It was like the sun breaking out from behind a cloud, that smile was. And his Enid was absolutely glowing with happiness.

He had to blow his nose a couple of times to get over it all.

★

Todd walked Leah back to Spring Cottage because Ben said he'd rather spend the night near his wall and be ready for the next day's work as soon as it grew light.

She stopped by the pub. 'Don't you want to go and get some sandwiches? I'll be all right going home from here, you know.'

'I'm not letting you walk back on your own, Leah. Your fizzy drinks workers will have gone home by now and for all we know, those two men who escaped might have come back across the moors.'

'Rosa will be waiting for me. I saw her go past on her way home from school earlier on. I shan't be alone.'

'Your sister won't be much use if someone attacks you.'

She shivered involuntarily. 'No. I suppose not. Thank you, then.'

'Be sure to lock all your doors after I leave you.'

He wanted to make sure he had a future with her so he added, 'And Leah?'

'Yes?'

He said it quickly before he lost the courage. 'Once you've had the baby, will you let me court you?'

She stopped dead, staring at him.

'We get on well and I . . . I like you very much. I don't think you're indifferent to me, either.'

She stood there for so long he was suddenly worried he'd read the situation wrongly. So he waited, praying as he'd never prayed before that she would one day come to care for him in the same way.

'I can't do anything about, er, that sort of thing. Not until I've had the baby, Todd. It'd not be respectful to Jonah.'

'I agree. But *after* you've had the child . . .' He searched desperately for a convincing way to put it and could only come up with, 'Will you give me hope?'

Her eyes searched his face as if she was trying to read his thoughts. 'We'll have got to know one another better by then, what with you and Charlie working together. And yes, I'd like us to start seeing more of one another, then find out where it all leads.'

'Jonah would have wanted you to be happy. He told me to take care of you.'

Her voice came out more sharply. 'Are you doing this because you promised him that?'

'No. I'm doing it for me, because I care for you.'

'Good. And in case you think I'm heartless even talking about this so soon, it was never a love match between me and Jonah. But oh, we became such good friends that I miss him terribly.'

'A lot of people in the valley will miss him. He did a great many small acts of kindness to folk who were struggling. Charlie always said— Oh, hell!' Todd stopped mid-sentence. 'I didn't remind Harry that Charlie needs him to phone urgently. I think he's got work and no one else can do it, so this is important for both of them.'

'You can remind Harry about it tomorrow.'

He let out a snort of laughter. 'Do you think he'll be able to concentrate on anything tomorrow except getting his new home into place? I doubt it. That man can hardly walk straight for worrying.'

'Poor fellow.'

'Look, Ben said I could sleep on his sofa but I want to get back to help with the carriage early. Do you think you could phone Charlie tomorrow morning and tell him how things are up here? Tell him I won't forget to remind Harry again once the carriage is in place.'

'Yes, of course I can phone. I might even do it tonight. Charlie doesn't go to bed early.'

As they stood by her front door, Todd looked down at her and though they didn't touch one another, it was almost as if he'd given her a farewell embrace.

He stepped back quickly before he made a fool of himself and bade her good night.

When he stopped at the door to Ben's quarters across the yard and looked back, she hadn't moved.

She raised one hand and he did the same. Only then did she go inside.

He felt hopeful about the future, though, because she definitely hadn't said no.

# 38

Harry slept patchily, starting awake a few times, but hearing only the natural sounds of the night whenever he raised his head to listen. As the sky began to lighten just a little, he heard footsteps coming down the road and jumped up to see who it was.

Wilf loomed out of the misty pre-dawn greyness. 'No trouble, then?'

'None at all. Isn't Enid coming?'

'Ah. Well. She's taken in Judson's children and she's seeing to them. She wants to . . . um, let them stay with us.' He had difficulty saying the next word, but forced it out. 'Adopt them.'

'Right. I see. And you?'

'I want her to be happy and they seem nice enough. That girl looks after her brother like a little mother, and her only five. Enid's always wanted children and . . . and so have I. Those two have no one else now.'

'Your wife has a kind heart and so do you.'

'Get on with you! Now, we must—'

Faint footsteps sounded from up the hill and they turned to watch two figures transform from dim outlines into Todd and Clarry.

'Ready to start work again?' Wilf asked.

'Very ready.' Clarry looked bright and cheerful, as if having something to do had revitalised him.

The two men went straight down to the retaining wall,

where Ben had already started work. He must have got up even earlier, Harry thought.

The baker's lad came up the hill and cycled past them, slowing down to take a good look at their progress. The aroma of fresh bread wafted back to them as he moved on.

'Last night I ordered some more loaves,' Harry told Wilf.

'You're being generous.'

'If I was really generous I'd pay these chaps proper wages, but I daren't run my money down more than I have to. I've a child to feed.'

'No one would expect you to.'

'Lily said she'd make up some jam butties and send them down.'

Work began, with Clarry insisting on throughstones being used. These were usually used to tie the two sides of a dry stone wall together, but here he wanted to tie the wall more deeply into the bank of compacted earth.

'Is that necessary?' Harry asked, worried it'd add to the time needed to finish the wall.

'It is if we want our part of the wall to last. Dost think that town council down in Rivenshaw will be sending up men to build us a new wall if it collapses on us? No, they won't! They ignore Ellindale as much as they can, them lot of paper shufflers do. I'd like to see them build a wall *or* plough a field. I'd like to see some of them even lift one of my stones.'

Still muttering, the old man got on with his work.

Ben winked at Harry and continued to follow Clarry's directions, tactfully finding ways to lift up the heavier stones for him.

Gradually, people came down from the village to sit on the slopes and watch, ready to help if they were needed. A few people even walked up from Birch End, and a little later, when the morning bus came up from Rivenshaw and had to stop before it got to its usual destination in Ellindale, another two or three people got out and came to sit with friends to watch the day's happening.

The driver complained when he couldn't get the bus past the carriage, but the rest of the passengers accepted it more philosophically. After they got out, he reversed slowly to where he could turn round and the passengers had a good look at what was happening as they walked past the carriage on their way up the final stretch of road to the village.

While Ben and Clarry were finishing the wall, Wilf did a final thorough check on the ropes and chains and in the brighter light of morning, he found that more of the ropes had been cut than he'd realised, so reconnected them carefully.

Lenny had slept in his tractor cabin and gone back there to sit out of the still-chilly breeze after he'd eaten a sandwich, so Wilf called him out to show him. 'We'll need to redo these lashings before you move off, Lenny. Can you lend me a hand?'

The farmer nodded. 'Aye. Mad sods, them fellows were, eh? What good does this sort of thing do anyone?'

'No good at all. I'd like to get my hands on them lot all over again and punch them black and blue, I would that.'

After about two hours' work Clarry patted the copestones on top of the wall as if they were part of a living creature. 'There you are, lads. It's as good as we'll get it without starting from scratch. Get that soil tamped down behind it. I've sloped the copestones backwards as well as the wall. The grass will grow over them and help hold it together.'

He and Ben took a rest while the others filled in the gap. Harry moved forward to help move in earth and small pebbles, wondering how stones without mortar could hold together well enough. But when he looked across the moors during one of his short breaks from digging, to allow others to stamp down the earth, his gaze fell on the many other dry stone walls climbing up and down the slopes. They seemed to be telling him that they'd been there for decades and the newly repaired wall would be, too.

Once everyone moved away from the new wall, Lenny looked round. 'Is it finished, then?'

Clarry gave it a proprietorial glance. 'Aye.'

'Well, you've re-tied the ropes as best you can, Wilf, so let's see if we can move this carriage up the hill for Mr Makepeace.'

Wilf called out loudly, 'I want some volunteers to walk in a line at each side of the carriage. If it seems to get wobbly and I yell, "Steady it!" do that in any way you can. It probably won't be necessary, but the road is uneven and twists a bit, so you can't be too careful.'

It was mostly men and a few of the younger, sturdier women who lined up along each side of the carriage.

Harry saw Cathie tugging at Nina's hand, clearly wanting to walk next to it with them, but Nina spoke quietly to the child and she stopped asking. He was glad to have Nina looking after his daughter, eh, he was that, because he had so many things to worry about during this final stage, he didn't know whether he was coming or going.

Wilf was suddenly beside him. 'Ben and I will walk behind each line, to keep an eye on things. You should go at the front of the tractor and lead the way. It's your home, after all.'

Harry nodded and moved forward, beckoning to Nina and Cathie and pointing to the hilly side of the road. 'You can walk in front near me if you keep right out of the way of the tractor.'

Cathie nodded and beamed at him.

Behind him the tractor engine coughed and spluttered,

then took hold. Very slowly, the ungainly vehicle started to move forward.

Harry kept a little way ahead, turning every step or two to check on it, sometimes even walking backwards. All the time he prayed that all would go well.

*Please let it go well! Please let it go well!*

It all seemed to be happening unbearably slowly, the carriage edging forward inch by meagre inch. Had it moved this slowly yesterday? Had the carriage shaken about so much? He shot a worried glance back at Wilf who gave him a cheerful wave, then carried on leading the way. It'd be all right. It had to be.

Nina and Cathie kept pace with him along the side of the road.

The two lines of men and women walked slowly, pausing occasionally because it was hard to walk at such a snail's pace.

Behind the carriage Ben and Clarry were driving in Ben's truck, and they were followed by a raggle-taggle group of people from the valley.

The carriage rose and fell with the bumps in the road. Things rattled or creaked, and it wasn't always clear what.

At one point Wilf yelled, 'Brace it!' at a particularly bad pothole on a sloping bend, and the hands went out to make sure the cumbersome load didn't get jolted to the side.

'All right now. You can let go.'

A collective sigh of relief went up.

When his land came in sight Harry hurried ahead. More villagers were standing around near the entrance and he called, 'Could you move back up the hill a bit, please? We'll need plenty of room to manoeuvre the carriage into place.'

Obediently they shuffled back a few yards. Even old Simeon was there, with two younger men giving him a hand to walk.

He raised his walking stick briefly in an encouraging gesture and a few others called, 'Good luck!'

As the tractor approached the entrance, Wilf came forward to take over and direct the helpers. He held up one hand and the tractor stopped.

Ben had stopped too, and was quickly out of the cabin of his truck, getting the special jacks down from the tractor and, since they were so big and heavy, he enlisted the help of a burly man and called for pairs of strong men to take each one and stay with it. 'Lean them against the wall and be ready to bring them where we tell you when the trailer's in place.'

Ben and Wilf moved forward off the road into the flat area. 'You did well, Harry, to make this space so wide. Can you get your motorcycle out and park it further up the road?'

'Eh, I should have thought of that myself,' Harry exclaimed.

'No one can think of everything.'

Wilf seemed able to, Harry thought. By the time he'd got the tarpaulin off and driven his machine up the road a bit, Wilf had paced out the ground yet again and made marks in the soft dirt with his heel. He then got up onto the tractor to speak to Lenny, pointing out exactly where he wanted the tractor to stop so that they could unhook the carriage at the nearest point to its final resting place.

Then Wilf went back to the people lined up beside the carriage. 'After Lenny's moved it just a little further up, I'll unhook the tractor and we'll see if we can pull the carriage along on the trolleys. It'll need a good few of you to do that, I should think, but it's the only way to get it into place. Will you have a go at it?'

There was a rousing cheer and shouts of yes.

'The people to be in charge of the jacks need to be ready, for when we get it next to the place it's going to stand. But they may need helpers to lift them. I want four others to be ready with the biggest stones you can lift as we move the carriage along. If I yell "stones", shove them behind the rear wheels on the trolleys to stop them rolling back.'

When they were all ready, he braced his shoulders, breathed in deeply once or twice as he did a final scan of the situation, then yelled, 'Go!'

There was dead silence from the spectators now.

It all happened so very slowly that the tension increased and spread over the scene like an invisible cloak.

Harry felt like yelling, 'Hurry up!' or falling to his knees and praying, or simply burying his head in the ground till it was over. But of course he didn't. Instead, he went to take his place, ready to help pull the carriage along with all the strength he could muster.

Lenny moved the tractor slowly forward till Wilf gave the word.

'Stones!' Wilf yelled.

The big stones were thumped behind the rear wheels of each trolley.

Then Wilf unhooked the first trolley from behind the tractor and passed out rags to wrap round the chain to give a better grip and protect the helpers' hands. There were more than enough willing folk.

'Right, as we start pulling, take them stones away and bring them along by the side of the trolleys, in case we need them again,' Wilf called.

Once again the trolleys started rolling, moving the carriage like a strange, ungainly ship that bobbed its way into the open space at the bottom of Harry's land. It came to a halt parallel with the space cut out and prepared for it.

# 39

Cathie and Nina were now standing on the other side of the road opposite the entrance. She tugged Nina's hand. 'Can't we get closer? Please?'

'No, dear. You'll see inside it soon enough.'

'But someone might get inside the carriage before me an' Dad.'

'He won't let that happen. Keep hold of my hand. We'll move closer as soon as it's safe, I promise you.'

Nina could understand the child's impatience but she took her responsibility to keep Cathie safe very seriously indeed, so her grip was firmer than usual. The child seemed to sense her determination and stopped struggling, but sighed from time to time.

Todd was behind Harry in the line along one of the chains, grunting with the effort of pulling the huge carriage up the slope.

It was still happening as Wilf had planned, Harry thought. It was. It really was.

Then there was a bump and the first trolley stopped moving. Harry's heart nearly stopped moving too.

'Stones!' Wilf cried out.

The stones preventing the wheels from rolling back were in place within seconds.

The carriage hadn't reached its final stopping place yet. What was wrong? Harry wondered. He stood on tiptoe but was unable to see the obstacle from where he stood.

'There's a rock just under the surface here,' Ben called. 'We'll need to get it out. Someone fetch me a crowbar and a spade.'

A man ran to get them from the pile of tools which Wilf had told the women to lay out carefully on the grass to one side of the entrance 'just in case'.

It took Ben a few minutes, then he managed to lever a huge stone out of the ground and as he stood back, other men shovelled a mixture of gravel and earth into the hole without needing to be told.

When that was done and the earth tamped down, Wilf yelled, 'Take up your chains again!' followed by, 'Stones away!'

And they were off once more.

'Stop!'

Harry looked back anxiously to see what was wrong and it took him a few seconds to realise what had happened.

There was nothing wrong, nothing at all. As planned, the railway carriage was aligned next to its final resting place. He closed his eyes for a moment in sheer relief. *Thank goodness! Oh, thank goodness!* Now there was only one big hurdle to climb – raising the carriage.

He opened his eyes again, watching Wilf. They were all watching Wilf now.

The lower end of the site was built up with Ben's wall to about two foot. The ground inside the marked area was level and well tamped down. The rest of the railway sleepers were pinned in place around the edge of the place where the carriage would rest.

'Now we need to get them special jacks set up and raise the carriage so that the trolleys can be taken away,' Wilf called.

The four men responsible brought the huge jacks forward, each with an assistant to help carry such heavy objects and help set their broad bases in place. People had never seen anything like them.

Harry swallowed hard as Wilf personally supervised the placing of each jack in turn, then they were raised till the men could remove the trolleys from underneath.

Spectators had crept forward to stand at the entrance, with Nina and Cathie at the forefront. Everyone was silent, seeming fascinated by what was happening.

'Right! Pay attention!' Wilf yelled. 'We're only going to lift one end at a time, so that we don't try to carry the full weight of the carriage. The jacks are designed to allow that. I'm going round to adjust them now. Before I do that, let's see how many men we need. We'll just lift this end up a few inches and down again to see how it feels.'

They did that, and it took the ten strongest men to lift it and set it down, with much grunting and groaning. Harry was not included among them, because of his less muscular build. A couple of the men pretended to show off their muscles afterwards and this caused a laugh.

He couldn't join in the laughter, just couldn't.

'Right, now we'll swing the bottom end of the carriage across the sleepers and set it down on them. You can stand at the other side, Harry lad, and see how well it fits. Yell out when we reach the spot.'

He moved obediently, glad to have something to do.

It happened more quickly than he'd expected, again thanks to Wilf's careful planning and guidance. The man was a miracle worker, seeming to know instinctively how to move things so that they fitted into place and – just as important – how to give clear instructions.

Harry stood the other side and yelled out when the bottom end of the carriage was in place.

Wilf came round to check it and said he'd judged it well, which cheered him a little. Now there was just one big step to go.

'Right, lads!' Wilf called. 'We've only got the top end to move.'

They were halfway through this task when one man stumbled and fell. The end of the carriage wobbled as the extra weight took its toll.

The crowd made a soft oohing sound and Harry stuck his fist in his mouth to prevent himself from calling out and distracting them.

The minute they saw what was happening two younger men ran forward from the crowd and took over to steady the carriage, without being told. The crowd made another soft sound, this time in relief.

The man who'd stumbled got up and realised he'd twisted his ankle, so called a friend to help him out of the way.

Wilf called, 'Lift it again. Slowly, slowly. That's it.'

Harry called, 'It's there.'

'Set it down.' Wilf ran round to check the other side.

Of course the final placement didn't satisfy Wilf, who wanted it moved another inch or two to align it perfectly with its supports.

Then he stepped back and said, 'Right. That's it. She's home.'

There was dead silence for a long moment as everyone stared at the carriage, then someone let out a loud hurrah and everyone began to cheer and whistle and yell.

Harry couldn't move, could do nothing but stare at his new home. Was it really in place?

A voice beside him said quietly, 'Come on, lad. It'll hold firm now. You should be the first to get inside it. Then I think we'll let all the lads have a turn to look round. They've earned it, don't you think?'

Harry nodded, then looked across the crowd and called, 'Cathie! Come into your new home with me.'

She ran across to join him and together they walked across to the top end, where the door was the easiest to get into.

Eh, he thought, there are six doors, three on each side. Why didn't I notice that before? Who needs six doors?

Trust Wilf to think of everything, he thought, as he saw that a short piece of a sleeper was being set in place to use as a step up into the carriage.

Still he hesitated. 'You're sure it's safe now?' he asked Wilf.

'Aye, lad. Go on. Don't keep that little lass waiting or she'll burst.'

Taking a deep breath Harry climbed carefully up and opened the door. Wilf helped Cathie to follow her father.

'Home,' they both said at the same time and laughed.

He managed not to weep for joy. But only just.

The carriage was dusty inside and at this end the damage showed. But as he'd noted the first time he saw it, there was only damage to the top layer, the upholstery and padding. Nothing structural had been damaged. At first, there seemed to be more of a mess than there really was for only the first pair of seats had been charred. The other three pairs of seats spaced along the carriage were untouched and looked fine. He could unbolt them from the floor and use them as seats.

'Let's walk to the far end.'

Cathie nodded eagerly.

He showed her the toilet compartment, discovered a cupboard at each end of the long space, something he hadn't noticed before, and suddenly, reaction set in. His legs wouldn't hold him up any longer, so he plumped himself down hastily on a seat.

Cathie sat down across the aisle from him, beaming and leaning her head back. 'Isn't it *comfortable*?'

It was. Very. He'd like to stay here for an hour and recover from the ordeal. But there were people outside who deserved to see the home they'd helped set in place. Some had managed to find a perch from which they could peep inside.

He realised that Wilf had stuck his head through the door and was watching them. He beckoned. 'Come inside, lad. You've more than earned an early viewing.'

Before Wilf could do this, Enid called, 'There's someone else who's come to watch what happened. Without his special jacks we'd have had a lot of trouble getting it in place.'

Harry looked out of the dusty window and saw Dan Oakham come forward through the crowd. 'I found I could stay on in Rivenshaw a day longer,' he yelled, 'so I thought I'd collect my jacks and save you the trouble of delivering them. And I have to confess I wanted to satisfy my nosiness as well.'

'Tell him to come inside,' Harry told Wilf.

'All right. Would you mind if my wife came in too? I'd never hear the last of it if Enid had to wait to see things when I'd been one of the first inside.'

'Why not? Tell her to bring Nina. I daresay the whole village will be in and out before today is through.'

'They'll have to take their shoes off,' Cathie said. 'There are *carpets* all over the floor.'

'They can wipe their feet on the scorched part near the entrance. We'll not be keeping that.'

He was right about everyone coming to see what it was like. Even old Simeon was hoisted inside for a look round.

Then it was over. People went home. Dan drove off with the jacks and a promise to be in touch, and the ones left were the ones who'd been at the heart of things.

Wilf made sure everything had stood up to groups of visitors tramping in and out, then came and sat down on a trolley next to his wife, with his arm round her shoulders. Nina was sitting next to Cathie. Harry was up and down saying farewell to people, or simply walking round his new home for 'just another quick look'.

Ben had seen Clarry off the site and promised to visit him the next day. Todd had managed to sit next to Leah, and Marion and Charlie had been spotted on their way up the hill to view the carriage.

'It's lovely, isn't it, Dad?' Cathie whispered. 'Look at that long window running along the ceiling.'

'It's called a clerestory window, I don't know why.'

'It's beautiful. Some of the glass is coloured.'

'The most important thing is, I'm sure we'll be happy here.' He glanced at Nina. 'And I hope you'll come and see us often.'

She stared back. 'I'd like that.'

It was a promise of much more, they both knew, but they hoped others didn't realise that.

It wasn't until Harry saw Wilf wink at Enid and Leah smile fondly at him and Nina that he realised he was holding her hand. Well, why not? Even if he hadn't done that, they'd have known, of course they would. In a village like this everyone would soon know your business.

And Nina hadn't pulled her hand away.

He turned to Wilf and the others. 'There's so much to be thankful for,' he said. 'But I couldn't have done it without your help, Wilf, and that of others, so I'm most thankful of all for good friends.'

It was as close as he could get to a speech.

When Charlie arrived, he took a perfunctory tour of the carriage and left Marion in it sitting chatting comfortably to Leah.

He tugged Harry outside. 'I'm sorry to interrupt, but I'm desperate for your help. Flewett cheated me, or perhaps his assistant Stanley did. I've asked Sergeant Deemer to investigate. In the meantime I have customers waiting for repairs I can't get done. And they're asking to buy goods when I don't know which to choose from the catalogues. So I want to offer you a job. Todd says you're a skilled electrician, army trained, and that's good enough for me.'

'A permanent job?'

'Yes, of course.'

'Full-time?'

'Yes.'

Harry closed his eyes then opened them and said in a voice grown suddenly husky with emotion, 'We'll have to talk about wages.'

Charlie clapped him on the back. 'We'll decide tomorrow. I pay my special people well, and they don't usually leave me. Ask Vi, who runs my pawnshops.' He held out his hand. 'Agreed? You'll work for me?'

Harry shook it. 'Agreed. I'll come down tomorrow for a few hours and see what's needed, but I have to get this place set up for us to live in before I can work full-time.'

Beaming, Charlie turned back to the carriage. 'Can I go in and have another look round? This time I can really take in what it's like. I was too worried before.'

For the first time that day Harry was left on his own. He breathed in deeply, brushed away a tear that had escaped his control and turned to find his daughter and Nina had come across to stand beside him. It felt so right to have one on either side.

There was still a lot to sort out, but it felt natural to put an arm round each of them and say, 'Isn't it going to be wonderful living here?'

'Yes, it is,' Nina agreed. 'Ellindale is a very special place to live. It didn't take me long to realise that.'

Cathie couldn't stand still for more than a minute, so when she walked off to go round the carriage, he dared to place a kiss on Nina's soft cheek, and then on her lips.

'We'll do well here, lass.'

'We?'

'The three of us. If that suits you?'

'It suits me very well.' She hesitated and added, 'I don't want to wait.'

His heart lifted. 'Nor do I. Not a day longer than I have to.'

'Let's tell Cathie.'

He beckoned to his daughter. 'I hope you'll be pleased. I'm going to marry Nina as soon as it can be arranged.'

She gave a little skip on the spot. 'Hurrah!'

When Nina bent to kiss her, Cathie flung her arms round her neck and gave her a big hug. 'And we'll all live happily ever after in the carriage?'

He looked at Nina ruefully. 'It'll be a bit rough at first, I'm afraid. Perhaps we should wait?'

'We can camp out here if necessary. But I don't want to leave Leah in the lurch at the youth hostel. I'll tell her and you talk to Wilf about the carriage. If anyone can see the quickest way to make it liveable, it'll be him. I'll see what we can arrange.'

He gave his two women a hug, feeling as if the whole world was sparkling for joy. He couldn't remember the last time he'd felt so happy.

Todd walked Leah and Rosa home from the railway carriage to Spring Cottage, exchanging greetings with various people as they passed through the village. When the three of them arrived at the house, Leah told her sister. 'You go inside and get ready for bed. I want to ask Mr Selby something.'

'All right. It was an exciting day, wasn't it? Good night, Mr Selby.'

She didn't wait for an answer, but went inside, leaving the door half open.

Leah pulled the door shut and turned to Todd. 'Could you put your arms round me? I felt so alone today.'

'If I had my way, you'd never be alone again.'

She put one finger on his lips. 'Shh. We have to do things properly till the baby is born.'

'I envy Harry and Nina.'

'I don't envy anyone at the moment.' She laid one hand on her stomach. 'I've wanted a baby for as long as I can remember. The thought of this child is making me very happy.'

'Yes, of course. I'm just being selfish, wanting to be with you.'

'Todd, I rushed into marriage with Jonah. This time I don't want to rush into anything.'

'You haven't changed your mind – about us?'

'No. But I want to be courted, to get to know my future husband before we get married, to feel loved.'

'He loved you, Leah.'

'Not in a madly passionate way.' She took his hand. 'And I always had to hold my feelings back, not love him too deeply. I wanted more . . . in bed. Much more.'

He sucked in his breath audibly.

'Am I being too forward about this?'

'No. If we can't talk frankly, we shouldn't get married.'

She gave a little nod. 'I agree.'

'May I kiss you?'

'Oh, yes. And please don't treat me as if I'm a fragile piece of china. I'm not.'

When the kiss ended, they stood there for a while, his arms round her, her head on his shoulder.

After a while she asked, 'Have I shocked you?'

'No. You could never do that. Actually, you've delighted me. I don't want a wife who only puts up with me in bed. When our time comes, Leah, I'll show you how deep my love is.'

She took his hand and raised it to her lips.

There were footsteps coming up the lane and she sighed as they moved apart.

Ben called good night across the yard.

'You'd better leave now,' she said.

Todd whispered, 'Good night, my dearest love.'

She carried the warmth of his love into the house with her.

# *Epilogue*

A month later Nina got up and dressed in her very best, staring at her face in the mirror. She'd not spent long in the youth hostel, but Leah said it didn't matter. She'd decided to take over temporarily herself till she found someone.

With a final touch to her hair, Nina put on her hat and turned to Leah and Enid, who were acting unofficially as bridesmaid and matron of honour. 'How do I look?'

'You look beautiful,' Enid said.

Leah nodded agreement. 'We'd better go now. We don't want to be late.'

Once again Todd had managed to hire a bus to take everyone down to the registry office in Rivenshaw.

Nina got in and joined Harry at the front. No motorbike for him and his daughter on a day like this. Cathie was sitting behind her father, smiling broadly and looking rosy and well.

The ceremony itself was very brief, then the man conducting it said, 'Now, you're just as married as if you'd done it in a church.'

Harry and Nina exchanged amused glances at this. Neither of them cared about the fuss or how they got married, only the life they were going to build together.

Afterwards, the wedding party was driven back to Ellindale, where a village celebration had been planned for at The Shepherd's Rest. The party was lively and happy, but it seemed to go on for far too long, Nina thought. It was a relief when she and Harry escaped and strolled down through the village to their new home. Cathie was going to stay with Leah tonight and didn't seem to mind.

Harry surprised Nina by lifting her across the threshold into the railway carriage. 'I'm sorry I've not got a better home to offer you, my lovely lass.'

'I don't mind. At least you own this and no one can throw us out. What's more I prefer to be involved in making everything nice. And anyway, it's you I've married not this railway carriage.'

He pulled her into his arms and sealed their day with a kiss, then felt the moisture on her cheeks and held her at arm's length, looking at her in dismay. 'What's wrong?'

'Nothing. Nothing at all. I'd better warn you that I always cry when I'm happy. I haven't had much joy in the past few years and now my life is full of it – you, my darling, and Cathie who is *my* daughter as well now. And, if fate is kind, we'll have more children.'

'If I have my way, you'll be doing a lot of happy crying from now on.' He pulled her to him for a long, loving kiss. 'Welcome home, Mrs Makepeace.'